The Rebellious Earthling:
Tale of The Turquoise Mirror

By Andi Hayes

ISBN: 978-0-692-13289-0

CREDITS:
Front & back cover graphics by Andi Hayes
Oil painting of Andi in Flames by STACY

Evil must be completely exposed and brought into the light for scrutiny, not simply doused with perfume and thrown back into the drawer – Andi Hayes

Eternal love to **Bratskulla, The Magical Cat**, whom I have loved forever; and to my two brothers, who remember what real clouds used to look like.

In loving memory of my soulmate Thomas A. Ybarra, aka **T.A. Black of The Web**, who passed on to the Afterlife (February 26, 1962 – October 17, 2017)

Mr. T.A. Black 1962-2017

CONTENTS

CHAPTER 1

WHAT LIES UNDERNEATH

As the praying mantises slogged and bashed away on their various musical instruments, the trolls began shuffling their feet awkwardly, as if trying to locate the beat. Some grabbed their dance partner by the hair, pulling hard and yanking out tangled oily chunks by the roots. They aggressively shoved each other while swaying unsteadily on their gnarled tree-trunk feet. Bending forward, they let their long, spindly arms graze the floor while violently butting the top of their heads against their partner's forehead. It wasn't long before the floor was covered in a greasy black slime, which I realized to my disgust was their blood.

This is utter depravity! I thought to myself. Although completely repulsed, I was unable to tear my eyes away from the theater of violence unfolding before me.

Several yards away, Fairuzo was engaged in what appeared to be a heated discussion with the one known as Darceva. She was angrily gesturing and pointing in my direction. Try as I might, I could not make out what they were arguing about over the noise of the band.

After a few moments, Fairuzo abruptly reached out and wrapped his large, powerful hands around her throat in a vice-like grip. He began vigorously throttling her until her face began to turn various shades of red, mauve, then dark purple. Finally, he released his hold on her and she crumpled to the ground like a discarded burlap sack, lying there motionless.

He then reared his right foot back and delivered a well-aimed kick to her lumpy backside with the pointed tip of his stiletto-heeled boot. The impact made such a loud crunching sound that it could be heard even over the music.

He stood there looking down on her with the most satisfied grin on his face, as if he'd been wanting to do that for the longest time.

Fairuzo strode away then, leaving Darceva in a moaning, defeated heap on the floor. Positioning himself beside me in the center of the room, he made a motion for the band to stop playing. He then called for everyone to gather around. They jostled and pushed each other, competing for the space nearest Fairuzo.

He then yelled, "Varlet! It is time!"

The trolls all turned to look expectantly at a small door panel to the right of the Mirror. After just a few moments, an albino-looking creature appeared. He had pale skin the color and texture of white corn and the rubbery amphibious body of an aquatic salamander, with a shovel-shaped head and little frilly pink gills in the place of ears.

He was walking upright on poorly-developed hind legs, balancing himself with his finned tail, while delicately holding on to a round silver serving tray with his tiny front paws. I could tell by the way he cautiously moved forward that he was blind, his eyes regressed and undeveloped in their sockets. He was apparently using some sort of sonar to make his way towards us.

Around his neck was a black box contraption attached to a wide red collar. Every so often the salamander would stiffen up and come to a full stop, tilting his head to one side while trembling. When he began moving again, it was in a different direction. I noticed that each time, right before this happened, a troll following closely behind him would jab a knotted finger at something being held in the palm of his hand.

It soon became clear that a remote control device was being employed to send little jolts of electricity through to the salamander's neck collar. A loud buzzing sound could be heard, and then the creature would nearly drop his tray in painful reaction to the shock. The trolls watching would then all laugh uproariously, as if this was the funniest thing they'd seen all day. I was sickened by not only this display of cruelty but that they found the blind salamander's distress to be fodder for hilarity.

Fairuzo turned to me and said, "Here comes one of our cave-slaves now with some of those delicious refreshments I promised you. You'll notice he's blind as a dust mop and needs a little buzz now and then to help him find his way around."

He gave a wicked chortle and the trolls standing close by all guffawed right along with him. The realization that Fairuzo found the suffering of the blind creature to be in any way humorous left me with a queasy feeling in the pit of my stomach.

In fact, the more he revealed this ugly streak of mean-spiritedness and sadism, the less desirable he became. I was now beginning to see past the seductive charisma and striking good looks that had so bedazzled me before. Up until now, he had managed to submerge and keep well-hidden this monstrously deviant side of his character; but now it was becoming far too obvious to ignore.

At least there's nothing deceptive about these trolls, I thought. *They are just as ugly on the outside as they are on the inside.* Not so with Fairuzo, though; for it was becoming clear that he had only been showing me his most beguiling side while deliberately keeping his true self hidden. But he was certainly no longer making any effort to conceal it now.

I began to feel trapped, as if I were standing in a rapidly-sinking pit of quicksand surrounded by minefields in every direction. I felt almost ashamed to have been so gullible, so naïve, so trusting, to have actually believed that Fairuzo would protect me from these nasty creatures, when he himself was one of them.

I knew then that somehow I had to escape this hellish place and find my way back home. Indeed, it was my only hope of survival.

And this was even before I saw what was on the tray the salamander was carrying.

CHAPTER 2

THE GOBLINS OF DARK HOLLOW

$\mathfrak{F}$ar from the pervasive evil that had once plagued and ruled their lives, the Dark Hollow Goblins were now safe – or so they thought. Forced to flee their beloved temple on the summit of Mount Hermon, they had managed to find refuge in a cluster of caverns on the other side of Earth. They believed that such a great distance would surely protect them from the tyrannical tentacles of the Cabal of Nations, the elite coven of Luciferians who had risen swiftly to power in their homeland.

As their former mountaintop home had been awash in the perpetual sunshine found above the clouds at such lofty altitudes, it had not been easy to adapt to their new lives underground. But the goblins were grateful they'd had the prescience to escape when they did – for the rest of their fellow countrymen were now trapped there, enduring dreary lives of shackled enslavement with no possibility of liberation.

The Dark Hollowians were a cheerful and benevolent clan, beloved by all who came to know them. A handsome, graceful people of noble countenance, they were of average height with dark, luxuriant hair. With so much of their time now being spent in torch-lit caves, their once-deep-olive complexions had faded gradually to an attractive greenish-alabaster, virtually the same color as the limestone slab markers they used in their burial grounds. Overall, they were a striking tribe of people, possessing both inner and outer beauty.

Never once had they ever been involved in war or in the bloodshed of any living creature, choosing instead to live and abide by strict ethical codes. They lived solely off of the vegetation that grew on the surrounding hillsides of Culpepper County, Virginia, the small mining community they now called home. They were so charming and endearing, in fact, that the copper miners working in the adjacent Azurite Mines shared their morning bowls of porridge with them. They also brought them apples and peaches from their bountiful orchards back home, leaving them outside the goblins' portal holes in little tin canisters.

Nearly every evening, the goblins would go on treasure-seeking missions outside the entrances to the mines, collecting the tiny chunks of quartz, malachite and azurite that had fallen out of the miners' wheelbarrows. They especially cherished the azurite, which they referred to as "The Stone of Heaven" for its magical healing properties and its ability to open celestial gateways. They believed the powerful energy that emanated from the azure-blue stones enhanced telepathic communication while aiding in extracting insight and wisdom from nightly dreams.

The goblins would place several chunks of azurite carefully in a circle just inside the opening to their caverns, with great faith that this would help protect any entering souls from demonic influences. They also believed the sacred stones would guide those souls departing from the Earthly realm into the Afterlife.

As gratitude for the food that the miners shared with them, the goblins would carry bowlfuls of pristine water from the nearby Dark Hollow Falls over to the Azurite Mines. They would also fashion intricate, hand-crafted jewelry out of the glittering quartz-stones, malachite and copper chips for the miners to take home to their wives, lady-friends and daughters. So pleased were the miners with these favors and gifts that they encouraged the goblins to keep any chunks of azurite they found for their own personal delight and spiritual rites.

The goblins also had close-knit relationships with the many animals that inhabited the hillsides and who wandered freely in and out of their caverns. On their journey over from their motherland, the goblins had brought with them a family of beloved rock badgers. These hyraxes were treasured for their companionship as well as their wisdom in securing safe housing and arranging elaborate sentry systems warning others of danger. Upon their arrival in the new land, the rock-dwelling creatures had adapted spectacularly to the sandstone cliffs while getting along surprisingly well with the local Trout Cave voles and Artic shrews.

But there were many other fascinating species here: Cumberland Cave pocket gophers, flying squirrels, lemmings, sloths, hares and caribou, as well as saber-toothed cats, cougars, jaguars, tapirs and dire wolves, all co-existing peacefully together.

Not generally known for mingling socially with others outside their genus, the big-eared fruit bats from the nearby limestone caverns would swoop down to eat slices of pears right out of the goblins' outstretched hands. In return for these treats, the bats protected them from the swarms of mosquitoes that fluttered uninvited into their cave openings on the humid summer nights, swatting them away with their massive and impressive wings.

All in all, it was a very harmonious and congenial atmosphere between all living creatures, and life was good... that is, until the Day of the Explosion, when nothing was ever the same again.

It was late summer, and the leaves had not yet begun turning autumn colors. It was a little before high noon, and the miners were just about to put down their pickaxes and step outside for their lunch break. The goblins were returning from their Falls water errand when the ground beneath their feet began to rumble and shake. First, they heard a muffled boom and then an incredibly loud blast, throwing them all violently to the ground, the water drenching them as it sloshed out of the buckets.

After a moment's confusion -- *had there just been an earthquake?* -- the goblins all looked at each other in terror, simultaneously realizing the horrible truth: the mine had just exploded. They all scrambled to their feet and rushed down to the scene of the disaster. But it was too late: the entire mine had been demolished and flattened by the blast. There was not much left other than scattered piles of dust and rubble. There did not initially appear to be any survivors.

The goblins scurried home to grab their shovels, then ran back to dig frantically through the debris, hoping to find at least one miner still alive that could be saved. They did come upon a few who had managed to survive the blast, but they were on their last breaths, bleeding profusely from missing limbs or fingers. Most had horribly charred and unrecognizable faces.

A couple of days after the tragedy, the Mining Authority came to clear out the rubble, cart away the dozens of decaying bodies, and officially board up the Azurite Mines.

The goblins fell into various states of shock, mourning and grief. Desolation and gloom settled over the entire community. Not only did they miss the camaraderie with their miner friends, but life suddenly seemed empty and purposeless without the daily excursions to the mine to bring water and collect stones. The pleasurable, productive evenings they'd spent lovingly crafting unique gifts of jewelry were now spent moping listlessly about the caverns and wistfully reminiscing about the good times that they now believed were gone forever.

They had also grown quite accustomed to the tin canisters of fruit the miners had so generously supplied them with, and now would have to go back to foraging for themselves. Although the pomegranate and prickly pear trees were plentiful, picking the fruit among the thorns made their hands bleed. They did not relish the resumption of this task.

Then one day a mysterious stranger arrived at the

Dark Hollow Caverns. He had wavy coal-black hair that fell past his shoulders; sharp, aristocratic features; a wisp of a mustache and a tufted, neatly-trimmed beard. His eyes were bottomless pits of black that glittered in the sun like those of a wolf spider's. He was dressed in the type of flowing garb that implied a representation of papacy, with the standard embroidered pallium over the white chasuble. His shoes were of the finest bark and cloth, artfully adorned with glistening gems and beads that formed esoteric symbols.

He went directly to the cavern home of Azazyel, the eldest and most respected goblin, forcefully pushing the portal door open and stepping in without the courtesy of ringing the entry bell. Inside, the family was gathered around the dining table. They were just about to sit down to their evening meal of freshly-picked arugula and watercress, rhubarb pie, prickly pear sauce and sun-dried figs.

The stranger aggressively pushed his way past Azazyel into the cavern's living quarters, loudly announcing that he represented the Board of the Mining Authority and was here on official business.

For a moment, Azazyel felt a sense of impending doom and genuine foreboding that the man might actually have been sent by the Mount Hermon Cabal of Nations, come all this way to deport the wayward, disobedient goblins back home for certain punishment and imprisonment. But whomever he was, it was apparent he had not come for any sort of pleasant chat and visit, but was here for an ulterior and most likely nefarious purpose.

The stranger brusquely informed Azazyel that he had come to inspect all of the goblins' quarters for contraband and to confiscate any items belonging to the Mines. To prove he had the authority to do so, he reached into his pocket and extracted a wrinkled piece of hemp paper, throwing it casually onto the dinner table for inspection.

Azazyel peered at it, and it looked to be some sort of official decree. The words "Order to Search and Seize" were written in bold, heavy lettering at the top and embossed with what appeared to be an official seal of gold.

When Azazyel reached out to pick up the paper for a closer examination, the man swiftly grabbed hold of his arm, twisted it behind his back, and then shoved him hard against the cavern wall, knocking the breath out of him.

"You will not be touching my things," hissed the man, a menacing look on his face, which was just inches away from Azazyel's.

Upon seeing this act of brutality, the children became afraid and began to cry. They had never before witnessed any display of violence, and were not at all accustomed to it.

"Shut those children up now, or else!" yelled the man with ferocious intensity.

Azazyel looked toward his wife, Lamia, who was standing close by and shivering in fear. He quietly besought her to take the children out of the way so that he could speak privately with the man. She did so slowly and with hesitancy, expecting the man to stop her at any moment with another show of force.

"What name shall I be addressing you by, sir?" the elder goblin asked politely, in his most respectful voice, hoping this might calm the man down some.

"Call me Phegor," the man replied curtly.

"And how may I be of assistance then? If you would kindly tell me --" began Azazyel, when Phegor rudely cut him off.

"Let's get straight down to business, shall we?" he said. "I haven't any time to waste with your useless pleasantries. I'm here about the treasures."

"What treasures are you speaking of?" Azazyel asked, truly puzzled.

"Don't play simpleton with me," Phegor sneered. "You know exactly what I'm talking about. These very baubles that you have lying all about here – where have you got all the rest stashed?" And with this, he grabbed a small pile of azurite stones from a nearby copper bowl, letting them slip through his fingers to clatter noisily upon the table.

Before Azazyel could even fashion an answer, Phegor barked out the order that he was to have every single goblin in the village gather up every bit of azurite, copper and quartz they had within their possessions. These all belonged to the Mine landowners now – not the goblins. He then informed Azazyel that he would be returning with several officers of the Authority to perform a thorough search of every dwelling on the premises.

Phegor then rudely reached onto the dinner table and grabbed a large piece of the rhubarb pie, shoving it into his mouth and chewing loudly. After making a show of swallowing, he said, "I'll be back within a fortnight's time to collect every stone your little village has in its possession. And it will do you no good at all to hold out, as we will be sure to dig up every single gem you try to hide."

All during this exchange, Azazyel's wife had been standing meekly over by the portal door with the children, slumping down as if she were trying to shrink herself into invisibility. Phegor strode briskly over to her, grabbed ahold of her shoulders, then pressed his lips roughly against her neck for a couple of moments. She reacted with a startled cry of surprise and pain.

Azazyel gasped and leapt forward to intervene, but Phegor had already released her. She fell back, cradling the palm of her hand over her neck, tears welling up in her eyes.

Phegor turned around to leer at Azazyel, daring him to make a move, then said, "And remember, my weak and insignificant little goblins: no longer will life be a bed of roses for you as it has been in the past. You will no longer have the protection of your little miner friends, for we have seen to it that they won't be returning.

"Oh, and that little mining explosion?" he added. "Did you really think that was accidental?" Here he gave a wicked, high-pitched cackle, reveling in their shocked expressions.

"Mark my words," he continued nastily, "from this day onward, you will touch nothing but thorns. And don't waste effort wishing to go back in time; for what once was yours will soon be all mine!"

And here he threw his head back and laughed diabolically, then cupped his hand under his chin to blow a vulgar kiss at Lamia. She shuddered in repulsion, still holding her hand protectively over her neck, which was now beginning to bleed.

He made a show of swishing his capelet then and walked to the door of the cavern. He deliberately kicked the protective circle of azurite stones out of his way. He took two steps out into the bright sunlight and then just seemed to vanish. It was as if a vortex had swept him up, for he was simply no longer there.

The goblin family wordlessly exchanged glances. Azazyel went to comfort his wife, who was now quietly sobbing. "What will happen to us now?" she cried.

"Don't worry, Lamia," he said soothingly. "We have two weeks with which to gather the stones he wants and then he should leave us alone."

"But what if he doesn't?" Lamia sobbed. "What if he keeps coming back and is never satisfied?"

"We will deal with that when the time comes," Azazyel replied firmly, although not without his own lingering doubts.

News of the ominous visit spread quickly throughout the caverns. The entire village of goblins met that evening to decide upon a proper course of action. They discussed the various positive and negative aspects for and against complying. They finally unanimously agreed it would be best just to placate the brutish and intimidating man. It was apparent he was more than capable of causing some very grim things to happen if they chose to defy him.

And now, with the stranger's boastful admission that the explosion had not been an accident after all – even insinuating that he had been behind its planning and execution – they certainly had every valid reason to fear that the same destructive action could easily be taken against their own cavern homes.

CHAPTER 3

THE POISON SPREADS

All that night, Lamia continued to weep uncontrollably. She kept wiping her mouth over and over, as if attempting to clear her tongue and saliva of something vile. In the middle of the night she had a coughing fit and sat up, whereupon a dark stream of rancid-smelling liquid came spewing out of her mouth. As Azazyel helplessly witnessed his wife's torment, he smelled something foul and evil permeating the air, like a slowly leaking cesspool.

The next morning, Lamia complained of a severe headache and nausea. Her normally pleasant and cheerful temperament was noticeably absent. Instead, she was irritable and short-tempered, and nothing at all seemed to agree with her.

She began cursing and muttering ireful threats under her breath when the children did not obey her quickly enough. It was not long before she took to hitting them when she felt they misbehaved. At first, it was just swats with the palm of her hand against their backs; then she took to shoving them roughly and for no reason. Finally, she began picking up heavy plates and cups to throw viciously at their heads as they ran away from her in terror.

In fact, her hateful, baleful attitude quickly became her perpetual disposition. There was now constant strife and disharmony within the household where once there had been nothing but cheeriness and laughter. Soon, it was as if the entire village had become infected with the same ugliness in spirit. They all now began constantly bickering and quarreling with each other over the pettiest of grievances.

Although they had meticulously gathered every gemstone in the entire village per the stranger's instruction, they were still filled with a nameless dread, uncertain as to what would happen when he did finally return to collect. This sense of imminent doom only exacerbated the tension and discord already prevalent.

Once so upbeat and industrious, the goblins now developed attitudes of laziness and resentment towards doing chores. They especially loathed having to do anything that caused them any extra work. They grumbled, groused and complained, feeling pity for themselves. They squabbled over who would make the daily excursions to the Dark Hollow Falls to bring back the buckets of water. No longer did they enjoy bathing in the waterfalls. They seemed to have developed an aversion to cleanliness, preferring instead to be slovenly and live among filth, as it involved the least amount of effort expended.

The children were heavily affected by the tense, unhappy atmosphere that now prevailed throughout the entire community. Not quite yet able to comprehend the concept of death or understand exactly why the miners would never be returning, they continued to badger their parents for the porridge and apples they had grown accustomed to eating. They whined when they were told they would now have to do without.

Instead of being grateful and appreciative of each meal as they had before, they now picked at their plates and sulked at the dinner table. They grumbled that the figs or berries were not ripe enough or that they wanted something different to eat. It soon became common for one or both parents to slap the children when they began complaining, which then led to crying and tantrums and all-around unpleasantness.

Early one evening, when Azazyel returned home from a trip to the Falls, he came upon his wife crouched on the floor by the dining table, ravenously feeding upon what appeared to be the remains of an animal. She looked up at him wildly, her eyes glowing red in the dusk, as if she'd gone feral and mad. She then went back to her voracious gnawing and chewing as he stood there in horror – for he immediately recognized the carcass as being one of their precious hyraxes.

"What on Earth is it that you are eating?" he cried in horror and revulsion, although he already knew.

"Come, taste it for yourself, and stop being such a whining prig," she snarled with her mouth still full. "It is much tastier than those boring twigs and leaves you've been bringing home lately," she added, sneering.

With only a small amount of hesitancy – for it did look rather enticing, and he was quite hungry – Azazyel leaned over and gingerly took a severed piece of leg off of the plate on the floor. The blood was still warm and trickling as he stuffed the freshly-killed, once-beloved animal's flesh quickly into his mouth.

"This is delicious!" he cried in surprised delight, in between bites. "Why have we never thought of having this as a meal before?"

Lamia just leered at him, too busy dipping her fingers ravenously into the pools of blood and flesh, and eagerly scooping up more entrails. "Wait until you taste the innards," she said with a sly cackle, after she'd swallowed another mouthful.

It was quite obvious to Azazyel then that this was not Lamia's first time eating the corpse of an animal. He could not help wondering then just what other secrets she'd been keeping from him.

It would not be long before he found out just what.

One day shortly thereafter, having just been out on the hillside for a short while to gather some rhubarb, Azazyel stepped back inside the cavern and heard loud grunting noises. He followed the sounds to the room where he and Lamia slept, and there in the bed lay his wife with the stranger from the Mining Authority heaving himself on top of her.

"What is going on here!" he shouted, and Phegor spun

his head around to look at him with a lascivious grin. Lamia gave a wide smile, as if pleased he had caught them together.

"How long has this been going on?" Azazyel cried.

"Long enough for it to be obvious you are a village idiot for not knowing about it," retorted Phegor with a snicker.

He rolled off of Lamia then and slithered past Azazyel into the hallway like a worm wiggling out of a half-eaten apple. Lamia showed no remorse or shame, not even attempting to cover herself as she got up out of the bed and nonchalantly put back on her clothing.

That night she casually confided to Azazyel that it had been Phegor who had suggested the idea of killing animals and consuming their flesh. She said it hadn't taken much convincing after he had showed her how easy it was to accomplish, and how rewardingly tasty it was.

First, he had taught her how to snap the neck of a baby hare – that being one of the quickest ways to kill – although the first time she'd attempted it, she did not do it properly, and the poor animal writhed around on the floor in agony, whimpering and crying pitifully for several long minutes until, finally, he lay still.

While watching the death throes of the animal, Phegor had laughed with great hilarity, making it apparent that he immensely enjoyed the animal's discomfort and pain. Lamia had quickly joined in with peals of her own derisive laughter. She felt an odd sense of pleasure intermingled with exhilaration at the sudden power that such a vile and cruel act filled her with. It felt good to have such undisputed dominion over such a small, helpless creature. She began to look forward to participating in future kills with her new lover.

Phegor then also taught her how to sink her teeth into the animal's neck and move her tongue and lips in the most efficient manner so as to create enough suction to siphon out the blood.

"Much more effective than letting the animal bleed out," he'd advised. "You see, this way, you don't waste any of the beneficial life's blood in some meaningless purifying ritual. When you directly drink the blood, you obtain all of the animal's dreams and their last dying emotions, which you can then absorb and utilize for enhanced mental powers and strength."

The very first time Azazyel killed an animal was in front of the children. It was one of their beloved hyraxes, and they had wailed and cried, begging him to stop. Just as it had carnally affected Lamia, it had also filled him with a perverted lust. As he licked the blood off of his hands, he began having twisted visions of all sorts of vulgarities. This wickedness excited him so much that he fell lewdly upon Lamia in the bed immediately afterwards in full view of the children.

But soon the children, too, could not help but be curious what the taste of flesh was like. After their first plateful, they quickly lost their initial aversion as well as any innate feelings of tenderness towards the creatures they had once cared so deeply about.

They gradually begin exhibiting cruelty towards any bird or animal they came across, throwing stones and kicking them. They now thought of them as no more than objects to be abused and killed. They even grew to enjoy the pain they inflicted upon the poor creatures.

It wasn't long at all before the entire village began to consume animal flesh, especially after realizing how effortlessly the smaller, more docile animals could be overtaken and killed, and how quickly the meat filled their growling bellies. It was certainly much easier and less tiring than picking fruit all day out in the hot Virginia sun. They soon learned to ignore any twinges of guilt or remorse whenever the animal struggled frantically to escape or gave out desperate cries of terror and pain.

It was also not long before meat had become their sole

diet. In fact, they could not seem to get enough of it, always wanting more, never sated. It was as if they had all fallen prey to some type of infectious and uncontrollable carnal lust, releasing an avalanche of gluttony and perverted pleasures that only the touching and eating of flesh would satisfy.

Not only were all the goblins now affected but also the bats they had once enjoyed sharing slices of pears with. They now could be seen swooping down to feed upon the blood of grazing animals, sometimes taking chunks of skin. Even the sweet songbirds joined in the depravity, dipping down to pounce on voles and shrews, piercing them with their sharp talons. They were no longer content with eating seeds and herbs.

As now even the animals had begun to devour one another, it had become commonplace for the goblins to come upon piles of carcass bones outside the caverns and all over the hillside. Wicked was the rancid blood that ran through the veins of every creature, their former way of life now completely corrupted.

Phegor had brazenly taken up permanent residence in the Dark Hollow Caverns, relegating the male goblins to the smaller back-caves while claiming the largest and roomiest caves for himself. By now, he had seduced all of the goblins' wives, leaving his beastly mark on each of their necks with a territorial branding, so they could be identified as property belonging exclusively to him.

Several female goblins lived with him in his spacious cavern quarters. They constantly bickered and fought over whose turn it was to sleep with him. Their husbands did not seem to mind at all, as they sometimes stopped by to watch the steady stream of bedroom intimacies. Sometimes they even joined in, if given the signal to do so by Phegor. After each session, the men came away with the same tell-tale puncture wounds on their necks as their wives had.

There was now a select group of goblins designated as

the colony's hunters and providers of flesh. They had been hand-picked specifically by Phegor for their swiftness and craftiness in the stalking of prey. Their job was to bring home as many carcasses as possible to create a stockpile.

Soon, they had amassed so many animal corpses that they found it necessary to begin storing them in the cooling waters of the Dark Hollow Falls. This would help to decelerate the inevitable process of putrefaction. Unfortunately, this resulted in the contamination of the once pure water they also used for drinking; but this did not seem to concern them.

Phegor taught them how to effectively start long-burning bonfires, so that they could utilize the ever-growing pile of bodies more efficiently. In this way, the goblins developed a taste for the cooked flesh, even though they still enjoyed tearing into the raw, bloody meat and gnawing on the bones of a fresh kill.

In this atmosphere of blood, death and wanton debauchery, the goblins soon began to distrust one another. They now found it necessary to add bolts and latches to their doors to maintain privacy and hamper pilfering. They held grudges, they told lies, and they gossiped cruelly behind each others' backs. Any semblance of loyalty, integrity or piety ceased to exist; these were now undesirable and unnecessary traits that no longer mattered.

They began choosing sides against one another, and the hatred and resentment grew to such a fevered pitch that, soon, a full-scale battle broke out between them all. Now, instead of using the copper pieces for creating beautiful artifacts of jewelry, the goblins utilized them to make swords, knives and breastplates for war. This was done under the tutelage and supervision of Azazyel, who seemed to have a special knack and adeptness for such things.

The women were eager to join in, using their long fingernails as claws to scratch out eyes and leave deep grooves upon their rivals' faces. Rifts grew between all of the goblins, with brothers pitted against brothers. Nothing was sacred any more, not even the blood being spilled between families.

And Phegor never did collect the treasured stones he claimed he'd come for on that initial visit. Rather, it had become quite clear he'd had a much more sinister intention in mind all along: for he'd managed to turn the entire clan of sweet, kind-hearted goblins into a hateful, vicious, warring mob constantly at each other's throats. He'd also introduced them to the idea of killing and consuming the innocent animals whom the goblins once cherished and considered friends.

The holy azurite stone rituals had been replaced with bloody sacrifices of young animals, where the goblins rabidly feasted upon the body parts and entrails afterwards. They began to engage in all manner of iniquities, including incestuous relationships between brothers and sisters, and even nonconsenting ones between father and child.

After a year of these perversions, and a diet now comprised solely of animal carcasses and blood, the women goblins began bearing children with a multitude of deformities: stunted limbs, crooked torsos, round and lumpy backs. Their heads were oversized and misshapen, and their bodies were covered with unsightly warts and growths. Their features were now coarse and gruesome, their ears saggy and pendulous. Their skin was a dull, lifeless gray, and their once-luxurious hair was now sparse and brittle.

And so the goblins, once pure of heart, noble and joyous, had transmuted into an unholy, hideous and repulsive breed, full of hate and maliciousness, and devoid of all joy.

Before, when their community had been harmonious and trusting, they'd had no need of a leader. But now, they required constant monitoring of the thievery and fiendish acts that ran rampant, and mediation of the daily fights and battles that continuously broke out. And so it was now accepted and undisputed that Phegor was their new leader and ruler. He was the one whom they now all looked to for every permission and decision. No one dared question his absolute authority.

But what the goblins did not realize was that Phegor was actually from the Mount Hermon Cabal, and he had followed them here. And what he had in mind for them next would be far drearier and more oppressive than what they had fled from.

CHAPTER 4

A PARADE OF BELOVED CREATURES

My mother had been so sure he was dead. Spirited away by the Grim Reaper, handed a one-way ticket to board that Last Train to Glory. If he wasn't already singing with the Invisible Choir upstairs, he was simply biding his time in the dirt, awaiting the verdict on whether he was in possession of a soul or not.

Not for one rational moment did she expect he'd ever wake up again, not while lying so still in his final, watery grave. And yet I knew the truth all along: that he had indeed long departed this mortal coil, and that I was witnessing a genuine, mind-blowing miracle with my very own eyes.

I must confess that I'd always preferred the company of animals to that of most humans. Even as a child, I had been innately fascinated with just about every living creature I came upon in the forest. And it wasn't just animals but reptiles, amphibians, fish, birds, and even insects. Unfortunately for them, I was not content to simply observe from afar, but felt compelled to capture and carry them home in little jam and pickle jars.

I held firefly/lightning bugs hostage just to watch them flitter and glow while trapped inside the glass, treading air like fairies cradling miniature lanterns. I was able to cram one rather large bullfrog inside a jar until he began inflating like an angry balloon about to pop. He looked so aggravated that I thought I'd better let him out before he exploded.

I would also gather up tiny sand crabs at the beach, placing them lovingly in shallow bowls of ocean water. But they rarely survived the ride home. I finally stopped taking them prisoner after my mother reminded me of their high mortality rate. She was probably more concerned about the decaying crustacean smell inside the car. She wasn't too happy about having to dispose of them after they perished either, which usually involved the multiple flushing of a toilet.

If someone had simply explained to me how cruel and selfish it was to hold these creatures captive, I believe I would have let them go immediately. But in my naiveté, I assumed that poking holes in the top of the jar lid would ensure their comfort until I eventually released them.

For quite some time, my yearning to bond with each and every one of them did not coincide with the ability to empathize with their abrupt loss of freedom. I simply was unable to comprehend the terror they must surely have felt at being suddenly scooped up and abducted by a large, monster-like hand. I would not obtain any sort of genuine empathy until many years later, following an epiphany that allowed me insight into what they must have undergone as my nonconsenting new playmate.

But before that moment of realization, there were little tell-tale signs all along the way, hinting that my love for these creatures was not in alignment with how I was unwittingly treating them.

For dinner one night, a piece of meat was placed upon my plate that looked unfamiliar. Upon biting into it, I was so repulsed by its bitter taste and squishy texture that I nearly spit it back out. When I asked my mother what it was, she told me it was lamb.

"Lamb?" I asked, confused. "Do you mean the animal, the baby lamb animal, the one that leaps around in the meadow?"

Now, I had only known of lambs from illustrations and movies, but to me, they were the epitome of innocence and high-spirited playfulness. So, when my mother reluctantly admitted that, yes, this pinkish-gray lump of flesh and congealed blood on my plate was one and the same as the animal, I became extremely upset and refused to take another bite. I felt mentally sickened and physically nauseous, as if I had been simultaneously tricked, lied to, and punched in the stomach.

Why hadn't I been told beforehand that this was what I was being given to eat? What if it hadn't tasted so bitter or unpleasant – would I have continued eating it, never finding out what it actually was?

From that day onward, I would refuse to eat lamb whenever I recognized its hacked-up remains on my dinner plate. I viewed it now not as something to be chewed and swallowed but as a symbol of a tragic and sorrowful demise. However, I still did not yet connect the dots to the hordes of other once-living creatures that took the lamb's place upon the plate, all of which I dutifully ate.

As for my beloved pets, I was allowed only one species at a time, and then only ones that could be contained in small cages or bowls that did not take up much space. A parade of animals crawled or swam by in my life in quick succession: a hamster, then a turtle, then a pair of goldfish, then an African dwarf frog, then an iguana.

None of my cherished pets lived very long in their tiny makeshift prisons. One even made a desperate but spectacular escape. Although his break for freedom had undoubtedly hastened his death, it at least had mercifully shortened the amount of time he was forced to spend trapped in what must have been an unbearable confinement.

My African dwarf frog was meant to live an entire life underwater. He did occasionally need to rise to the surface to breathe air, as he had lungs, not gills. He was barely an inch long and perfectly formed. He had a little pointed snout and an exotically spotted complexion like an aquatic oncilla. I imagined he was very similar to a sea monkey, which I was also enthralled by. But that was before I discovered they weren't really monkeys at all, but brine shrimp eggs that rarely hatched.

I was particularly fascinated with the frog's long, elegant legs that he would kick vigorously as he swam back and forth, up and down, in a miniscule bowl that contained nothing but water. His entire world had a circumference of not much more than nine inches.

In the ocean, he could have lived 20 years or longer; in captivity, less than five. Under my misguided, benighted care, he barely made it past a few weeks.

One day he went missing. The flimsy mesh netting barrier, secured at the top of the bowl by one thin rubber band, had been knocked off. Like a zebra discovered running frantically down an interstate highway in a daring attempt to escape a miserable life at the circus, the frog had no concrete plans of where he was absconding to. He only knew that he wanted out.

But sadly, like the zebra, the frog did not get far. He was found lifeless and desiccated a few weeks later by my mother while vacuuming in the next room. When she presented him to me, he looked like a sad, flattened replica of his former self. He resembled a deflated cicada orchid that had been pressed and dried between the pages of a book. Any trace of moisture once present in his cells had long since evaporated. I could only hope he did not suffocate too long or suffer too greatly.

I believe I did receive a glimpse then of how unhappy he must have been to have wanted out so urgently. He had only attempted what any thinking, feeling creature would have in order to change his surroundings. It makes me sad even now to think of the tiny space he was forced to live in. Although I had loved him dearly, I had been his captor and the cause of his misery. In my own defense, the truth is that, as a child, I knew no better.

But of all my captive pets, my favorite was a black moor goldfish named Popeye. He shared a tiny globular bowl with a yellow-colored fish-mate, Goldie. Perhaps Popeye was so special to me because he appeared misshapen and deformed, with huge, bulging eyes protruding abnormally from the sockets on either side of his head. I felt a sympathy and a tenderness towards him. I wished more than once that I could hold and kiss him, but at least had the sense to realize he needed to remain in the water.

The very first thing I would do upon arriving home from school each day was to check on my two friends in their bowl on the dining room table. But one fateful day, I came home to find Popeye floating motionless on his side on top of the water. One of his bulbous eyes was staring dully and unseeing up at me, glazed over with a misty film. His gills were neither lifting nor inflating.

Even at my young age of eight years old, I knew that could only mean he was dead.

As I stood looking down on him in the bowl, my mother came into the room, solemnly informing me that he'd been dead for several hours. She'd discovered him like that shortly after I'd gone to school that morning. She told me she had left him there undisturbed, just as he was, so that I could witness his death for myself and give him a proper burial. Although she herself was not at all fond of any of my pets – or of non-human critters in general – she did realize how much Popeye meant to me.

It was all so unexpected. I'd never even considered the possibility he would ever die. I'd never thought to plan ahead or even wonder how I would react to this inevitability. But, then again, what child does?

I knew what I had to do then, and I ran upstairs to my room: I was going to ask God to bring him back to life.

I don't even remember exactly what I said in the prayer, only that it was a desperate and heartfelt plea. I do remember kneeling beside my bed, crying and pleading with God to bring Popeye back. I not only believed that it was perfectly feasible for his death to be reversed, but I had complete faith that it would happen if I just prayed hard enough.

And, sure enough, when I came back downstairs, Popeye was swimming around the bowl again as if nothing out of the ordinary had transpired. It was simple: I had expected him to come back to life, and he had. I don't even remember feeling surprised, only happy that he was no longer dead.

When I called out to my mother that he was alive and swimming again, she came back into the room with an air of total disbelief and the opinion that such a thing was impossible. But when she saw the proof for herself, she was at a loss for words. I explained to her how I had prayed for God to bring him back, and He had.

At first, she seemed confused, unable to grasp or absorb the idea that he had come back to life. She told me he must not have been dead after all, that he was merely sick and had suddenly gotten better.

But that made no sense to me. I had seen for myself how his entire body was rigid and lifeless, his eyes misted over and utterly void of vivacity or spark. I had instinctively sensed that Popeye's spirit was no longer there. He had gone somewhere else far, far away. In fact, my mother had herself confirmed he had been floating immobile for so long in that position that he was most certainly dead.

And even if it were true he had just been feeling ill all that time, why would he abruptly start swimming around again the very moment I came back downstairs?

I remember wondering why someone – one who so consistently endorsed and encouraged the act of praying, and otherwise had such steady and unwavering faith – would then find it so difficult to believe that my prayer had been answered. Did you not pray for help and to receive answers?

I was also puzzled by how my mother could doubt such an undeniable miracle. In fact, it had been she who had first read to me the story of Lazarus, how he had been pronounced dead but had miraculously come back to life after four long days. I had not found the notion of it spooky

38

or strange at all, but wondrously uplifting. It was actually my recollection of that tale of resurrection that had fueled my belief that Popeye, too, could be brought back.

Perhaps my mother had such a hard time accepting Popeye's return from the dead because he was a mere fish. After all, he was not a human like Lazarus, and therefore not entitled to an immortal soul.

But although she was unable to concede or accept that my prayer had been answered – or that a fish could actually have a soul – I never had a moment's doubt that Popeye had been quite dead. I firmly believed that he had only come back to life because I had prayed for it to be so, along with the unfaltering conviction that it was possible.

For some reason I have no memory, vivid or otherwise, of when either Popeye or Goldie did actually and in finality succumb to death. But whenever it was, I apparently realized the futility of repeating that same prayer; I understood intuitively that this particular type of miracle could only occur once.

I must also have known that it was simply their time to pass over into a place much more expansive and glorious than their sad little fish bowl, and that even my love for them could no longer detain them on this physical realm.

CHAPTER 5

VANITY: THE TAUNT OF
THE MIRROR'S REFLECTION

It was just biding its time, waiting for me to come along. Like a vulture waiting for the hot sun to fry up his noonday lunch.

Propped up against a stone garden wall, the Mirror had a large "For Sale!" sign taped onto one of its corners. It caught my eye as I drove by, the glass glittering brilliantly in the sunlight like a smooth slab of pyrite. Although its ornate wood frame was a nondescript beige, I immediately envisioned it painted a vibrant shade of turquoise.

I lost no time in bartering with its current owner to take possession of it. The woman seemed overly eager to sell it, as if she couldn't wait to be rid of it. After hurriedly loading it into the back seat of my car, she spun on her heels and ran inside her house without another word. I heard the door slam behind her, then the click of a lock, as if she was afraid I'd change my mind about buying it.

On the way home, I felt incredibly pleased with my purchase. It was obviously an authentic antique of the highest caliber that I'd gotten for dirt-cheap. The thick glass was undistorted and ripple-free, and the wood had been intricately hand-carved. However, I did feel a bit guilty. I had just moved into my first home-away-from home and really couldn't afford to be spending any money on things I didn't need. I already owned two other perfectly functional mirrors, so my only excuse was that this had been purely an impulse buy.

Once I got it home, I fell to work decorating it. It wasn't long before I had transformed it into a work of magnificence. The frame was now a stunning oceanic-blue turquoise, and I'd glued a swirling mosaic of seashells, rhinestones and faux pearls all around its scalloped edges.

It was a heavy piece, but I was able to secure it on top of my dresser at just the right height. But I soon began noticing something very unsettling about the way it seemed to throw shadows upon my face where, in reality, none existed.

And even though this mirror seemed to reflect my features in the harshest light, it was the one I felt most compelled to gaze into. It began to both fascinate and repulse me with the way it seemed to magnify the faintest of lines and imperfections, and yet I could not seem to turn my head away each time I passed it.

Perhaps it was because I half-believed that having created this mirror that it in turn had created me. I wondered if it were playing cruel tricks with its unforgiving reflection or if it were actually revealing a somber truth – that the talons of time were now leaving behind perceptible rake marks and scars.

Gazing into its glass had become a painful experience, as if I were being stung by the prickled nettles of my own thwarted vanity. And as time went on, I began to dread facing this harbinger of my fading looks and what horrific new revelations it would impart each day; to fear the power, the hold it had over me, how it dictated my moods, my very self-image.

And I realized that this mirror, the very same mirror I had so proudly and lovingly crafted with my own hands, had become the very bane of my existence.

But even as I became uncontrollably obsessed with preserving my youthful countenance, I now, more than ever, desperately sought sleep. This I knew to be the elixir of vitality, yet it cunningly eluded me. And each night I tossed and turned only to awaken each morning to be chastised by the Mirror's mocking exaggeration of my weary and crumpled brow.

I began jealously guarding my pale, fragile skin from the malignant rays of the sun. I resented every moment I was subjected to its savage scrutiny and found myself avoiding the light of day. I was convinced that permanent lines were being carved indelibly by the claws of that stealthy vulture of youth.

I would not step outside now without darkly-tinted sunglasses shielding my delicate eyes. The fifteen-minute drive each morning to my place of employment soon became a daily tortuous excursion that I dreaded and endured.

Even as I began to withdraw from the outside world, my house became my unwitting tomb. And even as I hid from the sun and its wanton havoc, my sleepless nights were taking their toll. I felt helpless to slow the hands of a clock gone haywire, with time itself doing a cruel dance upon my face: not a slow, graceful one with soft, satiny ballet slippers, but a vicious tap dance with sadistically spiked heels.

It was painful and debilitating to see what my once-smooth, lineless complexion had become unless I took some immediate, drastic action – or would soon become, I should say. For I was now nearly convinced that my accursed mirror was not reflecting what now was, but whispering prophetic warnings of what would soon be.

I only knew this to be true because my other two mirrors reflected my appearance quite kindly and reasonably. It was only this one, this Turquoise Mirror of mine, that dared show me in such an unflattering light.

I came to regard it as both my best friend and my worst enemy – much like a trusted confidant revealing an unsettling secret under the guise of benevolent concern, then offering neither advice nor consolation, electing instead to sneer at my resulting distress.

As my obsession with my appearance grew, I found myself less and less capable of taking care of those small, tedious details that are involved in tending to one's business in life. I was unable to concentrate on anything but the most basic of necessities, which entailed getting up in the morning, plodding through work, and then returning to the gloomy, sunless refuge that had begun to feel more like a prison than a home.

For hours I sat upon my sofachair in front of the mind-sapping drone-box with its banal portrayals of life. I would stare listlessly at the screen with the sound muted, ignoring the ringing of the telephone. I no longer had anything to say to anyone – anything coherent, that is.

For even as I felt I was going mad, I still retained a thread of sanity that restrained and prevented me from blurting out the confession that a simple piece of wood and glass was holding me captive in my own home.

It's not that I cared if anyone thought I was losing my mind. No, I was far past caring what others thought now! And even in my disorientated state, I was well aware of the advice that I surely would have been given: Simply get rid of the damned thing!

But I knew this was something I could not do. It had become such an integral part of my life – albeit a source of interminable disquiet – that I felt as if I would lose a vital piece of my self if I were to get rid of it.

Perhaps I even thought I would *not* be able to get rid of it, that it would come back again and again to haunt me. Perhaps I feared it would return with a vengeance, knowing it had been reviled and cast out, infiltrating its sinister self into one of my other mirrors. Such collusion I knew I could not bear. For as much of a hold as this one mirror had on me, I still derived some small comfort in the reflections of my two other mirrors.

But even as they consoled and reassured me that all was well – that I was neither rapidly aging nor actually developing a haggard appearance – I still found it impossible to ignore the Turquoise Mirror's foreboding message:

What now you see, soon you shall be.

Each night I would delay going into my bedroom until the latest possible hour, dreading having to pass by the Mirror on my way to the bed. I would wait until my eyes had grown so heavy that I felt like I could not help but fall into a deep sleep once my head hit my pillow.

It was on one of those nights, not unlike any of the nights preceding it, that I arose from my chair in front of the drone-box with a curious sensation very similar to anticipation. Almost with a sense of wonderment as to why I felt so eager to go to sleep this evening but too mentally exhausted to question it, I went almost willingly into my bedroom, as if I were being led by the hand.

On my way to the bed I caught a shimmering glimpse of the Turquoise Mirror out of the corner of my eye. Even as I was determined not to succumb to its malefic influence this evening, I hesitated for a moment, puzzled by its placement on my dresser bureau. It now appeared to be tilted, as if someone had rearranged the glass inside the frame.

I stepped closer to examine this curious development. As I did so, I heard a faint crunching sound, then felt a sharp pain shoot through the bare heel of my right foot – although I must say it was more like a jolt of electricity than the pricking of some pointed object. I cried out loud, more in surprise than actual pain, then bent over to examine what it was I had stepped upon.

At first I could not quite make out what it was. Then, as I ventured a closer look, I saw it was a broken seashell that had stabbed me with its jagged edge. I bent down to pick it up, and upon doing so, noticed it was surrounded by a minuscule pool of sticky liquid. It was of a vile consistency, transparent light-brown in color, and looked as if it might be the remains of a flattened cockroach's entrails.

I drew back in revulsion, relieved I had not touched it. I did not need to wonder from whence the shell had come, for I could see quite clearly the indentation left on the mirror's frame where it had once been ensconced. How peculiar, I thought to myself, that it had fallen in such an angle so defiant of gravity!

It was then that I knew this was the Turquoise Mirror's doing, that the seashell had not simply fallen off of its own accord. The clammy fingers of terror grabbed ahold of my throat and squeezed. Simultaneously I felt at once totally alone and yet as if I were being watched by someone or something. I stared in abhorrence at the Mirror, then felt an anger rise up within me: anger at myself for allowing something so lifeless, so inanimate, so laughingly harmless, wield such control over my life.

Stop it! I screamed inside my head, though I was not sure if the directive was aimed more towards myself or at the Mirror. What I was certain of was that I had vowed I would get a good night's sleep and was determined to let nothing deter me from this much-needed rest – not tonight. And even as I thought this, I felt my anger subside and a great fatigue overtake me.

Wearily then I made my way to my bedside table. I clicked on the red ceramic owl lamp which served as my nightlight. It cast an eerie, crimson glow across my bed like smoldering embers from a dying fire. Yet I did not find its dim, bloody fluorescence to be ominous. On the contrary, its warm, comforting illumination thawed the icy chill in my heart.

I reached for the switch of the bright overhead bulb and snapped it off with a harsh click of finality. As the glare of the white light receded into a faint red incandescence, I climbed into bed. I arranged my head comfortably upon the pillow, pulling the sheets up to my chin. This evening I would do whatever it took to have an uninterrupted and restorative night of sleep. I blinked my eyes hard in an attempt to clear my mind of any biting gnats of worry.

Within seconds, I had fallen into a deep state of unconsciousness. Not only was it the deepest and most enchanted sleep I'd ever been embraced by, but one that would forever change the course of my life.

CHAPTER 6

A NOCTURNAL VISITOR

𝕴 must have slept for several hours. Upon rousing myself from my semicomatose state, my first perception was that I was not yet awake but still dreaming. The surrounding walls seemed to pulse and throb with a strange intensity, enveloped in a swirling, vaporous translucent-blue haze. I felt as if I were floating weightless under thick glass or immersed in the tranquil depths of some vast, lifeless ocean.

Then again the noise assaulted my ears, and I realized that it was this very racket that had jolted me out of my sleep. It was an abrasive sound, much like the claw of a hammer being dragged across glass. As it grew louder and more insistent, I struggled to lift my eyelids, which felt as if they were weighted with ten-pound penny bags. Even through my bleary, unfocused eyes I was quickly able to determine that the Turquoise Mirror was indeed the source of this alarming ruckus.

I watched with a fixed, morbid fascination as a crack appeared to lacerate the mirror's guts, widening into a jagged, serrated crevice. The ugly gaping gash resembled a freshly scapeled Caesarean section just prior to being sutured shut.

The scratching sound progressed into an ear-splitting, tumultuous din, not unlike that of a freight train roaring out of a tunnel. As I shielded my ears with my hands to protect them from this near-deafening cacophony, the noise then reached a crescendo. It erupted into a feverish, high-decibeled shriek that sounded for all the world like thousands of lost souls screaming as they were being burned in the fires of Hell.

Then, as abruptly as it had escalated, the clamor diminished in volume until it had ebbed away to a feeble wailing, like the siren of an ambulance fading off into the distance. Thereupon commenced a high-pitched hissing sound, like the shrill warning herald of a viper hidden deep in its lair-pit. When that too had faded away, there remained only a menacing silence, punctuated by small tufts of smoke floating nebulously from deep within the by-now massive chasm in the Turquoise Mirror.

Then, over the edge of the broken shards of the shattered mirror, a tiny clawed hand materialized. Its bony, elongated fingers were tipped by long, curling, blood-red talons. It was frantically scratching, endeavoring to claw its way out of the glass abyss. The top of its head next appeared and then its face. Oh, its face! It was a face of such perverse grotesquery, far beyond any mere Halloween mask, every feature a distorted anomaly; a visage of a most loathsome, hideously deformed and repulsive creature.

Covered with light-brown matted fur like a hairy cockroach, its huge purple-veined eyes were nearly bulging out of its head. It had a fat, bulbous red nose dotted with cancerous-appearing moles and warts. Its blubbery, slobbering lips hung limply, accentuated by a crooked line of bright red as if crudely drawn on with a cheap crayon, out of which protruded rotted, black teeth and a long, green serpentine tongue, which it flicked in and out of its mouth, causing obscene strands of spittle to form and hang.

Its belly was distended as if it had just gorged itself. It was covered in peeling, bead-like, brownish-yellow scales like those of a Gila Monster, intermixed with what appeared to be fresh scabs. It rested on two spindly little legs, which hardly seemed at all capable of supporting its swollen corpulence. Its feet were webbed and clawed, like those of a chicken's. It emitted a foul stench which permeated the room, the odor putrid enough to inspire an involuntary retching and covering of the mouth so as not to breathe in its noxious gas.

I stifled a scream as I saw the thing was crawling over the dresser bureau with obvious intent to come closer to me and invade my bed-space. I could do nothing but pull the bed sheets up to my chin and tremble with dread at what this revolting little goblin-creature had in mind.

It hopped off the dresser onto my bed like a cat, surprising me with its nimbleness, it having such an obese, jelly-like body. It squatted there on all fours, staring intensely into my eyes with its own watery, bloodshot eyeballs, sizing me up as a predator would its prey.

As it crouched there, I felt paralyzed, as if compelled into a stunned cataleptic trance. I could neither move nor avert my gaze. As I stared frozen with repulsion into its vulgar face, its orbs began to shake and vibrate as if the thing were having convulsions or a fit of some kind. Its tongue lolled out of its mouth and it bent its head sideways, twisting its stumpy little neck and rolling its eyes.

Then its pupils began to narrow until they had become vertical, coal-black slits. Its irises gleamed, emitting a surreal glow, thereupon turning a brilliant hue of turquoise. The contour of the eyes took on an exotic, oblong, almond shape until finally they quite resembled those of a wildcat's.

The rest of its face then appeared to melt, each feature undergoing a remarkable transformation: the fat, red, diseased-looking proboscis tapering into an aristocratic nose of a delicate slimness and nobility; the shapeless, hanging lips losing some of their fleshiness and dissolving into ones both well-formed and full, and of an attractive shade of muted violet. The revolting facial hair receded entirely to reveal a pale olive-gold complexion, creamy smooth and of an unblemished perfection.

Above its perfectly-shaped lips lay tiny wisps of black hair-strands, suggesting whiskers rather than a mustache. These were to be found on its chin also. The hair now covering its head was of darkest ebony, crowned by a glossy blue-black sheen and falling in soft, curving waves that encircled its face and curled 'round its pearly, shell-shaped ears.

Within seconds, the hideous troll-like creature had metamorphosed into the most devastatingly gorgeous being I had ever laid eyes upon. And though I could tell it was not of human origin – and most certainly not of this Earth – its gender was unmistakably that of the male sex.

With a languorous and virile sensuality he then stretched himself upwards from his crouched, panther-like position on the edge of my bed until he was literally towering over me, allowing me to gauge his considerable and most impressive height.

The skin on his bare, taut-muscled chest glowed like fine, gilded-lime porcelain interspersed with tiny black tufts of thorax hair. When he threw back his majestic head, the thick veins on his long, elegant neck protruded like throbbing ropes of azure.

He smiled at me then, his cat's-eyes glistening like fiery alexandrite in the red glow of my night lamp, his teeth flashing iridescently. And for just a moment, I thought I detected fangs.

His shoulders were enshrouded with a diaphanous black cloak, the glossy filminess undulating in shimmering ripples each time he flexed his sinewy torso. His legs were tightly encased in a gold spangled fabric patterned so as to simulate the scales of a reptile.

As he raised a translucent hand to his face to brush a wisp of hair away from his eyes, I saw he was endowed with extraordinarily long fingers, ferociously tipped with claw-like talons of dark crimson red.

He made a soft purring sound then sinuously slithered even closer to me, like some reptilian-cat creature, till he was but an inch away from my face. He buried his head into my neck then, his silky hair fanning airily across my face. As I was enveloped by him, I felt a rustling softness like velvet bat-wings glide across my shoulders.

I felt his moist tongue push itself insistently into my ear, and once again I trembled, this time not with dread but with pleasure.

It was then that he whispered: "Lie still, Ermina; I am not here to harm you, but to release you from your torment."

He continued his purr-like breathing in and out of my ear, in a hypnotic rhythm that was slow and soothing, and having such a seductive effect that I felt I could refuse him nothing. Each time he exhaled, a foggy cloud sprang forth from his lips, and a gelid mist fell upon my face like a meltwater spray escaping from glacial ice.

Again, he commenced whispering into my ear: "Do you not wish to remain young and beautiful forever, to never again lament the ravages of time?" I opened my mouth to reply, but no sound would come forth. I so desperately wanted to cry, "Yes!"

He whispered once more: "I can give you the eternal youth you so crave, if only you do not resist me."

I felt his frigid breath upon my neck then, followed by a sharp jab as if I were being administered a medicinal syringe. Then a fiery jolt surged through my entire body like a bolt of lightning. I stiffened in excruciating pain as a searing electrical current tore through my burning veins like hot, molten lava.

Just when I felt the torment nearly too much to bear, a wave of exquisite tranquility washed over me. It alleviated my agony and supplanted it with a blissful serenity the likes of which I'd never before known. I sighed with a deep ecstasy that emanated from my very soul.

After a few moments of reveling in this wondrous new bliss, I opened my eyes to gaze once again upon the ethereal creature whom had so enraptured me. But, alas, I saw only a faint blue light illuminating the spot where he had once lain.

And before I could wonder where he had vanished to or if indeed he had ever existed, I fell back into a deep, dreamless sleep.

CHAPTER 7

THE AWAKENING

When I opened my eyes the next morning, it was as if I were slowly coming back to consciousness from a prolonged delirium or coma. My head felt like a leaden block of concrete that had sunken deep into the pillow. The right side of my neck – particularly in the vicinity of my jugular vein – throbbed and radiated a sensation painfully reminiscent of an Asian Hornet's pulsing, voltaic sting. When I gingerly reached up to touch it, my fingers came back oozing a viscid syrup which I instinctively knew to be my own blood. As it slowly dripped like treacle upon my bedsheets, I was puzzled as to why it was now the deep blue color of azurite.

As I wearily sat up and pushed aside the covers to rise, I felt a wave of nausea assail me. My head began to strobe and pound as if there were an electric nail being driven into it by a ball-peen hammer. My heart began beating so rapidly I feared it might literally spring out of my chest.

I felt an abrupt blast of frigidity, as if a freezer door had been yanked open and its innards were wafting towards me. For a moment it felt like my lungs had lost their ability to inflate with air. I had to take several short, frantic gasps in order to catch my breath. I also detected a curious taste of sulfur on the tip of my tongue. It was quite nasty, like rotten eggs.

Overall, I felt as if I'd just taken a long, arduous hike to the utmost peak of a mountain while simultaneously battling a horrific hangover, and was now being subjected to all the resulting symptoms of altitude sickness. My vital organs felt as though they were being slowly and deliberately crushed in a vise.

After the pounding and nausea had abated somewhat, I attempted to get out of bed, holding onto the bedside table for balance. I felt disoriented and dizzy, and I was still a bit out of breath. Each step I took was a tedious effort, as if I were being forced to wade through a lake of muddy, waist-high water.

As I made my way laboriously across the room, random thoughts began popping rapidly into my head, as if someone sight unseen were speaking them directly into my ear. In no particular order, I heard the curious assertions that: air has a certain weight and is a cycle of ever-changing molecules; there are hotwater vents located at the bottoms of deep seas; all forms of energy, including light, will cause gravitation; photosynthesis converts light energy from the sun into fuel, and so on and so forth.

I could make neither heads nor tails of the purpose of these thoughts – particularly in my present state of confusion and unwellness – other than they appeared to be edifying instructions of some sort regarding scientific matters for which I had no use nor interest in. I was very relieved when they ceased just as abruptly as they had begun.

As I made my way slowly down the hallway, I realized that, although my stomach felt completely deflated and empty, I did not feel any hunger. What I did feel was an almost desperate thirst, as if my sleeping body had been aspirated and was now depleted of all liquids.

As I approached the entryway to the kitchen, I began hearing what sounded like muffled cries of anguish. They were accompanied by a frenzied scratching, as if many tiny creatures trapped inside a catacomb were calling out for help. The closer I got to the refrigerator, the louder and more urgent these cries grew. The sound itself was, in fact, so distressing, I was afraid to open the door for fear of what I might find. But my curiosity soon got the better of me. I wrapped my fingers warily around the handle, bracing myself for what might lie inside.

As I opened the refrigerator and cautiously peered in, I found nothing out of the ordinary: a jar of strawberry preserves, a glass bottle of lowfat milk, a half of a loaf of wheat bread, and the remains of a blueberry pie. Satisfied that there was nothing amiss or unusual, I reached for the bottle of milk to quench my ferocious thirst. But just as I did so, the wailing began again, this time so loud and insistent that I threw my hands up over my ears to shield them.

But what I saw next made me wish I'd covered my eyes instead – for several torso-less heads began to materialize inside the bottle of milk, floating around like little animated gumballs with their mouths opened wide in mid-scream. At first glance they appeared to be the tiny heads of children. But as my eyes focused, I saw they were the severed heads of animals, more specifically of baby cows, their eyes bulging and terrified.

I recoiled in horror and took a step backward, for seeing something alive inside was the last thing I'd expected to find. I could now feel all of their eyes burning into my face, beseeching me to help them.

It was then that one of the heads stopped wailing and, looking directly into my eyes, cried out, "Help us! Please help us!" Another of the heads then pleaded, "Please take us out to the orchard so we can go home!"

"But how did you get in here?" I cried out, shaken and confused.

"Don't you remember?" one answered. "You carried us here."

"But how can you be alive? And why have I not noticed you until now?" I asked, still perplexed and frightened.

"You were asleep before with your eyes shut tightly. But now that you are awake, you can perceive reality for what it truly is, and this enables you to see and hear us," one explained, quite sensibly.

"Yes," another head said, "and we've been waiting for

you to take us out to the orchard and set us free."

Still puzzled as to how these animals could have possibly gotten themselves into my refrigerator, I felt compelled to comply with their urgent requests. I took ahold of the bottle then and gently lifted it out, carrying it over to the door that led to the back yard.

As I stepped outside, the ultraviolet rays of the sun hit me full in the face. But instead of recoiling with my usual phobia of its potent beams searing and damaging my skin, I felt an electrifying jolt of energy pass through me. Along with it came a distinct uplifting of mood. Instead of fearing any maleffect, I now experienced these shafts of sunlight as having a preternatural healing impact.

I also noticed that my eyesight had intensified so remarkably that I now had the ability to see through solid objects as though they were translucent. It was as if the sun's electromagnetic radiation had transformed into waves of X-radiation. Even whilst marveling at my incredible newfound clarity of vision, I realized that the nausea and dizziness I'd experienced earlier was no longer present. I felt better than I had in years.

I walked up the hill to the crabapple tree orchard, still gently cradling the bottle of milk with its precious cargo. The little heads inside were now silent, although I could still see them bobbing and floating like the figureheads of little ships in a white frothy sea. The look of terror on their faces had been replaced with wonderment. Their eyes were darting excitedly everywhere around them as if they were discovering a strange and wondrous new land.

When I reached the top of the hill I spoke to them, asking what they wanted me to do next. One of the heads answered, "Just pour us out upon the ground and we will find our way back home."

"Our mother is waiting for us there," another announced gleefully.

I removed the lid and, with great care, poured the

contents of the bottle out onto the ground. As each one of the little heads settled into the dirt, their bodies began to slowly materialize: first their necks, backs and bellies, then their legs and hooves, until they were each tiny, perfectly formed little calves. They began to leap and gambol about joyously for a few moments, as if they were testing out newborn limbs.

One looked up at me and said with great delight, "You have made us all so very happy! And now we can go home and be with our mother!"

As I looked down at the others all gathered around me now, they had ecstatic smiles upon their faces and were nodding their heads most enthusiastically. Then, in unison, they began running as fast as their little legs would carry them to the outermost boundary of the orchard. They began to leap nimbly up into the air, soaring in a giant arc as if they were vaulting over the edge of a rainbow. One by one they began to dematerialize, then disintegrate into the stratosphere, until soon there was nothing left to see but thin wisps of curling smoke rising vaporously from the ground.

CHAPTER 8

FROM THE CAVERNS TO THE KINGDOM

Although Phegor was by now quite comfortably ensconced in the Dark Hollow Caverns, he realized the time was swiftly approaching when he would be moving the entire community to a much more suitable and clandestine locale. There would be a lot more space to spread out and multiply.

This had been the agenda of the Mount Hermon Cabal all along: to permanently relocate the goblins to their new cave-digs deep within the nethermost realm of the Tartarus Underground; to permanently mark each goblin as property in order to monitor and obtain control of them; and to encourage incestuous couplings between family members in order to mutate and expand the population as aberrantly as possible.

The Cabal was also in the process of building a new branch in the Underground that would expand its domain. It was even considering relocating several other divisions of its Headquarters there one day as well, including one of its laboratories. This would make it most convenient to conduct covert missions undetected and undisturbed in the deepest core of the Underground while overseeing and controlling Earth from its highest summit point.

Since Tartarus was virtually another planet – and considered to be the Negative Parallel Universe of Earth, or Earth's Dark Mirror – it was the perfect location for the Cabal to set up shop. It allowed them to rule by absolute, unadulterated evil and darkness.

Phegor was now merely awaiting the signal from Headquarters when the time was right and the new kingdom was ready to inhabit.

Administering The Mark to each of the goblin wives

had gone as smoothly and efficiently as a well-greased assembly line. Phegor had had absolutely no problem coaxing any of them to crawl under the sheets with him where they could be injected quickly and stealthily. In fact, it was they who eagerly sought out his attentions. There was no pursuit whatsoever required on his part.

Once he had gotten them into his bed, he would stab their necks with his fangs at the very moment he would shove his long scaly member into their mildewy cave-holes. His serpent-bite would leave behind a putrid-smelling dribble of saliva along with the tell-tale Beastly Mark: a double vertically-curled crest of royal purple that stood out boldly as if embossed.

As Phegor panted and grunted lewdly on top of them, they would swoon and howl as if he were making the sweetest, most romantic love to them. What they failed to notice was that the entire time he was inside them, he had an ugly sneer on his face. It was as if he found them too repulsive to even look at. And the moment he was finished, he withdrew from their embrace as if they had leprosy, quickly hopping out of bed like a frog on springs. But this they did not seem to notice either, for he had left them in a stunned, trance-like state.

When the wives finally noticed the double puncture wound in a looking-glass, they did not find it invasive or disfiguring at all. Rather, it evoked a great carnal and visceral response. It reminded them of the long, wild night they had just spent with the greatest lover they had ever had. And when they returned home to their own caverns the next morning, they could not stop themselves from bragging to their husbands about the incredible hammering they'd received all night long from Phegor.

The husbands would react with curiosity rather than jealousy. They would then go 'round and pay Phegor a visit themselves, with the hope of receiving their own lecherous instruction from the "Master of All Things Lustful," as he half-jokingly referred to himself.

And after watching him going at it with one of their wives, none of the husbands would dare even dream of disputing he deserved that title.

Phegor's system of infecting the male goblins worked like a charm as well: while they were preoccupied plying their newly-learned lascivious skills on whomever's wife was occupying Phegor's bed, they barely even noticed when he would sneak up behind them and sink his fangs deep into their necks. And even if they *had* noticed, they would not have dared complain. They were far too grateful for the never-ending sexcapades Phegor was providing them access to.

In no time at all, Phegor's quarters had become a continuous orgy of both male and female goblins coming and going. It ceased to matter to any of them whom their partner of the moment happened to be.

These multiple couplings soon resulted in the births of many children. They were all unwanted and just barely tolerated. They were offered just enough attention to keep them alive. Even the babies that weren't products of incestuous relationships or familial molestations were born with grotesqueries and deformities. This made them even more resented and rejected by the mothers and fathers.

The older children, who were always present to witness these sordid activities, soon learned to imitate the foul grunting noises they heard constantly emanating from the bedrooms. It seemed that the goblin parents had become so immersed in their own lustful cravings that they no longer had time to teach the children anything of value, including language, etiquette or morals. The children would simply point and grunt whenever they wanted something. They would then throw screaming fits when they were ignored (which was most often), or when they were unable to rouse their slothful parents out of slumber long enough to attend to their most basic of needs.

As for ensuring that all of the children received The Mark as well, Phegor would creep into their rooms while they were sleeping. He would personally administer the injection himself. If they awoke shrieking or complaining of pain afterwards, they would just be told they were having a bad dream. They would be given a quick meat treat to shut them up.

By now, the entire family of rock hyraxes brought over from Mount Hermon were long dead. Their once-beloved companions had been shoved into the goblins' greedy mouths to be chewed upon for a few moments, then expelled out their backsides as waste. Even the precious baby animals were gone, consumed for quick snacks by the bored children.

In fact, by this time, the hunter goblins had pretty much decimated most of the wildlife in the entire area with their new arsenal of weaponry. This resulted in many of the species becoming extinct, including the once-plentiful passenger pigeon and the dire wolf. This situation of sparseness also made it necessary to employ new methods of obtaining enough meat to feed them all. They no longer had any interest in the fruits and vegetation still growing freely and abundantly on the hillsides.

Phegor's solution was to teach them how to build traps and crude cages in order to capture and hold hostage various species of birds. They could then be bred to replenish their dwindling food supply.

As the birds huddled silent and miserable in the crowded cages, the goblins found it to be a constant source of amusement that their wings were now useless. They'd taunt them with cries of, "Let's see you fly now, you stupid bird!" They'd shove sticks and pebbles through the bars while waiting impatiently for them to grow plump enough to kill, all the while complaining how hungry they were. They were too lazy to go pick the fruit right outside their caves.

Although Phegor had his choice of any one of the goblin wives, he had specifically chosen Lamia to be his main mistress. It mattered none that she was already married to Azazyel. Phegor only meant this partnering to be a casual common-law arrangement of convenience. She would be providing the physical vessel for the gestation and birth of his one and only son, the all-important heir to his legacy.

No small part of making this decision had been the fact that Lamia was well-known throughout the Caverns for her habit of devouring other people's children. To her credit, she did at least leave her own offspring off the menu. Therefore, by designating her as the mother-to-be of Phegor's own son, it would ensure that his heir would not one day wind up on her dinner plate. It was an extremely prudent strategy.

But as much as Lamia enjoyed consuming children, she derived even more pleasure in the ritual of seducing them. She detested innocence and wanted to see it abolished in the community. But aside from these charming habits, Phegor found Lamia's serpentine attributes to be quite useful in advancing the pervasive wickedness he foresaw for his entire kingdom. She was the epitome of a gluttonous slattern: sly, greedy, slovenly and sluttish.

And as she had been the first-ever goblin Phegor had chosen to infect with The Mark, she was constantly reminding the others of just how this distinction entitled her to receive preferential treatment and privileges. She exhibited the most narcissistic, sociopathic traits: superficial charm and a most grandiose sense of self. She was parasitic and paranoid. She was opportunistic, conniving, calculating, manipulative, and willing to do whatever it took to assert her dominance over those she considered to be weaker.

In short, she was everything Phegor was looking for in a mate.

She was also one of the first goblins he had taught to partially-shapeshift. Her serpent's tail could sometimes be seen dragging along behind her on the rare occasions she decided to get out of bed. This, too, she used as leverage and bragging rights, and as proof of her superiority over the other goblins.

But even though Lamia had succeeded in convincing the other goblins of her supremacy, in no way did Phegor deem her to be anywhere near his equal. To him, all females – as well as animals and other species – ranked far beneath him in importance and intelligence. He had yet to encounter an exception.

And having chosen her to be the future mother of his son did not prevent or hinder Phegor in any way from cavorting and cohabiting with as many of the she-goblins as he pleased. In fact, he found Lamia to be no more attractive than any of the other wives. Indeed, he found them all to be equally repulsive.

They were certainly far below the lofty standards he'd grown accustomed to over at the Mount. There, a plethora of alluring succubi had been available to routinely service the officers of the Cabal. But the fact that none of the goblin wives physically appealed to him did not stop him from deriving intense carnal pleasure out of each coupling he initiated and participated in.

Aside from being the first one he'd infected, Lamia had also been the first to be taught the skills and pleasures of killing and flesh-eating. More than anything else, he felt this made her the most experienced. She was also the most compliant and the most easily persuadable. In fact, he was convinced that she would go to any lengths to please him. She would do whatever it took as long as she could continue to share his bed, even knowing she was just one of the many faceless dozens who did.

In fact, sometimes it seemed as if she were in direct competition with him in her willingness to perform just about any perverted act he had in mind, either in or out of the bedroom. He actually found this to be quite stimulating. He could always count on her to do something one of the others might balk at or find unsavory. Whatever immoral task he had in mind for her to accomplish, he felt certain she would obey his orders promptly and without question.

But he did occasionally recall how stunning Lamia had looked that day on his first visit to the Dark Hollow Caverns. In fact, it had been on sudden impulse that he had given her the serpent-bite just before he'd made his exit. His initial plan had been to wait until his return to start the fang-injections and spreading of poison.

There was something pious and stately about her that he was keenly impatient to corrupt and mold to his own standards of wickedness. He had perceived quite rightly that she would one day become extremely useful to him.

But it had only been a matter of days afterwards that her looks had begun slipping and deteriorating into a grotesque mockery of her former self. Her features became troll-like and distorted. Her back became hunched, humped, and lumpy. It was as if the putrid bile and vileness inside her intestines had crawled outwards from every orifice to infect the surface layer of her skin. It seemed to reflect and reveal the hideous monstrosity lying deep within.

Not so with Phegor, of course. He was still as strikingly handsome as the day they'd met. But, then again, he was one of the Twelve Elite Blue-Blooded Lords from Xibalba, whereas she was a mere second-generation black-blood from Earth he'd infected and mated with.

Azazyel was completely accepting and supportive of this arrangement. He had pretty much voluntarily ceased all contact with Lamia. He had grown exceedingly tired of her constant nagging and ill-tempered belittling of what she considered to be his inferior manhood in comparison with Phegor's.

Besides, he had become fully preoccupied with the various duties that his job as Lieutenant of Weaponry and Warmongering entailed. He was now Second-in-Command of this division. He was in charge of making and distributing the tools of the war trade, including brass knuckles, finger knives, daggers, swords, breastplates, spears, javelins, pickaxes and blowguns. And this significant position gave him great influence in the community.

In addition, Azazyel had proven himself invaluable to Phegor. He provided him with all kinds of scuttlebutt and inside prattle relating to the other goblins' personal affairs. Essentially, he had become the unofficial Community Snitch. He kept this second title to himself, of course. No one was the wiser as to whom among them was the informant.

He had no qualms about being engaged in what most might consider betrayals of confidence, as he no longer had any loyalty to or affection for the other goblins. His allegiance was solely now to Phegor.

And just to keep things stirred up and chaotic, Phegor had devised a system of awarding meaningless titles to the feuding goblins. This resulted in igniting suspicions among them that some were receiving perks like job promotions in exchange for snitching. Really, this ploy had succeeded quite splendidly in making them distrust, envy and despise each other even more.

As a result of all of this turmoil, there was a constant clamor for weapons. Each goblin wished to outdo his opponent by using the most sophisticated instruments of combat. In addition to scratching among the dirt for tidbits to tattle, all of this providing of weaponry kept Azazyel very busy. And no matter the outcome of each battle, it was certainly a win-win situation for him every time. He was generously rewarded with many favors for his endeavors, both from the goblins and from Phegor himself.

In his previous reign as Lord of the Moabites, Phegor had been instrumental in erecting the immoral institutions of both war *and* incest. It was not at all surprising, then, that he was also known as "The Disputer" and "The Destroyer." They were both well-deserved and apt descriptions of his expertise in sowing seeds of discord, fanning the flames of disputes until they were raging battle-blazes, and destroying the very fabric of a decent society. Instigating dissension, strife and depravity among the underlings was something Phegor thrived upon.

He also realized that the more splits, disunity and infighting he encouraged among the goblins, the less effort it took to deceive, manipulate and control them. And, if he was anything, Phegor was certainly a Master of Deception, Manipulation and Control.

But his specialty was infecting and sickening the blood of Earthly mortals. Indeed, that was the most effective way to spread evil, and he was damned good at it.

CHAPTER 9

THE TUNNEL TO TARTARUS

The time had come: Phegor had been given the green light from Headquarters to proceed with the relocation process. He had already recruited several of the less indolent goblins to forge ahead with pickaxes and tunnel their way down. It had not been an easy relegation, as most of them had become extremely lazy. They had to be bribed with promises of rank promotions and medals in order to even agree to perform any sort of manual labor.

In general, they had turned into a village of apathetic layabouts. They were no longer interested in doing much more than eating, sleeping and copulating when they weren't bickering and at war with each other. They were all feeling irritated and imposed upon. Although they grumbled about the bothersome effort and disruption to their lives, they knew better than to refuse to obey orders.

Phegor had announced that they would be leaving just about everything behind except for what he considered essential items: weapons, lanterns, clothing, and various sundries. Fortunately, the goblins had kept their living quarters sparse and uncluttered with only the barest of possessions.

It was also fortunate that the children had never been given any toys to play with, as these would have been left behind as well. And since the goblins' furniture had only been makeshift at best, they did not have to worry about lugging any of this along either. However, they were not pleased at all when they found out they would be transporting Phegor's heavy Royal Bed, even though it would be disassembled for the journey.

Phegor had requisitioned Azazyel to concoct the simple but volatile formula for the explosives that were to be tossed down the vertical mine shafts ahead of the diggers. He had been fastidiously instructed as to the proper way to blend together the sulphur, red phosphorus, potassium chlorate and ground-up glass. These ingredients made up the incendiary powder keg of what Phegor fondly referred to as "the bomb stew." In fact, it was the same recipe that the Mining Authority had always used for preparing the hillsides for excavations. It had never failed to achieve its goal of annihilation, permanently flattening the once-picturesque mountainous landscape.

Of course, by now, it was no secret to anyone that it had been Phegor who had set off the deadly explosions that day in the Azurite Mines. But the goblins were long past caring about any of their dead miner friends. In fact, they now blamed the miners for having brought such a horrific fate down upon themselves. They believed it had been their own faults for working in the mines in the first place.

After all, who in their right mind besides a fool would want to dirty their hands and break their backs at any type of arduous job involving such extreme physical exertion? They had conveniently forgotten about all the gifts the miners had given them, along with the holy azurite stones and other gems they had once been so fond of collecting.

All they found to be of value now was the copper, as it was the material needed for making the all-important weapons for war. Treasures that glittered in the sun, items of loveliness that exalted the spirit – these things meant nothing to them these days. What they had previously found so precious just seemed dull and meaningless to them now.

Of course, it made no logical sense to blame the victims, but Phegor had had no trouble at all in convincing the goblins that this was a rational and valid viewpoint. He could twist the simplest thought process into something so convoluted that they found it required just too much effort to argue against. It was much easier not to question or even think at all when being given information with a possibly biased perspective, especially from someone as persuasive and guileful as Phegor.

Eliminating the miners from the overall picture had always been a crucial part of the Cabal's agenda for Dark Hollow. All hailing from different parts of the countryside, the miners' scattered presence would have interfered in the localized depravity and corruption that was Phegor's perverted vision specifically for the goblin community. And once they were settled into the Tartarus Underground, this concept would become a reality. Every iniquitous detail would come to fruition and cement their destiny.

But for now, not much made sense in the lives of the Dark Hollow Goblins. They existed in a constant state of anxiety and confusion. It was like they were in limbo.

However, Phegor *had* succeeded in sparking a tiny particle of interest in them about what their new home would be like. As much as they had grown to despise the sun where they were now, they couldn't help wondering what it would be like to live completely without it so far underground.

When one of the goblins timidly voiced this particular concern to Phegor, he had been informed that they would still occasionally be allowed to visit Earth and its hot plasma star whenever they needed certain provisions. Phegor had declined to expound further upon what these particular provisions would be exactly. His answer served to satisfy the goblin's curiosity, though, and he then went back and passed the information on to the others.

On the day of the move, Phegor began barking out orders: first, the goblins would toss the explosions crafted by Azazyel down the burrowed holes; then the diggers would begin tunneling. The remainder of the goblins would take up the rear carrying the essential items.

Of course, Phegor would not be lifting a finger throughout this entire pilgrimage. In fact, he had arranged for four of the tallest and strongest goblins to carry him on a pallet-bed blanketed in the softest Irish moss, mullein leaves, and the fuzzy flower plumes of fountain grasses. This carriage of royalty would ensure him a luxuriously comfortable ride down. As well, his fancy hand-cobbled boots would be protected from soilage. None of the nasty cave-dust would be allowed to mar or muss his luxuriant head of hair.

When the question of food was brought to his attention, Phegor snapped his fingers. Several of the hunter-goblins appeared, all carrying cages. Some were full of birds and others were full of baby gophers. He informed everyone that this was to serve as their food on the voyage down. He added that there would be no fancy bonfires and none of this waiting until the food-animal had reached ultimate plumpness. These meals would be served raw, as-is, and on a first-come/first-served basis. Of course, he realized the goblins would be fighting like demented savages over the limited amount of live caged prey. He looked forward to this entertainment, anticipating much spillage of blood.

He had prepared for his own provisions by stuffing his pockets and personal knapsacks full of squirming voles whom he'd stunned and sedated with neck bites. He would most definitely be well-fed. He had absolutely no plans to share his rations with anyone.

Of course, Phegor realized it wasn't even necessary to travel the same tedious route as the peons and peasant-goblins. He could assume any shape he wished in the blink of an eye and be teleported instantaneously to the target site. But he could not trust the shiftless, incompetent goblins to find their way on their own without his authoritarian presence and guidance.

There was Azazyel, of course, who could possibly take charge while Phegor flitted ahead, but he was too busy preparing the mixture for the explosions. He briefly considered Lamia, but rejected the idea outright. He realized that the other goblins would simply sneer at any attempt she made to assert authority.

As yet, she was still completely unaware that she would be the one to bear his heir. This was deliberate. She had no need to know until right before the conception seed was to be implanted. This would occur right after their arrival on Tartarus.

After it was made known to the others that she would be the new Lord's mother, she would more than likely be accorded a bit more respect from the community. But being fully aware of her current temperament, Phegor could not imagine how much more obnoxious, demanding and full of herself she might become after being informed of her new role and elevated status. As it was, she was extremely disliked by just about everyone. They already found her level of perceived self-importance far beyond grating and insufferable.

There was no guarantee that she could be trusted to properly mother the child either. But at least she would not be considering him edible. If she became intolerable and too difficult to manage, however, he'd have no problem with bringing in a nanny/surrogate to raise his son. After all, Lamia was really only needed temporarily for the incubatory accommodations of her womb.

Essentially, what would happen to her afterwards would all be contingent upon how she behaved herself. He certainly would not be putting up with one iota of dramatic nonsense from her. He would have no problem tossing her aside as a nuisance and banning all future contact with his child.

Phegor had meticulously calendared out the gestation period: his son would be born precisely in time for the Winter Solstice. This was already an event of great celebration, it being the longest night of the year. But now it would be even more of a distinguished and momentous occasion, as it would mark the birth of the heir to the new Kingdom: the one and only true son of Lord Belphegor Cuchumaquic of Xibalba.

CHAPTER 10

THE SERUM AND THE SOUL

All this time Fairuzo had not left Ermina's side. Having literally transformed himself into the proverbial fly on the wall, he flitted effortlessly and undetected from room to room before following her outside. All the while, he was observing her with his extraordinary set of compound eyes and ocelli.

And he was not at all pleased with what he'd seen so far.

From her visceral reaction to the creatures in the milk bottle, along with her newfound predilection to sunlight, he had every reason to suspect that her soul was still intact. If this was indeed the case, he would soon have a critical situation on his hands.

In fact, she was not exhibiting any of the customary behavior that the scores of neophytes before her had upon their Awakening. In all of his centuries of unholy soul-gathering, this had never before happened. He was puzzled as to what could have possibly gone awry. He would have to carefully monitor and guard her now to ensure she did not influence any of the others. There was a very real danger of mutiny once he transported her to the colony.

The potent hydrozoa serum that Fairuzo carried in his saliva and secreted from his fangs during an Injection/Infection procedure had never before failed to produce full transformation. The tell-tale signs of a successful soulless rebirth would always appear the next morning. The most prominent was an aversion to the rays of the sun and a dramatic dulling of empathy so essential to a devoted predator.

Fairuzo had always been very careful to select and seduce only those who were alone and unhappy with their lives. He made sure they had no familial or binding Earthly tethers.

He was particularly attracted to those who exhibited traits of vanity and narcissism. He was able to feed upon these attributes and utilize them as portals of entry. These distinguishing features of self-absorption made his newly-infected victims much more compliant and grateful. They had very few misgivings about having to leave Earth behind, and were much more willing to accept and embrace both him and their new world.

Never before had there been any indication of reluctance or resistance on the part of a fresh recruit. They were most eager to begin their new existence in the Netherworld of The Defiled and The Eternally Forsaken. They had no qualms regarding their renunciation of all ties with their former lives. They welcomed any tutelage from their new Lord and Master, who informed them of the edicts each would now be expected to abide by.

The problem was that most of these steadfast decrees of conduct applied only to those no longer in possession of their souls. And the discarded soul-shell, typically shed immediately upon the newly-infected's initial arising, was nowhere to be found in Ermina's house.

In just about every case, the shell would be shrugged off onto the floor-space right beside the bed. It would lie there rejected and quivering like an abandoned pet: a flattened, oblong-shaped, reddish-green slough-blob still damp and pulsing with the life's blood. After being exposed to the air, it would take but a few moments for it to begin to oxidize and decay, bubbling and wrinkling and forming a thin layer of crust. Finally, it would turn limp, black and lifeless.

Fairuzo would scoop up the flimsy viscous tissue with his own hands and carry it over to the dresser bureau. He would fold it neatly like a contraband kite into a tiny square bundle. He would then slip it securely inside his cloak pocket for safekeeping until he could return to the colony.

Once back home, he would pay a visit to the locked and heavily guarded Soul Warehouse, of which only he had inside access to. There, he would carefully wrap the folded soul-shell in gauze. He would place it in a solution of formaldehyde inside of a serially-numbered glass jar with the name of its former owner. He would then position it beside the thousands of other jars lined up diagonally in what resembled a vast basement wine cellar.

About the only proof that the serum had had any effect at all upon Ermina was that the blood oozing from the injection site had transformed in color from an oxygenated crimson red to a deep, rich blue. But what was most puzzling was that blue blood was found only in non-human Earthling species like the octopus or tarantula. However, in transmogrified humanoids, this was indicative of royalty. Most specifically, it was in a first-generation Neph-Biter spawned on Tartarus, descended directly from the Dark Hollow Caverns and Lords of Xibalba lineage. Heretofore, only Fairuzo was known to carry this blood type inside his veins.

In stark contrast, the life-sap of all the other initiates, infected by either the Mount Hermonites or their hybrid Neph-spawn, resembled the coal-black waters of the Acheron River of Woe. It was completely void of all hue or light.

And now, as Ermina stepped back inside the house after having released the cow-creatures, Fairuzo knew her time was running out. It would be but a matter of moments before she would begin to gasp for breath. For even with an intact soul, her interior organs no longer functioned as they had when she was mortal. Her lungs were no exception.

For her now, the Earthly atmosphere was the equivalent of water for a dolphin, only able to hold breath for brief periods of time before finding it crucial to come up for air. And an atmosphere with an altitude low enough to provide enough oxygen could now only be found in the deep underground caverns of Fairuzo's kingdom. This was where she would be spending most of her time.

Henceforth for Ermina, Earth would no longer be a place to live, but one where she and the other inhabitants of the colony would visit but briefly to seek prey for sustenance. And whenever the sating of hunger necessitated a visit to Earth, there would always be an overriding urgency to finish the task before running out of oxygen.

There were always warning signs when the allotted time was up. First, it would feel like there was a heavy weight pressing upon their chest. Shortly thereafter, they would begin to struggle for air and find it exceedingly difficult to catch a breath. When no breath at all could be caught, they would then enter a Death Zone similar to that of a mountain climber when reaching an altitude too high for sufficient oxygen. The ensuing frantic gasping would then inevitably lead into the slow, agonizing process of suffocation.

After many moments of such torment, they would finally and mercifully lapse into a type of paralyzed half-consciousness, whereupon they would shrink and disintegrate until they became less than a speck of dust. They would then either completely cease to exist or wind up trapped between two worlds in a kind of hideous Purgatorial existence. Blind and mute, they would be unable to cry out for help or even fathom how to escape – a fate one should wish only upon their worst enemy.

This grim possibility awaited all of The Defiled. It was the one terror that made their hedonistic existence less than ideal and far from idyllic. Sometimes they were forced to return to the colony prematurely and with voracious hunger, having been unable to procure a prey's life-blood, so terrified were they of overstaying their visit. Some even grew to greatly resent having to travel to Earth for this very reason. Nevertheless, they had no choice; it was either that or starve.

But Fairuzo had planned ahead for this very moment. He had brought with him a very special container of botanicals that would give Ermina back her breath. It was a blend of black bindweed, deep scarlet witchweed, vines of kudzu, and minced leaves from Mary's Gold Flower of the Dead. The effect that inhaling this potent mixture of weeds and foliage would have upon her would be the equivalent of a fast-acting oxygen mask.

For mortals inhaling its scent, it had the effect of taking one's breath away; but for a Defiled, it would literally give breath back. Indeed, it was the secret to prolonging a stay on Earth that very few but he knew about. He was also fully aware that restoring her breathing would serve to endear him to her as savior and healer while adding an element of indebtedness to the relationship.

After swiftly transforming from fly to his own recognizable form, Fairuzo grabbed the canister of medicinals from the bedroom closet where he had stashed it away. With impeccable timing, he would step out into the hallway to where Ermina would just be beginning to clutch her chest and gasp for air.

Her eyes, already wide with panic, would nearly pop out of her head when she saw him standing in full three-dimensional form before her. He was prepared for her shocked reaction, as he was certain she recalled him as nothing more than a vivid dream.

It was also not lost upon Fairuzo that it was indeed the ultimate irony he would now be rescuing her from an affliction that he himself had deliberately created in her.

CHAPTER 11

THE POTION AND THE PORTAL

As I stepped back inside the house, I was immediately struck by how dark and gloomy it all felt, especially after having been outside in the bright, cheery brilliance of the sun. Odd how I had grown so accustomed to living in such dreary surroundings. I'd had only the dimmest of lights as illumination, my thick, opaque curtains drawn tightly over murky windows streaked with dirt. It was almost like I was stepping into a once-familiar place that no longer felt like home, as if someone else lived there now, and not me.

There was definitely something different about the way I felt today. I wondered if it had anything to do with that strange dream I'd had last night. Even now I questioned if it had been merely a dream, so vividly real it had seemed.

The entire experience with the baby cows felt completely surreal yet so intensely genuine as well. It had awakened in me a curiosity towards things I'd never before given a moment's thought to. For instance, I now could not help but wonder if every bottle of milk contained more baby cows trapped inside, or had it just been this most recent one I'd purchased? And were other people able to see them as I had? At any rate, I decided I would never again buy any form of cow's milk, as it seemed to be linked to distress and suffering; I could certainly do without it.

Compared to the lucidity I felt at this very moment, it was as if I had been sleepwalking my entire life up until now. It was all quite puzzling, yet freeing and elating at the same time.

But just as I was pondering all of this, my chest began to suddenly seize up. It was as if there was a great weight upon it pressing downwards, preventing me from inflating my lungs. As I struggled to catch my breath, I thought, *This is what a panic attack must feel like!* My mind raced in terror, desperately trying to figure out how to get my lungs to fill with enough air to gulp in another breath.

Even as I stood there frantically gasping, I became aware of a presence in the hallway. Out of the corner of my eye I could clearly see there was someone standing a few feet away from me. I suddenly had the shocking realization that it was the man from my dream. But how could he be real? And what was he doing here?

There was a swishing sound and, suddenly, he was standing right next to me, having traveled several feet in the blink of an eye. He was holding in his hand what appeared to be a small cylindrical container. He bent over and exhaled, directing his breath inside, and a plume of smoke-vapor arose from within. He then shoved it directly under my nose.

It had a strong floral fragrance. It reminded me vaguely of the rose water that I put on my face each night. But underlying that was a peculiar musky smell reminiscent of marigolds potted in freshly-dug dirt shoveled over a coffin.

The man spoke: "Quickly now, you must take deep breaths."

I inhaled deeply and gratefully then. My limp and flattened lungs quickly responded by filling with blessed air. I continued to breathe in the scent. It became increasingly pleasing until it was like heavenly nectar from the ripest serendipity berry. I felt a calmness descend over me, and my anxiety evaporated, spreading a feeling of relief throughout my entire body.

"We grow those, too," the man from my dream said. I glanced at him questioningly, having no idea what he was referring to.

"The serendipity berries," he further explained. "You were just thinking of them. We're able to grow them in our underground datura gardens, which have the low altitude required for them to flourish." And here, he gave a cryptic smile that bordered on slyness, as if hoping he had shocked me with his apparent ability to read my thoughts.

After a few seconds more, he withdrew the vial. I was now able to breathe normally again on my own. As I focused my full attention upon him, I saw it was definitely the same stunning man-creature who had lain next to me in bed last night in what I thought had been a dream.

But I could not deny that he was here standing next to me now, and that this seemed as real as anything I'd ever experienced. I certainly had no doubt that the frightening ordeal I'd just undergone of not being able to catch my breath had been undeniably real. And what was in that miraculous concoction that had given me back my ability to breathe?

Just as I was about to ask, his hand touched my waist and there was a distinct spark of static electricity. But even in such close proximity, I felt no warmth whatsoever emanating from his body, and this I found to be quite peculiar.

Wordlessly, then, he took ahold of my hand with his own frigid one and led me into the bedroom. He brought me over to the dresser bureau, stopping in front of the Turquoise Mirror.

"Look at yourself now," he said, letting go of my hand and gently pushing me forward.

As I peered directly into the mirror's glass, I could hardly believe what I was now seeing: all of the unsightly lines and flaws so obvious before were no longer visible. Instead, my face looked like fine porcelain, smooth, velvety and flawless.

There was something remarkably different about my eyes as well, for they now appeared to be emitting an eerie phosphorescent luminosity. In fact, the pupils themselves seemed to be radiating glowing blue beams as if being directed from the tip of a laser pen.

Even as I was marveling over this curious effect, I

suddenly realized that I was seeing only my own reflection in the mirror; the man no longer appeared to be in the room. But when I turned my head, I saw that he was still standing right beside me.

"Why doesn't your reflection appear in the mirror?" I blurted out suspiciously.

"It doesn't need to; I already know what I look like," he said, laughing.

But that doesn't explain why I can't see you, I thought peevishly to myself. Suddenly his image *did* materialize in the mirror, as if it were something he could turn on and off and control at will. Just as I was wondering how he was able to manipulate his own reflection, that odd voice spoke directly into my ear again, and it said:

"A mirror is glass coated with a crystal network of atoms which vibrate when light attempts to penetrate, thus reflecting the light from the surface."

It was the same type of random, pedantic thought as the ones I'd had earlier. Those, too, had seemed to originate from a source outside my own head. But the man's lips had not moved the entire time the voice spoke, so I was fairly certain it had not been him.

I looked around the room but saw no one else there. When I looked back into the mirror, both the man standing beside me and his reflection had vanished.

Then I heard his voice, and it was coming from inside my closet. He said, "Come here, my dear, I have something to show you."

There he goes again, I thought, *whisking himself away like an invisible dragonfly. How does one move that quickly without even being seen leaving or arriving?*

I walked over to the closet, instantly curious as to what it was he was so eager to show me.

He slowly slid open the closet door as if it were a theatrical curtain. Directly behind him on the wall inside I was surprised to see a small, octagonal-shaped door. It had certainly not been there before; for as many times as I had been in my own closet, I would surely have seen it!

"Behold this portal that will take you to my kingdom," he said grandly, gesturing with a flourish at the mysterious entry panel. "For I am Lord Fairuzo, Ruler of The Land of Turquoise.

"And now, if you would allow me the honor of escorting you to your new home, let us be on our way," he said as he reached for my arm.

"My new home? But where are we going?" I asked in confusion, while allowing him to pull me inside the closet. I had a funny feeling in the pit of my stomach akin to fear, but intermingled with excitement.

"Come, come, now. All of your questions will be answered on the way there. Until you have become acclimated to the Underground, you will not have the ability to teleport. So, unfortunately, we have quite an extensive and tedious descent ahead of us."

"Teleport? The Underground?" I repeated feebly, feeling perplexed. This was all moving a bit too fast for my liking. And it really did seem as if he were starting to speak a different language, one that I was having a hard time comprehending.

As if to confirm this, he then said what sounded like, "Glabish sum lata. Wobellum zim talis pilloto."

"What?" I asked in bewilderment. "I did not understand what you just said." I couldn't help feeling a bit foolish and dim-witted, as if I should somehow already be fluent in this unfamiliar language he was speaking.

"I said they are all waiting for us and are quite eager to meet you, so let us not tarry. They will be growing quite impatient if we do not appear soon," Fairuzo replied.

He then reached over to the portal door to unlatch it, and it swung open easily, albeit with a slight creak. I was nearly blinded by the intense blue light that sprang forth from the opening. As my eyes became accustomed to the glare, I could see it was a cavern of some kind. There were many wooden steps leading down that looked roughly hewn and precariously placed. The stairs seemed to endlessly spiral until they disappeared into a thick grayish fog below.

"That looks pretty steep," I said warily. "Are you sure I won't fall, going down all of those steps?" I was not all that comfortable with great heights, especially ones in strange places that did not appear to have any sort of safety nets nor even a rail to hold on to.

Fairuzo replied, "As long as you are willingly making the descent by your own choice and of your own volition, there will be no gravity pulling you downward. Therefore, it is highly unlikely that you would fall."

I wondered how such a thing could even be possible, this lack of gravity. But even odder still was his apparent need to openly establish that I was coming with him of my own free will. Or was I? It could almost be argued that I was under a hypnosis of some kind, so eagerly did I want to acquiesce to whatever he suggested.

And what if I *did* refuse? Truthfully, that option had not even entered my mind. In fact, I found myself quite eager to go with him to wherever it was he wanted to take me. Again, this attitude was not at all like my former cautious and fearful self, and I quite liked it.

"Besides," he added, "I will be right there to guide you every step of the way. Trust me." He gave me a most captivating and seductive smile then, and this time I was absolutely *positive* that I detected fangs.

CHAPTER 12

THE DESCENT

Just as I bowed my head to slip through the portal door, I heard the sound of many bells ringing – or should I say tolling, for they had a forlorn, funereal tone rather than a joyous, celebratory one. As I paused to listen, I heard that odd voice again, as if it were my own loud thoughts. It said:

The sun is the healer, not stealer, of soul
So banish the void and make whole of the hole
An unholy fear can be vanquished by light
A bell tolls one last time for eternal night

What could that possibly mean? I wondered. I suddenly felt as if I were leaving something precious and irreplaceable behind once I stepped through to the other side of this door, something I would one day sorely regret and mourn the loss of. But for the life of me, I could not figure out what. I was eager to go somewhere new, and there was nothing for me here, of this I was certain; so what was this sudden sentimentality?

"Come quickly! They await us!" Fairuzo commanded, interrupting my thoughts. He stretched out his arm, and I allowed him to grab ahold of my hand and pull me forward. As I lifted my right foot to step through the door, a powerful gale sucked me inside, lifting me up over the portal's edge. I then experienced a steep drop as if I were on a mad roller coaster ride plunging over a vertical cliff.

Immediately I sensed an absence of light, as if a black curtain had suddenly dropped behind me. When I looked back over my shoulder, I saw that the door I had just come through no longer existed. There was nothing there now but total darkness.

I looked around for Fairuzo and saw he was floating above me like a long-legged helium balloon, his feet dangling and not quite touching the stairs. He seemed capable of swimming through the air as if it were water, gyrating around me like an electric eel. When he had positioned himself directly behind me, he placed his hands firmly upon my shoulders.

"Go ahead," he urged. "Have no fear of falling; I'm right here with a secure grip on you. And remember: the only gravity present now is your belief that you will not float away. The deeper you descend, the lighter you will feel; and the more steps you go down, the easier it will all become."

I could see now that the glowing blue light was emanating from inside intricately scrolled lanterns ensconced upon the cavern's craggy, stone walls. It illuminated the twisted, spiraling cylinders hanging from the ceiling alongside miniature knobbed mineral clusters. I cautiously peered down but could see nothing beyond the foggy mist that stretched out below. I concentrated on placing each foot carefully on each plank of wood and tried not to think about losing my balance.

After I'd gone down several steps and was starting to feel more sure of my footing, I asked, "Now can you tell me where it is we are going?"

He replied, "Wait until we have gone down a bit more; then I will explain those things to you that you need to know. For now, let's just keep your full attention on taking it one step at a time."

We both were silent then as I slowly made my way down. After awhile, I began to notice different colored beams of light piercing through the mist below like probing lasers. They were blinking and pulsating in a distinct rhythmic pattern. It reminded me of the electronic Simon game I used to be so fond of playing as a child – flashing from green to yellow, then red to blue, then blue to green, in various sequences.

Soon, I began to hear a loud rhythmic thumping, much like the tribal pounding of many drums. It was intermingled with what sounded like an orchestra playing discordant, out-of-tune notes with no discernable melody. Deep bass tones throbbed robotically, as if programmed and relayed by a machine. What sounded like a chamber organ was emitting sinister spasms of minor-key chordings, all overlaid by rapid and repetitive high-pitched arpeggios.

"What is that music?" I asked.

Fairuzo answered, "That is the sounds of The Insect Pulse. They have the most magnificent manner of stridulating, and they are skilled musicians as well. They will be in charge of performing the music in your honor at the Turquoise Hollow Ball.

"And as I've told you," he continued, "the Hollowians are eagerly awaiting for you and I to arrive, upon which time I will be introducing you to everyone. There will be refreshments and music and dancing, and then you will be properly initiated into the colony in the customary manner."

When he said the word "initiated," it immediately conjured up disturbing images of brutal gang jump-ins and vicious prison hazings for new inmates that I'd seen re-enacted in movies. It did not sound at all pleasant. In fact, it sounded rather alarmingly violent. I now felt a vague uneasiness that where I was headed might be even more life-threatening than descending these steep stairs without a guardrail.

As we wound our way further down the increasingly-spiraling stairs, I began to hear a loud droning sound above the music. It was as if many voices were mechanically and monotonously chanting the same phrase over and over.

I could not make out the words. They appeared to be in a foreign tongue, although they did seem to have some sort of rhyme to them.

"What are they saying?" I asked curiously.

"You'll know soon enough," replied Fairuzo cryptically. "You won't be able to understand the Turquoisian language until we reach the Underground level."

He then gave a quick, joyless chortle, as if he found something ironic in my not being able to comprehend what they were saying. When I turned my head to gauge his expression, he had a sly smile on his face, as if harboring a secret he wanted to keep to himself.

I then noticed with great alarm that all behind him was a vast expanse of nothingness. It was as if we had just crawled out of the belly of a Black Hole mass. The stairs we had just descended had completely vanished, along with the cavern's walls. The only illumination now was the pulsing lights emanating from below.

I was hit by a wave of panic. I suddenly had the most horrific realization that I would never be able to go back home again – or at least where I once thought had been my home. Even though I hadn't felt welcome or comfortable there for the longest time, at least it had had a modicum of familiarity and comfort. Again, I felt that same sense of foreboding, of melancholy longing, of something forever lost, as I'd experienced right before stepping through the closet's portal door.

As the swirling mist around us began to dissipate, I could now clearly tell we were nearing the bottom of the stairs. I could not only see the beams from the pulsating lights with greater clarity but finally hear what it was they had been chanting.

And it was this:

"Another Soul to Dust Bring her down to us!"

A soul being returned to dust could only mean one thing, I thought to myself. *And that was being placed in a coffin and buried in the ground! Was that what I was being brought down here for? My own premeditated death at the hands of these strangers waiting to meet me?*

It certainly sounded ominous, and I began to shiver uncontrollably. At first I thought it was simply from fright, but then I realized I was incredibly cold. It was the type of bitter, bone-numbing chill where your body has lost all semblance of heat. I could literally see ice stalactites dangling from the low cavern ceiling just above me, and my breath was visible in short bursts of arctic frost.

Just then Fairuzo shouted in a thunderous voice so loud it was as if it were being delivered on a public address system: "We are here!"

The voices stopped in mid-chant and the throbbing music went deathly quiet. After a few moments of eerie silence, I heard the distinct sound of a gong being struck that echoed and reverberated, ricocheting off the cavern walls like a sharp crack of thunder.

"Ahhh, you hear that, my dear?" Fairuzo exclaimed. "They are announcing your arrival! I do believe they are expecting the Queen of the Netherworld!" He laughed, as if he found this to be highly amusing.

But far from finding anything humorous in the situation, I was filled with apprehension and dread about what might possibly be in store for me. I was deep within the bowels of some underground realm, and this impending initiation now began to feel like a specter looming overhead, with the blade of a guillotine poised right above my neck.

The gong I'd just heard certainly did not sound celebratory or heralding, but had a decidedly more sinister and portentous tone. Ultimately, though, it made me think of a dinner gong, as if announcing a meal about to be served.

I then had a most frightening thought: what if I was being brought down to this place for the purpose of being the evening's main course – an exotic delicacy to be served upon a platter – and Fairuzo was in charge of delivering me to those hungrily waiting? Was *this* to be my initiation?

I did not know then how close I was to being right; only it would not be me served upon the plate.

CHAPTER 13

THE SQUABBLING GOBLINS

Phegor was growing increasingly annoyed. He was no longer finding the goblins' incessant bickering to be entertaining in any way. There always seemed to be something to argue about, whether it be over food or whose turn it was to heave the shovels. Their disputes went on endlessly with no sign of resolution, and he was constantly having to intervene. All of these interruptions were beginning to interfere with the timetable, and it was imperative that they arrive on schedule.

Even after pulling the combatants apart, it had become a real chore having to then coax them into resuming their digging duties. In fact, in his myriad of assignments over the centuries, he had *never* had to deal with a lazier, more worthless bunch of imbeciles. He himself was no fan of manual labor, but was at least crafty enough to convince others to do his work for him. Besides, he shouldn't have to dirty his hands or bend his back: he had risen to a position of great power and importance on the sheer merit of his clever wit and cunning skills of manipulation.

When Phegor had been assigned to the Dark Hollow goblins, the core agenda had been to make it easier to monitor and control them, but not so much so as to render them completely useless. They were still needed to perform all of the menial tasks required in keeping a planet operating smoothly. And although he had succeeded in transmogrifying a village of independent, hard-working, astute and compassionate souls into a pack of apathetic babbling idiots who unquestioningly obeyed orders, he was beginning to see indications that some elements of the stratagem might have backfired.

At the next Council meeting, Phegor would definitely mention his concerns and observations that the goblins hadn't quite turned out as planned – or at least not optimally – and that there had been a slight deviation in anticipated results. He would then recommend having the Mount Hermon lab re-evaluate the ingredients of the hydrozoa saliva serum. Surely there was a way the formula could be tweaked in order to avoid such counterproductive effects as the total annihilation of brain cells.

At the same time, new synthetic additives for the serum needed to be developed that would effectively accomplish a mass sterilization of the population for when it reached its maximum desirable limit. The last thing the Cabal needed was a horde of unrestrained, brainless goons with dementia running amuck while overpopulating.

Phegor was aware that the scientists back at Headquarters were always looking for new and exciting ways to cause grotesque physical deformities and chronic afflictions – more even than the usual aberrations naturally resulting from inbreeding. He would be interested in finding out just how much progress they'd made on that end. There was also talk of adding even more disease-riddled animal blood to the serum to increase trans-species mutations.

He found the entire topic of genetically engineering the goblins to be fascinating, especially involving the cross-breeding with animals to create monstrous new strains. He strongly felt that bestiality – or zooerastia, as it was also known – was unfortunately underutilized as of yet, and he was extremely keen to bring it onboard and introduce it universally into the mainstream.

But now, this is what he was currently dealing with: a tribe of sluggish, half-witted buffoons who could not handle even the simplest of tasks without constant beratement and supervision. It was to be expected that they were a festering blight upon whatever space they inhabited, but he resented having to even associate with such obtuse dullards.

However, he had no choice but to see this project through to its conclusion, at which time he could then return to Mount Hermon for a much-needed respite and vacation. He might even fit in a visit to his planet of birth, Xibalba, for some good, old-fashioned, evil fun. After that, he would place a bid on a new contract of his own choosing for his next assignment. *Anything* would be better than being stuck here with this aggravating lot of numskulls.

It was just one reason why he was so anxious to spawn an heir, someone he could then hand over the reins of Lordship to. He would be so relieved when his work here was done and the Kingdom of Turquoise was successfully established on Tartarus.

He especially wanted to get back to his juicy succubi, who provided such winning services at any time of night or day. In comparison, the she-goblins he had to make do with here were gnarled stumps of unattractive features, putrid breath and stinking body odor.

Admittedly, they had all been extremely pleasing to look at when he'd first bitten and bedded them, but their allure had long since faded – gnawed away and rotted by the infection. It was an unfortunate side effect but one that, thankfully, he would not have to deal with much longer.

Speaking of which, he would have to implant his seed into the distasteful, overbearing Lamia almost as soon as they reached their destination, which was the reason now for the haste and urgent need to be on schedule. It was getting precariously close to the deadline for what was formally known as The Royal Seeding Ceremony. Such an epochal event required the utmost attention to detail and meticulous preparations to be set up properly.

As the rays of the sun did not reach Tartarus – yet another reason it made the perfect location for the new city – the ceremony had been scheduled precisely at the time of Earth's sunset. The onset of dusk would then symbolize The Eternal Darkness that Phegor's son would be conceived in. It was only fitting that the first Royal Neph-Biter spawned would be born on the blackest of planets so close in proximity to Earth.

If it so happened that the goblin party still had not arrived at their destination by the scheduled time, Phegor had even considered flitting ahead with Lamia and making do without any preparations or ceremony – just the barest minimum of getting the deed done. But he'd had to reject this idea as being entirely unfeasible, as she was only partially able to shapeshift and incapable of assuming any useful form like a flying insect.

She was also completely ignorant of the advanced process of molecular dematerializing and cellular reconstruction required for teleporting. In fact, only the Cabal was privy to that knowledge, and they had strictly forbidden Phegor to share it with any of the lower-caste drudges. Even though Lamia's body would be used as a vessel for incubating his own son, she was not to be trusted with classified information of such a sensitive nature; none of the goblin-peasants were. And, lest she forget, she was still just one of the peasants.

So now it was absolutely critical that Phegor take some sort of drastic action to ensure they arrived on schedule – for if they did not, the blame would rest solely upon he who was in charge, and his entire mission would be classified as a fail. If that happened, he very well might lose rank or even tenure, and he needed to do everything within his power now to avoid that.

He issued the order that, from here on out, any further fighting would be grounds for a permanent banishing; there would be no exceptions. This put the proper fear into the goblins. And, although they mumbled and grumbled under their breaths, there was nary a word uttered aloud after that. They now concentrated fully on tossing explosives down into the shafts and tunnel-digging, as they should have been doing from the very beginning.

Maps and makeshift compasses were now being properly consulted so as not to lose any more time. And, in very short order, they began to see red and blue lights flickering in the fissures of the rocks below them. Phegor knew these to be the plasma and ionized gasses of a handful of stars that revolved around the planet. This meant that, very soon, the expedition would be at the point where they could simply freefall the short distance onto the surface of Tartarus – for this was how close to Earth it was.

In fact, when the Cabal's head astrologist, Barkayal, had discovered that the planet Tartarus was not visible by mortals viewing the sky from Earth, they realized it would be the ideal relocation for their new hidden civilization. It was made even more appealing by the fact it could only be viewed by those burrowed deep within the Earth at a precise point, and even then only by an expedition being led by a Mount Hermonite.

Once the goblins had touched down upon the outer surface of Tartarus, it was simply a matter of tunneling for a few miles more until they reached the underground city. The Cabal had already prepped the area by remotely bombing it with Centaur – one of their powerful long-distance, 2-ton kinetic weapons. The explosions had leveled the hilly regions and carved crude living spaces among the resultant craters and ridges, effectively creating a primitive foundation upon which to construct a future kingdom.

When they arrived at the precipice where they would be plummeting down into space, Phegor began briskly pushing each of them off into the inky blackness. One by one, each goblin fell howling and screaming in terror for three-quarters of a mile. But it was a surprisingly soft landing, and they even bounced a few times from the low gravity.

After making certain that every last one of them had been evacuated, Phegor propelled himself over the edge. Upon his landing, it was official: the Goblins of Dark Hollow could no longer claim Earth as their home-planet; they were now citizens of Tartarus.

With the combination of sunless sky and clouds of nebula dust covering the surface of Tartarus, it was nearly impossible to make out much of anything but the murkiest of shapes. The goblins panicked in the darkness, and Phegor ordered the lanterns be lit.

He then reminded them they still had a few more miles of digging left to do, and they needed to get back to work. After weeks of tedious tunneling, they would soon be in their new city.

CHAPTER 14

THE SPAWNING AT THE STROKE
OF ETERNAL DARKNESS

𝕿he goblins resolutely set to digging and tunneling through the planet's exterior crust. Soon, there remained just one last barrier-wall to break through before reaching the underground caverns. After the final chunk of limestone had been pick-axed into crumbs and they had a clear view of what lay before them, they could hardly believe their eyes: the bombed-out rubble that greeted them was nothing like what they'd expected or envisioned. It was far from being any sort of glittering crystal palace or anything even remotely resembling opulence. In fact, it looked more like a deserted war zone than a place suitable for a kingdom – or even for inhabiting.

Before the goblins could begin their grumbling again, Phegor reminded them there was only one day left to prepare for the Seeding Ceremony. The Royal Chambers needed to be set up, and quickly. There was simply no time to brood and moan over the disappointment in their new surroundings.

As the goblins reluctantly shuffled off to ready the room, Phegor pulled Lamia aside. He brusquely informed her that she had been chosen as the vessel for his seed and that the ceremony would be commencing shortly. She immediately began to cackle and swagger, shoving the other goblins out of her way and announcing her important new role. She was quickly admonished by Phegor that if she didn't keep her obnoxious gloating and boasting to herself, he would have no problem choosing another in her stead.

She then demanded that she be given a beauty make-over and pedicure for the ceremony. A few assistant-goblins were assigned to appease her. She also requested a new piece of lingerie to wear for the occasion, and one was quickly fashioned for her out of rags. She did not seem to notice that the fabrics used were absolutely filthy and the shape not at all flattering.

Phegor did have himself a good chuckle at the thought of her requesting a facial. Her face would be the last thing he would be looking at! He would have his eyes tightly closed, fantasizing about the nubile succubi who had spent many hours pleasuring him back home on the Mount.

The appointed time was quickly drawing nigh. There was a great rushing around as the goblins began hastily finalizing Phegor's Royal Chambers. After many aborted attempts, they'd managed to drag in all pieces of the heavy canopied bed and get it assembled properly. Even this task could not be easily accomplished with ten of them all working together, awkwardly tripping over each other's cloddish feet in the process.

Pyres were placed at strategic points around the bed and set ablaze. This would ensure that the participants were kept in a constant state of perspiration and that the proper body temperature was maintained. The appropriate ceremonial chants were chosen from the Royal Handbook, and the Conception Clock was located and displayed prominently.

The appointed time of fertilization was 5:44 p.m. on March the 20th, which would be the official Sunset on Earth's Mount Hermon, the Day of the Vernal Equinox. This would allow for nine months and one day of gestation, with the date of birth being December 21st: the Day of the Winter Solstice.

It was twenty-five minutes until the hour, and Phegor was already undressed and lying naked on top of the sheets, impatient to begin. His eyes were glowing with lust, every strand of hair standing out wildly from his head like a thicket of black barlow. His body was glistening with oils lavishly rubbed on him by the goblin attendants; he did not require much preparation to become excited.

Lamia finally rushed into the room with just minutes to spare, panting and anxious. Her face was garishly painted and her crusty, unkempt hair tangled up in absurd ribbon-rags. She was frantic that Phegor would be greatly displeased at her tardiness – as indeed he was.

When he saw her, he growled, "Where the Hell have you been, you nitwit? Do you even realize how important it is that this start exactly on time? Now get into the bed and quickly, for the countdown is about to begin!"

She climbed clumsily onto the bed with flushed face and flared nostrils, deeply inhaling the pungent scent of his musk. As she hungrily drank in the sight of his unclothed body and exposed hardness, her lumpy rolls of flesh began to shake and quiver with feverish excitement like mounds of curdling jelly.

Phegor sat up and ripped off her flimsy nightgown with one quick yank. He then grabbed ahold of both of her arms, twisting one of them behind her back, expertly flipping her over onto her stomach. He got on his haunches behind her and deftly spread her flabby thighs apart, brushing his hand roughly against her entry-hole to make sure he would have no problem inserting himself.

She moaned as he did so and he slid easily into her. He immediately began ramming himself in and out as she began to wail and scream in pleasure, although the sounds were muffled with her face buried in the mattress.

Phegor quickly worked himself up into a fevered pitch and began to emit loud grunts. The goblins excitedly moved in closer to get a better view, elbowing each other in their eagerness. The one who had been instructed to keep an eye on the clock began to count down from twenty seconds: "Twenty, nineteen, eighteen..."

Phegor grew even wilder in his gyrations, and Lamia's moans nearly matched his own primal grunting and bellowing. The chanting of the goblins grew louder, then reached a crescendo:

"Vun Nott braz vi donn! Vun Nott braz vi donn!" they shouted.

At exactly sixteen minutes before the hour of six o'clock, a loud tolling of a bell sounded. Phegor's body stiffened, then he gave one last forceful thrust. He emitted a loud gasp to let all know that the deed was done: the seed had been successfully implanted.

He lay there completely still for three and one-half minutes afterwards, demanding complete silence from the goblins. He warned Lamia not to move or even twitch a muscle. He held her down so firmly she could go nowhere even if she'd tried. It was critical that the newly-homed sperm not be jostled or shifted by any sudden motion or disturbed by any noise.

When the time was up, he slowly and carefully withdrew himself and sat upright. A victorious and celebratory cheer went up from the crowd of goblins.

Phegor slowly got up off the bed, the sweat pouring off of him in rivulets. There was a huge, self-satisfied smirk upon his face. When Lamia twisted herself around to receive her own accolades, there was no one paying the least bit of attention to her. They were all clapping Phegor on his well-oiled back and congratulating him on a job well-done.

Several of them began toweling him off with cloths. Azazyel stepped forward with Phegor's special pipe. After lighting it and handing it to him, he said solemnly, "Vun Nott braz vi donn: The Lord will be born."

Two female goblins appeared on either side of Lamia. Deemed trustworthy enough to have been appointed as nurse-guards, they were in charge of ensuring nothing happened to the fetus now developing in her womb. They had also been warned that she was to be closely guarded and continuously monitored.

Although they were well aware of Lamia's reputation for being a voracious devourer of others' children, they were even more concerned about a potential visit by Obyzouth. She was an especially noxious Mount Hermonite who spent most of her time on Earth directly infecting pregnant women in order to cause still-births. Another of her nasty habits was killing newborns sleeping alone in their cribs with just one serum injection from her deadly fangs.

She was able to gain entry into households by shapeshifting into the form of a lost child appearing on their doorstep, whom the mothers would trust and take pity upon. They would invariably invite her inside – much to their later horror and regret.

Obyzouth considered no infant off-limits, even one of the Cabal's own offspring. She was known to materialize on Tartarus from time to time, and the trolls guarding Lamia had been thoroughly warned to be on the look-out for her.

The nurse-guards grabbed ahold of each of Lamia's arms and pulled her forcefully off the bed. They sternly informed her that she was to come with them to the private room that had been made ready. Lamia mistook their presence as proof that she was now important enough to merit her own servants, and immediately began ordering them around. They quickly set her straight.

"We are not your servants, you ugly twat. We are here to make sure nothing happens to the baby. It's him we are here to look after – not you," one of the goblins said snippily, giving her a rough shove from behind.

They then hauled her off to a tiny, securely-locked room with a bare mattress. One stood guard while the other left the room to empty the chamber pot. She was fed three times a day and received water four times a day. She would be kept sequestered from all others for the full term. She was warned that if she complained, the baby would be surgically removed and implanted in someone else. She would then be forbidden contact – if she survived the surgery, that is.

Lamia quickly learned to keep her mouth shut and do as she was told; but inside, she was seething. She vowed that after this was all over and the baby was born, *someone* was going to pay. They might be getting away with treating her like this for now, but she would be getting her revenge one day, one way or another. On this, she would stake the child's life.

CHAPTER 15

THE ARRIVAL

As I trod the last few wooden planks, I felt as if I were being escorted down to my own scheduled execution. *Dead woman walking*, I thought somewhat self-pityingly.

Suddenly I remembered reading of a botched electrocution in a state death chamber. The prisoner's head and leg had caught on fire, and the burning flesh could be both smelt and heard as it sizzled and popped. This thought did absolutely nothing to bring me any comfort.

Fairuzo was close behind me, his hands still firmly upon my shoulders. But now his touch no longer felt reassuring. Instead, it felt as if he were restraining me to prevent me from escaping – as if there were anywhere now to escape to.

"Keep going," he urged. "Just a few more steps and we are there."

I continued down the last two steps and my feet came to rest on the cavern's limestone floor. Fairuzo zipped around to my right, grabbing firmly ahold of my elbow. He steered me in the direction of an enormous wooden door with a long metal bolt drawn across it. Although there was no longer any music, the bright lights poured out of the cracks in a flood of colors, still pulsating.

When we reached the door, Fairuzo pulled the bolt back and slowly opened it. I was nearly blinded by the intense rainbow of multi-colored lights that poured forth out of a large cavernous room.

In the center of the ceiling hung a great, glittering dome seemingly suspended in mid-air. I could see now that this was the source of the brilliant laser-like beams pulsating and radiating outward in every direction. The rounded walls were iridescent. The floor had the look of a frozen lake, shimmering with millions of tiny silver flecks of light.

There were several-dozen beings gathered inside. Even with their incredibly poor, slumped-over posture, each one looked to be nearly six feet tall. They were all standing in pairs. They slowly turned, almost mechanically and in unison, to face us. When they began inching closer, their faces came into sharper focus. I could see that their features were crude and exaggerated, as if they were all wearing masks.

Their tiny, beady eyes were radish-red with severely dilated pupils that gave them the look of automatons. Their skin was a drab greenish-gray marked with splotches of purplish-red. They had crooked, misshapen noses with wide nostrils set just above their open-hanging mouths. I could see most of their teeth were either rotted or missing. Their ears were huge and pointed at the top, then hanging down loosely in a way that suggested a lack of cartilage.

Their hair was a jumbled tangle of dull grayish-brown. The thick, wiry strands stuck out from their heads like a knotted nest of diamondback rattlesnakes. They were all wearing tattered and ill-fitting tunics or gowns made of well-worn satin and velvets. Cheaply-made costume jewelry was bunched up around their necks and arms. Not a one of them was wearing any shoes. Their monstrous feet looked filthy and unattended, full of bunions and ragged, overgrown toenails.

Jutting out of each of their backs was a pair of black veined wings like those of a fly. The appendages hung limply as if they were rarely, if ever, used. Some wore ridiculously oversized floppy hats decorated with mounds of gawdy plastic flowers, like one would wear to a horse-racing spectacle. Others wore cheap crowns or tawdry tiaras, as if they fancied themselves to be royalty.

Suddenly I felt something akin to pity for them all.

They were so desperately trying to be elegant and failing so miserably, completely unaware of how they might appear to others.

As I stood there not quite knowing how I should react or behave towards these troll-creatures, I began to hear murmurs of what sounded like they were talking amongst themselves. When they spoke, their mouth-holes gaped open and contorted in a most conspicuous manner, like deflated tires flapping noisily along an unpaved road.

"Oh, she does not look like one of us at all," one hissed in disapproval.

"No, she will never do. What in the Tarnation of Tartarus was Fairuzo thinking, bringing this one down to us?" another one said.

"She'll soon be knocked off of her little throne," another said with a snicker. Several others joined in with peals of cheerless laughter.

"Yes," another affirmed, "for we all are fully aware of whom the throne rightfully belongs to."

At this they nodded and exchanged knowing glances, turning their heads towards one of the more feminine-appearing creatures standing in the middle of the group. She had a more regal demeanor. Her carriage was a bit more upright, her hair a bit less disheveled. She had at least put forth some effort in an attempt to prettify and glamorize her innately unappealing facial features.

"What do you have to say about this new one, Lamia?" asked one, looking directly at her.

"Don't call her by her gob name," another chided sharply. "She goes by Darceva now; remember?"

The one known as Darceva said nothing, but I could feel her eyes burning into my face with what was an utter and undeniable hatred. I had no clue as to why she would loathe me so intensely and instantaneously, only that she looked as if she wanted to tear my head off with her bare hands.

Just as another started to speak, Fairuzo let out a

shrill, ear-piercing bark, like a coyote warning his pack. He then clapped his hands together sharply. "Enough!" he yelled. "Enough of this chatter! You will not speak rudely and out of turn to our new initiate. If you continue doing so, it will be at your own peril," he warned menacingly.

He made a show then of wrapping his arm intimately around my waist, as if making it apparent that I not only had his unequivocal approval but his promise of protection as well. And as much as I'd felt a bit suspicious of his intentions back on the stairs, I was much more wary of these beings who clearly despised me and considered me a foe, for whatever reason.

And to be honest, his arm around me did fill me with a small sense of comfort and security. I was even beginning to get used to the coldness of his touch, even if it did not completely offset the escalating sense of hostility directed towards me. I felt like an intruder who had crashed a party and was being informed by the unfriendly attendees inside that I was neither invited nor welcome. For it was apparent they were all extremely displeased at my presence – especially the one known as Darceva, who was emitting tidal waves of animosity directly at me.

I had certainly not been expecting this most inhospitable reception bordering on malevolence when Fairuzo had mentioned their eagerness to meet me. Their rancor and resentment towards me was so blatant that it was literally palpable.

Fairuzo then announced, "This is Enmira. She is now one of us."

Enmira? I thought. *Why was he mispronouncing my name?* He had called me by my correct name that very first night, so surely he knew what it was.

"And if anyone wishes to question my choice, they can take it up with me directly here and now," Fairuzo declared sternly, then paused, looking around the cavernous room, as if daring anyone to object or offer any resistance.

"Speak now or forever hold your peace!" he shouted, but there was only silence. Suddenly the formerly so talkative and disagreeable beings had nothing at all to say. Most of them were looking down abashedly at the floor while shuffling their clumsy, lumpy bare feet – except for Darceva. She was staring defiantly straight ahead at both Fairuzo and I, her nostrils flaring wildly as if they might take flight and flutter away.

Her mouth was opening and closing, then twisting into a bitter pucker. It was obvious she was having a devil of a time holding her tongue. Her complexion was the burning color of a beet soaked in gasoline, as if red hot lava might start erupting out of the top of her head at any moment.

I felt relieved that no one openly objected – although they had already made it perfectly clear how much they resented my being here. *Perhaps if I just stick close to Fairuzo,* I thought, *I can steer clear of these unpleasant creatures – at least until I can figure out why they hate me so much.*

I felt that as long as I had Fairuzo at my side to act as buffer and protector, I would be able to avert the rising tide of resentment angrily nipping at my ankles. Without him, however, I sensed that this disagreeable mob could easily turn vicious, goaded on by the one who looked like she wanted to eat me alive. And with all of them pitted against just the one of me, I wouldn't stand a chance.

CHAPTER 16

THE INSECT PULSE

It was then that I noticed a large raised platform in the far left corner of the room. Several tall insect-like creatures stood on their hind legs in the center of it, each holding a different musical instrument. Some posed in front of stacks of module boxes while others stood behind huge sets of kettledrums.

With their triangular visage, feather-like antenna and pious stance, they reminded me very much of praying mantises, except their bodies were a gleaming metallic silver rather than the customary green. Their large compound eyes were black and bulging, and they had two sets of multicolored wings jutting out of their backs.

The insect-creatures seemed anxious and ill at ease. They were nervously twisting their heads around and rubbing their spiked forelegs together in a manner similar to hand-wringing, as if they were unsure what to do next and were awaiting instruction. Directly to the rear of them I could see the large metal gong that had been struck earlier. There was also some sort of piped contraption as well as many oblong-shaped boxes and modules with blinking lights.

Fairuzo then said, "Now that we've gotten that established, let's get the Ball started." He clapped his hands again and barked out an order: "Bring down the Mirror!"

One of the mantid creatures hurriedly pushed a button on one of the modules. A large screen began descending from the ceiling, stopping just a few inches shy of the floor. The aperture in the middle began sliding open, revealing a large mirror. To my astonishment, I realized it was a gigantic reproduction of my very own Turquoise Mirror. It had been diligently duplicated down to every last rhinestone and seashell adornment.

Fairuzo grabbed my hand and pulled me forward. The crowd parted hastily in synchrony to allow us passage.

"Come!" he said. "You will be very pleased at what you see here in this mirror. It is even more flattering than your own back on Earth."

As we approached the mirror, I could see that my complexion now appeared to be a pale olive-gold shade. My casual attire of jeans and t-shirt had been transformed into an exquisitely detailed gown of deepest turquoise. It had a full taffeta skirt and satin bodice. Decorated with many glittering gems and shells, it seemingly replicated the mirror down to the most minute detail.

But I was even more amazed to see I had somehow sprouted a pair of the most brilliantly-hued iridescent wings, like those of a Blue Morpho butterfly. They were bright turquoise edged in brown and marked with white eyespots. I felt their slight weight resting vibrantly upon my back as if they were independently alive, possessing a separate set of muscles and tendons similar to having two extra limbs.

What was also remarkable was that, in this mirror, I could clearly see Fairuzo standing right beside me, appearing in the glass just as he did in reality; whereas in my own mirror, he had faded in and out of visibility.

Then I heard the murmuring behind us begin.

"Do you see that? She has a reflection!" I heard one mutter in disbelief.

And it was then that I realized that, although the troll-creatures were all gathered right behind us, not a single one of them could be seen reflected in the mirror. It was as if Fairuzo and I were the only ones in the room. I cocked my head a bit to more closely hear what they were saying, but tried not to appear as if I were listening.

"How can this be?" one asked indignantly. "Just what makes *her* so special that she can be seen in the Mirror along with Fairuzo?"

"Do you think she still has her soul?" whispered one incredulously, as if almost hesitant to say it aloud.

"That's impossible!" another exclaimed.

"All I know is that as soon as I saw her, I knew she was definitely not one of us," another sniffed in disapproval. "I mean, just look at how short and unattractive she is, with that stringy blue-black hair and that tiny nothing-of-a-nose! And that atrocious gown – it looks like something half-eaten that crawled out of a garbage dump!"

"And would you get a load of those wings?" another spat. "How gaudy and tacky! Those bright colors hurt my eyes! Is she some sort of sun worshiper or something? They're nothing like our own stylish black ones!"

I looked at Fairuzo to see if he was listening to these disparaging remarks, but he was paying no attention. He was gazing steadily into the mirror at his own reflection as if mesmerized.

I suddenly heard a thunderous bang, as if someone had just dropped a hammer into a steel sink from a great height. I then saw that a mallet had slipped out of the grasp of one of the insects and fallen onto a kettledrum. The poor creature was frozen in fear, as if dreading punishment for his clumsiness. He then cautiously began swiveling his head all around to make sure no one had noticed.

The loud sound succeeded in shaking Fairuzo out of his reverie. He turned towards me and pointed at the band. "This is The Insect Pulse. They are not descendents of the Hollowians but are original members of the Devil's Horse Tribe. We captured them from Earth and brought them back here to be bred as cave-slaves. They were given musical training so as to entertain us, and you will derive much pleasure from their sound.

"But you must listen closely to the lyrics, Enmira," he admonished. "I have written them especially for you and for this occasion."

I could not contain my curiosity any longer and

blurted out, "But why do you keep referring to Earth as if it were another planet? And why do you keep calling me Enmira? My name is Ermina!"

Fairuzo gave a crooked grin like a sinister jack-o'-lantern. His long, yellowish fangs flashed distinctively under the glittering dome overhead.

"Are you not aware that the Realm of the Tartarus Underground *is* another planet?" he asked.

"And as for your name, it is quite obvious that we are facing a mirror, yet you still find it necessary to ask me that?" he questioned with a deriding laugh, as if I were being deliberately silly or thick-headed.

"You are now in *my* kingdom where good is evil and evil is good," he continued. "You will soon learn the art of Reflective Reversal. In fact, I predict you will become quite adept at it. You will find this skill extremely useful on the occasions you visit Earth."

Before I could even inquire as to why evil being interpreted as good could at all be considered something to be desired in any way, he turned away from me abruptly to face the crowd.

"Let the merrymaking commence!" he shouted with great gusto, signaling for the band to start playing.

Several of the mantid musicians began swinging mallets against the kettledrums in unison, while another scraped a metal stick along the notches of a hollow gourd, producing a ratchet-like sound. Yet another began banging a tambora drum with what looked like a pair of ice tongs. The overall effect did not sound musical at all, but more like the head-pounding noise of a multitude of jackhammers tearing up concrete.

I wanted to put my hands over my ears to shield them, but thought it might be interpreted as a rude gesture. And since I was already treading on thin ice with this crowd as it were, I just stood there and bore the din, hoping it would soon become less abrasive and more listenable.

One of the insects punched a few buttons on a module, and the rapid progression of arpeggios I'd heard earlier started up. He then walked stiffly over to the piped contraption. It had a small keyboard, which consisted of black and white bars, similar to an organ or piano. He began pawing the keys with the tarsus of his right foreleg in a rather primitive and uncoordinated fashion, coaxing out only the most discordant of chords. The unpleasant sound blared out of a large speaker-box off to the side.

Another of the mantids pressed a series of buttons. A deep bass tone began pulsating in an off-beat behind the kettledrums. It created a sort of delayed arrhythmic effect that was jarring rather than cadent. I then heard an amplified whirring sound, much like the moan of an artic wind whipping through a desolate glacier. I thought at first it might be coming from somewhere else inside the cavern.

Then I noticed a couple of the insects had started rubbing their green and yellow-spotted fore-wings together, much as you would expect a cricket to do, except the sound being emitted could hardly be considered a musical chirp. It was at a much lower pitch, like the groaning of someone either in agony or ecstasy – I could not tell which.

Then one of the insects stepped up to what looked like a triangle mounted on a stick at the front of the stage. He opened his mouth-hole and appeared to be blowing through the opening, as if attempting to inflate a balloon.

I then heard these words being droned over the music in a monotone:

We welcome you to caves of blue
Through deepest portal hole
Once you've been bit, you must submit
And release to us your soul

It is ordained we eat all flesh
For this is good and right
For in this land, you understand
The darkness is the light

Where good is bad and bad is good
The Mirror is our Eye
And all you thought was beautiful
You'll see now was a lie

To enter gates one must have key
No life allowed except through me
And you will worship only one
Embrace the dark, reject the sun
And you will worship only one
Embrace the dark, reject the sun

CHAPTER 17

THE INITIATION AND THE SACRIFICE

Darceva was starting to stir from the prone position she'd been lying in since the beating. The trolls had all ceased their violent dance ritual and were now crowded expectantly around Fairuzo and I. A sudden hush fell over the Ballroom, with all attention focused on the blind salamander slowly making his way towards us carrying the tray.

As he approached, I could see there was a small, white-furred creature curled up in a fetal position on a platter in the tray's center.

"Give the tray to me," barked Fairuzo, impatiently grabbing it out of the salamander's tiny paws. The crowd surged forward eagerly, maneuvering in position for a good vantage point, as if in anticipation of a highly-touted show.

It was then that I realized it was a baby lamb lying on the plate. I was overcome by a sorrowful wave of distress and nausea. He appeared to still be alive, parts of his body twitching. His eyes were open but staring dully, as if momentarily stunned.

Fairuzo then turned to me and, nodding at the lamb on the tray, said, "What you see here is merely a sampling of the tasty hors d'oeuvres we will be serving this evening. But this specimen is for your lips and delight only, Enmira: a delicacy captured on Earth and brought back specifically for your enjoyment on this special occasion.

"Now, I do apologize for the cliché of a lamb sacrifice; but, really, it is the best choice all around for its tender meat and undisputed symbol of innocence.

"Besides," he continued, "these lamb-creatures do not make proper cave-slaves at all. It is much too troublesome to get them to hold still in order to tame them properly. And believe me, we've tried every method from electric prodding to bayonet hooking. The stupid creatures just do not respond nearly as well to obedience training as do our insect and amphibian specimens."

He paused and looked around at the trolls, who began nodding their heads vigorously, as if they agreed completely with all he'd just said.

"I suppose by now you must be absolutely famished," Fairuzo said, looking at me with what appeared to be a semblance of concern. "So, please, feel free to dig in without fear of engaging in improper etiquette. No utensils are needed, of course; and most of us here have already eaten."

"Oh," he added, as if in afterthought, "and don't let us stop you from saying grace before the meal. Just be sure to address your thanks directly to me and not to the other useless lord."

Here, Fairuzo began to laugh diabolically. The others all quickly joined in, their fat bellies shaking in fiendish mirth at his clever quip.

I could do nothing but stare in horror at the tray. Did they really expect me to eat this pitiful, innocent creature? *My God*, I thought, *he is still alive! A dead lamb on a plate disguised as food was sad enough; but to eat one while still alive was beyond monstrous! I am surrounded by wicked, primitive monsters!*

As I stook there frozen in place, the lamb began to move his limbs feebly, as if attempting to stand, a look of fright and confusion in his eyes.

"You must not delay the sacrifice!" Fairuzo warned heatedly. "It is beginning to wake now and I certainly do not want the trouble of having to subdue it again!"

The crowd then began to chant over and over in unison, steadily growing more and more frenzied:

"Taste the blood of innocence
Pulsing through the vein!
Bite the neck and savor
Every morsel of the brain!"

Darceva, who was now back on her feet and standing directly behind Fairuzo, was ferociously leading the chant. Her mouth was open so wide I could clearly see her long yellow fangs draped in spittle on either side of rotted black teeth-stumps.

I began backing away, shaking my head in abhorrence.

"Why do you hesitate?" one troll cried out. "It would surely eat you, you fool, if it had half a chance!"

This made absolutely no sense to me, as this was a meek, timid creature who was far from being a man-eating carnivore. Even so, I had absolutely no desire to eat him, either living or dead.

"I will not eat a lamb!" I cried. "I just won't!"

"Are you actually attributing value to the life of this stupid thing? It is of no more significance than a speck of dust!" a troll yelled at me.

"Did I not tell you? She is an imposter! An infiltrator! She is not one of us!" shouted Darceva. "And if she refuses to eat it, then I will jam it down her throat myself!"

Fairuzo's eyes flashed in anger. "You know damned well that she must partake of this voluntarily or the entire ceremony is in vain!" he screamed at her.

"I don't care! You're just going to let this sacrifice go to waste? And why do you insist on coddling this bitch?" Darceva yelled back.

And with that, she roughly shoved two fellow trolls aside to stand next to Fairuzo. She reached into the platter with her long jagged fingernails and brutally ripped the head off of the lamb. For a few horrible seconds the poor creature screamed in anguish. I then heard the sickening sound of tearing tendons and flesh. Blood splattering everywhere, Darceva stuffed nearly the entire head into her mouth, as if she could not wait another moment to gorge herself.

As she voraciously gnawed and chewed on the little lamb's head, I felt the tears welling up. I could not stop myself from sobbing. It was one of the most heartlessly savage things I had ever witnessed. I was almost certain that I was the only one here who felt despair at the animal's suffering and demise.

"This one still retains tears?!" a troll asked incredulously.

"That is because she is still an Earthling! I keep telling you! And I will bet that she still has possession of her soul too! Why is she even here?" yelled Darceva, red rivulets of lamb's blood dripping down her chin and half-chewed pieces of flesh spraying out of her mouth.

"Shut up at once or you will be banished!" Fairuzo screamed in warning at her, and the trolls collectively gasped. This was the worst punishment that could be meted out to any one of the Eternally Forsaken. It was far worse than even a Purgatorial existence, and they all lived in dire fear of its very mention.

Being banished meant being sent to The Frozen Lake of Cocytus, where the exiled were reduced to nothing more than a paralyzed head jutting out just above the ice, unable to close their eyes or even scream. They were subjected to a never-ending hailstorm of razor-edged rocks the size of small meteors, while being struck intermittently by bolts of lightning that would set their hair and faces on fire. They could only wish for an end to their existence – but one that would never come, for they were not allowed to perish.

They also realized that Fairuzo voiced this threat only once before acting upon it.

Fairuzo placed his hands on either side of Darceva's head and violently slammed her face-first onto the ground. The sound of breaking teeth could be distinctly heard along with the crunching of bones. Her body went limp. She lay there like a worn-out dishrag, a thin black stream of blood trickling from her fractured mouth. She made some gurgling noises then murmured something very faintly that sounded like a cross between a curse and a plea.

After a few moments, Darceva attempted to stand. A couple of the trolls nearby grabbed ahold of her arms to help steady her, but she brushed them rudely aside. "I don't need anyone's help. I can stand by myself," she snarled.

She looked around, as if searching for something. Then her narrowed, bloodshot eyes zeroed in on me and she knitted her brows together in an intense scowl of hatred.

"You!" she shouted. "I'm not through with you, you ugly bitch!" She made a beeline towards me. As she got within a few feet, she lunged forward with both of her clawed hands extended towards my face.

Fairuzo casually stuck out his foot. She tripped over it hard, slamming headfirst into the ground. This time I heard a few snickers from the crowd, as if they were really beginning to enjoy the spectacle. She lay there dazed for a few moments, then slowly and shakily stood back up again. It reminded me of one of those silly wrestling ring matches, where the loser refuses to acknowledge he's been beaten, insisting on repeatedly getting back up for more punishment.

She was missing even more teeth now, still bleeding rather profusely from a deep cut in her lip. She glared at me for a few moments, as if deciding whether to make another lunge, then seemed to think better of it. It was clear that with Fairuzo at my side, she wasn't going to have too much luck tearing me in half like she obviously wished she could.

She then announced belligerently, "All right, that's it. I'm *out* of here. I didn't want to come to this piece of shit Initiation to begin with. It's all *yours*."

She gave me one last look of contempt, then swept past me with as much dignity as she could muster. She roughly and deliberately brushed up against me on her way out of the cavern hall.

"Watch your back, bitch," she hissed as she passed me. "Philanus is *mine!*"

Philanus? I wondered. *Who the hell is Philanus?*

I had absolutely no idea whom she was referring to. All I knew was that she would do her damnedest to cause me great harm if she ever caught me in an unguarded moment. I would most certainly be watching my back from now on – unless I fancied having a machete stuck into it when I was least expecting it.

CHAPTER 18

A DETHRONING AND
A CULTURE OF BLOOD

As Darceva flounced angrily out of the cavern hall, I couldn't help but notice that no one seemed too visibly upset to see her go. The group overall seemed to display some sort of pack mentality, but there was a palpable lack of camaraderie amongst these beings. And although Darceva appeared to have a good amount of influence over the other trolls, none of them seemed to be too terribly fond of her.

Although she didn't seem to have any comates who would openly sympathize with her, she seemed extremely effective at riling the crowd by unifying them in hatred. And since her focus seemed to be primarily stirring up animosity towards me, I wondered if I even stood a chance at persuading any of the others I was not the villain being depicted here. I was well aware that a horde of venomous cretins allied in such malevolence could easily turn into a very dangerous lynch mob situation. And in this potential scenario, I had every reason to be worried.

There were certainly plenty of trolls shooting me dirty looks as they shuffled past me, but they did not radiate anywhere near the degree of barbed hostility as she had. This made me suspect that it was something personal that was fueling her loathing of me. At any rate, I needed to find out who this Philanus character was and stay far, far away. The last thing I wanted to do was toss petrol into a trash can already on fire. However, it did not seem too likely she could despise me any more than she already did.

Although I felt relief that she was gone, I was still badly shaken by the horrific cruelty I'd just witnessed. In the space of just a few minutes, I believe it was more than I'd seen in my entire lifetime.

The image of her viciously ripping off the baby lamb's head and shoving it into her mouth had imprinted itself on my mind like a harrowing scene from Hell. To me, a lamb had always symbolized the utmost in purity and innocence. I felt certain that anyone capable of committing such an atrocity must surely be completely devoid of a conscience. At the very least, she lacked the empathetic capacity for discerning the difference between a living animal and a rock someone had carelessly tossed on the ground.

However, if these demented people wanted to bash each other's heads in while participating in some freaky dance ritual, that was their choice. And the way Darceva had kept coming back for more blows almost seemed as if she were inviting the violent treatment, even deriving pleasure from it.

The manner in which she'd been an active participant made me wonder if there existed such a thing as consensual violence, versus an involuntary, unwilling involvement of an innocent victim – such as had been the lamb. There seemed to be a span of immeasurable distance between a faultless victim and the end result of a deliberate and complicit provocation.

The truth was that even had she not obviously detested me so much, I still would not have been able to summon much sympathy for her. For as severe a beating as I'd seen her being given, she seemed almost deserving of it.

And when Darceva had brushed past me and hissed that warning, her mouth had reminded me of a swirling black cesspool flushing into a bottomless pit. I had truly felt as if I were in the very presence of pure evil.

I was also wondering why the trolls seemed so stupefied as to the possibility I still had a soul, as I had overheard them whispering – as if the possession of such a thing here was a rarity and an anomaly. Did not every living creature have a soul? It was certainly something I had always believed and had no reason to question.

Perhaps it was just my own perception, but there did seem to be a whole lot less tension crackling in the room since she'd taken her leave. And once the band started up again with one of their crashing, meandering noise-symphonies, the trolls quickly lost interest in all prior adversarial drama, vigorously shaking and nodding their oversized skulls like manic bobble-heads.

Some of the praying mantis bandmembers were rubbing their forelegs together as if they were drawing bows across violins, while others frantically pushed buttons on modules and banged away on kettledrums.

I couldn't help wondering about their status as "cave-slaves," as Fairuzo had referred to them. Were they really being held here against their will? And why didn't they all just rise up and rebel? To be fair, they did seem outnumbered and outsized; although I suppose, at the very least, they could have put their heads together in private to discuss the possibility of escape.

Not so the blind salamander. He seemed quite alone in his plight. He did not seem to have any allies or even the ability to see a way out. I wondered if he had ever tried to remove that cruel shock collar from around his neck. The way I had seen him being mocked and targeted as the butt of a vicious joke, I highly doubted any of these beings had ever tried to help him in any way.

As the band began to increase in tempo, the trolls resumed their deranged head-butting ritual with their partners. Some began spinning like frenzied tops with arms extended until they fell over from dizziness, clumsily tripping over their own feet. It reminded me of a group of dysfunctional kindergarteners whose teacher had left the room, taking advantage of being left to their own devises absent any supervision.

Suddenly I became aware of Fairuzo standing right

next to me, having apparently launched himself across the room like a desert locust wind-borne in a sandstorm. He reached out and gently brushed my elbow with his hand. I was surprised at his tender touch, having just moments earlier seen him kicking the hell out of Darceva and planting her face-down on the limestone floor.

Although he had yet to exhibit any violent tendencies directly towards me, I was still wary of him and his intentions. He had exhibited such a lack of empathy towards the lamb and the blind salamander that I could not help but suspect any kind-hearted gesture now might be simply an act with an underlying ulterior motive.

"Enmira," he whispered seductively into my ear. "Are you enjoying yourself now that our unpleasant little friend has taken her nastiness elsewhere?"

I laughed in spite of myself, nodding my head in affirmation. "Oh, you have no idea how glad I am that she's gone," I confessed.

Realizing that now would be a most opportune time for me to try to find out what was behind Darceva's intense animosity towards me, I asked him: "Why does she despise me so much? What could I have possibly done to make her hate me so?"

Fairuzo replied matter-of-factly, "It's quite simple, really. She resents your presence because my bringing you here has taken the limelight off of her. She's used to getting *all* the attention. In fact, she fancies herself the Queen of the colony."

"But is she?" I asked. "I mean, *is* she the Queen?"

Fairuzo laughed derisively. "Oh, hell, no. Darceva is no more a queen than any of these other repulsive creatures around here. She has delusions of grandeur, but it's strictly in her own thick-knotted head. And the fact that you possess the beauty that she once herself had makes her even more consumed with jealousy.

"My father once even —" And here, Fairuzo stopped

himself, as if realizing he must choose his words more carefully. After a pause, he continued: "Let's just say that she once played quite a significant role in my family, but she was removed from that position a long, long time ago – and for very good reason."

It did seem quite understandable, really, that she would be resentful and envious of the sudden appearance of a newcomer shoving her off her self-proclaimed center-stage throne. It was also not at all surprising that she would consider such an interloper as both enemy and rival. Nonetheless, it was extremely unfair to place any of the blame upon me.

There appeared to be nothing I could do to change her attitude, short of befriending her and convincing her I was not the bad sort she imagined me to be. But this I had absolutely no desire to do, as her toxicity seemed most infectious. I decided, therefore, that the best course of action would be to just stay as far away from her as possible – while watching my back, of course.

I could not resist asking one more burning question: "And who is this Philanus that she referred to?"

For a moment Fairuzo appeared startled, as if the name awoke something in him that had long lain dormant. Recovering his composure, he said sternly, "Now you are asking far too many questions, and this is simply not the place nor the time. I have something much more pressing to discuss with you at the moment: it concerns proper decorum here in the Land of Turquoise.

"I realize this is only your first day, but there are certain ways we require things be done around here. For instance, there is the matter of the sacrificial offering. That was an extremely important component of your Initiation, and I apologize that you did not have an opportunity to participate. However, even before that boorish little slag so rudely shoved her way in and grabbed what was rightfully yours, I sensed a strong reluctance on your part to partake.

And I'm quite curious about this sentimental attachment you have to certain objects."

"Do you mean the lamb?" I asked, feeling sick and saddened all over again.

"Yes," he replied. "And to some, your refusal could be interpreted as inexcusable rudeness. You see, this is a crucial part of our culture here. It is our firm belief that if you butcher the sacrificial offering yourself *specifically* for the purpose of consuming every last bit of it, you have adhered to the ceremonial laws of purification while not letting any of its valuable elements go to waste."

I did not quite know what to say. In fact, I was quite appalled at such logic: that ripping the head off of a living animal to then eat all of its parts somehow validated the heinousness of the act, even bestowing upon it a virtuous trait of purity.

"You must realize that you are in a new world, one that requires you to look at things differently than you had before. We are no longer on Earth; this is Tartarus," he reminded me.

"Remember the lyrics I wrote for you that The Insect Pulse sang? Did you pay close attention to them, as I requested?"

And before I could reply, he began to recite: *"It is ordained we eat all flesh, for this is good and right; for in this land, you understand, the darkness is the light."*

Before, I hadn't paid much attention to the lyrics when the praying mantis had intoned them; but hearing Fairuzo speak the words now, I understood all too well what they meant.

I felt a nausea wash over me at the realization that I might yet be forced to participate in this barbarity. Fairuzo had made it abundantly clear that it was part of the culture here and that it would be considered unforgivably rude of me to refuse it. It was practically decreed that one must cooperate and engage in such an act.

"I need to make you aware that flesh is the only food procured, served, and eaten around here. So if you have some type of aversion to it, I suggest you get over it, and quickly," he said sternly.

"Our sacrificial meats are of the finest quality and imported directly from Earth, and I can assure you that each morsel is a mouthwatering taste explosion," he added ebulliently, almost as if he were a salesman pitching a top-grade commodity.

"In fact," he continued, "I simply cannot comprehend why you are not attracted to the blood and tendons of living beings. Does it not make you salivate at the very thought of it?" He seemed genuinely perplexed.

"No!" I exclaimed. "It actually repulses me. And although it's true that I ignorantly considered animals to be food for many years, at least they were cooked and unrecognizable while on my plate. In fact, I preferred not to know what they used to be and even went out of my way not to think about it. But it's been quite a few years since I've even eaten any meat at all – nor do I ever want to again," I said firmly.

Fairuzo seemed shocked. "I have never heard of such a thing! Of *course* everyone on Earth enjoys eating the cooked corpses – at every meal! And some even enjoy eating the flesh raw and still bloody! In fact, it is one of the rituals I find most impressive about that planet – that, and the constant wars that are so cleverly drummed up to cull the most useless of the population," he said, snickering.

"Why, I've seen for myself the thousands of food warehouses that stockpile and preserve the bodies the hunters drag in. And is not the barbecuing of multiple carcasses deemed a joyous occasion and celebration there? So, please tell me: how is it even possible you could go without – or even *want* to go without – these delicacies for so long?"

"Well," I explained, "it's really just a matter of

realizing that the eating of corpses is actually quite disgusting and unnatural, and that it's not that difficult to find other foods to eat that are much more appealing. And once you discover what's actually involved in the whole process of turning animals into food, it becomes increasingly harder to pretend that meat is something that just grows on trees."

Fairuzo cocked his head and gave me a long look of scrutiny, as if trying to ascertain whether I was toying with him. Seemingly satisfied that I was being sincere, he then shook his head in bewilderment, as if unable to even fathom what I was saying.

"I really am trying to understand your way of thinking, Enmira, because I am becoming quite fond of you. I even believe you'd make a valuable contribution to the colony. But I must say that you are the first Earthling who has joined us here that has not only questioned our delicious Initiation offering but actually refused it as well.

"And I must admit I cannot understand your affection for these creatures: they cannot think or speak, they cannot reason; they do not feel pain, and what else are they good for? They are merely non-feeling machines dropped into the world to serve and please us.

"And biting into them raw is *extremely* pleasing to the palate, let me tell you – while the blood is still vibrantly oozing and pulsing, it allows their organs to be fresh, moist and juicy. Perhaps, for you, it is just a matter of needing a little bit of encouragement and time to acquire a taste for this delicacy? Because, believe me, you would not be able to deny its exquisite flavor after just a few mouthfuls," he finished with great exuberance.

Again, I got the feeling that he was trying to sell me something that I was certain I did not want nor would *ever* want. I wanted to tell him that he was just wasting his time trying to change my mind, and that it was not a matter of acquired taste at all. I would continue to reject their execrable idea of cuisine for as long as it was offered; I only hoped it would not be forced upon me.

But how could I possibly make him understand? How could I convince him that I needed to be made an exception of here and be allowed to opt out of this barbaric ritual?

I was actually quite surprised at how patient he was being in giving me the opportunity to explain my position, even though he still didn't seem capable of grasping it. If only I could manage to persuade him to at least respect my beliefs, half the battle would be won.

But even if I could somehow convince him to suspend this deeply-entrenched custom for me, there was still the matter of these easily-agitated trolls who did not require much provocation to be shoved over the edge into mass hysteria and violence. How would I handle them? For surely they would greatly resent my being granted special privileges and immunity from the rules they were all expected to comply with.

It was really beginning to look as if I might be forced into participating in this abhorrent bloodbath of innocent creatures, and this I simply would not stand for. The feeling of being trapped in waist-deep quicksand returned. I knew my only hope was to escape from this horrible place before the boggy noose tightened around my neck.

CHAPTER 19

THE GESTATION

The time passed tediously and interminably for Lamia. She could do nothing but wait for the day when she would finally be rid of this accursed burden growing inside of her. It felt like the fetus had hijacked every inch of her entrails, kicking and pummeling at random, all hours of the day and night.

Being stuck in this room was like having water slowly dripping onto her forehead while watching a snail trying to climb backwards up a slippery wall. She had neither the patience nor the stamina to endure this relentless privation, and was simply frustrated and bored out of her skull.

She was not allowed to do a bloody thing all day except lie in bed and wait for meals to be thrown at her. Usually that would have suited her lazy temperament just fine; but being locked up in this tiny, dingy pit with these nurse-guards constantly eyeballing every move she made was excruciating. If she even looked like she was opening her mouth to yawn, they wasted no time in yelling at her to shut her hole.

She filled her days plotting her revenge for being treated like a used rag from a refuse pile, and her rage constantly simmered. If only she could get her claws into something or someone and just rip them apart. She was *royalty*, for screaming out loud! Yet she was being pushed around and shaken off like the dregs in a fecal bucket.

She looked forward to the time she would be released from this prison of a room, no longer under lock and key, being scrutinized and guarded every minute by these priggish, bone-headed dullards.

She longed to get back to her hunting playgrounds on

Earth. She sorely missed sucking the life's blood out of the easy animal prey she found in the forests. She missed sneaking through open windows and sinking her fangs into the necks of babies she found sleeping peacefully in cribs, then gnawing on their young, tender flesh. She missed stalking the unsupervised children she grabbed from yards and then molested in the basements of their own homes.

She was being driven nearly insane with exasperation at being left out of all the wild orgies that were surely proceeding without her outside of this room. She especially hungered for the erotic touch of her lover Phegor, although she was growing increasingly resentful that he had not once took it upon himself to even come visit her. After all, this was *his* seed she was carrying. He should be showing her the proper respect and gratitude for the humongous favor she was doing him.

She had just assumed he would be staying with her at least part of the time to keep her company. She had no idea he would be completely ignoring her, leaving her here to rot away in this dreary place with absolutely nothing to do but brood and sulk.

She had quickly grown to despise the invasive thing growing inside of her. She could feel the embryo hungrily sucking up what little nourishment she was given to eat. She resented having to share any of it with this unwelcome trespasser in her uterus.

One of the nurse-guards had mentioned that she would be kept here for nine months, as it was how long the gestation period would last. Although she had little concept of time nor any sort of grasp of what each stage of pregnancy entailed, that had sounded like an eternity to her. All she knew was that her belly was rapidly growing uncomfortably thick and sphere-shaped, far surpassing the quivering, pulpy rolls of flab she'd been carrying around her midriff prior to the conception.

She was curious what would happen to her after the

baby was born: would she go to live with Phegor in his Royal Chamber then? Even though there had never been mention of any type of wedding ceremony, formal or otherwise, as far as *she* was concerned, she considered herself his wife, for all intents and purposes. And why not? She had been specifically chosen to be the mother of his heir. She believed that gave her the right to claim the title of not only mother and wife, but also now as member of the royal clan.

When Phegor had informed her she would be the recipient of his seed, her already-oversized head had immediately inflated to the circumference of a pumpkin, filled to the brim with fanciful notions of grandeur. She believed she would, at long last, be awarded a position of significance and prestige, as she rightfully deserved.

Although fully aware of the legions of admirers Phegor had at his beck and call, ready at a moment's notice to climb into bed with him, she'd always viewed herself as being far above them – and even more so now. She'd had to put up with entirely too much backbiting and jealousy from the other smitten she-goblins back at the Dark Hollow Caverns, all vying for his sexual attentions. But now, having ceremoniously been given his seed to carry, *surely* that meant she was entitled to have him all to herself!

She certainly hoped that she wouldn't actually be expected to take care of this pest ballooning up inside her once it finally dropped out. She cared only for the official title of Lady and Royal Mother, not the chores or tiresome drudgery that would be involved in playing nurse to some clinging, needy chit. But now she was questioning if she would be receiving any kind of perks or benefits at all, and beginning to wonder if she was just being used as a receptacle.

Sometimes she almost wished she'd never been selected for the task. But she had to admit that The Royal Seeding Ceremony had been incredibly exciting. She had been the star and center of attention – all of those eyes focused on her as she performed on the royal bed, doing what she did best! But it had been over far too quickly. And, immediately afterwards, she had been forcibly dragged away, then shunned and quarantined like a leper ever since.

She still recalled the humiliation she'd felt at having been forced to sign a formal Notice of Compliance with the promissory oath that she would not even *think* of eating this baby once it was born. Did they really think she'd consume her own offspring, the one thing that entitled her to claim royal standing? That would be a bit like biting her own head off, wouldn't it?

Of course, she had achieved quite a bit of notoriety in the colony with her reputation for devouring children. This was mostly due to the fact that this particular preference was neither the status quo nor commonplace. The majority of inhabitants preferred animal corpses for all of their sustenance and nutritional needs.

And although she certainly never minded the taste of beast flesh, dining on freshly-killed human baby meat just seemed so much more taboo and decadent – and it filled her belly faster, too. At any rate, it was her own business and her own personal choice.

Phegor had even given her praise for indulging in this penchant for deviant cuisine, telling her that he found it refreshingly bold and original. She took this, of course, as a supreme compliment. He'd told her how he'd sampled the infant meat himself a few times, but it had just been too bland and dry. He preferred the more seasoned, robust flavor of wild forest creatures or, for quick snacks and even easier pickings, their farmed cousins.

He'd also explained how taking the life of an animal was so much more thrilling and gratifying, just in the way they each struggled so desperately to live, resisting so ferociously until that last moment when they could no longer delay their death. Simply inhaling the scent of their terror and anguish filled his whole being with a glorious sense of domination and omnipotence. Their suffering was like the finest gourmet condiment or spice.

Whereas, in comparison, snuffing the life out of a human baby presented so little of a challenge and took such minimal effort that the all-too-brief procedure was pretty much an uneventful bore. And Phegor was always up for a good, stiff challenge.

The document Lamia had been forced to sign also warned that the consequences of breaching this covenant would be instantaneous banishment – but she would have to be a fool to even think of risking *that.*

Besides, she looked forward to basking in the acclaim that producing such an offspring would automatically merit. And, of course, she would be taking full credit for the perfect spawn that would surely result from the fruitful coupling of a bona fide Lord of the Cabal and a Dark Hollowian Diva-Queen of Orgies!

No, she had *other* plans for this baby that didn't involve utilizing him as a meal. Whether she acted upon those plans or not was completely contingent upon how she was treated by Phegor after the birth. In fact, the targeted recipients of her fantasies of revenge so far only included the two nurse-guards and, of course, that pretentious prig of a goblin-husband, Azazyel. He now apparently thought too highly of himself to be seen associating with her.

She had convinced herself that the reason he'd initially begun distancing himself from her was because he was simply eaten up with jealousy over her highly vocal preference for Phegor. But that wouldn't explain the way he had then pledged total allegiance and loyalty to him, nor how he had fully ingratiated himself by becoming the Community Snitch.

At any rate, Azazyel was number one on her score-card of those who had slighted and rejected her, and whom she would definitely be exacting revenge upon. She was sure she'd be adding many more names to that list soon enough.

Sometimes she passed the time trying to envision what her older sibling Philatanus was up to. She hadn't seen that leering bastard for eons, not since she'd been removed from all the action. He had been one of her frequent traveling companions to Earth. He now spent the majority of his time there, having achieved the status of trustee.

His main duties entailed being in charge of infecting and recruiting males for the Tartarus population. He was also entrusted with ensuring the ratio of females to males remained perfectly within balance. It was only logical that if each troll had a partner to occupy themselves with, it would greatly hinder them from forming rebellious gangs comprised of their own gender.

Occasionally, he was still called back to Tartarus to act as chaperone for not-yet-trustworthy recruits. Whenever they needed to go on their Earthly feeding missions, he was in charge of escorting and monitoring them.

He had taught Lamia just about everything she would ever need to know about sodomy and pedophilia. She had observed him in action on many occasions. They had gone on many successful and exhilarating molestation expeditions together. She had him to thank for all that invaluable knowledge and experience.

In fact, as a token of gratitude, she had decided she would be giving the baby an abbreviated version of his name. It would also serve as a nod to his area of expertise. She would be including her own slightly revised name, as well. She figured that melding the family names together would serve to formally wedge a slice of her own genealogy into the royal lineage.

So, after giving it quite a bit of thought, she would be naming the baby Philanus Lamianus Phegorus.

She wasn't even quite sure what Phegor's actual surname was, as she'd never gotten around to asking him; but Phegorus seemed as good a guess as any. Besides, it was *her* baby, so she could name it whatever the hell she pleased.

But even as Lamia was becoming increasingly resentful over Phegor's continued absence, she was growing less certain that her fantasies of living with him in his Royal Chambers afterwards would ever come to fruition. And even as she alternately stewed and pined over him, she had no idea that he had actually been just a few yards away from her this whole time.

In fact, Phegor had been keeping extremely close tabs on Lamia from the moment she'd first been taken into the room. Completely unbeknownst to her, he had been surreptitiously monitoring every move she made. He was utilizing a peephole in the wall that afforded him a most opportune view of what she was up to inside.

He didn't observe her doing much except lying on her flabby backside all day long, occasionally muttering under her breath whenever the nurse-guards turned their heads away for a moment, or busily shoveling food into her mouth whenever a bowl of bloody, pre-mixed gruel was brought in.

He was making damned sure that she remained in the room at all times. He would not tolerate her participating in anything that could potentially endanger his son or interfere in any way with a smooth and victorious birth.

It was a real shame that he was having to do all the monitoring himself, but he knew full well that if you wanted something done right, you had to get in there and do it yourself. You could never fully trust the help either. They were of inferior intellect and usually resentful of their lower position as drudges, invariably leading to insidious and retaliatory passive-aggressive behaviors.

He had to admit, however, that the nurses were doing a pretty impressive job of keeping Lamia quiet, ensuring she uttered nary a word. He got a real kick out of watching her frustration at being prevented from speaking. In fact, it was the first time he'd ever seen her when she was not endlessly running her mouth while saying absolutely nothing of importance or merit. It was a real nice change of pace.

But he was also on the look-out for a visit by that Hermonite outcast, Obyzouth, who relished thwarting pregnancies by causing sudden fetal demise. He'd initially found her fixation on racking up high volumes of stillborns quite amusing – when she'd confined her targets to pregnant Earthling mothers, that is. He even found her handiwork quite practical, as it was an extremely efficacious way of culling the population.

But when she began to extend her circle of victims to members of the Cabal's own offspring, it no longer seemed so amusing or advantageous. In fact, what she had been caught doing – attempting to decimate the royal bloodline – was forbidden and merited severe punishment.

Obyzouth had foolishly confided in one of the Hermonite snitches that her motive had been pure revenge: having grown to despise the duty of having to constantly bear children by multiple officers of the Cabal, she had sworn that, as a form of retribution, she would dedicate eternity to killing the unborn of others.

Not only could what she had done be considered an act of treason, but Phegor was especially appalled at her attitude of ungratefulness. It was a high and distinguished honor to be chosen as womb-vessel, and Obyzouth had been offered the position a multitude of times by the highest-ranking Cabal members.

Did she think she existed for any other purpose but to service the men? He found that mindset of feminine entitlement with delusions of equality simply outrageous.

But even though her personal attacks within the ranks could be considered tantamount to mutiny, the law decreed that, since she had been the consort of so many high-ranking officials, she would be granted partial absolution. So, instead of sentencing her to banishment, the Tribunal had decided simply to ban her from the province of Mount Hermon – with anywhere else on Earth still being fair game, of course.

Having cast his own vote to have her banished,

Phegor unfortunately had been outvoted. That had burned him; he did not like having his opinions or recommendations dismissed. So, he actually carried a bit of a personal grudge against her for having escaped the sentencing he felt she deserved.

And since Tartarus was such a newly-established territory, it had not yet been officially defined as off-limits for her activities. However, after being sighted once in the vicinity, she had been duly warned that the ban did extend here also.

And so it was wise to be especially vigilant now whenever the birth of any sort of royal offspring was imminent. He also knew that if he or any other Cabal member caught Obyzouth anywhere near Tartarus during this period of gestation, there would certainly be no question of her being banished at that point. He could probably even talk Headquarters into allowing him to set up a cozy little farewell torture party before her final departure.

The truth was that Phegor really had very little use for *any* of these smelly, clinging she-trolls like Lamia, other than for sexual gratification. Once again, he thought nostalgically of the succubi back home at Mount Hermon. They certainly knew how to treat a Lord as Master and then just gracefully disappear until needed again.

In contrast, the annoying trolls here were like molten glue after a sexual session, suddenly growing extra tentacles that clung and grabbed all over him until he had to physically kick them away just to extricate himself. They were too knot-headed to take the obvious hint that he just wanted them gone and had zero desire to canoodle and spoon.

Finding them all so equally repulsive, it had not been a simple decision to select any one of them as womb-vessel to incubate his heir. But more and more, he was really beginning to regret his choice of Lamia. In fact, he was already making plans to replace her immediately following the birth.

If she still insisted on causing problems and refusing to stay away from his son, he would seek a Tribunal decision to have her banished altogether. But since that process could take weeks or even months for a final decision, he would pursue that avenue only if all else failed.

What he had in mind first was simply convincing Lamia that the duties of mothering would not only be an immensely time-consuming and annoying job, but one that would greatly interfere with her pleasure-seeking activities. Once she saw the reality of that, he would then explain to her how the role of motherhood would be best accomplished if taken over by someone else with more matronly attributes.

He would then reassure her not to worry, that she would be given full credit and all corresponding perquisites that the mother of his heir would be entitled to. Of course, this would be said merely to placate her; it would be a promise he had no intention of keeping.

He'd already made his decision as to which nurse-guard he would appoint as the full-time nanny in her stead. He would assign the other as second-in-command, who would be in charge of monitoring both the baby *and* the nanny.

He'd decided that at no point would his son ever be told who his real birth-mother was. Instead, he would be led to believe it was the caretaker who had raised him. It would be made crystal clear to Lamia that she was forbidden to reveal she was actually his biological mother – *ever.*

Indeed, it was best for all involved that Lamia be given as little contact with the child as possible. He wanted his son to grow up with class and distinction, and with absolute loyalty to the Cabal. For an heir and Lord of his stature to be associated in any way with a crass and skanky bumpkin like Lamia was now beginning to seem completely unthinkable.

Honestly, he had no idea now what he had been inhaling at the time to have chosen her – other than the tangy, pungent aroma of her labial musk-scent. He had allowed himself to become beguiled and blinded by her most impressive talents in bed, and flattered by her unrestrained eagerness to please him.

He could even use the excuse that, since he'd been so new to his assignment at Dark Hollows, he hadn't taken as much time mulling over the decision as he should have. Perhaps he'd made his choice a bit prematurely. Then, of course, there was also the overwhelming distraction of being constantly nose-deep in all that fresh female-meat he'd been surrounded by. What virile male could think clearly at a time like that?

But his time in the Caverns all seemed like ages ago now. It was unfortunate that he'd been led by his lusty lower jewels into making a hasty and regrettable decision, one that could adversely affect the entire future of the Kingdom.

He would be making no mention of this little lapse in judgment in his reports to the Cabal, of course. It was therefore imperative that he resolve this problem quickly and efficiently on his own – and as discreetly as possible.

CHAPTER 20

THE BIRTH OF THE ROYAL HEIR

$\mathfrak{F}$inally, the date of the royal birthing arrived: it was December 21ˢᵗ, the Day of the Winter Solstice.

A special delivery-room had been set up next to the Royal Chambers. A large, rectangular bale-mat made of woven hemp and straw had been positioned strategically on the ground in the center.

Here, Lamia would be placed, then instructed to squat and push. Phegor had already arranged for two of the strongest male trolls to be standing by. They had been instructed to forcefully restrain and escort her away as soon as the baby was born.

Since he was uncertain as to how long a newborn could go without blood to suckle, he had collected large vial samples from each of the trolls to start a donor pool. In the event the baby refused to drink that particular blood type – Black X Negative – a multitude of hunter and carrier trolls had already been dispatched to Earth to bring back vats of animal blood, which was now being kept fresh in the underground cavern spring.

Phegor and the entire congregation of trolls now waited impatiently inside the birthing-room for Lamia to be brought in. Her cursing and screaming could be heard all the way down the outer corridor as the nurse-guards dragged her in. She was kicking violently in all directions and yelling out obscenities at the top of her lungs, apparently reacting to the waves of contractions hitting her in the belly and groin – along with simply being her usual disagreeable self, of course.

Upon Phegor's orders, a rag was quickly stuffed into her mouth to stop the obnoxious caterwauling. He did not wish to have the baby's arrival disturbed in any way by her tantrums or unruly behavior.

The nurses grabbed her arms tightly in a vise-like grip to keep her as still as possible in one spot.

"Push, you moron!" they screamed at her. "You want it out, don't you?"

But Lamia kept struggling out of their grasp. Every time she attempted to flop herself down on her back, they had to keep dragging her back upright into a squatting position.

Finally, with very little help from Lamia, the head of the baby began to emerge on its own. First, a thick crown of luxuriant blue-black hair was revealed, then a flawless complexion of an alluring shade of light olive green. Next, a most perfect nose and mouth, and the most exquisite seashell-shaped ears.

However, its eyes were so tightly shut that the hue of the irises could not readily be discerned. Phegor hoped that they would be large glittering pools of tar-black to match his own and nothing like Lamia's hideous beady red ones. Already, though, it was clear to all that the baby possessed only his most strikingly handsome features. There was not a hint of the repulsively coarse and unsightly genetic traits that an ugly troll like Lamia might pass on.

As soon as the baby's head had cleared Lamia's claustrophobic canal, he let out a spine-paralyzing scream as if he had just been stabbed by the point of a razor-sharp object. A glistening drop of deep-blue azure appeared on the infant's neck. Phegor eagerly knelt down and, leaning forward, swiftly lapped up the lone droplet with his elongated reptilian tongue.

Sitting back on his haunches, he gave a self-satisfied smirk as two of the waiting trolls reached in to pull the baby's torso out from between Lamia's still-convulsing legs. He slid easily into their outstretched hands like a raft catching an ocean wave, as a viscous stream of black liquid gushed out alongside him.

One of the nurse-guards then plucked him out of the trolls' hands, gingerly holding him away from himself as if he were a leaking sack of wet potatoes. Phegor ordered him held tighter and more securely, then peered intensely at every inch of him to make sure he had all appendages and that no part of him was deformed.

He then announced, "For he is born! Henceforth, he shall be called Lord Fairuzo Cuchumaquic of Tartarus, Ruler of the Land of Turquoise."

The trolls gathered around then all intoned solemnly and in unison, "Lit sala pran vumona Nott Fairuzo!"

The two waiting guards took this as their cue to quickly step forward and grab ahold of Lamia forcibly on either side. As they began roughly dragging her out of the room, the globules of black blood still oozing out from between her legs created a greasy trail behind her that resembled burnt slug slime.

When she realized that she was being taken against her will yet again, her eyes widened in frenzied rage. She glanced frantically over at Phegor, but he seemed completely unconcerned that she was being manhandled and kidnapped by these ogres. For all she knew, the bastard might have even ordered this be done to her.

Out in the corridor, she suddenly let her body go completely limp. The two guards were forced to drag her heavy weight behind them like a three-hundred pound bag of limestone. She occasionally let loose a scream so ear-piercingly loud that it was only slightly muffled by the rag still stuffed into her mouth.

Finally, they arrived at their destination: it was the same room she'd been confined in during the gestation period. She was to remain there until Phegor got a chance to pay her a visit, whereupon he would proffer insincere apologies to soothe and appease her.

He would then put on a most convincing performance

designed to leave her literally begging him to have the baby taken out of her care. He would persuade her to have the responsibility delegated to someone else more prudish and less inclined to attend every single orgy.

To cement the arrangement and put the icing of enticement on the cherry pastry, he would give her a good going-over in the sack for old times' sake. Of course, there would be absolutely no indication given that it would be the very last time he ever planned to touch her.

It was prudent for him to allow her to retain slivers of hope that he would still want anything to do with her. This way, she would remain compliant – that is, until she realized that he would not be keeping a single one of his promises and was completely done with her.

When the guards had gotten Lamia securely ensconced in the room and had the door firmly bolted behind them, one of them removed the rag from her mouth. Immediately she bellowed, "Where is Philanus?"

"Who the hell is Philanus?" one of the guards asked, in genuine befuddlement.

"It's the name of the baby, you idiot!" Lamia yelled.

"What are you even talking about?" the guard spat back contemptuously. "Did you not hear what Our Lord and Master Phegor christened him as? The baby's name is Fairuzo, you imbecile! So, no more of this Philanus nonsense.

"And what a silly, disrespectful name to be calling a Lord, anyway. Besides, he's no longer yours to be giving any such name to!"

At that, Lamia's face balled up in such constipated fury that it looked like a clump of ripe radishes dunked in a bowl of regurgitated tomatoes. Just as she opened her mouth to retort, one of the guards quickly shoved the rag back in it.

"I really do not see why Phegor selected this obnoxious twit to begin with," he remarked, shaking his head in bewilderment. "She's an utter pain in the ass."

"Not only that, but a back-stabbing troublemaker with delusions of eminence. I'd say the kid is much better off motherless," the other shrugged.

"Well," added the other guard, "she must have been damned good in the sack to have bedazzled the Master of All Things Lustful into thinking she was anything more useful than a quick lay."

"Well, he's sure done with her *now*!" the other said loudly and pointedly.

They both guffawed long and hard at that one.

CHAPTER 21

THE WHISPERER OF
HIDDEN KNOWLEDGE

𝕿here was a commotion in the back of the Ballroom. Some trolls had gotten into an altercation over a perceived affront. One of the trolls had violently slammed into another while twirling around and subsequently knocked him to the ground. Now their two female partners were going at it – viciously ripping out handfuls of hair and gouging each other's faces with their long ragged nails.

The two male trolls looked on in high amusement at their brawling mates, guffawing and cheering them on as if they were at a hockey game. Broken teeth and bits of shredded clothing were flying everywhere, with rivulets of black blood spurting like a cracked oil rig.

"Oh, look," exclaimed Fairuzo, grinning with glee, "the evening's *real* amusement has begun! We shall see how long they can hold up, and then the survivor will be awarded a facial and a pedicure administered by one of our cave-slaves."

I could not tell if he was being facetious or if there really was such a prize being awarded. All I knew is that I would certainly pity anyone forced to fondle any one of these trolls' odious feet.

All of the others were beginning to form a circle around the slugfest, boisterously rooting for the combatant getting the most savage blows in. Even the band had stopped playing after realizing their audience had stopped thumping and hopping around, and all eyes had turned away. The trolls' limited attention span had been easily hijacked by this exhibition of violence that clearly excited and delighted them.

There is something really wrong with these beings, I thought to myself. *They either overreact inappropriately or they are totally apathetic; they're just not right in the head.*

Fairuzo eagerly moved forward to get a more intimate view of the fray. I stayed where I was, wishing to keep my distance from the insanity. The clamor was annoying. I once again had the feeling of alienation, realizing I had nothing in common with any of these lunatics here.

Just then I heard that strange voice again speaking directly into my ear. It said: *"A magnesian stone produces a magnetic field that is invisible, possessing a force that attracts or repels others."*

I looked around and could see no one standing near enough to have spoken. But when I turned to look behind me, I saw a man staring back intensely, as if waiting for me to notice him. He looked so dissimilar to the other trolls, I wondered why I hadn't taken note of him before.

His facial features were slim and delicate. His eyes had an alert quality and a noticeable sparkle to them, unlike the trolls with their dull, bloodshot zombie-orbs sunken deep into their sockets. He had an extraordinary mane of silver that hung nearly to his waist like a thickly twisted rope, and he was elegantly dressed in a long pearly-gray satin robe with a gold tassled sash. His garb looked very similar to what a Knight of the Templar Order might have worn, but with a large red X in place of a cross emblazoned on the front.

He suddenly gave a little hop while twisting around to face the other way, then began swiftly walking backwards towards me as if he had eyes in the back of his head. When he came precisely within a foot of me, he spun around to face me. He quickly averted his gaze, as if he were too shy to look me directly in the eye.

In a voice so faint I had to strain to hear it over the din of the ongoing melee, he said, "Enmira, I have been waiting to speak with you. Well, actually, I have already been speaking *to* you; you just weren't aware it was I," he said, and laughed a bit self-consciously.

"First, let me explain to you who I am. I am Duke Procel, and I am the Gatekeeper of Hidden and Secret Knowledge here. That is my official job title. I have been feeding you tidbits of trivia here and there so that you would already be somewhat familiar with me once you arrived here."

"Oh! So that was *you* all this time?" I exclaimed. "But how did I hear you speak from so far away?"

"Well, that was a simple matter of thought transference," he explained. "You see, there is really no limit as to how far the communication of minds can travel, as it is beyond space and time. And it is instantaneous: the second I think it is the second it reaches your ears. It is merely a projection of energy that travels in the form of vibration.

"It is quite a simple process, really, once you are aware of the great Universal Laws of Mentalism, Vibration and Communication. You see, a thought is transmitted to the astral body through the mental plane and then transferred to the physical mind, where it is interpreted in the form of native language.

"And this then – oh, I do apologize," he said, interrupting himself with a grimace. "I just realized I must be boring you to tears. I have this tendency to just prattle on and on. I forget that no one is really interested in what I have to say," he finished weakly, with a dejected look upon his face.

"Oh, no, I was not bored at all," I fibbed, as I had actually been starting to wonder when he might stop talking. But I felt sorry for him; he seemed so timid and I felt a need to reassure him.

"In fact," I said, "I found most of your communications quite interesting, and they were certainly things I had no previous knowledge of. It's just that I was so taken offguard by how they suddenly appeared in my head, I did not get a chance to properly assimilate the information."

"Oh, but you are far too kind, Enmira, to not admit that you were indeed horribly bored," he said gratefully. "For none of the creatures here will even deign to speak to me. They accuse me of still possessing a soul because I don't have the same simple-minded interests as they, and so they want nothing at all to do with me."

My ears perked up at the mention of a soul. *This is something I've been wanting to find out!* I thought excitedly. And so I asked him, "But why would you or anybody *not* have a soul? And why is everyone here so concerned if someone has one or not? I mean, don't they all have one themselves?"

"Well," Procel replied, "it is a strict requirement of residency here that one relinquishes their soul before arrival. In fact, it is something that occurs instantaneously once the injection is administered on Earth. But it does so happen, on extremely rare occasions, that a soul is accidentally retained, and the trolls can immediately tell. It is like they can sense or smell it, as if it were an intruder.

"You see, the trolls are highly offended and repulsed by souls, as they believe having one interferes with their ability to have what they consider to be fun. Not much they do here requires an active conscience, or any sort of innate system that would alert them they were engaging in anything too wicked or morally wrong – as I'm sure you've clearly already seen for yourself."

I nodded my head in affirmation, for I'd certainly seen evidence of *that*.

"But I suspect there is also an element of jealousy and envy involved as well, the fact that someone else has something of inestimable value that they once had and never will have again," he added.

"But I don't understand," I said. "How does one give away a soul? Is it not permanently attached to one's self?"

"That is precisely what I used to think until I arrived

here and discovered differently, Enmira," he replied. "Apparently, somehow during the infecting and dehumanizing process, the soul is forcibly ejected and separated from the mortal essence. It basically disengages from the core and falls away, like an item of discarded clothing."

Here, he lowered his voice even further, so as to ensure what he said next would reach my ears only. "It is said that Fairuzo collects every one of these souls and puts them all in storage, each individually preserved. However, I have no idea what he personally plans to do with them. I do know where they are stored, though, and it is a place that is heavily guarded, you can be sure of that."

His voice then dropped to a whisper and I really had to lean closer to hear what he said next.

"Now mind you, this is not completely confirmed, but it is something I have overheard and suspected for a long time –" Here, he paused and looked around, as if afraid to continue. Then he blurted out, "I believe Fairuzo is one of the few here that still has his soul."

"But how do you know all of this?" I asked curiously. "And what does it mean that Fairuzo might still have his soul?"

"Like I said," Procel answered, "it is something I myself have suspected for quite some time. But then I overheard some very interesting conversation at one of the Cabal meetings – those take place when the top bloodsuckers from Headquarters pay the Turquoise Kingdom a visit. Occasionally even Fairuzo's notorious father – His Royal Highness, Phegor – rouses himself out of his own slothfulness to actually join the junket and show up at the assemblage; I suppose that's when they have something *really* important to discuss."

Hearing mention of Fairuzo's father took me by surprise. I was fairly certain I would have noticed any of his family members hovering about had they been present today, and so I'd assumed it was just the trolls, the cave-slaves and Fairuzo that made up the population here. I wondered why his father lived in a different part of the world. His mother was apparently elsewhere, too.

I was just about to inquire about his family when Procel continued: "Oh, the fuss that's made over the Cabal by the trolls when they pay a visit here. You would think that Belial himself had put in an appearance! The bowing and scraping that goes on is just ridiculous." He clucked his tongue in disgust.

"Although, I suppose, to the trolls, they *are* actually royalty," he added. "But to me, they are nothing more than parasitic leaches involved in the highest level of universal debauchery and evil." He frowned in heavy disapproval.

"As for Fairuzo, you noticed how you and he were the only ones whose reflections appeared in the Mirror, while all of the trolls behind you did not?"

"Yes!" I replied. "I found that extremely odd! But then, in my own mirror at home, Fairuzo seemed to fade in and out of the reflection, and I was very curious how he was able to do that."

"Well," said Procel, "he *is* extremely powerful and can shapeshift almost as impressively as his father; but just the fact that his reflection appears at all is a fairly reliable sign of a soul. I can assure you that his father's reflection does *not* appear in any mirror.

"Now I suppose one could presume that if Fairuzo *did* indeed still have his soul, then it would mean he is not irretrievably damned like the rest of these cretinous ogres devoid of all decency – and that could only be a good thing.

"I do so fervently pray that turns out to be true, for both your sake and mine, for it gives us something to hope for – maybe even another ally on our side, as far-fetched as that might sound. But how he could even have *half* a soul with that devil of a mother and father that he was cursed with..." Here Procel trailed off, as if wondering if he should best leave the rest of these thoughts for another time.

"As for myself, I have found it extremely prudent to stay far to the side whenever the Turquoise Mirror is dropped down, so that none of these nosy trolls can see whether my reflection appears or not."

I nodded, for it made perfect sense not to arouse suspicion. I only wished that Fairuzo had not led me up to the Mirror in front of all of their prying eyes, for they had already been looking for any excuse to distrust me. Perhaps, by showing that I still had a reflection, he was trying to prove some sort of point to either me or the trolls – or to himself?

"Oh, and just so you know," he added quickly, "in addition to being able to communicate telepathically, I possess a highly-developed sense of hearing. That is to say I can actually hear what's being said through many thick layers of rock simply by pressing my ear to the wall and concentrating."

Procel gave a tight little smile then, as if he were extremely proud of his abilities – as well he should be, for what he was capable of was quite extraordinary. I could see how this would come in very handy in revealing what those in control might have in store for the inhabitants here, including me.

"These trolls have absolutely no curiosity and could not care less about what is really going on around them, other than making sure that none of their sordid fun and entertainment gets interrupted. It is also why I have been so eagerly awaiting your arrival, Enmira, because I believe you and I are kindred spirits – ones that very likely still possess our souls, that is – and we can watch out for each other."

Procel paused, peering closely at the side of my neck. "Ahhh," he said, in a tone of satisfaction intermingled with relief, as if he'd just unearthed a long-missing piece of a puzzle. "It appears you have only a double-puncture scar instead of the complete bite-circle."

"But what does that mean?" I asked.

"It means that, for whatever reason, you have only been partially infected. This might explain why you have managed to hold on to your soul. It would also explain your natural aversion to the blood-drinking and flesh-eating that are the only items on the menu here."

"By the way," he continued, "when was the last time you ate something?"

I had to stop and think for a moment. It must have been the night before when I'd last actually eaten anything.

"I believe it's been over a day," I replied.

"And you are not famished? Or even the least bit hungry?" he asked.

"Well, now that you mention it, I don't believe I am at all. I feel a bit light-headed, but that's about it," I answered. And it was true: my stomach did not ache or even feel empty.

"Well," Procel said, "since you don't eat what they consider to be food around here, you will eventually need to return to Earth for sustenance."

"You see, Enmira," he explained, "if you are like me – and I think you are – then you will now be able to exist purely on the energy from the Earth's sun. All you will need to do for rejuvenation is place yourself directly in the pathway of its rays and immerse yourself in its healing light. Simply let the pores of your skin drink it in and let it permeate your being.

"Unfortunately, we are now on what's considered a dead planet, and there are no such restorative powers from the few and tiny stars in its orbit. But I must say that you are one of the very, very few who are immune to the poison that causes The Darkness in all of the others here, and I will tell you why –"

He paused for a moment and then continued: "–because a pure soul cannot be corrupted, even by the most potent of evils."

For the first time, he met my gaze directly and, as if for further emphasis, he reached out his hand and placed in upon my arm. It felt surprisingly warm to the touch, particularly in comparison to Fairuzo's icy cold one.

"You see, The Light shines even in the dark, but those enveloped in The Darkness are blinded by it. They complain that it hurts their eyes and makes their heads ache. Does this all make sense to you?" he asked.

"Yes," I said, "I believe I understand what you are saying." And I did, for the most part.

"Good," he said. "Now, I know those at Headquarters are far from pleased that our souls may have survived intact, and they are quite concerned about this possibility. You can be sure they are keeping a close eye on us and that there are informants all around us.

"But, as yet, they have absolutely no proof of any such thing. And I'd really like to keep it that way," he finished firmly.

I felt a tiny prickle of fear crawl up my spine at the thought that I was most likely being carefully watched and monitored. After all, through no fault of my own, I had apparently circumvented one of the strict rules of admittance here. The trolls had all caught wind of this merely through their own observance and suspicions. And if those simpletons could figure it out, surely the ones in charge of monitoring could easily enough as well.

I began to understand why Procel seemed so timorous and low-key in demeanor, making sure to keep to himself and remain in the shadows. For it was becoming obvious that anyone with an intact soul here was under very heavy scrutiny and most likely in grave danger.

CHAPTER 22

THE GOLDEN GOBLET ELIXIR

The battle between the two female trolls was still raging, with no sign of either one tiring or conceding defeat. By this time, the ground they were grappling on had become completely soaked with viscous pools of slippery black blood. As they lunged and pecked at each other's eyes with sharp nail-talons, huge chunks of hair and shredded bits of clothing floated on top of the thick puddles like wayward bird's nests.

Fairuzo had been so engrossed in the entertainment that he hadn't even noticed Enmira was no longer by his side. Growing bored with all the repetitive gouging and splattering, he began looking around for her.

He really should have been keeping a closer watch on her; after all, she was a long way from being considered trustworthy at this point. On just her very first day here, she was already causing problems with her decidedly unrepentant, contrarian attitude. It was also lessening the likelihood of the Cabal deeming this particular candidate's initiation a success. If he was to get her anywhere near the proper mindset of an Eternally Forsaken, he must work harder to indoctrinate her into the 'do unto others what thou wilt' philosophy of true hedonism and debauchery.

The way she was now, she seemed to be thoroughly enmeshed within the dreary, dead-end cogs of morality and empathetic feelings. What possible fun was there in that? It was imperative that this unacceptable outlook of hers be corrected as soon as possible.

One *could* rightfully accuse him of being a bit biased on her behalf, however. She seemed to possess a certain quality that made him not only want to tame and corrupt her, but to also protect her. In fact, he did not recall feeling like this about any of his other Earth-Tarts – ever.

Then, again, the others had all been willingly compliant from the very first moment, without even a speck of resistance. Perhaps it was her very defiance that so intrigued him – which was quite illogical, as her refusal to cooperate and submit should normally have aroused his ire.

He knew there had to be some sort of clever maneuver or ruse that would entice her into embracing The Darkness with all of its immoral pleasures. He was thinking the Golden Goblet Ceremony just might do the trick, which he had planned next for the evening's festivities.

This was a customary and critical part of each initiation. Without exception, every neophyte before her had eagerly partaken of the Goblet's liquid – some even swigging it down with great relish – but he couldn't help wondering if she might once more balk and refuse to cooperate.

When he saw for himself how the Turquoise Mirror had revealed her reflection even after the Descent, he was not at all surprised. It had confirmed his suspicion that she had somehow retained her soul.

He now needed to focus all of his powers of persuasion on convincing her to let go of this stubborn and annoying hindrance. For the souls of mortals served only to lock in chaste values while interfering in the enjoyment of licentious behaviors and wicked abandonment.

If only he could get her alone in a quiet place, far away from all this din, he would be able to probe her mind and get a better scope on her inner mechanisms. But, until then, he was certain that just one decent gulp of the special nectar would shatter her inhibitions faster than a wrecking ball could demolish a castle's parapet – if he could just get her to voluntarily drink it, that is. It was a potent elixir, containing trace amounts of his own saliva serum, along with other powerfully transformative chemicals, that would surely get her shedding that pesky soul in no time.

As for now, the last thing he needed was for her to go wandering off into any of the restricted areas of the Kingdom. There were certain places he needed to keep her away from as long as possible. In her present state of mind, he had no doubt that she would be completely appalled at some of the things and conditions she might discover.

Most certainly she would be extremely displeased to see the quarters where the cave-slaves were kept. Their living space was, quite frankly, really not much more than a bleak and filthy dungeon. He'd never seen the need to coddle the slaves or provide them with any sort of extravagant surroundings. After all, they required only the most basic of amenities that would keep them functioning and fulfilling their purpose of serving all of his needs.

He was perplexed at the pity Enmira seemed to extend towards these lower creatures; they were clearly not worthy of such wasteful and stifling emotions. He really must rid her of this groundless notion that inferior beings deserved any mercy or had any intrinsic value at all. He found this to be a most absurd concept.

Fairuzo was of the opinion that a slave beholden to his master worked that much harder to please him. In fact, the blind salamander should consider himself lucky to have been given a job that kept him so useful and busy – unlike some of the others who were never let out of their chains. For that alone he should be grateful.

He also had no doubt that she would heavily disapprove of how the cave-slaves were routinely trained and disciplined. She would regard the electrocutions, whippings and beatings as inexcusably cruel. She would be incapable of comprehending that these methods were indeed the shrewdest and most effective ways of keeping the slaves obedient and in line.

Fairuzo was even beginning to wonder if perhaps the difficulties he was beginning to encounter with Enmira's non-cooperative attitude might warrant him reaching out to his father for advice. Phegor had many unpleasant traits that he felt no urge whatsoever to imitate, and it was only on very rare occasions that he wished he was more like him. But he did have one skill that he greatly admired and did his best to emulate, and that was his amazing ability to seduce and subdue every single species of female he'd ever encountered.

It was as though he were able to hypnotize them into doing whatever it was that he wanted. He easily broke their wills as if they were brittle twigs just begging to be snapped. His tales of conquests over the centuries were not just idle boasting. No one would even think of disputing the validity of his self-proclaimed title "Master of All Things Lustful."

Fairuzo realized that he was still just a novice at this game of seduction. He had a long, long way to go before he could even begin to rival Phegor's fool-proof wiles and astronomical number of successful seductions under his belt. Fortunately, he had inherited his father's strikingly handsome looks. It was this distinct advantage that he was able to rely upon most to beguile his selected prey.

Up until now, this attribute had never failed him. However, in Enmira's case, he was becoming increasingly exasperated with her impenetrable wall of resistance at just about every turn. He was beginning to see how much it was preventing him from achieving full domination and control over her.

He glanced around the room and spotted her off in a corner, engaged deeply in conversation with Procel. He was not at all surprised to see that they had already met and were speaking together. Procel had quizzed him nonstop about her – what she'd been doing in her house the entire time Fairuzo had been watching her from the Mirror, when she would be arriving here, and so on.

Fairuzo was well aware that Procel had been sending her thought-transferences. He even knew exactly what each one of them had been, as he'd been explicitly instructed by

Headquarters to monitor them all. So far, he'd only overheard references to mundane scientific trivia – Procel's specialty – none of which could at all be considered a breach of confidentiality or a threat to the security of the Cabal.

And even though he'd been ordered to keep him within his line of sight, Procel had never given Fairuzo even the slightest indication that he might cause any sort of trouble. He was fairly certain that Procel's sense of logic and guarded restraint would prevent him from using his vast reservoir of cryptic knowledge to reveal any innermost secrets of the Kingdom. This was, of course, strictly forbidden. All in all, he believed that Procel was basically harmless.

Although Procel was the firstborn son of Allocen – one of the original Dukes of Mount Hermon – he was a meek sort. He was certainly not known as one for making waves. It was obvious that he was much more comfortable keeping to himself rather than inciting any kind of disturbance.

He was also considered one of those who had "slipped through the cracks," as he had never been subjected to any of the usual disciplinary actions for regulatory infractions. Any other resident here who had flouted as many rules as Procel had would most definitely be considered insubordinate. These transgressions specifically included his refusal to participate in any of the orgies or in the blood and flesh feasts. But since he was the spawn of one of the Cabal's own, he was given the kind of leeway that would be considered prejudicial or special privilege if it were to be granted among any of the troll population.

It must be noted, however, that although their mutinous behavior appeared to run in a similar vein, the crucial difference between Procel and Enmira was that he was given a permanent free pass due to his heritage, while her refusal to comply would only be temporarily tolerated.

Fairuzo even felt a bit of a brotherly kinship with Procel, as they were both royal heirs. In fact, Procel's

Dukedom title technically outranked Fairuzo's Lordship. But, for whatever quirky personal reason, Procel had adamantly declined to involve himself in any leadership role after being sent to Tartarus. In fact, he'd voluntarily handed off all governance powers to Fairuzo, who had immediately accepted this generous but most unexpected transfer of appellation.

In the view of the Mount Hermonites, this made Procel even more of an oddball. For who in their right mind would not crave and eagerly accept such limitless power over an entire kingdom? And although Fairuzo had essentially inherited the Land of Turquoise from his father, he was well aware that Procel had been first in line to be considered for the position. As Fairuzo had already resigned himself to the idea of existing as a mere underling in the chain of Procel's command, he was especially grateful for the opportunity to take the reins of authority.

On numerous occasions, Fairuzo had been told the story of how he'd been conceived and born right here on Tartarus, but he'd always been led to believe that the nurse-maid who'd been hired to take care of him had actually been his mother. He'd only discovered the truth completely by accident. He was incensed that this had been kept hidden from him for so long. In fact, being deliberately lied to by those he trusted felt like a monumental betrayal.

It was this chief traumatic event in his childhood that had irreversibly scarred him, prompting him to adopt an entirely new worldview. That one shocking revelation had forced open his eyes, smothering the once brightly-burning flames of blind trust, leaving nothing behind but the smoldering ashes of doubt. In its place sprang forth a constant, wakeful wariness and a questioning of all things. He came to regard the intentions of his own family members and their devoted satellite of sycophants with mounting suspicion.

He gradually and steadily began to separate himself

from the Cabal's one-sided web of allegiance. Instead of unquestioningly embracing their absolute authority and irrefutable sagacity, he found himself growing more and more disgusted with their self-serving motives. This had became something of a dichotomy with him, though, as he was still deeply attracted and attached to all of the wicked diversions and recreations he'd become accustomed to. But there was now a part of him that wondered if he weren't just playing a role that fell right in step with their agenda.

He also couldn't help wondering if there was perhaps a deeper reason why Procel had refused to accept the ruling crown. It would certainly not be far-fetched to believe that he might know something that Fairuzo didn't. He had yet to think of a way to quiz Procel about this without seeming to pry into his private affairs, but it was definitely something he needed to probe further, and soon.

In contrast to Fairuzo's entire lifetime on Tartarus, Procel had been born on Mount Hermon, and had spent all of his childhood there. It could even be said that, in comparison, he'd lived a life of opulence and luxury. Even more importantly, he'd always known exactly who his real birth-mother was.

It was odd, then, having come from such disparate environments, that they both now harbored such remarkably similar disdain for their ancestral lineage. But it might also be noted that both he and Procel had opted out of being injected with the Beastly Mark, whereas all of the other Neph offspring had eagerly volunteered to receive it, without exception. To them, forever discarding their consciences had been a more-than-fair exchange for a life free from guilt, remorse or empathy, and from ever having to feel any conflicting emotions like joy, hope or optimism.

Fairuzo had been clever enough to realize that holding on to his soul gave him a distinct advantage over those who had given theirs up, that it actually gave him power over them – contrary to what the Cabal wanted anyone to believe.

He'd even found a way to circumvent the unfortunate morality effect that a soul could have upon the enjoyment of wanton pleasures, while still remaining in total control.

He had also personally observed that those who were now soulless had very little insight or clarity of mind. They were quite often confused and anxious, and were, in fact, extremely dense and doltish. This was clearly a side effect that he did not at all see as any sort of asset.

So, was the administration of The Mark and the resultant soul-shedding the cause of their regression into a far less intelligent, primitive species? Or was it the pre-existing condition of their souls prior to the injection that had been the causal factor? And when he did finally manage to convince Enmira to relinquish her own soul, would she, too, begin to degenerate into one of these repulsive beings?

These thoughts crept into Fairuzo's mind more and more often lately, and he'd had little luck in trying to avoid or ignore them.

Procel constantly complained of being stuck on Tartarus with the dim-witted trolls, every one of whom he thoroughly despised and refused to interact or mingle with. Fairuzo could easily see his point. He himself sometimes dreaded returning here after one of his many visits to Earth.

That was one of the advantages he had over Procel – that he could flit back and forth to Earth whenever he pleased. Granted, he had to use one particular portal that was monitored, but Procel had to ask permission each and every time. Fairuzo suspected that this was because Headquarters did not completely trust him to return afterwards.

During his many journeys between the two planets, Fairuzo had noticed that, even though Tartarus was said to be the negative polar opposite of Earth, there did seem to be quite a few obvious similarities insofar as corruption, debauchery and just plain evil. However, Earth did have the advantage of an abundance of spectacular scenery – forests and mountains and oceans – in stark contrast to the dark, dank, endless caverns of Tartarus.

And, of course, Earth had a seemingly unlimited and ever-expanding population of both human and animal flesh to choose from. Whereas, here, there was strict adherence to a maximum number of inhabitants, with culling achieved mostly through banishment. However, as the populace on Earth began reaching all-time highs, culling was rapidly becoming much more popular and prevalent there, particularly among the wildlife deemed as pests, the chronically infirm, the incarcerated, the indigent, and the elderly.

Although Fairuzo innately despised the light and heat of the blazing sun on Earth – even keeping to a night schedule as much as possible whenever he visited – Procel claimed that being in the pathway of its rays actually revitalized him. Fairuzo had dismissed this claim as illogical nonsense – that is, until he'd seen for himself how it had energized Enmira when she'd gone outside.

He did find her visceral reaction bothersome, as it indicated she might still retain some fondness for certain elements of her former planet. Therefore, he would need to make sure to inform her that she could only survive in Earth's atmosphere for short periods of time now, due to the limited capacity of her altered lungs. He would explain to her about the Death Zone, and then remind her of the incident in which she'd literally lost her breath.

If she happened to inquire about the botanicals he'd revived her with, he would have to plead ignorance. For if he was to ensure she continued returning to Tartarus after each visit to Earth, she must never learn the secret of the breath-restorative qualities of the medicinal weeds or where to obtain them.

Aside from the annoyance of the sun, Fairuzo did thoroughly enjoy his Earthly safaris. He found great pleasure in the pastimes of stalking animals and hunting new female recruits – or "the procurement of assorted fresh meats," as he liked to refer to each of the activities. He would feast on a few carcasses first, then continue on his prowl for nubile bedmates to infect and collect. Although he was quick to grow bored with each conquest after a few days of sex play, he always found the actual quest to obtain souls to add to his extensive collection utterly exhilarating.

As for Procel, save for the occasional supervised visit to Earth here and there, he was pretty much trapped on Tartarus. And Phegor had made it crystal clear that he would never be welcome back at Mount Hermon. Procel's openly rebellious attitude and blatant disapproval of the Cabal's agenda had branded him an exile. Even though Fairuzo was beginning to think very closely along the same lines as Procel, he understood the prudence of shrouding and concealing any insurgent views he might harbor.

Although Procel pestered Fairuzo about each new initiate he brought back to Tartarus, Enmira seemed to be the only one who had immediately sparked his approval – and seemed to have retained it, judging from the way he was so deeply engrossed in conversation with her now.

Procel had once explained that, as a mystagogue, it was essential he forsake all carnal pleasures and remove all temptation of physical cravings, so as to immerse himself completely in the acquisition of knowledge. This, he valued above all else, claiming to be interested only in the cerebral part of existence.

Even amidst all of the wantonness, the willing sexual partners, and the orgies constantly in progress all around him, he had voluntarily chosen celibacy. And so, for most intents and purposes, Procel could be considered a monk of sorts: one living outside his own kind, in a den of iniquity rather than a monastery. Therefore, Fairuzo felt it fairly safe to assume that Procel posed no threat as a potential romantic rival.

Fairuzo, of course, had no such inhibitions or

boundaries, and held the totally opposite view: he felt it was complete lunacy not to take full advantage of every single worldly perversion and opportunity of lust-fulfillment that presented itself. However, there *was* a part of him that couldn't help but admire Procel's ironclad will and extreme sense of self-control.

Whenever Fairuzo saw a new beauty on Earth, he had to have her; he simply could not stop himself. And although he would never confide this to anyone – especially his father, who mocked such things – he sometimes secretly wished to one day find an Earthling who would make his heart quicken with excitement past the initial serum injection, past the two-day seduction-courtship, past the Initiation ceremony, and even past the climax of the inevitable Consummation ritual.

So far, it seemed quite possible that Enmira just might be the one to outlast all the others. Even though she was his polar opposite in so many ways, so uncompromising and stubbornly willful, perhaps it was this very friction between them that made her such an enigmatic puzzle to him. She was a fascinating labyrinth with so many hidden chambers and twisting alleyways that he hardly knew where to begin.

His father never tired of reminding him how these Earthlings began to grow unattractive immediately after they'd been infected by the serpent-bite, deteriorating rapidly once they'd arrived on Tartarus. It even seemed that the sunless atmosphere only accelerated the uglification process. And since this result was inevitable, his advice was to get all he could out of the relationship as soon as possible, and then casually dismiss and dump the ogre once she had become too hard on the eyes.

Fairuzo could only hope that, somehow, Enmira would be the one exception to this downward spiral of grotesquery.

Procel had presented him with his own peculiar theory that, in addition to the serum's poison, it was the sole diet of corpses that made the Earthlings disintegrate into hideous trolls. Fairuzo was still not convinced that had anything at all to do with it. And if it did, that would be a real shame – as there was no way that part of the Turquoisian culture would *ever* be altered or abandoned. He simply would not allow it.

Fairuzo himself was so heavily attached to the diet of animal carcasses that he could not possibly imagine sating himself with any other fuel. Drinking the blood gave him a lusty thrill, and the flesh provided the most amazing texture for chewing. He loved the sensation of rolling the muscles and tendons over his tongue while crunching the bones with his razor-sharp fangs. He especially savored the satisfying squish of the eyeballs after plucking them out of their sockets and biting into the orbs' succulent tissue.

Indeed, what else would they be living off of: air? He had heard of such an existence but knew it to be pure nonsense, no more than an urban legend of mythical proportions. It was beyond absurd to believe that any beings could exist simply by inhaling the layers of gasses found on Earth, comprised of nitrogen, oxygen, argon and carbon dioxide. And there was certainly no sustainable air to be found here on Tartarus!

But enough of these profound thoughts; they made his head feel like a hot, swirling, bubbling cauldron about to blow its lid off. What he needed to do now was get closer to Procel to hear what was being said.

Fairuzo quickly transformed himself into a gnat and alit on Procel's shoulder, just in time to hear him warning Enmira that she was being watched.

Well, that's certainly true enough, Fairuzo thought wryly to himself. *I'm watching both of you right now!*

He observed the look of worry upon Enmira's face, and felt a bit irritated that Procel was causing her distress with his usual dour outlook. He then heard Procel go on to declare that there were snitches all around them and that they needed to be very careful.

All right; that's enough of <u>this</u> depressing conversation, Fairuzo thought in annoyance. *This was supposed to be a celebration; not a Dysphoric Convention!* He quickly materialized into his recognizable form, startling both of them. Procel stopped in mid-sentence and Enmira's mouth gaped open in astonishment at his sudden appearance.

Fairuzo grabbed ahold of Enmira's arm, pulling her in the direction of the bandstand.

"Come," he urged. "It's time for the Golden Goblet Ceremony."

He tugged at her sleeve to hasten her along. They approached a long banquet table, whereupon a huge crystal punch bowl sat, filled with a frothing, gold-colored liquid. On either side of the bowl were two large golden wine goblets, shining resplendently like polished ammolite beneath the pulsating dome light overhead.

Just before they reached the refreshments, Fairuzo came to a sudden stop, grabbing hold of one of Enmira's wrists and peering closely into her face.

"Wait – you do drink wine, don't you?" he asked warily, suspecting that her answer might be something he did not want to hear.

Enmira took a few moments to reply, then said with some hesitancy, "Well... I used to."

"What do you mean, you used to?" Fairuzo asked sharply. Already, again with her, he seemed to be hitting another wall of resistance.

"I mean that I used to drink it quite regularly; but after awhile, I started resenting the deleterious effects it had upon me," Enmira explained.

Fairuzo was puzzled. Deleterious effects? But the effects were all quite wonderful! The wine made your head spin in the most delicious way, and allowed you to surrender to desires that you otherwise would never have even thought of exploring.

He began to feel a sense of frustration overtake him then at his utter powerlessness and inability to exert control over her. This was something he'd never dealt with before with *any* of his initiates, and he loathed feeling this way.

But herein lie the dilemma: he could not force her to participate in any of these ceremonies; her involvement must be totally voluntary, or else the act would be meaningless and accomplish nothing. True, the initial infection-bite had been forced upon her; but after that, everything she did must be entirely volitional.

He realized how crucial her partaking in the Golden Goblet ritual was. He was certain it would be the *one* thing that would loosen her inhibitions once and for all, and, in so doing, pry loose that bothersome soul she was so obstinately holding on to.

"What effects did you not like?" he asked in a rather patronizing tone.

"Well, for one," Enmira explained, "it made me feel so sick afterwards."

"Oh!" said Fairuzo, brightening a bit, for he could easily assuage her fears over this point of contention.

"There are no worries like that with this wine!" he exclaimed. "It is entirely different than anything you've ever sampled upon Earth. There are absolutely no after-effects or sickness; no harm, no risk, just a warm, cozy glow that makes you feel like you can fly!

"In fact," he continued enthusiastically, now warming even more to his sales pitch, "you see those gorgeous wings upon your back? If you take just a few sips from the Golden Goblet there, you will actually be able to use those to fly! Just think of the hours of fun you will have!"

But Enmira still did not seem convinced. Now Fairuzo was beginning to lose his patience with her, wishing he could just tilt the goblet up to her lips and force the potion down her throat. So far, she'd only actually chosen to participate in one item on the agenda, and that had been descending the stairs down to Tartarus. Since then, circumstances seemed to have spiraled beyond his control and come to a stalemate, at the mercy of her most stubborn will.

He propelled her forward to the table, whereupon he picked up one of the goblets – the one meant specifically for her that contained his special serum. He graciously handed it to her as if it were a most exquisite bouquet of belladonna.

Enmira accepted the chalice full of the effervescent liquid, holding it gingerly in her hands. She bent her face down to it and took a cautious sniff of the contents. "It smells like poison," she announced, turning up her nose in disgust.

"Oh, no," Fairuzo argued fervently, "it is far from being poison. In fact, the taste is quite delicious – even better than the nectar from a honeysuckle flower in Spring!"

Enmira continued to stare at the goblet in her hand for what seemed like an interminable amount of time, as if frozen with indecision. Finally, and with great reluctance, she slowly lifted it up to her lips.

Oh, yes! Fairuzo thought elatedly. *She will drink the elixir now and will soon be discarding that prim exterior!* He waited eagerly for her to take the first sip, as did all of the trolls who had gathered around by now and were intently watching her.

She looked as if she were just about to take a swallow, then suddenly jerked the goblet away from her mouth. Turning it upside down, she swiftly poured out all of its contents onto the ground.

Upon seeing her do this, the trolls collectively gasped in outrage at this bold act of insolence.

"How dare she!" one exclaimed indignantly.

"What nerve this one has!" another angrily shouted.

At this point, Fairuzo lost his temper. "You ungrateful little girl!" he yelled. "You have wasted the precious sacrament! This wine is thousands of years old and cannot be easily replenished!"

But Enmira was not listening to any of them. She was staring intently at the goblet in her hand. It had begun to vibrate, and then to shake more and more violently. A look of horror came over her face and she let go of the cup with a loud gasp of revulsion. It fell with a clatter onto the ground, whereupon a writhing mass of serpents came slithering out – dozens of tangled, undulating ophidians, slipping and gliding and making their way deliberately towards the pools of black blood, as if they were returning to their swamp-pit.

"What is going on here?" one troll shouted petulantly. "This one has already been given powers of turning wine into serpents on her very first day here? Why, the rest of us have had to wait months and months for *our* promised powers – and are *still* waiting!"

"Oh, yes, she is a special one, all right," another sneered.

Fairuzo was glaring angrily at Enmira, trying to decide how to handle the situation. He really wanted to just throttle her, and it took every ounce of restraint he had within him not to.

Again, he felt an overwhelming sense of impotence and wondered: *Why is everything turning upside down now to where she seems to be holding the reins of power? Meanwhile, it would appear that I'm rapidly losing my grip! How can I possibly rectify this to where I am back in control?*

He could not allow this humiliation to continue. He needed to regain his domination and retrieve his sense of self-respect, once and for all.

CHAPTER 23

EN ROUTE TO THE HIDING PLACE

As I stood watching the wriggling mass of serpents slither away, I sensed that I had come perilously close to stepping upon a snare trap that would have catapulted me headfirst into an abyss.

Apparently the snakes had been hidden inside the wine all along. Had I not thrown the goblet down when I did, I would surely have been bitten. In fact, they would be taking up nasty residence in my gullet right now, knotted and coiled and hissing, had I not resisted.

The truth was that I *had* been curious to see if the liquid would indeed taste like the nectar of honeysuckle, as Fairuzo had advertised. But only for the briefest of moments had I considered taking even the most tentative of sips. For, right as I was about to raise the goblet to my lips, I'd suddenly heard that loud voice in my ear telling me to throw the cup down, and quickly, for it was a potion meant to entrap me.

Had that been Procel warning me? I wondered now. I was almost certain it had been. I looked around but did not see him standing anywhere nearby.

Even before I'd heard the voice, I'd already had a strong sense of foreboding, especially after smelling the liquid – for it most definitely did reek of toxic chemicals. And after the voice had warned me, I was even more convinced I should not swallow it. When I raised it to my lips, I had only been pretending to consider drinking it. The truth was that I feared someone would force it down my throat if I did not at least look like I was making the effort.

The trolls now loudly complaining and insisting that I had been given some supernatural ability to turn liquid into snakes were sadly mistaken. If only that were so, I would have put those powers to so much better use – like finding a way out of here and flying back to my own world with these wings upon my back!

I still had not had a chance to ascertain whether these appendages would actually enable me to fly, or if they were solely decorative. This was definitely something I needed to explore. It did not seem likely, though, as I had the distinct feeling that anything that might encourage my leaving here would be highly frowned upon and most certainly not made readily available. And it was quite obvious that Fairuzo seemed utterly determined to keep me here with him in this desolate place.

Aside from the voice of warning I'd heard, what had also prevented me from drinking the wine was the haunting feeling that, after I'd taken that first sip, there would be no turning back; I would be forever trapped here. Once again, I recalled the lyric I'd heard just prior to stepping through my closet's portal door and embarking upon my descent, foretelling of the bell tolling one last time before the falling of eternal night. This realm I had blindly and impulsively blundered into certainly seemed to be one where the sun did not exist, although I still clung to that microscopic thread of hope that I might somehow escape.

My immediate concern was seeing how furious my having spilled the wine had made not only Fairuzo, but the mob of livid trolls now shrieking all around me. They were loudly asserting that I was an infiltrator, an interloper, an imposter who did not belong here – and, on that point, they were certainly correct. I was as out of place here as a lost seagull stranded in the middle of the Atacama Desert, surrounded by vultures.

It seemed that my unwavering rejection of each and every refreshment offered me had only ensured I continued to make enemies here. But I refused to participate in their bizarre rituals. All that was acceptable here went so greatly against my most basic morals and conscience.

I now began to suspect that Fairuzo was deliberately trying to deceive or taint me in some way. I was certain he must have known there were serpents in the goblet he'd offered me. Why was he so insistent that I drink it?

But I still could not figure out what his true motives were. On the one hand, it was blatantly obvious that he held no fondness for any of the trolls here; yet on the other, he seemed to want to alter something in me that would result in my more closely resembling them. And I then had to wonder: if I were to become more like them, what would prevent him from losing all interest in me as well?

Whatever it was he was trying to either forcibly take from me or convince me to surrender, it seemed that my determination to cling to it was the one critical element working in my favor now. It made sense that retaining my sense of autonomy would continue to give me a position of barter and leverage, and I resolved to do everything I could to hold on tightly to it.

It made me shudder to imagine being anything like these despicable creatures. They seemed to hold nothing sacred and they had no concept or boundaries of morality. I saw no redeeming qualities in any one of them.

I glanced over at Fairuzo now and could literally see the rage ferociously simmering in his face like a gas-soaked rag being lowered into a vat of explosive chemicals. It did frighten me, as I'd seen firsthand how capable he was of extreme violence; he'd certainly had no qualms in kicking and pummeling Darceva into a bloody pulp. Yet even in his intense anger towards me, I sensed a restraint, as if he were physically holding himself back.

The trolls shuffled closer, mumbling and grumbling, some jutting out their bony elbows to jab viciously into my back as they lumbered past me. I was somewhat relieved, though, to see that more and more of them were becoming increasingly interested in what was on the banquet table, stumbling clumsily towards it to sample its wares.

Many of them were already swarming around the punch bowl, leaning down to voraciously lap up the liquid with their long yellow-and-black tongues like frogs slurping up mosquitoes. They acted like boorish oafs with their usual lack of manners, all shoving and jostling each other to get in position to suck as much wine out of the large crystal basin as they could.

I looked over at Fairuzo and he was holding his arms stiffly by his sides like two matching wooden boards, his hands balled into solid fists. He seemed as much frustrated as he did enraged, unsure as to his next course of action. I slowly began to back away from the angry mob, swiveling my neck in all directions to search frantically for Procel, but he was still nowhere to be seen.

Just then, I felt someone behind me tugging on the sleeve of my dress. I felt a flood of relief, thinking that it was surely Procel coming to my aid. But when I turned around, I was startled to see that it was one of the female trolls trying to get my attention. She had a look of utter wretchedness and misery embedded in her heavily-lined face, and her deeply furrowed brow was set in a frown of perpetual worry. When she spoke, it was in a plaintive, high-pitched whine.

"Enmira," she said, "you need to give up all hope of anything good ever happening here. It only gets worse. There's nothing to look forward to and you will never escape. There is no one who will help you, either.

"I was once beautiful like you – or at least I think I used to look really good. Fairuzo certainly found me attractive. I was his favorite at one time, too. He constantly told me I was special. But then when I lost my looks, I was just cast aside and he replaced me with another. That will happen to you, too. Even if you ever managed to escape back to Earth – which you never will – there is no hope there either. The world is hopeless, I am hopeless, and you should be hopeless too."

"Oh, my," I said, "I don't think it's quite *that* bad!" I really did not know how to properly respond. Such dire pessimism was certainly the opposite of what I wanted to hear now. I had actually been feeling quite optimistic about finding a way out of here ever since meeting Procel, who had really lifted my spirits and seemed to be a kindred soul. I also truly believed he would do everything he could to help me.

Part of me instinctively felt sorry for her. I wanted to give her some sort of advice that might help lift her out of her horrifically depressed state of mind. Yet another part of me wanted to run far away before her pervasive despondency could take root and germinate in me as well.

"How can you say it's not so bad? What would *you* know, anyway?" she practically spat back at me. "And, by the way, everyone here hates you," she continued matter-of-factly in her increasingly annoying whine, "especially Darceva. And she has good reason to, as you've stolen Fairuzo from her."

"But I did not steal anyone," I protested. "It was he who chose me, and it was he who brought me here. I had no idea at all that he belonged to anyone."

"Oh, you stole him, all right, and it was on purpose. He belongs to Darceva. Do you even know who she is?" the troll asked antagonistically.

"No, I don't know who she is; only that she hates me for no valid reason," I replied.

I was beginning to wish I'd never initially responded, and had just turned and walked away. Her bitter dysphoria felt aggressive and infectiously toxic, like a shedding virus contaminating all who came in contact with it. It was clear she was only here to argue and accuse, to try to drag me down to her level of hopelessness and transparent hatred of life.

In fact, I was wasting precious time getting involved in this sort of futile personal confrontation that could only end badly. What I needed to do now was either locate Procel or find some way to get out of this place, somewhere away from these horrible trolls, before things started to get dangerously physical.

"Darceva's not just his lover, you know," the troll said with a taunting sneer. "She's his own flesh and blood, and she owns every part of him."

"What do you mean?" I asked, my curiosity suddenly piqued, even though I really wanted to just end this uncomfortable exchange.

The troll snorted then laughed derisively. "Figure it out yourself, princess. Oh, and you never heard that from *me*," she said, jerking her head dismissively and turning on her gnarled heels to amble away in the direction of the banquet table.

I stood there for a moment, watching the back of her lumpy, hunched body retreating. *Well, I certainly didn't see that coming*, I thought, still in a bit of shock at the extremely unpleasant interaction. And to think I had felt sorry for her!

Honestly, I now felt almost foolish for having wasted any time or emotions on her. It was apparent she'd chosen me as some sort of target at which to direct her overall virulence. I just happened to be the perfect person here to lash out at, too, as there was no doubt I had somehow been unofficially elected the newly designated focal point of hatred just by virtue of my being here.

In fact, I was actually getting rather used to being disliked around here. In a way, I suppose it was even a bit of a compliment to be regarded with this much uniform antipathy by such an incredibly nasty group of folks! Would I even want such disagreeable and malevolent beings to *like* me?

I looked around one last time for Procel, then decided my best option would be to furtively inch my way over to the bandstand and crawl up onto where the insect musicians were standing. From there, I was going to try to get to the door behind them, the portal from which the blind salamander had emerged.

When I reached the platform, I grasped its edges and pulled myself up and over to where the insects stood. They all looked at me with abject terror in their eyes.

"Oh, please, Miss, don't bring us any trouble," one of them pleaded with me. "They'll punish us if we try to interfere with anything going on. We're just here to play and stay out of everyone's way."

"I'm so sorry," I replied, as I certainly did not want to cause these poor creatures any more distress than they were already dealing with. "I was just trying to get to this door behind you," I explained apologetically.

"Oh, but you mustn't go in there!" one exclaimed in alarm. "That is the slave's quarters and it is off-limits to all but the captives and Master Fairuzo!"

"Please stay away from there, Miss," another said with great fear in his voice, "or you might just end up like us."

Just then I heard my name being called – or whispered, rather. "Enmira! Enmira! Here! Look over here!"

I peered past the bank of monitors on the stage and saw what looked to be none other than Procel crouching beneath the bandstand.

"Oh, there you are," I said with great relief. "I've been looking all around for you."

"Yes, it is I – Procel. Here, let me help you down," he said in a voice just above a whisper. He grabbed ahold of one of my hands while I leapt the short distance to the ground.

"Now come quickly," he urged. "This mob could turn vicious any second now – especially after they've drunken their wine – and I know a place where you can be hidden for awhile."

I glanced behind me and was relieved to see that most of the trolls were now busy around the banquet table and, for the moment, seemed to have forgotten about me.

The door through which we were to make our exit was already ajar, and Procel propelled me forward, following close behind. After it swung shut, he grabbed a large brass key hanging on a long, satiny cord around his neck and jabbed it into its lock, firmly twisting until it clicked.

We began to walk at fast pace down a cobblestone pathway inside a narrow, twisting hallway with a low-hanging limestone ceiling. The only illumination was the occasional torch flickering on the wall, casting long shadows that looked like giant ogres were pursuing us. As we hurried along, I kept glancing over my shoulder to make sure no one was following.

After just a few moments, we arrived at a large, oval-shaped wooden door. Procel fumbled inside of a pocket in his robe and pulled out a large ring of copper keys. He jangled them around until he recognized the correct one. He inserted the key into the round metal lock and the door swung open easily.

He turned to peer at me with a concerned look upon his face, then said, "I need to warn you that there are things in here that you might find extremely frightening; but it is imperative that you do not scream or make any loud sounds. You must be quiet. We do not want the trolls outside to hear you."

"What is this place?" I asked, now beginning to feel quite anxious.

"This is not only where the slaves are kept; this is also where the Cabal keeps one of its laboratories," he answered. "There are monstrosities here that never should have been allowed to exist – but they do. Do you think you're ready to proceed?"

"Well, I suppose I have no choice," I replied, "if you believe this is the best place to hide. But are you sure no one is following us? Or might be back here to possibly intercept us?"

"Oh, no worries of that," Procel confidently assured me. "I locked the door behind us and only Fairuzo has another set of keys. And you can be sure there is no one else back here but you and I, as everyone is at the Initiation still – except for the troll Darceva, of course, and she is safely ensconced in her cave in another part of the Kingdom."

"Well, she is the *last* person I'd want to run into here. But if you're sure she won't suddenly be popping up..." I tapered off uncertainly.

"As a matter of fact, that's where I was just prior to meeting you: I paid a little visit to her cave to make sure she was there – and that she remained there," Procel said firmly.

"So, I must ask you – is it true Darceva has some sort of close family connection to Fairuzo?" I blurted out, unable to contain my curiosity, especially since he had brought up her name.

"Where did you hear that?" Procel asked, looking at me with an odd expression.

"Some troll out there mentioned it to me, but then refused to give me any more information," I replied.

"Ahhhh," responded Procel knowingly, "I observed you speaking with Achlys, whom I have given the nickname of 'The Viral Lamenter' for very good reason. I was wondering what you two could possibly even find in common to converse about. She is the embodied spirit of misery and sadness, existing solely to spread the concept of hopelessness and the never-ending night. Nothing but woe and wretchedness from that one. Given half a chance, she will suck every drop of happiness out of you like a bitter, thirsty sponge.

"But the story of Darceva and Fairuzo is a very long and involved one, and we certainly don't have time to get into that now. I do promise you, however, that I will fill you in on the specifics after we get to the hiding place."

I nodded, looking forward to hearing all the details, as sordid as they might be.

"Okay, then," he said decisively. "Let's go."

We entered through the doorway and, immediately, I heard the screams. Up just ahead on our right was an arched doorway, and it sounded like this is where the cries were emanating from. As we got closer, the wailing grew louder, interspersed with low-pitched moans.

"What on Earth is that?" I cried, not sure I really wanted to know, for it sounded like the suffering of many beings trapped in the dungeon of some torture chamber.

"You mean what on Tartarus – not Earth," Procel corrected me. "Although actually they perform these same atrocities on Earth too. In fact, my father once took me on a tour of one of the facilities there – the very first laboratory the Cabal ever built. It was rather small back then but has grown to immense proportions. It now employs thousands of Earthlings who have been promised great fame and wealth to participate in what goes on there.

"In comparison, the one we have here is quite miniscule – perhaps only 1/100th of the size. But aside from the difference in dimensions, there is another rather distinct dissimilarity. Here, the routine infliction of pain is boldly admitted to be nothing more than wicked sport to relieve boredom and assert dominance. It exists purely for sadistic control over what they view as the weaker beings, whom they keep in tiny, barren cages.

"Whereas the abominations that are legally permitted in the laboratories on Earth are actually promoted as being beneficial. They are perceived as acts of heroic philanthropy even, and generally accepted as being for the good of all, with both valuable and honorable merit.

"The scientists there realize that an agenda of evil based solely upon ill intent is most successfully promoted under the guise of altruism. And through the gullibility, blind trust and denial of the masses, it is then most surreptitiously implemented and accepted.

"I'm not even sure which I despise more: the deceit and denial behind proclaiming that the heinous experiments are necessary and useful, or the openly brazen admission that the procedures are completely unnecessary and useless,"

Procel said, shaking his head in disgust.

"You seem to know so many things," I said admiringly. "Did you have to go to some sort of University to learn all of that?" I asked.

"Oh, no," Procel said disdainfully. "I don't believe in Higher Education, but rather the education you get from being high – the enlightenment type of high, that is. Empirical knowledge has so much more to offer than classroom courses of indoctrination and propaganda fed to the mindless hordes by those with an ulterior agenda."

Procel shut and locked the door behind us and we continued on our way. I began to dread what I might see up ahead, for the sounds alone were horrific enough without whatever the accompanying visuals might be.

When we were just a few feet away from the opening, Procel turned to me and said, "Perhaps it is better that you close your eyes when we pass this doorway. Otherwise, you may never be able to erase these images from your mind."

I was torn between not wanting to look at all, and feeling as if it were something crucial that I needed to see. When we were right by the entrance, I decided I would just take one quick peek and then look away.

But I was not at all prepared for what I saw in that room inside the dozens of cages lined up along the wall.

Just as I was summoning up the courage to take another look inside – for in truth, I did not want to believe what I had just seen – I heard a loud crack, like a ball made of gunite being smashed with a steel bat. I then saw Procel crumpling limply to the ground beside me. A pool of bright blue liquid quickly began to seep from beneath his head, fanning out in little rivulets, while he lay completely motionless.

I was just about to lean over him to see if he was still breathing when I felt a sharp and painful blow to the back of my own head. Immediately I saw a tar-black sky swirling with stars, and all kinds of planets whizzing by at dizzying speed, like I had been hurled inside a vortex that was spinning out of control.

Apparently there *had* been someone following us, after all.

CHAPTER 24

CREOBOROS AND THE HISTORY OF MONSTROSITIES

When I regained consciousness, I was lying on a cold, hard floor. The back of my head was on fire and throbbing mightily, as if someone had walloped my skull with a sledgehammer. The last thing I remembered was seeing swirling stars and planets, and then nothing but blackness.

Through blurred vision, I could just make out a man standing over me. He was saying my name repetitively, which may have been what had roused me out of my unconscious state. As the filmy veil of haze obscuring my eyesight began to gradually dissipate, I recognized Procel's satin cloak, his distinct facial features, and his long, roped hair, and felt relief that it was he.

Then the memory came flooding back of him falling limply to the ground beside me, bleeding profusely from what looked to be a critical head wound – right before I myself was knocked out. It puzzled me how he could have gotten back on his feet so quickly, when I was having such trouble just getting my eyes to stay open.

"Procel, is that you?" I asked hopefully, still trying to raise my heavy eyelids a bit more.

"Yep, it's me," he replied casually. He stuck his hand out and said, "Here, let me help you get up."

As his fingers wrapped around my wrist, I noticed his touch was devoid of all warmth, having the frigidity of a block of ice.

"Oh, your hand feels so cold!" I exclaimed.

"Uh, no, not really. I mean, it *is* pretty cold in here," he said evasively. "But never mind that. We need to get out of here now before they come back."

"Before *who* come back?" I asked.

"Never mind, I said," Procel answered sharply. "We just need to hurry up."

He grabbed my other hand and yanked me up off the floor so quickly it made my head spin, and I nearly lost my balance.

"Who was it that attacked us and where did they go?" I asked, as I shakily followed him, still unsteady on my feet.

He turned to look at me with an odd glint in his eye, then said, "Never mind that either. It's not anything you need to be concerned about."

As I followed him to the door, I heard a sudden scuffling noise behind me, then a muffled cry.

Just as I turned my head to see what the commotion was about and who else might be in the room, Procel snapped, "Keep your eyes facing front, lady, and watch where you're going. I keep telling you we have to get out of here right now."

How impatient and irritable he is being! I thought to myself, my feelings a bit hurt. *Perhaps his head is still aching and that is what's causing him to act so brusquely.* My own head was certainly still causing *me* quite a bit of discomfort.

I ventured a quick sideways glance at him but his expressionless face gave away nothing.

He didn't say a word as we hurried along the hallway, and I began to notice that we were going back to the place we had started from.

"Are we going to a different hiding place now?" I asked. "Because it looks like we're going back the same way we came before."

He made a noise that sounded like a cross between a growl and someone clearing their throat.

"Damn you, did I not tell you to stop asking so many questions?" he barked furiously. "Is it at all possible for you to walk without speaking?"

I glanced over at him with surprise at how he was behaving towards me. It was certainly not the same kind and courteous Procel I'd spoken with earlier. Something in his demeanor had changed dramatically. Although he was wearing the same clothing and had the same outward appearance, he seemed like a totally different person – and not one that I was growing too fond of, either.

As I took a closer look at his face, I noticed his eyes had a reddish glow, making him look decidedly fiendish. I could tell that this was not simply a reflection from the flickering torches overhead.

I then began to notice something very creepy: the skin around his cheekbones and eyes had begun to elasticize, stretching and pulling as if it were made of rubber or putty. Bits of flesh then began to slide and drip slowly down his face like wax from a fizzling candle stub. His mouth was set in an unpleasant, leering grimace. I could see his long, yellow and jagged teeth jutting out over his bottom lip like the fangs of a payara fish.

His overall presence was now markedly sinister and decidedly non-friendly.

This is certainly not the Procel I first met! What has happened to him? And if this is not Procel beside me, then who is it? I wondered with rising alarm.

He suddenly reached up to his face and raked the long, sharp fingernails of both hands down his cheeks. The skin peeled and sloughed off like a shedding snake, revealing a hideously monstrous visage full of hatred and contempt. His complexion was a jaundiced yellow covered with huge, fresh boils and lesions. His chin was covered with what looked to be live lice nestling in the matted hairs that were clustered there.

"Hah!" he shouted. "I had you fooled, didn't I? You Earthlings are so stupid and trusting. I hate to tell you, but your adorable little Procel was not able to make it, so I have come in his place. Has not Fairuzo informed you yet of our shapeshifting talents here on Tartarus?" He laughed demonically.

My intuition had been right – this was not Procel at all but an imposter who obviously wished me great harm! But what other purpose did he have for wanting to deceive me into believing it was him?

Just then I saw the dark outline of someone standing shrouded in the unlit doorway up ahead.

"So, you have brought her to me, Dantanian. Good work!" Darceva said, stepping brazenly out of the shadows to reveal herself, an evil smirk upon her face.

"I don't recall dismissing you or giving you my permission to go anywhere. Did you think you were going to escape here before I had my fun with you?" she sneered at me.

I caught a whiff of her putrid breath and it was overpowering, even from several feet away. It stank of rancid bile and rotting carcasses. The vile stench seemed to waft and permeate the air around me like a cloud of freshly dumped sewage.

I had to at least make an attempt to get away from these ghouls, but in which direction should I run? If only these wings attached to my back were functional, I might even be able to evade them in flight!

I was now standing near the door where I had first entered with Procel behind the bandstand. I had absolutely no idea what lay in the shadows behind Darceva. Therefore, I felt it would be wiser to take my chances going back into the Ballroom, as this is where I believed Fairuzo would most likely still be.

Although I had no concept of how much time had elapsed since I'd been knocked unconscious, there was a slight chance that he had gotten past his anger at me by now. If that were the case, he might even be inclined to intervene and protect me from the vicious, vindictive Darceva, as he had so readily before.

Then, out of the corner of my eye, I saw someone at the other end of the passage who appeared to be Procel – *again*. Was this just another mirage, more shapeshifting trickery? Or was this the *real* Procel?

Just then I saw a bright flash of light like a meteoric ball of fire, and it lit up the entire area where the man was standing. I then heard a loud whirring sound that culminated in an explosion, like a train barreling down a track that had smashed headfirst into a tornado. The figure then began spinning faster and faster like an automated top, whirling at such supersonic, breakneck speed down the pathway that he was nothing more than a blur.

Although it was obvious he was aiming directly for the imposter-demon and Darceva standing just ahead and to the right of me, I sidestepped quickly to get out of the way, just to be safe. First, he knocked the demon to the ground like a bowling ball striking a pin, and then he slammed into Darceva. She dropped like a hefty sack of logs, and they both lay there motionless like felled trees.

Procel stood over them, his hands on his hips, surveying their silent bodies.

"Oh, my! It looks like they are both out cold!" I exclaimed excitedly. "But is that really you, Procel?"

"Yes, it is I, Procel," he affirmed, reaching his hand towards me.

Instinctively, I flinched and backed away, still not completely sure it was him.

"But how do I know it is really you now?" I asked warily – although he *had* just knocked out both of the menacing demon-trolls, a feat which had undoubtedly saved my life.

"Take ahold of my hand and you will see how warm my blood runs," he answered.

I gingerly reached out and touched the tips of his fingers, and they were indeed a comfortingly warm temperature. He clasped my hand and held it firmly, and I could feel the heat of his emotions pulsing and coursing through, unlike the icy cold hand of the demon-imposter.

"It is how you will always know it is really me," he said gently. "Dantanian is a cold-blooded demon with many faces, but he can only shapeshift his outward appearance. He cannot conceal the fact that he is dead inside. His black blood is frigid and stagnant in his veins, and he cannot thaw or mask the ice in his heart."

"Plus your eyes do not glow red," I said, laughing weakly, so relieved to be sure that it was really him.

We turned and started back in the other direction towards our original destination. After a few moments, I looked back over my shoulder. I was comforted to see that both Darceva and the shapeshifter Dantanian were still lying like inert objects on the ground.

Upon seeing me glance back, Procel remarked, "They should be out for a good eight hours, which will give us plenty of time to hide and to bide our time."

"That is good to know," I said, relieved that at least we did not have those two to worry about for now.

"Now you must tell me, Procel – how did you ever manage to escape with your head bleeding so badly?" I asked curiously. "The last time I saw you, I was afraid they had killed you. But I must say you look completely unscathed."

"Oh, I was merely engaging in thanatosis," Procel replied nonchalantly.

"And that is --?" I asked, having never before heard the term.

"That is tonic immobility, also known as apparent death. It is what you Earthlings refer to as 'playing possum' – although possums are far from the only species who participate in it for self-preservation.

"It is a spur-of-the-moment instinctual behavior," he continued. "It deceives your aggressor into thinking you are no longer drawing breath and therefore pose no threat. It is a ploy that convinces them to move on to other prey. In short, I simply laid still where I fell to make them think I had either perished or had been knocked completely unconscious."

"Oh, that was very clever of you!" I exclaimed admiringly. "I don't believe I would have even thought to do that, had I not blacked out upon impact. But how did you manage to survive your injuries and recover so quickly?"

"You see," Procel explained, "one of the benefits I have as the offspring of a Cabal Duke is that I heal almost instantaneously. In fact, my inner fluids replenish themselves the instant they flow out of any sort of wound. It is a bit like my body has a built-in waterfall that rains its own healing liquids into a creek that has dried up after a drought."

"Well, that is certainly a very handy thing to have," I said.

"You might be receiving that ability very soon yourself – or you may even already possess it," said Procel thoughtfully. "Here, let me see."

He stopped mid-stride to peer closely at the back of my head, gingerly parting my hair with his fingers.

"Ahhh," he said, "I do not see any vestige of a wound whatsoever. And that is a very good indication of your rapid healing."

"Oh, that is good to hear," I said. "In fact, I have just now noticed that my head has almost completely stopped hurting. But what about this horrible Dantanian demon – was it he who actually attacked us?"

"Well, he was in on the ambush," Procel replied, "but the one who actually wielded the club was a scientist named Asmoday, one of the laboratory workers imported from Headquarters. It was he whom I had the skirmish with, right as you were being tricked by Dantanian into leaving the room with him."

"Oh," I said, "I *thought* I heard some odd noises."

"Asmoday is also a Duke in the Cabal, as well as being

a close colleague of my father's, unfortunately," Procel said. "I should have known that he would be the only one back here not expected to attend the Initiation.

"He is currently obsessed with a special project he has been working on around the clock. I overheard him bragging about it one day to another laboratory worker, and I've seen firsthand the results of these diabolical procedures. It is a hideous experiment that defies everything natural and pure and good."

"So, what *are* these experiments he's working on?" I asked, almost fearful of his answer – for I now vividly recalled the horrors I'd caught a glimpse of earlier, of the rows upon rows of tiny cages with what looked to be mutilated animals cowering in the corners of each enclosure.

"Asmoday specializes in cloning and transplantation," Procel replied. "At present, he is attempting to graft various dog heads onto the shoulders of other dogs. He then observes them to see how long he can keep their hearts beating. In fact, the demonic freak has three heads himself – that of a bull and a sheep, with his own evil skull holding court in the center.

"His actions could even be considered quite the narcissistic endeavor, as if he were trying to recreate numerous variations of himself, like a distorted funhouse mirror reflecting cloned organisms."

"Oh, no!" I exclaimed in disgust. "He sounds like a real monster – not only in what he looks like but in what he's involved in."

"That he does indeed, Enmira," Procel agreed, pursing his lips in disapproval. "He was mentored by Bune, the son of the notorious and highly-revered Balam – another three-headed demon. He was taught many vivisection techniques, including how to effectively restrain and subdue specimens without aid of anesthesia.

"Balam's other son, Creoboros, is the infamous flesh-devouring, three-headed dog who guards the main gate of

Tartarus, so that all who enter may never leave. He symbolizes the corpse-consuming Earth. Each of his heads represents one of the Three Evil Roots or Poisons: greed, hatred, and delusion.

"You see, after the Eternally Damned reach the end of their Reincarnation Cycle of Chances, their bodies are then buried and swallowed up by the ground. The soul-shells are then shuttled across the Acheron River of Woe. The dungeon where they are all kept is actually not too far from here. I've seen the stairs leading down to its entrance myself.

"But since Creoboros can only guard one portal at a time, Asmoday is attempting to create even *more* three-headed dogs. They can then be employed as gatekeepers at all of the other portals that need sentries – which is why we are so pressed for time. When these dog mutations are finalized and placed at their posts, there will be no exit left unguarded that we can escape from.

"And after carefully studying all passageways that lead in and out of Tartarus, I am aware of other routes out – but they will not exist for much longer."

"What part of Tartarus does the dog guard?" I asked. "I did not see anyone guarding the door Fairuzo brought me through after we came down the stairs."

"Oh, that is because you came in through a Cabal-approved entrance portal with Fairuzo as chaperone – not an exit. They are only concerned with those trying to escape their fate, not with those being escorted inside the Pit," Procel explained.

"But where do they get these dogs that they experiment on?" I asked.

"Most are captured on Earth and brought back here," Procel explained, "but there is also a breeding facility back at Headquarters. The laboratory here is specifically set up to house the animals they use for surgical experiments – the head grafting, the organ transplanting, the replacement of body parts with various metallic elements, the implantation of radioactive transmitters, trackers and microchips, and so on. Whereas the main laboratory at Mount Hermon is mostly designed to house and breed the animals they test the various poisons to be sold as medicine to the Earthlings.

"Awhile back," Procel continued, "the Cabal hired the ogre known as Demonkhov to oversee these experiments. He had become fairly well-known on Earth for managing to graft one dog's head onto another dog's body for a very short period of time. This was the infamous 'two-headed dog exhibition.' Of course, the surgically-created monstrosity was a complete failure, the poor creature living only a few agonizing days.

"In fact, since Demonkhov was unable to figure out how to properly connect the spinal cord with the donor body, the dogs were left paralyzed below the neck. There was also the matter of the unconnected stump of the esophageal tube just dangling."

"Oh, dear God!" I exclaimed. "That sounds so demented and sadistic!"

Procel nodded vigorously in agreement, then continued: "Demonkhov initially grafted the head, shoulders, and front legs of a puppy onto the neck of a large German shepherd. He then went on to create a total of twenty of these two-headed dogs. None of them lived very long, of course, as they all inevitably succumbed to problems arising from tissue rejection. I believe the record was not quite a month, with most of the dogs only living a few days at most.

"He later began fiddling around with heart and lung transplants in various animals, but every one of these experiments were abysmal failures also. Even so, they were deceptively portrayed as heroic and life-saving, as well as leading the way for the acceptance of organ transplantation in human Earthlings. In fact, it has quickly become an extremely lucrative and sought-after procedure there.

"Of course, the humans don't fare much better than the animals, as the immune system immediately rejects the incompatible organ and begins attacking its own cells. The patient either succumbs to a massive infection originating in the lungs or the lethal side effects from the myriad of toxic immunosuppressant drugs they are given afterwards.

"Unaware of this outcome – or perhaps in deliberate denial of it – the Earthlings still line up in desperation for these operations, literally begging to have it done to them. They are willing to pay exorbitant fees for what they perceive as a privilege and a cure. Even after realizing they will never again experience any semblance of quality of life or vitality, and that the replacement organ will eventually fail as well, it still does not deter them."

Upon hearing all of this, my thoughts and emotions were all jumbled and conflicted. It was almost too much to take in at once. It seemed so unequivocally depraved. I simply could not comprehend how anyone could commit such pitiless crimes against these innocent and unsuspecting creatures.

It was clear to me that these experiments certainly served no purpose except to cause suffering. There was no doubt at all that the animals suffered greatly throughout their horrific ordeals, as then did the humans who believed the laboratory animals had medically paved the way for them. It was all so unnecessary and barbaric.

I then noticed that we had arrived at the entrance to the room where we had been attacked.

"I do hope we are not going in *there* again," I whispered. "I don't even want to look inside."

"Don't worry, Enmira," Procel reassured me, "I took great care to ensure that Asmoday would not be up and about any time soon. But, at any rate, we will not be going in that room again. And I believe it best this time that you not look inside, even for a few moments."

"Oh, yes, I quite agree," I said, feeling relieved. I still remembered all too well what I'd seen before.

"So sad to see all those cages, and not a thing we can

do about it," I added regretfully.

"Well, there may not be a thing we can do about it *now,* but later might be an entirely different story," he replied, with the slightest hint of a smile.

CHAPTER 25

THE MONKEY'S HELMET

As we passed the room, I made sure to keep my eyes focused straight ahead, not even allowing myself the tiniest peep inside this time.

"Actually," said Procel, continuing his train of thought, "there was another nefarious scientist who specialized in transplantation grotesquery, heavily inspired by Demonkhov. Asmoday was quite taken with his handiwork as well. He, too, was employed by the Cabal.

"He was known as Doctor White. He derived great pleasure from slicing up and reassembling dogs and monkeys. Most specifically he was known for transplanting rhesus monkey heads onto the paralyzed bodies of other monkeys."

"That sounds absolutely deranged!" I exclaimed. "Did Doctor White have three heads too?"

"No, he just had the one. But, believe me, that one head was evil enough. After decades of performing these atrocious experiments where the monkeys only lived for a few hours, the Earthling government finally decided to cease the funding of his research. He was then forced to seek financial support elsewhere – which is when the Cabal stepped in to hire him.

"Oddly enough, they did not seem overly concerned with all of his failures. Rather, they were much more impressed that he had no boundaries when it came to morality or decency, and that he was well-practiced at the art of deception – which is, of course, of utmost cruciality in his line of work.

"You see, when presenting himself to the public, Dr. White made sure to give the impression that he was a Godrevering, devout Roman Catholic. But behind the closed doors of the laboratory, it was a different story altogether. He would lead his team of vivisectionists in a group prayer as part of his regular, established pre-surgery ritual. Except he was not praying to any Almighty God. No, he was actually offering up the animal on the operating table as a sacrifice to his Luciferian deity.

"In fact, if an animal did not manage to survive the surgery, the day the death event occurred would actually be noted in the lab report as 'Date of Sacrifice.' This descriptive terminology is still used even today in all vivisection labs on Earth. And would you believe that this Satanist was also advisor to the Pope?" Procel shook his head at the absurdity of it all.

"Very few are aware that the Vatican is a vital promotional branch within the Cabal, where the Darkness is portrayed and promoted as the Light," he said.

"I can't even fathom that," I said. "Who would even think of praying right *before* deliberately committing such a heinous act? It would make much more sense to pray *afterwards* for absolution and the easing of one's own conscience!"

"Well," Procel replied, "I think it would be safe to say that Doctor White was never haunted by anything even remotely resembling a conscience. I doubt he was even aware that such a thing existed.

"I would also venture to say that his ostentatious little pre-sacrifice prayer-ritual served as the ultimate public relations coup: promoting the perception of piety by participating in public prayer. This sadist was deliberately depicted as some sort of benevolent saint involved in only the noblest of altruistic deeds, fervently dedicated to the Greater Good of all humanity."

Procel grimaced and let out a disgusted snort at such deceitful effrontery.

"It was also a way of perpetuating the Luciferian

tradition of the Sacrifice of the Innocent that is inherent and embedded in the most corrupt of demonically-conceived religions.

"So, after the pretentious and offensive sacrilege of the group prayer, followed by a grueling 18-hour-long surgery, the horribly-disfigured monkey wakes up. It is immediately clear to anyone observing that he is distressed, disoriented, and terrified. But most of all, he is furious – no doubt due in large part to the intense pain he is in.

"He attacks the nearest assistant. He then visually tracks Doctor White's movements around the room with his eyes, silently seething. He snaps his teeth at him, attempting to bite him whenever he comes near. Even in his confused and tormented state, the monkey seems cognizant of just exactly whom is the primary cause of his suffering.

"One of Doctor White's own cohorts, who personally observed this particular surgery, later admitted that what he saw truly disgusted him. He witnessed the monkey's facial expressions of fear and anguish, and confirmed that it was more than apparent he was in a great deal of agony.

"He also remarked that it was an experiment that should never again be duplicated. Of course, it goes without saying that it should never have been conceived of in the first place, much less attempted at all."

I shook my head, picturing the monkey waking up from the mutilating surgery terrified and wracked with pain, the scientists and doctors all around the table gaping and gawking at him. It both sickened and saddened me.

"It is a self-evident truth that no good can ever come of evil, nor has there ever been such a thing as an evil that was necessary," Procel said sagely. "Yet this is what these demons lean upon. It matters not the wake of suffering left behind; only that they are perceived as heroes and pioneers and geniuses, reaping undeserved accolades and obscene financial rewards.

"But there *is* something that you might find a bit

comforting in all of this, Enmira," Procel said with a slight smile, "which is that, in the end, Doctor White's own karma literally came home to bite him.

"It seems that a monkey in the doctor's own laboratory managed to work himself free from his cage one day, get ahold of a scalpel lying upon a desk, and then apply it to the doctor's own neck when he was least expecting it, slicing his head nearly clean off with one swift stroke.

"Our heroic doctor did manage to survive for several anguished hours with his head practically severed. He weakly gurgled for help in vain before finally succumbing to a death that surely entailed a whole lot of unpleasant karma for his lifetime of unrepentant wickedness.

"After that, the monkey finished off the job of decapitation and began parading around with White's head upon his own. He wore it just like one would a helmet – much to the amusement of his fellow primates, who had all been let out of their cages to participate in the fun on this long-awaited Day of Reckoning.

"It was indeed a karmic victory for these enslaved and abused creatures. They then managed to escape the laboratory altogether and find their way to the nearest forest that would serve as their new home."

"I certainly like the ending of that one!" I said, smiling.

"Oh, there's more," Procel said. "There was also a notorious torturer known as Doctor Christian, who prided himself on experimenting upon obscene numbers of dogs in unsuccessful heart transplants. His claim to fame was that he went on to perform the first publicized heart transplant on a human. But this, too, was a dismal failure, with the human only surviving 18 days, painfully drowning in the bacterial fluids of his own lungs.

"Although these heart transplants are touted as life-saving operations today, the majority of patients are still dying of the same tissue rejection and viral pneumonia infection as

Doctor Christian's first casualty. It is a testament to a very successful propaganda machine and to the gullibility of the masses who blindly trust in the treacherous snake oil of allopathic medicine.

"But, once again, karma came home to roost with its trademark sardonic sense of irony: the ignominious Doctor Christian himself, who had forcibly removed so many hearts from unwilling victims and caused so much suffering, died of a massive heart attack! It seems his widely-heralded operation could not save his own black and merciless heart."

Here, Procel managed a wry but disgusted chuckle.

"Perhaps he realized that his own operation was so pointless that it would only delay the inevitable without any real benefit," I offered.

"Precisely, Enmira," said Procel. "He knew better than to subject himself to the pain and trauma of such an operation doomed to fail, yet it was perfectly fine for the hordes of unsuspecting, paying customers who served as disposable generators of revenue.

"Now, I believe you heard some of the dogs howling right before we went into that room. Those are the ones being used in Asmoday's experiments. I should have realized that meant that the demon bastard was actually in there inflicting pain on them right at that very moment."

"So how far along do you think Asmoday is in these experiments?" I asked. "I mean, how much time do we have until they start placing these three-headed dogs all around the exits as guards?"

"Well," said Procel, "I will have to listen in on the next Cabal meeting to know for sure, but I would estimate we have perhaps a week or two at most."

We continued on in silence while I thought long and hard about all of the disturbing things Procel had revealed. I had known vaguely of the existence of such horrors, but had never given them much thought.

As for the laboratory experiments being performed, it

was not at all surprising that these wicked miscreations had been kept so well-hidden from any curious or prying eyes, sequestered in inaccessible and heavily-guarded dungeons of torture. I could now see clearly the insidious spin involved in the rotisserie of deceit, as the animals were skewered alive on the rotating spit by soulless demons who relished inflicting great pain upon them.

Masquerading as valid science, this cruel, twisted mockery of life had been exalted and deified, neatly packaged and marketed to the public as gleaming models of goodness and benevolence, suspended far above the shrouded cesspools of evil bubbling below.

I suspected that if the futile and sadistic nature of these barbarous experiments was ever thoroughly exposed, many others would be as righteously appalled as I was – except, I supposed, those who wished to remain ignorant and in denial.

For I was beginning to realize that sometimes a newfound truth was not always so comforting, and was quite often very bothersome to acknowledge.

CHAPTER 26

A BRIEF FLUTTER OF
EMERALD-GREEN WINGS

𝔉airuzo watched intently, and with quite a bit of displeasure, as Enmira climbed over the bandstand and was met on the other side by Procel. He was not at all surprised that Procel had come to her aid, but spiriting her away from her own Initiation was entirely unacceptable.

The trolls were continuing to enjoy themselves and the festivities were still going strong. It was crucial that Enmira be present to take part in the last two scheduled events, not the least of which was the Consummation Ceremony. Preceding that would be the unveiling of a specially-prepared, delectable dessert that contained a mood-altering flavoring that was even more potent than the wine.

The powerful concoction of chemicals in this dish would be highly effective in removing all of Enmira's inhibitions once and for all – but, as per dictum, she must first voluntarily partake of it.

Even the smallest of mouthfuls, once swallowed and safely inside her belly, would obviate the necessity of any sort of seductive cajoling on his part. He knew that once she fell under its influence, it would be an effortless toboggan ride down a well-iced hill then to simply slip her in between the sheets in his bedchamber. It would virtually ensure an unopposed and enthusiastic coupling.

Although the seduction-courtship process traditionally took place over a two to three-day period, Fairuzo realized that an acceleration of the scheduled timetable was in order. He had failed so far to iron out the deeply-embedded wrinkles in Enmira's unyielding uniform of obstinance. He was quickly running out of time. Soon, circumstances would begin spiraling even more out of his control than they already had.

As for the Consummation ritual, it was customary that it be performed in full view of all inhabitants. Their spectatorship lent the event the exhilarating atmosphere of a live theatrical production. Afterwards, all trolls present were invited to join in the erotic activities with the new initiate.

However, in light of all the resistance he'd encountered so far from Enmira, Fairuzo was quickly realizing that he was going to have to completely waive the audience participation in this particular ceremony. In fact, he had decided that the entire deed would not be performed in the Ballroom at all, but completely in private in his own Royal Chambers.

The truth was that he wanted this one all to himself. He did not wish to share Enmira with any of the trolls, as was the usual custom. Besides, he could think of no worse scenario than of the drug wearing off mid-Ceremony, with her suddenly coming to her prudish senses only to find herself part of a public spectacle. In his detailed fantasy of a perfect union, there would be no struggling or scrambling out of bed involved whatsoever; it would be entirely consensual from start to finish.

It was to be expected, of course, that the trolls would grumble vociferously at being excluded, but they had no say in the matter. He was the Lord here, and it was entirely his decision where the event took place and under what circumstances.

But, first, this situation with Procel – having taken it upon himself to rescue what he perceived to be a damsel in distress – needed to be addressed and resolved tout de suite.

He understood all too well the mutual attraction between the two. After all, they were the only inhabitants who had retained their souls – other than himself, of course. But this type of mutiny was exactly what he had suspected might happen once they met up.

At least he no longer had to worry about the possibility of Enmira convincing any of the other trolls to join her in any type of mass revolt. It was clear how much they disliked and resented her being there. In fact, loathing and despising would be a more fitting description of how they felt towards her.

Even more so than the male portion of the population, the female trolls exhibited an intense jealousy and animosity towards her – in particular, Darceva.

But that was to be expected.

Darceva had despised and caused trouble for every single new wench he had brought back with him from Earth. She had done everything she could to sabotage each of his courtships with them, disrupting each of their Initiations in some way, and most of all, doing her damnedest to interfere with the Consummation ritual.

But, of all the neophytes he had been temporarily infatuated with over the centuries, she seemed particularly vindictive and acrimonious towards Enmira.

Fairuzo could only presume that this was because Darceva saw in Enmira all of the desirable qualities that she herself had once had but would never have again, having lost them eons ago: not only her outward beauty, but that unique element of purity and untarnished innocence that Enmira exuded from within.

This absence of guile and deception seemed to increase Darceva's own vitriolic hatred towards her, an ever-present and toxic irritant that must have stung and burned like bile being churned in a vat of sulfuric acid. Fairuzo liked to say that Darceva had three primary moods: seething, steaming, and boiling over.

Her constant fits of jealous rage most likely also had a lot to do with the undeniable fact that Enmira had somehow managed to retain her soul. This must have gnawed and grinded away at Darceva, especially since her own soul had been shed and relinquished almost instantaneously after being given The Mark.

In her case, the infection had spread as rapidly as a lab-created virus following a sly and unexpected poke of a syringe, rapidly consuming and corrupting her insides with its cascading rivulets of poison.

Even Fairuzo could not figure out just how Enmira had managed the heretofore impossible feat of holding on to her soul after being infected. Did she have prior knowledge of how souls could be used to great personal advantage and leverage? Or was it something within her that had spontaneously and instinctively clung onto it so tightly that it was prevented from shedding itself?

He had no doubt that many of the trolls also resented Enmira's consistent refusal to participate in any of the activities that they themselves all freely engaged in, as if she were somehow better than the rest of them.

But Fairuzo had yet to see much, if any, evidence that Enmira thought that highly of herself. From what he had observed so far, she seemed confident but not conceited, while maintaining an air of modesty and unpretentiousness.

Even though he had given her many hints as to how attractive and enticing he found her, she did not seem to respond in kind. At any rate, she seemed neither aware of the power she held over him nor of her own allure.

The fact that she displayed little to no gloat or smugness in her demeanor puzzled him. He was so accustomed to dealing with the most egotistical, self-absorbed braggarts, both in the troll community as well as in the Cabal. His own father was especially insufferable, puffed up with vanity and consumed by narcissism. In stark contrast, Enmira was like a breath of fresh air in an overflowing septic tank.

Even so, her ambivalence and impassiveness towards him seemed to precipitate an enfeebling and dilutive sapping of his own power and authority. It had almost a see-saw-like effect: the more her confidence grew, the weaker his own became.

The trolls had made it clear that they perceived Enmira as an enemy, a disrupter, an infiltrator not to be trusted. But to Fairuzo, she was an enigma with a mysterious, magnetic lure.

He was beginning to wonder if perhaps getting inside her head might not just be the key to getting inside her body. But where was the secret crevice that concealed the lock he needed to pry open?

What Fairuzo needed to do now, though, was follow her and Procel into the passageway to see just what sort of gobbledygook he was filling her curious head up with. He watched as they both slipped through the door into the corridor leading to the laboratory and the slave's quarters.

He then gave a quick glance around him. He was relieved to see that the trolls were all still busily lapping up the alcohol from the punch bowl. They would certainly not be paying the slightest bit of attention when he abruptly vanished after shapeshifting.

For basic stealth observance, he favored the form of the white-headed flesh fly with its mobile head and large, dichoptic eyes. In fact, it was this shape he found most useful on Earth whenever he needed to monitor the Awakening of a freshly-defiled victim inside her bedroom. It also came in especially handy when he craved a few quick sips of blood from an animal body.

However, when in close proximity to those he wished to eavesdrop upon – and, of course, did not want to be spotted doing so – his favorite metamorphosis was that of the chalcid fairy wasp: the Earth's smallest known flying insect.

But when he wished to inflict pain upon those he was observing, he would transmute himself into a female Pepsis wasp. This convenient form gave him the advantage of being able to rapidly unsheathe and plunge his stinger into whomever was saying something he either disagreed with or found objectionable.

The red-hot burning sensation of the sting served to immediately divert them, thwarting and derailing them from their original train of thought. In fact, the pain was so unbearable and overpowering that they usually forgot whatever it was they were just talking about.

Then, after paralyzing them with a few quick jabs, he would insert his stinger under their skin in order to lay eggs inside of them. When the larva began emerging, it would then proceed to eat the victim from the inside out.

He saved this little parlor trick for special occasions.

He was curious to find out just what would make Procel think he would be able to escape from the planet this easily. More likely, he was simply taking Enmira somewhere to hide her away for awhile.

Now just where that would be, was the question: *surely* he was not thinking of secreting her in the slave's quarters? There was only one entrance there which also served as an exit, and it was monitored constantly by guards.

With Procel's vast array of insider information, Fairuzo had no doubt he had already mapped out all of the unguarded exits on Tartarus. But even so, he must surely be aware of the multitude of surveillance cameras placed all around that were vigilantly overseen by the Cabal. Fairuzo was extremely curious to discover just how Procel was going to engineer and pull off this Great Escape he was apparently planning.

And had not Procel thought ahead to what he would do *after* he'd helped Enmira escape? He might be able to avoid punishment, courtesy of his royal status, but he would certainly no longer be welcome here on Tartarus; he was already blacklisted on Mount Hermon. Furthermore, Fairuzo doubted Procel would be at all interested in returning to his planet of birth, Xibalba, where indulgence in evil was the sole pastime. It was just not Procel's style.

That would leave only one inhabitable planet: Earth. And since he would undoubtedly be accompanying Enmira on her journey back home, it was very likely that he would just remain there with her.

Briefly then, for just a moment, a fluttering suspicion flapped by on emerald-green wings, reaching out to slash him with a jagged shard of jealousy before elusively zig-zagging away. It came upon him so quickly that it took him by surprise. He could not help but consider the painful possibility: was Procel harboring romantic aspirations towards Enmira?

But he quickly flicked away this nipping midge. It was simply too disconcerting to even entertain right now, as well as being completely unfounded. In fact, he had heard from fairly reliable sources that Procel had taken powerful medicinal herbs which had rendered him impotent, effectively castrating him and leaving him with zero libido and void of all salacious desires. So, for all intents and purposes, he was an asexual monk who had taken vows of chastity that he was not only unwilling mentally to break but physically incapable of as well.

If he did somehow find proof that Procel's intentions towards Enmira went beyond the platonic, it would certainly make matters a lot more complicated than they already now were. For one, he wondered: would she be inclined to reciprocate? He hadn't a clue. The way she felt towards Procel was just as hard to get a read on as it was trying to figure out how she felt about *him*.

He did not know quite how he would react if that turned out to be the case. But it would be one hell of a dilemma. He would have to choose between his only real friend in the universe – one whom he greatly respected and had grown quite close to – and the first female wight whom he had ever developed genuine emotions for, feelings that went far beyond the physical cravings of lust.

These thoughts he tried to suppress, but they kept

bobbing up like buoys in an otherwise placid ocean. The cozy pair having left the Ballroom together had added a whole new element to an already complex conundrum.

Honestly, if he weren't so fond of the both of them, he would simply petition the Cabal to have them banished right now, just to have the entire quandary over and done with. The truth was that they were each, in their own way, really beginning to cramp his style.

Just look at how the Initiation was turning out! He had looked forward to this for weeks; and now the most climactic portion of it might possibly have to be aborted. Not only that, but his control was being slowly but surely siphoned, usurping the authority he had over his own Kingdom.

This would not do at all.

But, for now, he was wasting good time. He was missing out on their conversation, and he needed to get in there and hear what was being said.

Quickly transforming himself into the tiny body of a fairy wasp, he slipped through a crack in the door in time to catch them walking briskly down the passageway. Propelling himself forward with his wings, he landed gracefully on Procel's shoulder, holding on to a strand of the long ropes of hair with his forelegs.

The first thing he overheard was Procel explaining to Enmira how he, Fairuzo, was the only other one in possession of a set of keys that would gain him entry into these rooms. He almost had to stifle a laugh at this, as he found it absurd that *he* – the Lord of Turquoise – would even require a set of *keys* to unlock any of the doors in his own Kingdom.

Keys? He sneered at keys. He could practically go through *walls* with just a flick of his wings.

Of course, he *did* utilize keys whenever entering or exiting in full view of the nosey trolls, but it was solely for appearance's sake. It was just so much more expeditious and clever to travel around Turquoise sight-unseen in whatever form he chose.

Surely, Procel was aware of Fairuzo's shapeshifting abilities? Then, again, Procel most likely had never observed him transforming into various shapes. And since Procel did not indulge in shapeshifting himself – he had neither the ability nor had ever expressed any interest in it – perhaps he did not give the skill much thought.

Rather, Procel had other talents he found to be much more useful, like his fountain of esoteric knowledge and his mountain of cryptic secrets. Then there was his odd habit of reversing direction – although that could be considered more an eccentric quirk than an actual talent.

Next, he overheard Enmira asking Procel for details about what kind of familial ties Darceva had to Fairuzo, alluding to something that the insufferable busybody Achlys had blurted out.

Fairuzo had already fielded questions from Enmira earlier regarding Darceva's relentless and excessive animosity towards her, even mentioning that she'd once played a significant role in his family. Fortunately, he had caught himself just in time from revealing something he shouldn't have about her relationship with his father. He had thought her curiosity had been sated then. But now, she seemed to have become privy to some sort of new information pertaining to the family secret – thanks to Achlys and her big mouth.

He was relieved, then, to hear Procel reply that he did not have the time just then to explain the situation fully, promising to give her the details later when it was more convenient. Fairuzo couldn't help wondering just how much Enmira knew at this point. Although he'd witnessed her brief encounter with that whining sourpuss Achlys, he hadn't been close enough to be able to hear the specifics of what was being discussed.

What *was* clear was that the few tidbits of information

that Achlys *had* fed her had obviously served to awaken and pique Enmira's curiosity even more. He swore, that troll was nothing but a prying gossipmonger and a griping spoilsport.

Even though, at the time, he had still been stewing with rage over Enmira's refusal to participate in the Golden Goblet Ceremony, watching her slowly backing away from Achlys and her annoying whine had caused him to nearly laugh out loud despite himself. It was as if she feared being infected by a highly contagious germ – which actually wasn't too far-fetched of a concern. If one stuck around Achlys long enough, sopping up her negativity, infernal wretchedness and self-pitying, one could certainly catch a bad case of the commiserating cooties.

At any rate, the full details of the family secret had not yet been divulged. And even though it was forbidden for Darceva to ever reveal the truth herself, it was a different matter for Procel. He could speak of it at his own discretion, just as long as doing so did not constitute or cause a breach of security.

Although Fairuzo would personally like to see the whole story buried as if it had never happened, as long as Enmira was going to find out about it eventually anyway, he preferred to be the one to provide her with the details. The last thing he wanted was for her to get any kind of wrong idea about what had really transpired. He needed to explain that he himself had been blameless, and had played no other role but the victim.

As Fairuzo rode along on Procel's shoulder, he heard him explaining in vivid detail the past and ongoing experiments in the Cabal's laboratories. He was relieved that uhey had moved on to other topics, and that his dirty family secret was not being spilled – not yet, anyway.

As he listened in, his mind began drifting away, wandering back to that fateful day when he had discovered the ugly truth that had been hidden from him his entire childhood.

Even centuries later, he was still flooded with disgust and humiliation at the memory of it. The only good aspect of the entire imbroglio had been that he'd found out the truth sooner rather than later or never. And although the lie he'd been told was monumental, it was at least something he could understand the rationalization behind, enough so to where he would eventually be able to move past it into some sort of begrudging acceptance.

But it was the way he'd found it out that was so unforgivable. He was almost willing to trade his soul away just to be able to forget it had ever happened.

CHAPTER 27

MEMORIES OF THE BETRAYAL

It was his twelfth birthday, and Fairuzo had been gifted the services of one of the finest succubi that Mount Hermon had to offer. Officially known as The Rite of Passage Ceremony, the entire evening was dedicated to the carnal solidification of his coming of age.

The celebration was meant to acknowledge his entrance into adulthood, with all of its attendant responsibilities and prurient pleasures. It was a bit like an Earthly bar mitzvah – the difference being, of course, that the activities involved were a lot more lascivious.

When the ravishing young nymphet arrived at the Royal Suite at the appointed time, she was ushered into young Fairuzo's private chambers by the two on-duty bodyguards posted outside his door.

She quickly disrobed and climbed into his bed, losing no time in beginning the lessons. Fairuzo was a quick study, and possessed the boundless energy of a very young and eager student.

She slid her soft, adept hands all over his muscular physique, then flicked her moist, supple tongue expertly over every inch of his hardness. When he began to groan and indicate he was ready, she skillfully climbed on top of him. At the moment of climax, she declared him officially deflowered.

But Fairuzo wanted more. He only required brief respites in between each new position, and would grab her around the waist to signal that he wanted to go again.

After a couple of hours, she had taken him to the point of exhaustion. The assignment complete, she climbed out of bed, quickly threw on her clothes, then sashayed over to the door to take her leave.

All this time, Lamia had been waiting impatiently just outside the room. She was seething with jealousy at the thought that she would not be the first to have her beloved's semen inside of her. She had been hoping to slip inside the bedchamber before the harlot had arrived, but she had beat her to it.

He was *hers*, and she was here to claim him, even if she had to settle for sloppy seconds. She would just have to come to terms with the fact that his first sexual experience had been with some random, anonymous hag instead of her.

They had been going at it inside the room now for a good two hours. Lamia could only hope that he would at least have some sperm left to share with her. If not, she would be back.

In fact, she planned to make this much more than just a one-time occurrence. She would make him *beg* her to return to his bed. It would be a simple matter once she spread her legs and demonstrated her oft-practiced sexual skills.

Lamia had already taken care of the two royal guards posted outside his door. At first, she had considered the idea of sexually bartering with them to grant her entry. But, since they both were already so close to the point of passing out from all the wine they'd drunken at the festivities, she'd only needed to give them a couple of good, hard blows to the head. She'd added in one more brisk whack for good measure, just to make sure they wouldn't be waking up any time soon.

She was very pleased with herself that she had had the foresight to bring along a heavy chunk of pyrite, just in the event that force would be necessary. It had come in extremely handy.

Now she was just waiting for the whore to get finished with her business. Arms crossed and angrily tapping her foot, she kept one eye on the door and the other eye on the guards to make sure they did not awaken.

When she finally heard the creaking of the floorboards inside the room, she knew that meant the succubus would soon be coming out. She got into a crouching position. Just as the door opened, she crawled inside on her hands and knees as stealthily as possible in order to avoid being detected.

Once in, she quickly peeled off all of her clothes. Her clammy hands were shaking with anticipation and lust, and her rancid, unwashed body was greasy. She was sweating like a child molester being given a polygraph in an interrogation room. Her eyes darted quickly around the candlelit bedchamber for something to towel off with. She decided to make do with a corner of the velvet duvet cover, which she swiped haphazardly over her torso.

As discreetly and unobtrusively as possible, she climbed onto the bed. She didn't want to startle him; he had his eyes closed, and it appeared he was either already asleep or very close to drifting off.

She noticed he had a big smile of satisfaction on his face, apparently still glowing from the succubus's visit. This aggravated Lamia to no end. *Just wait until he sees what I have to give him*, she thought spitefully.

As she crawled clumsily on top of him, she was literally holding her breath, hoping he would just assume the succubus had returned for more. She fumblingly managed to get him inside of her and then began rocking back and forth.

The weight of her body was oppressively heavy, her dry, scaly skin scratched roughly against his abdomen, and she exuded the most horrendous odor: he could immediately tell something was amiss.

It was definitely not the succubus come back for more.

Fairuzo's eyes flew open to find a hideous troll leering on top of him. Her red, welted face was just inches away from his, her black hole of a mouth emitting strong gusts of fetid breath that stank like sewage as she panted and grunted. She was awkwardly gyrating her hips and beginning to emit loud, raspy moans intermingled with shrill, abrasive screams that sounded like caterwauling.

He attempted to wriggle out from under her girth, but she was much too heavy for him. She quickly pinned him down, wrapping her large, fleshy arms tightly around him like a mosquito net trapping a butterfly.

Meanwhile, the succubus had definitely *not* missed noticing the ungainly Lamia worming her way past her into the room. But she had thought it best to just let her think she hadn't been seen. She had then continued on out into the hallway to alert the sleeping guards.

Once she had finally succeeded in rousing them, she began to animatedly explain how Lamia had snuck into Fairuzo's bedchamber and was in there right this very moment.

She was well aware of just who Lamia was, as were the guards; Lamia had quite the reputation for being an exceptionally obnoxious troublemaker. But it was still quite a shock that she would have the sheer, shameless audacity to pull off a stunt like this.

Even the succubus couldn't help but be appalled at her behavior. And for one who had seen and performed just about every perversion imaginable, for her to regard any sexual act as shocking or immoral was really saying something.

Their heads still aching, the guards flung open the door to find Lamia moaning and heaving away on top of Fairuzo. Even from their vantage point at the doorway, they could clearly see that Fairuzo, trapped beneath the mounds and folds of her pendulous flesh, was desperately trying to push her off of him and get out from under her.

"This is prohibited by law! Get off of our Lord this instant, you despicable whore!" yelled one of the guards in warning.

Lamia muttered, "Oh, go mind your own business.

I've got him now and I'm going to finish," bouncing even harder and faster.

The guards ran over to the bed and pulled her roughly off of Fairuzo, then began dragging her away.

"How did this repulsive troll get in here?" Fairuzo shouted. "And why?"

One of the guards paused, then looked at the other.

"Should we tell him?" he asked

"Sure, why not?" the other replied, shrugging. "He's going to find out sooner or later anyway."

"Tell me what?" demanded Fairuzo.

"This slag here that was just on top of you is Lamia," the guard answered, pointing to her, now struggling and wailing like a cornered banshee between them.

"And who or what is a Lamia?" Fairuzo asked, perplexed.

"Lamia is –" and here the guard paused so long that the other one finished the sentence for him:

"Lamia is your mother."

"My mother?" Fairuzo yelled after them as they continued dragging her out of the room.

"Yes," replied one of the guards, "your *real* mother. The one you were told had been banished since your birth."

Lamia let out a loud cackle. "Yes! I fucked my own son!" she yelled. "And what of it? I promised you all that I'd get my revenge one day! So what are you going to do about it?"

Fairuzo lay in shock and disbelief in the bed, his head spinning in confusion. Not only was he just now finding out that this disgusting ogre was his own mother, but that she had deliberately committed the forbidden act of incest between an infected Earth-troll and her Royal Neph-Biter son.

He would *never* have voluntarily let anyone so vile and revolting touch him. It was a double insult that she had forced herself upon him. She had known full well that incest was only allowed between members of Royalty to maintain the purest of bloodlines or amongst the trolls themselves with their own siblings and children.

For, although inbreeding was strictly forbidden between mother troll and her own Royal offspring, it was heavily *encouraged* between all of the trolls. In fact, they were ordered to participate in it as much as possible. It was all a matter of selective breeding: the trolls needed to be kept dumbed-down, mutated and crippled, and inbreeding amongst them did a fantastically efficient job of achieving all of these things.

It had been decreed that the bloodline of the elite Royal Nobility was to be kept unmixed at all costs, that troll females must only be used as vessels and allowed no sexual contact with their offspring. And Lamia had just tainted the pedigree and broken the forbidden code.

He felt not only tricked and eternally sullied by her, but betrayed by everyone who had lied to him all this time. And she was getting revenge against whom and for what?

After awhile he got up from the bed and walked over to the sink. He began scrubbing himself all over as hard as he could with a rough-bristled brush dipped in diluted lye-water. In an attempt to get her nasty stench off of him, he paid special attention to his private parts.

He then made a concoction of lavender, sage and lemongrass, which he rubbed firmly all over, not missing an inch of his body. Her nastiness had seeped into his very pores.

After several days, the putrid smell finally went away, but the memory would be burned into his mind for centuries. And just as she had promised to exact revenge one day, so would he. Oh, would he *ever.*

CHAPTER 28

THE SLAVES' LIVING QUARTERS

As we continued on down the passageway, Procel's vivid descriptions of mad scientists and their depraved experiments continued to haunt me. The horrific visions of dogs and monkeys with transplanted heads were made all the more real having seen for myself the animals huddled inside their barren laboratory cages, shivering and miserable, their eyes blank and staring, void of all hope.

What made it even worse was the powerlessness I felt at not being able to intervene, to release them all from their captivity and torment. I could not help but feel relieved that Procel was taking me somewhere not in such close proximity to where they were being warehoused. It was all so distressing to see, yet do nothing.

I began to wonder if Fairuzo had noticed by now that I was no longer at the Initiation. Surely, he must have seen Procel and I leaving the Ballroom together. For whatever reason, he had chosen not to follow us back here.

I hadn't the slightest clue as to how long we'd been absent, nor how long I'd lain unconscious. The concept of time had always puzzled me, so nebulous and fleeting. At any rate, I had not seen a single clock since I'd arrived here. In fact, it was almost as if time did not exist in this place – or at least it was neither needed nor desired.

As far as I could tell, anything even resembling order was shunned here; the trolls seemed to exist in utter chaos while feeding an insatiable lust for hedonism.

And what of the Initiation, I wondered: were the festivities still proceeding without me? I seriously doubted they would have considered curtailing any of their bloodletting or twisted notions of revelry on my behalf. It was obvious my presence had done nothing but put a damper on their deranged merrymaking and brawling. And they had been openly enjoying the wine, so at least you could say it was not going to waste.

Had Fairuzo known beforehand that Darceva and Dantanian would be lying in wait for us? And was *that* the reason he did not follow? Or was their ambush a plot the two of them had hatched without his knowledge? Perhaps I had made him so angry this time that he would no longer be interceding on my behalf, and had, for all intents and purposes, washed his hands of me.

Oh, he was such a complicated one to figure out! Just when he seemed to be showing me an intimation of decency and I was beginning to let down my guard, he would do something that would make me distrust him all over again.

I wondered why it had been so important to him that I drink that wine, and why he had become so furious when I'd refused it. Surely, he must have known there were serpents inside the goblet; was it possible he had been trying to poison me? Or perhaps the liquid had contained some sort of Rohypnol type concoction that would have rendered me senseless and put me at his mercy. Hardly acts of trust-inspiring benevolence.

Yet even as I pondered the plausibility of such devious intentions, I felt a bit silly that I might simply be yielding to unwarranted paranoia. It was true that the inexplicable hold he seemed to have over me caused me to balk instinctively and defensively. I even found myself consciously fighting to resist his cunning beguilement. But still, my suspicions that he might be harboring such injurious motives reminded me that I needed to remain ever vigilant in not succumbing to his most persuasive charms.

The truth was that if he hadn't been so devastatingly handsome, I could find it much easier to dislike him. This, I realized, was incredibly shallow of me – my being drawn to someone based solely upon their appearance. But it was more than merely his looks; there was also some sort of magnetic attraction, a potent chemistry between us that threw my mind into a tailspin.

I had begun to notice that whenever he was near, I felt heady and dizzy, as if some sort of scent or airborne signal were triggering a visceral response. And while this spontaneous reflex both exhilarated and excited me, it also gave me the uneasy sensation of being rapidly propelled into the deepest part of an ocean. I knew very little of what lay just beneath the choppy surface waves and absolutely nothing of what lurked at the shadowy depths of its bottom.

He seemed dangerously unpredictable.

In fact, I was beginning to realize that, quite honestly, I much preferred the company of Procel, with whom I felt comfortable and at ease with. Exuding a steadfast reliability, I trusted him almost implicitly. As yet, I had not detected any ambiguous or ulterior motives.

In comparison, Fairuzo was like a volatile powder keg that the slightest spark could set off. And although I might well be mesmerized by the blazing inferno that would invariably ensue, I had a chilling sense of foreboding that I could easily end up badly burned if I lingered too close to the flames.

We turned a corner and came to several steeply-cascading stone steps leading down to another level.

"Below here is the slaves' quarters," Procel explained. "The entrance is constantly being monitored by guards, but I know a secret way around the back where we can enter without being observed."

"Boy, you sure do know your way around here," I said admiringly.

"Well, I should certainly hope so," replied Procel crisply. "I've been living here for two centuries! Then, again, it does help that I have unrestricted access to all areas – except for one, that is. And that would be the warehouse where all the disembodied souls are kept.

"It is locked up airtight like a fortress and heavily guarded, constructed entirely of hammered copper. There is not a window or portal in sight, other than the main entry. And Fairuzo is the only one on Tartarus who is allowed inside."

"Oh, that sounds very mysterious," I said, "but I can't even imagine what one would even want with souls no longer attached to a body!"

"Let's just say I've overheard some of their agenda at a few Cabal meetings, and they are currently working on ways to splice souls together in newborn Earthlings," replied Procel. "Their goal is to create mutated creatures that are hybrids of brainless robotic machines and killer mercenaries, programmed to take orders and comply without question."

"Well, that's really creepy," I said. "They really seem to love tampering with humans and animals around here."

"Yes," agreed Procel. "Things you should not be tampering with – like life and nature."

"And you've been here two centuries?" I asked incredulously. "Is that how long this hellish place has existed?"

"Well, Turquoise was first established by Fairuzo's father about two and one-half centuries ago when he first brought the Earth goblins over to colonize Tartarus."

"The Earth goblins? But where are they now?"

"Oh, they're all here, but they are no longer called goblins. After they made the journey over and settled in, they were deemed trolls from that point onward."

"Well," I said, "I really don't know the difference between a goblin and a troll – is there any, really?"

"Oh, yes," said Procel, nodding his head enthusiastically. "There is an entire solar system of difference between the two! When the goblins lived on Earth, they were a noble, peaceful tribe of beings who wouldn't hurt a tsetse fly; they only knew of goodness and truth, and lived by the creed of doing no harm to any other living creature.

But after The Infection, they all became just as evil and corrupt as the one who had bitten them."

"The one who had bitten them? And who was that?" I asked.

"That would be Fairuzo's father, Phegor. He was in charge of transmogrifying all that was good into evil, and he did a damned good job of it. In fact, before that, the goblins knew nothing of flesh-eating, war, greed, lust, or even violence. They were as innocent and naïve as little children, completely unaware that evil even existed in the universe. They had no idea that there were vile and destructive entities out there who did not have their best interests at heart."

"And the trolls? How are they different from the goblins?"

"Well, that is what the goblins turned into after they were bitten and given The Mark – a mean-spirited, cloddish clan of violent, narcissistic trolls.

"In fact," Procel continued, "they were all given new names to symbolize their new lives and identities. The ones they had previously answered to were now referred to as their "gob" names; while the new names assigned to them would henceforth be their Turquoisian Troll names."

"Oh, so, it was kind of like letting them know they were officially leaving their old lives and ways behind?" I asked.

"Exactly," said Procel. "And to remind them that Earth was no longer their home. The names they were given reflected their new troll personalities, too.

"For instance, the one formerly known as Lamia was given the name of Darceva. Her old gob name meant 'gentle like a lamb,' while her new name meant 'Dark Deceiver.' "

"Well, I'd have to say that's a very fitting name for her," I said, frowning. "But you mean she was once a good and kind-hearted goblin who lived on Earth before she ever became a troll? It's hard to imagine that she wasn't just always pure evil."

"Hard to see it now, I know, but she was at one time a very pious and gracious goblin resident of Planet Earth before she ever turned evil – although she could certainly convince you otherwise with her nasty disposition," replied Procel.

After descending the steps, we came upon a thin, dirt pathway that encircled a large ramshackle building. It was constructed of limestone slabs and dull gray endellite crudely fashioned into lumpy bricks. Apparently this was where the slaves were being held.

Procel walked up to one of the filthy windows, covered with a heavy layer of dust. He spit into his hand, then smeared it across the murky glass. Using the edge of his sleeve, he meticulously cleared off a bit of the grime.

"Here you go," said Procel, turning towards me. "Take a peek in there. You'll get an idea of the conditions these poor slaves are forced to live in."

I didn't really want to look inside, afraid of what I might find. I reluctantly moved a bit closer to the window and, when I peered in, saw a cavernous room dimly lit by a few flickering torches on the surrounding walls.

As my eyes focused, I could see long ropes of heavy metal chains hanging from the ceiling. Hooks on the ends of these were attached to collars around the necks of about a dozen pale-skinned salamanders, all about my height and all swaying unsteadily on their spindly hind legs. With their recessed eyes and pink frilly gills fanning out just above their collars, I could tell they were the same species as the one who had been carrying the tray in the Ballroom.

Placed about two feet apart, many of them were jerking from side to side, almost in rhythm with each other, while others rocked back and forth or bobbed their heads incessantly up and down. They all appeared to be completely unaware of their surroundings.

"This species is what is known as the 'human fish,' the offspring of the cave dragon," explained Procel. "And as you've probably noticed, they are all quite blind, which makes them especially meek and malleable. The Cabal selects only the most docile creatures on Earth to stock their servant stable. They then bring them back here to physically and mentally break their spirits, brutalizing and terrifying them into submission.

"See the way they are swinging back and forth like that and shaking their heads?" he asked.

"Yes," I murmured, frozen to the spot. I felt as if I were peering into an insane asylum, where all the patients inside had gone completely mad and were no longer cognizant of where they were. What I was witnessing was surreal and beyond disturbing.

"But what is wrong with them?" I cried.

"They are exhibiting a neurosis called zoochosis," Procel explained. "It is an obsessive, repetitive behavior that allows the slave to mentally project themselves out of their surroundings, essentially going into a trance. It is both a coping mechanism as well as an instinctual reaction. Their reality is so painfully unbearable that they can no longer face it. This is the only way they can escape – inside their own heads."

"Oh, my God," I exclaimed, feeling my eyes begin to well up with tears. These poor creatures had literally gone insane from the sheer intolerability of the life they were being forced to lead. I could barely imagine what sort of hell their sightless world must be like and what they'd had to endure.

"I know you are just as upset at seeing this kind of cruelty as I am, Enmira – if not more so, as I have become all too familiar and accustomed to seeing it constantly," Procel said. "But don't you worry; it will not be for much longer. One day this abuse will stop, you can be sure of that – at least for these particular creatures in *here*, anyway," he said pointedly.

I looked questioningly over at him. He had a faint

secretive smile on his face, and I decided it best not to pry or ask any further questions. But for some reason, hearing him voice this vow aloud helped to lift my spirits a bit.

"Now, when we get around to the back, you're going to need to climb on my shoulders. Can you do that?" he asked.

"Well, I suppose so," I replied. If that was what needed to be done, I would do it – although I was not feeling at all confident in my acrobatic abilities at the moment. I was certainly not dressed appropriately for any sort of gymnastics either.

I looked down at the skirt of the dress I was wearing: its billowy circumference and bulky layers of tulle would certainly hinder anything that required more than the slightest degree of maneuverability. I could also see that the beautiful taffeta fabric was beginning to show signs of wear and tear as well as some soiling.

Just for a split second, I wondered if I was going to ruin it altogether, having to go inside such a dusty, filthy place. I immediately felt shame for having such selfish thoughts.

These beings are suffering greatly, I chided myself; *and what kind of person am I to worry about mussing up some silly dress?* No doubt, it was a most stunning gown – certainly more exquisite than anything I'd ever owned – but it was a mere lifeless possession, and one that could most likely be replaced or, at the very least, closely replicated.

I followed Procel around to the back of the building, where he pointed to a small octagonal opening several feet up the wall.

"See that aperture up there? That is where I will need you to slip into after I lift you up onto my shoulders. There will be a very short duct you will need to crawl through once you're inside. But, after that, it's a quick, short drop to the floor."

"But how will *you* be able to get in?" I asked, already beginning to panic at the thought of being left alone inside.

234

"Well, you'll be letting me in, of course. Just go inside the main room where the cave slaves are kept and you will see that first window we looked into. Simply unlatch it and I will be waiting right outside.

"Now, I suppose I could have forcibly smashed the window glass for both of us to crawl through, but I thought it best not to draw any attention to ourselves – nor do we wish to startle the poor blind creatures, either," Procel explained.

I took a look around and saw that trash was everywhere, piled high and strewn all about. The stench was just awful. It appeared to be some sort of refuse dump back here. I also saw – and smelled – what appeared to be several festering pools of sewage, containing both liquids and solids, and they were emitting a most foul odor.

Procel moved closer to the building, then bent forward facing the wall, motioning for me to climb up on his shoulders.

"And when we are safely ensconced inside," he continued, "I will tell you all about the Darceva and Fairuzo saga, so you will have a better understanding of their relationship."

"Oh, yes, please do!" I replied, relieved to have something to look forward to that would take my mind off of all of this filth and wretchedness. I had almost completely forgotten about his earlier promise to give me all of the sordid details.

I was curious to know just how Fairuzo and Darceva were related, and what his father had to do with it all. Were they brother and sister? Some sort of step-siblings with different mothers, perhaps? That would seem most likely, although Darceva certainly seemed obsessed with Fairuzo in a way that was somehow immodestly inappropriate, almost incestuous.

It was also obvious that he truly despised her for some deeply personal reason. At any rate, I'd be finding out very shortly.

Procel, still waiting, held his hand out towards me.

"Okay, Enmira," he said. "Climb on up now, and I'll try to balance you as much as I can."

Just as I took a step towards him, I heard a familiar voice behind me say, "I wouldn't go in there, if I was you."

I must have jumped a good foot up into the air. I turned around to see Fairuzo standing right behind us, a sardonic smirk upon his face.

So, he *had* been following us all this time, after all. We just hadn't seen him.

My first thought was, *I wonder how long he's been here, just watching and listening?* I could feel my face flushing, humiliation and embarrassment washing over me. I felt as if I'd been caught red-handed trying to slip something into my pocket that didn't belong to me.

I glanced over at Procel, and he appeared to be very busy studying his feet all of a sudden.

I wondered if I should at least attempt some sort of explanation as to why we were back here, but could think of nothing that would even begin to excuse what Fairuzo must clearly view as trespassing. I, for one, was certainly out of my element. I knew that where we were now was no doubt considered forbidden territory – especially for a newcomer to his Kingdom such as I.

Being caught like this certainly did not bode well for Procel either, as it was he who had led the way.

"Now what am I going to do with you two?" Fairuzo asked, an almost amused expression upon his face. Oddly enough, he did not seem too terribly angry, but rather more entertained by our audacity in believing we would actually be getting away with something behind his back. I'm sure he was enjoying our obvious discomfort at having been caught, as well.

He turned his attention towards me. "Did you really think I was just going to let you leave your own Initiation, Enmira?"

He shook his head slowly, as if he still could not believe I thought I could get away with such impertinence.

"You know, I could have easily stopped you before you even made it through the door, but I was well aware that the lovely Miss Darceva was back here waiting for you with her trap. And, if nothing else, I knew that would certainly curtail your flight."

I let out a gasp – so he *had* known about the ambush! I felt a sinking feeling in the pit of my stomach at the thought that he had known all along they planned to cause me harm, yet had neither warned me nor intervened to stop them.

Fairuzo shrugged. "I really did think it might teach you a lesson," he explained simply. "And I certainly didn't think they would actually hurt you. After all, I knew that Procel was back here with you and would step in the moment they tried to.

"And, believe me, I had absolutely *no* idea they would have the asinine effrontery to attack him as well – the son of a Duke, a Royal member of the Cabal – which, by the way, they will be both be dealt with severely and accordingly for that. But you really cannot just go around here doing whatever it is that you please, Enmira."

He turned towards Procel, his voice taking on a sharper edge.

"And that goes double for you, Procel. I thought you were my friend. You *knew* how long I've been looking forward to this Initiation, and yet you took her away right in the middle of it. If I didn't know any better, I'd –" and here Fairuzo trailed off.

Procel still would neither look up nor meet his gaze, and remained silent.

"Don't make me do something irreversible, Procel," Fairuzo said in a tone that sounded almost pleading. "I don't want to report you to the Cabal for this. I don't see any reason I should need to. We can settle this between ourselves. But this really does qualify as mutiny, and I think you realize you're already kind of on their shit list as it is."

Procel nodded then, seeming relieved, although still unable to lift his head to meet Fairuzo's gaze.

"Oh, Fairuzo, thank you for not reporting him!" I blurted out. "It was all my idea, really, and he was just trying to help me escape from the trolls and hide me out for awhile until things cooled down. You know yourself how much they all despise me."

I smiled uncertainly at him, hoping he would at least try to see my side of things and understand how threatened I'd felt.

"Well, Enmira," Fairuzo said, "in that case, you should have come to me for assistance instead of going behind my back."

I couldn't help but let out an exasperated sigh then.

"But you were still so angry at me for not drinking the wine! How could I have come to you when you would have surely snapped off my head!" I cried.

"I suppose you do have a point there," Fairuzo begrudgingly acknowledged. "I won't deny I was pretty damn upset. But you have no idea how much I was restraining myself from lashing out. "

Actually I do have an idea, I thought to myself. I'd seen the way he'd held his balled-up fists so tightly at his sides. The potential threat of violence towards me had been frightening and worrying, but at least I could see he was making an attempt to try to contain himself.

"But I had already given you way too many second chances!" Fairuzo cried. "And you've consistently refused every gift and treat I've offered you!" he continued, with an almost wounded tone to his voice.

For a moment I wanted to laugh out loud at the absurdity of what he'd just said – these gifts and treats, as he referred to them, were far from the romantic presents he seemed to regard them as. Why, they were downright offensive and repulsive, some of them even qualifying as completely psychotic.

I really couldn't imagine how any rational-thinking person in their right mind would not be incredibly insulted by the mere offer of them, all while wondering just what sort of sociopath would even think they would be acceptable as gifts for *anyone*.

I struggled for a way to relay this notion to him. I didn't want to appear ungrateful, but it was not an easy thing to explain to someone with such a different perception of what constituted simple common taste and decency. He found the offerings splendid, and I found them horrific; there could not have been a greater disparity.

"Yes, I know, but the things you offer..." I began, then stopped myself, unable to put my thoughts into words that wouldn't further aggravate him.

"So, let's just end this little side-adventure now and get back to the Initiation, shall we?" Fairuzo said, cutting me off sternly. "No more of this going off on your own. Are we clear?"

He paused, awaiting my response, and I obediently nodded my head – although, inside, I was thinking: *You may have caught me this time, but I will not promise that I won't try to escape again!* It made me feel better to think this; I was never going to give up hope that there was a way out of here back to Earth.

"And I'm fully aware that you feel sorry for those slaves in there," he said, jerking his head towards the building, "but they are only here because they are useful to us. They are not anyone's pets, so don't even think of getting attached to them!"

I was silent then, reminded once again of our vast differences in opinions when it pertained to the creatures he viewed as objects rather than living beings. I wondered if I would ever be able to convince him to see it from my perspective; for there was certainly no chance I would *ever* come to see it from his.

Just then, Procel spoke in a very meek voice, barely above a whisper.

"I am thoroughly sorry, Fairuzo. Truly I am. Please do not take it personally. You know I consider you to be like a brother. The last thing I want to do is to interfere in your pleasures or get you in any kind of hot water with the Cabal."

"Then let's shake on it, brother, and never let it happen again," Fairuzo answered solemnly.

He walked briskly over to Procel and they clasped hands vigorously. Then, almost impulsively, Fairuzo gave him a quick, hard hug and a couple of firm claps on the back. It was obvious they were both relieved that the tension had passed – at least for the moment -- and that a renewal of friendship while letting bygones be bygones seemed to be the best resolution.

"Now let us get back to the Initiation," Fairuzo said loudly, steering me towards him and beckoning to Procel to follow. "We have more festivities to enjoy!"

With that, he playfully pinched the side of my waist with his fingers, then took ahold of my hand. And I must say I rather enjoyed the sensation that it gave me.

CHAPTER 29

THE MORNING AFTER:
FATHER AND SON

The morning after the Rite of Passage Ceremony, Fairuzo awoke feeling disoriented and full of angst. Something in his life had changed irreversibly last night, and it had not been for the better.

Having subsisted on the insipid cacti of a bone-dry carnality desert up until now, he had finally gained entry into the moist and fertile oasis of endless lascivious pleasures. By all rights, he should have been humming and brimming with the potent virility expected after such a baptism of lust. Instead, he was overtaken by melancholy and a desolate sense of betrayal and doom.

He was not even allowed the luxury of reveling in his memories of the glorious hours spent with the sensuous succubus, for his mind was flooded with the ugliness of what had immediately followed: that grotesque creature sneaking into his chambers and lewdly forcing herself upon him. The one who had turned out to be his real mother.

The way she had slithered uninvited into his bed and coiled her odious, corpulent body on top of his was forever seared into his mind like a three-dimensional nightmare, marring and tainting what should have been a most pleasurable and memorable ending to a very special night.

During that evening's ceremony, his father had officially pronounced him The New Lord of Turquoise, handing over the reins of authority and all keys to the Kingdom. He had felt such an exhilarating rush of power at that moment. How long he had looked forward to becoming the ruler of his very own planet! But now, even that triumphant memory had been sullied and crushed.

As the New Lord, he would henceforth be granted all privileges and extraordinary powers that a full-grown Neph-Biter was entitled to as a birthright. But the new responsibilities that were part and parcel of his new position felt like nothing more than wearisome chores and nuisances now, weighing upon him like a ponderous yoke made of millstones anchored around his neck.

And with his father leaving today, from whom would he be able to ask for assistance when conflicts arose, as they inevitably would? There was very little he knew about taking charge of a kingdom. It appeared he was utterly on his own, and this thought did nothing to help lift his spirits.

Surely, by now, the guards had informed his father of Lamia's illicit nocturnal visit. He couldn't help feeling a bit resentful that his father had apparently not been concerned enough to even pay him a visit after the traumatizing event.

He did realize, however, that his father was busy packing in preparation to return to Mount Hermon. Indeed, it was all he had talked about for months – of leaving this place and getting as far away from it and its inhabitants as possible. And now that Fairuzo had come of age and had inherited the crown of Lordship, his father could indulge himself in a long vacation anywhere in the universe he pleased.

Then, again, his father had never been the mollycoddling type. Fairuzo had long ago stopped hoping he might ever one day reveal some deeply-hidden sentimental side.

He remembered all too vividly the first time he had taken him to Earth with him on his first hunting expedition. It was one of his earliest memories, and it had been far from a pleasurable bonding experience. In fact, it had made him fully aware of the extent of his father's cruelty and arrogance towards anything and everyone in his path – including him.

First, he had demonstrated the best method of

spotting and tracking animals in the woods. Then, he had shown his son how to shapeshift into a tick, whereupon he effortlessly leapt upon the neck of an unsuspecting deer to siphon out the blood.

He next took him to a small farm that had stacks of wire hutches in back of the barn, with dozens of rabbits being held captive in each cage. He opened the door of one of the enclosures, then reached inside and roughly yanked out one of the rabbits.

"Here," his father said, shoving the frantically struggling animal right in Fairuzo's face. "Just snap its neck. It's how the farmers do it."

Fairuzo stood there frozen. The rabbit looked terrified, desperately trying to get out of his father's vise-like grip. He felt no desire to harm the creature. In fact, all he really wanted to do was tell his father to put the rabbit down and let him go free.

"Oh, for all the damn milksopping pansies..." his father swore impatiently. In a split second, he violently twisted the rabbit's neck until there was a sickening popping sound. Then his father sank his fangs deep into the animal's back.

Fairuzo stared as the blood arced and spurted rhythmically like a still-beating heart that had been abruptly ripped out of a ribcage. The rabbit was still alive, whimpering, and his sad eyes seemed to be looking straight into Fairuzo's, imploring him to help him. Emotions of tenderness towards the creature welled up inside him and he began to quietly sob.

All these years later, he could still feel his father's black, merciless eyes burning into him with a look of abject disgust. He could hear his father's contemptuous voice ridiculing him: "Are you a true Neph-Biter and spawn of my loins, or a soft-centered vulva? Why, no son of mine could be acting the way you do! What are you, a spineless sissy crybaby? You make me sick!"

As the rabbit finally went limp, his father shoved the now-lifeless body into his son's face again, urging him to take a bite for himself. Fairuzo felt cornered, realizing he had no choice, knowing full well that his father would persist until he finally did as he was ordered to.

He reluctantly took a tiny bite out of the dead rabbit's mangled neck. Immediately, he felt an overwhelming reflex to regurgitate. He fought with all his will to suppress the urge; for he realized that if he vomited the flesh back up, his father would simply force him to take another bite.

Even though Fairuzo had essentially acquiesced to his demands – thinking surely that should have satisfied him – that didn't stop his father from berating him all the way back to Earth. Not for one moment did he let up with his tirade, focusing mainly on his questionable gender and manhood, even wondering about his legitimacy as son and heir.

"If I did not know for sure that you were the spawn of my own seed, I would swear you were pure goblin and did not possess a single drop of blue blood in you," he spat out scornfully. "And after today's pathetic demonstration, let's just say I now have some very valid doubts."

Fairuzo could only keep silent and submit to the relentless haranguing, all while hanging his head in shame for not living up to his father's expectations. He was torn between wanting to please him and not wishing to participate in the cruel, senseless deeds his father was insistent upon involving him in.

When they got back to Tartarus, Fairuzo felt the need to reassure his father that, next trip, it would all be different.

"It damn sure will be!" exclaimed his father. "And, by the way, your attendance will be required tomorrow night at the Sacrifice of the Innocent, which I've arranged.

"Now I'm warning you, Fairuzo," he continued sternly. "Don't you *dare* humiliate me in front of all of my subjects or there will be repercussions. You will do *exactly* as you are told from here on out.

"And as you may or may not be aware, I do not require permission from the Cabal to discipline my own son, so don't go getting any notions that you fall under their umbrella of protection. Any further disobedience will not be tolerated!"

When the next evening rolled around, the Royal Guards arrived at the appointed hour to collect Fairuzo from his chambers. As they escorted him through the long, winding corridors that led to the Ballroom, he felt a strong sense of doom, as if each step he took was bringing him closer and closer to his own beheading.

His father was waiting impatiently for him inside the large cavernous room, shifting restlessly from foot to foot next to an octagonal slate table that held a large cage. A massive crowd of trolls was gathered around the table as well, many with expectant looks upon their faces, some literally drooling with anticipation at the wicked fun that was in store for them.

As Fairuzo came nearer to the cage, he could see that tucked inside it was a magnificent alabaster-white swan. For a moment, he felt a tender pity for the trapped creature, intermingled with an awe and wonder at the bird's pure and unsoiled beauty. But this was quickly overtaken by an overwhelming sense of dread at whatever it was they were all expecting him to do next.

His father began chanting, and the trolls all quickly joined in with their shrill, raspy voices:

"Sacrifice the Innocent to feast upon the dead,
By his own hands, the blood of innocence is shed
Surrender to all darkness and extinguish all light
Eternal Night is his once he doth take the bite!"

Fairuzo's head began to pound. He felt as if the trolls were screaming right in his ear, and he was finding it hard to think clearly. All he could focus on was his father's warning of punishment if he did not comply. He knew there would be no way for him to opt out; he simply had no choice.

His father flung open the cage door, and the swan hastily shrank back with an expression that could only be interpreted as great fear and trepidation. The bird then stood trembling, as if realizing that what was about to happen next would cause her great anguish and pain.

"Behold, your sacrifice, my son," his father announced with a sneer.

By now, some of the trolls had moved to where they were now encircling Fairuzo from behind. They began crowding in and elbowing him sharply in the back in an attempt to shove him even closer to the table.

His father then pulled the frightened swan out of the cage, placing one hand firmly around the torso and the other tightly squeezing the bird's long, slender neck.

"Bite its neck, Fairuzo," he commanded. "Come on, don't be a pussy-boy. Go on, bite it. Sink your fangs in there. Kill and feed."

"Kill and Feed!" echoed the trolls robotically and in unison. "Kill and Feed!"

Fairuzo knew he could stall no longer. He leaned forward, closed his eyes tightly, and sank his fangs deep into the bird's neck. The swan reacted by screaming in pain and struggling to break free. But instead of being repulsed and nauseated as he had with the rabbit, Fairuzo was suddenly overtaken by an insatiable desire to continue biting.

Over and over he bit the swan's neck until there was no more movement and the bird lay still. His father then dropped the lifeless creature onto the ground with a dull thud, as if it were a sack of garbage to be disposed of at the city dump.

An unfamiliar feeling flooded over Fairuzo then: he was suddenly filled with an overwhelming torrent of hatred and loathing towards the swan. He hated the bird, he despised its innocence; he loathed the way it had aroused feelings of compassion and tenderness when he'd first seen it in the cage. He hated and blamed the swan for every lousy feeling he'd ever had that had made him feel weak and submissive.

In fact, it surprised him to realize that he loathed the bird even more than he despised his father. For some reason, this realization filled him with relief – for he did not want to hate his father; he wanted to love him. Almost as much as he wanted his father to love him back.

Directing his hatred specifically at the bird seemed to free him from the burden of these heavy, ambivalent thoughts and feelings towards his father. He was glad the swan was dead and that he had been the one who had taken its life.

And intermingling with this newfound hatred was a sense of power, of dominance, as if he now had the ability to force any being in the world to surrender to him. He did not want to let go of this feeling, for it seemed to electrify him with enormous jolts of revitalizing energy.

All of the dead flesh that had been served to him as food up until now had not given him anywhere near the empowerment that he felt now. He decided that, from here on out, he would only chew and feast on the flesh of the still-living-and-breathing. For it was now obvious to him that his razor-sharp fangs were designed for biting into blood still pulsing, tearing into gristle and muscle still twitching, and crunching through rock-hard bones encased in still-quivering marrow-jelly.

And, as an added bonus, the struggling of the animal desperately fighting for its life gave the whole feeding experience that extra kick and inimitable thrill. You certainly could not find any of these delights in a decaying mound of long-dead road-kill.

Perhaps now that he had become more like his father – cold-hearted, pitiless, emotionally detached – they would grow closer as father and son. Perhaps now his father would even be able to show him just how proud he was to have him as a son.

But here it was now, several years later, and Fairuzo had to admit that these hopes had never come anywhere near fruition. His mimicry of his father's cruel, heartless and murderous ways had not brought them any closer, nor had his father ever been able to express even the slightest amount of pride in him.

On the contrary, it had only served to make him feel even more conflicted and alienated. And what he was beginning to realize was that it did not really much matter that his father was leaving him behind now, for he had never really been there for him to begin with.

Not only had his emotional support been absent, but his physical presence as well. He was constantly flying off to Earth to hunt for fresh lovelies with which to populate the Kingdom and satisfy his lust for new erotic bed-mates. And when he returned with his latest conquest, he would then spend all of his spare time in bed with her – until the inevitable boredom set in and he quickly lost interest, which never took long at all.

As the poison from the serpent-bite each one received rapidly took effect, they began rotting from the inside, descending into grotesque caricatures of their former stunningly attractive and vibrant selves. Then, realizing they were losing their appeal, they would cling even more desperately to him in ways that annoyed him to no end.

Truthfully, Fairuzo was actually rather relieved that his father would be leaving today. He had pretty much given up trying to please him at all, as it seemed he could never satisfy him no matter what he did. He had grown weary of constantly seeking his father's approval to no avail, always failing. From this point onward, he would seek it no more.

He reluctantly got out of bed then and began dressing himself. He could not assume that his father would take it upon himself to come visit him before he left, even if just to leave him with final instructions or orders. Not even to bid his own son a fond farewell. Therefore, it was entirely up to Fairuzo himself now to pay him a visit – and quickly, before he flew off to other playgrounds on more pleasurable planets.

There were several things he wanted to clear up once and for all. And who knew when he might ever get another chance or, indeed, ever see his father again.

For one, he needed to find out how the Lamia situation was being handled. He could only hope that his father would have already expedited the matter, and that the Cabal was now involved in deciding upon and meting out the punishment.

All he knew was that the guards had dragged her away kicking and screaming, but to where, he had no idea. He could only hope that she was being held securely in a place where she could never again get anywhere near him.

In fact, he had decided that he himself, as the New Lord, would request her banishment. She deserved nothing less for the outrageous violation.

After he finished dressing, he opened the door of his bedchamber to find that the two guards from last night were still at their posts outside. At first, he was relieved to see them – until he remembered that it was as a direct result of their incompetence that Lamia had gained access to his room.

In fact, he would speak to his father about their transgression as well, requesting they be immediately dismissed for breach of security. What they had allowed to happen was far past a simple blunder; it was absolutely not acceptable. They had sorely failed in their duties of keeping him protected from all intruders, so why give them another chance to endanger him again?

When the guards caught sight of him, they each gave him an unmistakable look of pity. Seeing the way they looked at him filled him with rage – especially as it was they who were to blame for placing him in such a compromising situation. One that made him appear weak and not in control.

He realized now that, more than anything, he desired to be feared and obeyed, just as his father had before him. The last thing he wanted was their sympathy.

He would not let his emotions betray his diffidence and vulnerability now, as had happened far too many times in the past. Making an effort to conceal his disquietude, Fairuzo looked one of the guards squarely in the eye. When he spoke, it was with a newfound boldness and confidence: "So, where is that vulgar troll now? And is she receiving proper punishment?"

Fairuzo was surprised at the sudden surge of authoritative power he felt as he quizzed the guard. It was as if a mantle containing the essence of his father's brusque personality had been flung across his shoulders, manifesting and incorporating itself into his own persona. He greatly relished the overriding sense of supremacy this gave him.

It was true that, in the past, he had felt uneasy with the gruff manner in which he had seen his father deal with the underlings and agitators. It had just seemed so excessive. But now, he was able to see clearly how this ruthless assertion of forceful authority had instantly garnered him the respect and obedience he was entitled to as Lord.

Fairuzo never had any doubt that his father was the undisputed master at striking fear into even the most thick-headed and unruliest of trolls. He understood implicitly now that he would do well to emulate his methods so as to achieve the same effect.

Not surprisingly, the guards could immediately sense the change in his demeanor – his self-assured, almost overbearing manner – and the pitying looks on their faces quickly dissolved into ones of fearful respect.

"My Lord," one of them began to explain in a properly deferential tone, "Lamia has been dealt with and will not be interacting with you at any time in the future."

"In what way was the whore dealt with?" demanded Fairuzo impatiently. "I need details!"

"Well, we, uh --" stammered one of the guards nervously, "-- we escorted her straightaway to your father, Lord Phegor, to deal with her directly."

"And then?" asked Fairuzo, gesturing at the guard impatiently with a flutter of his hands.

"And then Lord Phegor pretty much beat the snotty black blood right out of her – I mean, to the point where she was actually crawling around on the ground sniveling and groveling for forgiveness," he replied.

"Yes," the other guard chuckled, "it was a damned thorough beating. She seemed remarkably submissive afterwards, bordering on contrite, you might even say – although I doubt at all that it was in any way sincere. Those of us who know what a cunning actress she can be are well aware of the trickery she will employ to get her way.

"All in all, though, the way Lord Phegor handled her was quite impressive," he finished, smiling fondly at the memory.

"He gave her a beating? A simple beating?" asked Fairuzo, growing increasingly irritated at the information he was being furnished. It was certainly not what he expected nor wanted to hear.

"Surely, she was punished more than that! She was not even banished?" he continued, his voice rising in agitation.

"Well, not exactly banished – not quite yet, that is," replied the first guard hesitantly.

"What do you mean – not quite yet?" exploded Fairuzo, losing all composure, the azure veins in his neck bulging like a straining parachute rope about to snap.

"I mean, she was given one last chance," explained the guard in a tone he hoped was placatory. "Due to her being technically part Royalty and all, you know, I suppose there's some clause that allows her one slip-up."

"But then Lord Phegor had a blood oath drawn up for her to sign," the other guard hastily interjected. "It was made clear in the contract language that if she *ever* crawled into bed with you again or told anyone of what had transpired inside your bedchamber, she would be immediately banished with no further warnings given. And then he forced her to sign it in blood."

"And that was not difficult to do at all, since she now had buckets of it available to finger-paint her name on the dotted line with," the first guard chimed in, fighting hard to keep from grinning at the visual.

Fairuzo shook his head angrily. He was extremely displeased that she was still on Tartarus and had not yet been banished. Should it not now be up to *him* to decide what the proper punishment for her should be, now that he was the New Lord?

Then again, perhaps there really *was* such a clause that entitled her to be given one more chance. It was definitely something that he would have to look into. And if that did indeed turn out to be true, there was nothing he could do to change the outcome. He could only hope that she tripped herself up somehow, and that it happened soon.

What he most needed was to hear the truth of their relationship from his father's own lips. He simply was unable to fathom how he could have possibly ended up in that hideous troll's womb. What had his father been thinking to bed her even once? Why, she was beyond foul!

It made no sense whatsoever, as his father had always prided himself on mating with only the most delectable succubi. He had never known him to even glance at or consider a lowly, smelly troll. And certainly not one as laden with warts, nasty rolls of flesh and stench as that one!

He still could not believe the audacity of the whore for believing herself exempt from the Cabal's one law forbidding fornication between Royalty offspring and the troll used as the incubation vessel. Did she actually think herself above the law that the rest of them were forced to follow? Was she *deliberately* trying to taint the bloodline?

Perhaps she had harbored the delusion that Fairuzo would find her so blindingly alluring that he would be willing to risk violating the taboo, all for the privilege of getting her between the sheets. Of course, he only would have known he was engaging in something forbidden if she had also revealed her true identity to him.

And if things had gone her way, perhaps she would have just been content with procuring his sexual favors, all while snickering to herself about how stupid he was not to know he was screwing his own troll-mother the whole time.

And what of his father? Had he also been planning to keep this secret from him his entire life? Why had it been kept from him at all? And if he had planned to reveal it to him one day, when would that have been, exactly?

The whole fiasco disgusted him so much he nearly felt like vomiting up all the wine and fresh, raw flesh he had binged on last night at the Ceremony.

Fairuzo slammed the door to his bedchamber behind him and stomped off down the hall that led to his father's quarters. One of the guards hurriedly locked the door behind him, then rushed to catch up.

"Hey, hold up there, Lord Fairuzo," he began, but the other guard quickly nudged and shushed him not to say anything more.

"It's just not our business," he whispered to him. "Let him find out for himself."

When they arrived at Lord Phegor's chambers, Fairuzo saw that the door was closed and appeared to be bolted from the inside. He drew his foot back and then smashed the lock with his boot as hard as he could. It disintegrated into a thousand tiny fragments, splintering the handle as well. He then shoved the door open so hard with the palms of his hands that it slammed against the stone wall behind it with a thunderous bang.

He no longer gave a damn what his father thought of his actions or what sort of punishment he might threaten him with. He had busted down the door to his private chambers instead of properly knocking: so what? He was damn pissed off and he wanted answers *now*!

Fairuzo rushed headlong inside to confront his father, then stopped short at the sight that greeted him: Phegor was bent over the bed with his pants down around his ankles. Upon seeing his son suddenly come bursting into the room, his eyes opened wide in surprise, then the corners of his lips twisted up in a self-satisfied smirk. He began laughing uproariously as if he found the situation incredibly amusing.

On the bed in front of him Lamia lay on her back, her fat, fleshy legs spread wide, her face still bloodied and swollen from the beating he'd given her the night before.

When she spotted Fairuzo, she leered. "Hey, come join in, honey! Let's have a three-some, keep it all in the family!" she cackled.

Fairuzo could only stare, horrified: what was *she* doing in the room? And with her legs opened wide for his father, yet! Had not the guards told him what she'd done to her own son last night?

Phegor did not look the least bit disconcerted or flustered at having been caught. He casually yanked up his pants and then roughly pushed Lamia off the bed. She fell headfirst in a heap on the floor with a loud thud.

"Now get the fuck out of here," he growled at her. "That's the last poking you'll ever get from me, you whore, so make the memory last."

He turned to the guards. "Get her out of here. Take her to the slave tunnel and shackle her, like we discussed."

As the guards grabbed ahold of her, Lamia began to protest, jerking her arms evasively behind her back in an effort to slip out of their grasp, but they quickly overpowered her.

"But you said you were taking me with you!" she yelled at Phegor. "You lying bastard!"

Phegor just guffawed again and waved her away, ordering the guards to silence her. They quickly located a sash to bind around her mouth as she continued to mumble and struggle.

"Just what the hell is going on around here!" Fairuzo yelled at his father.

Phegor shrugged. "I simply wanted one more piece before I left. One for the road, you might say. But don't worry, my lad, that was it; I'm completely done with her now. And I made sure that she won't be telling anyone that you two went at it last night."

"Nothing of the sort happened between us!" screamed Fairuzo. "It was all *she* who attacked *me*! I played no part in it at all!"

"Oh, okay, okay," said Phegor. "No need to get all bent out of shape. Maybe I got the story wrong. The way I heard it was that you wanted it. At any rate, she'll be taken and held downstairs for safekeeping where she can't come at you again – unless you want her to, that is.

"And hey, I don't mind at all that you had the hots for each other; but those are the Cabal's rules, you know? – no fornicating between the offspring of royalty and the dirty troll slut that took the seed," Phegor said. "No matter how good she is in the sack," he added, winking.

Fairuzo could only stare in disbelief at his father. He seemed determined to assume that his son had initiated the encounter and been complicit in it, and no amount of explaining seemed to convince him otherwise.

In fact, he was now almost certain that it had been Lamia who had twisted it around to where *she'd* been invited into *his* bed, when the truth was she'd snuck in there and forced herself upon him. He just couldn't understand why his own father would choose to believe that filthy slag's lies over his own son.

He now felt even further betrayed and violated all over again – but this time by a parent he had grown up with knowing for sure was his own father. As upset as he was now, he still needed to have some questions answered – like how such a repulsive troll had been chosen to be his mother in the first place, and if his father had ever planned to tell him who she really was.

He was actually rather relieved that his father's back was towards him now while he busied himself shoving articles of clothing and toiletries into knapsacks. He did not care to see the look of insouciance on his father's face nor did he wish for him to see his own hurt and bitter disappointment.

Fairuzo waited until the guards had dragged Lamia all the way out of the room and had closed what was left of the door behind them.

"So, how did this all happen? I mean, how did that hideous thing become my mother?" he asked, trying to keep his voice even without breaking.

His father slowly turned around to face him. Then, with a sigh of resignation, he said, "All right. Sit down, boy, and I'll tell you the story. I suppose I do owe you that much."

CHAPTER 30

THE PROTOTYPE AND THE MOB

As Fairuzo navigated the way back to the Ballroom, he kept his arm wrapped tightly around my waist. Although I could have interpreted this as an outward display of affection, the firmness of his grip felt more like a domineering ploy to prevent me from slipping off again, as well as a subtle way of letting me know I was under his control.

Still, it gave me a comforting sense of having a protector, which was becoming a necessity in this hostile, alien world rife with perils and pitfalls. Even Procel, with all of his knowledge, experience and kind intentions, had been helpless to shield either of us from the demon stealth-attack in the laboratory.

It did appear as if, for now, Fairuzo was letting me off the hook for all of my previous snubs, giving me this one last chance to redeem myself by cooperating. And the closer we got to the Ballroom, the more apprehensive I felt about the refreshments and festivities he had planned for me.

I wondered how I was going to wriggle my way out of participating again this time without the risk of reopening the floodgates of his fury – for I had absolutely no intention of engaging in any activity that went against my conscience and gut instincts. So far, I had found these inner guides to be extremely useful measuring tools with which to determine right from wrong, and they had never led me astray.

As we made our way back, I began to feel as if we were adrift in an endless labyrinth, wandering aimlessly through a maze of dead-ends and passageways branching out into identical-looking corridors. I began to wonder if we were actually going back a different route, as much of what we passed did not seem at all familiar.

As if reading my mind, Fairuzo asked me, "Does it seem to you as if we are going back a different way?"

I admitted that it did, and he laughed.

"That's because all of the tunnels and corridors are internally programmed to transpose and switch direction if a visitor passing through without a key is detected. It's a foolproof system for discouraging those foolish enough to believe they'll find a way out. They're guaranteed to encounter nothing but blind alleys, becoming hopelessly lost."

The system certainly seemed to be working, as I felt thoroughly disoriented. I doubted that I would have been able to find my way back on my own even if the tunnel infrastructure *hadn't* been altered.

As it was, I had never been blessed with much of an inner compass. I could barely tell east from west – which made it all the more imperative that I have Procel along to guide me when we did attempt our escape.

Fairuzo then introduced the topic of bounty hunters, which he proceeded to expound upon with great relish.

"The Cabal has set up a special task force of bounty hunters, each professionally trained in tracking down escapees from Tartarus," he explained.

"In order to locate these fugitives, a sophisticated global positioning system is utilized, which has been programmed to match cellular tissue extracted from the violator's soul stored in our Soul Warehouse.

"This system has been so effective that not one single renegade has ever managed to evade capture – not one. In fact, just recently, one troll – who thought he was being incredibly clever – went to Earth presumably for provisions but with the imprudent plan of not returning afterwards.

"Well, let me tell you, the bounty hunters instantly tracked his whereabouts. He was found decapitated, his head nowhere to be seen and his torso burnt to a crisp. His lungs had lost their capacity to inflate, and he had slowly and agonizingly suffocated while being fried in the sun like grease popping in a hot skillet."

Here, he paused for effect, swiveling his head to look deliberately at both Procel and I.

"You see, this dim-witted troll had foolishly forgotten about the limitations of his lungs and what occurs when one overstays the allotted time in Earth's atmosphere. And, as he had no soul with which to barter, he was not eligible for redemption or recycling. Therefore, he was sentenced to banishment. His missing head is now eternally entrenched in the purgatory of the Frozen Lake of Cocytus."

As Fairuzo finished relating this frightening tale, it was obvious it was meant to serve as a very transparent warning to the both of us, making it clear what would befall us if we decided to go through with our escape plans.

Cocking his head towards me, he remarked, "You know I only want what's best for you, don't you, Enmira?"

Rather than replying disingenuously or blurting out something that would most likely precipitate an argument, I remained silent. But what I *really* wanted to ask him was: how, then, could he be so insistent upon keeping me here in a place where I was obviously so unhappy?

Ensuring I could never leave certainly did not seem to be at all in my best interest, but rather a selfish desire designed for his own purposes. However, the implied threat in his message did not go unheeded – which seemed to be that if I were to attempt an escape, I would be immediately intercepted and then punished swiftly and severely – or worse. Even so, I still refused to give up hope that there was some way to outwit these bounty hunters and successfully make it back to Earth.

As we finally arrived back at the door that led into the Ballroom, I could hear the muffled beats and discordant music of the band, along with the wild cheering and yelling of trolls participating in whatever mischief they were now up to.

I could feel Fairuzo's grip on my waist tighten, as if he could sense my great reluctance to go back in. And his intuition was correct: I was suddenly seized with dread at what awaited me inside. It was indeed the last place on this Godforsaken planet that I wanted to be right now.

"You hear the fun they are having?" asked Fairuzo pointedly. "I just don't understand why you are having such a hard time enjoying yourself here, Enmira. I've provided you with everything that could possibly be desired for your Initiation – there's live music, delicious treats and all sorts of amusements! Do you not like being entertained?"

Again, I remained silent. I could only think to myself that my idea of entertainment did not include bashing each others' heads in and wrestling around on puddles of blood over petty quarrels. His idea of fun and especially what constituted edible treats was worlds away from mine.

Before I even had a chance to balk, Fairuzo propelled me through the door with one strong push, Procel following closely behind. After having been in the hushed shadows of the dim, torch-lit cavern tunnels for so long, the intense light inside nearly blinded me. The shrill shouting and pounding drums made my skull feel like earwigs were burrowing into it with pickaxes.

The globe dangling from the ceiling pulsated and glittered as it illuminated the chaos unfolding below. The trolls were in various states of undress, dozens of them piled on top of each other in a variety of sexual positions. Others were on their hands and knees watching and drooling while pleasuring themselves. Their moans and grunts could be heard even over the din of the music.

"Ahhh," cooed Fairuzo in a pleased voice. "The orgy is in full swing. Doesn't *that* look pleasurable, Enmira?" he asked, giving me a suggestive look.

Actually, it did *not* look pleasurable at all. The trolls' flaccid rolls of flesh shook and jiggled unattractively, and their genitals were on full display, covered with what appeared to be festering sores. Just looking at them made me want to retch.

I could only hope that they were so inebriated by now that they would not even notice my reappearance. But my hopes of this were soon dashed when Fairuzo clapped his hands and waved at the band, signaling for them to stop playing. The mantid musicians immediately halted the ruckus they were making, each carefully setting down their various instruments upon the stage.

"Okay, Turquoisians!" he shouted. "I do apologize for interrupting the fun, but we must move on to more delicious refreshments in honor of our guest, Enmira!"

The trolls carried on as if he had not spoken. Fairuzo waited a few seconds, then walked rapidly over to the table, picked up the now-empty punch bowl, and hurled it with full force a few-hundred yards away. It smashed against the limestone wall into a million shards of crystalline glass.

This immediately got their attention, and they looked up with startled expressions. Then, one by one, each slowly and unsteadily stood up and turned around to face Fairuzo, most not even bothering to pull up their drawers or cover their unsightly unclad bodies.

"Do I now have your full and undivided *attention*, all Turquoisian trolls?" he yelled, his voice booming and echoing around the cavernous room.

They all nodded obediently, chanting "Yes, Lord and Master Fairuzo" in unison.

"All right then. As I was saying, the time has come for the Dessert of Enticement to be served to our Guest of Honor and newest initiate, Miss Enmira," Fairuzo continued.

As he gestured grandly towards me, I could literally feel the collective animosity in the room. Their squinty little bloodshot eyes were all focused upon me with intense stares of hatred.

Fairuzo clapped his hands again and turned to face

the area behind the bandstand. The trolls all swiveled their stumpy necks to follow his gaze. Right at that moment, a creature appeared in the doorway carrying a tray.

Oh, no! I thought to myself in dismay, vividly recalling the horror of what had been on the last tray. I did not think I could bear to go through that nightmarish scene again.

Procel, standing just behind me, inched closer and whispered excitedly into my ear, "Look, Enmira, this is exactly what I spoke of! It is one of the first prototypes of the Creoboros mutations that will be guarding the exits!"

Making its way towards us was a dog with three heads. But instead of the expected canine body, each of the heads was attached to the torso of a large, furry tarantula with the eight tentacle-arms of an octopus. And in the place of orbs sunk into sockets, each dog-head sported two eyeballs on the ends of long, flexible stalks that resembled dual periscopes, continuously bouncing and rotating in all directions.

The pitiful mutant crawled slowly towards us, holding on to the tray with two elongated tube-shaped siphons attached to the front of its body. It swayed crookedly from side to side, and each of the dog-heads emitted tiny yelping sounds as if each step it took caused it great pain.

"The joints are not properly aligned," Procel said with a displeased scowl. "It's clear to see that the creature is experiencing a great deal of distress simply from walking."

"And take note of its body and legs, Enmira," he continued. "It is a combination of Earth's rarest of creatures: the blue-blooded mollusc and the blue-blooded arachnid -- not coincidentally the same color of blood as that which coagulates in the veins of all Mount Hermon Royalty.

"Oh, I see!" I exclaimed, simultaneously experiencing both horror and incredulity. "I can tell he is part spider and part octopus; but what a bizarre combination that is, especially with all of the dog heads!"

"Yes, it causes one to wonder to what ulterior purpose

that choice of blood will serve?" Procel asked. "Perhaps something to do with the future breeding of slaves to create a new subservient species with homogeneous bloodlines? That would make the most sense."

I could only stare in pity at the poor deformed creature, unable to even imagine what sort of horrible experiments he had been subjected to. Or was it a *they* -- three separate dogs, each with their own individual sentience? And which head was in charge of controlling the movements and the appendages of the body? It was all quite confusing – and disturbing.

I recalled Procel having told me how all of the head transplants attempted so far had failed to produce any sort of mobility, with the body left paralyzed below the brainstem after each experimental surgery. But apparently the wicked scientists had since made a bit of progress in fusing the necks together with the spinal cord, although it was still obviously not optimal or in its final, finished form.

What I was witnessing went far beyond unnatural; no one should have any right to do this to another living being. The sort of depravity entailed in conceiving and constructing these monstrosities was simply unfathomable. All of this mad tinkering with life just to exert power over these meek creatures and force them into a miserable existence of torment and slavery!

The Creoboros-mutant limped and winced his way over to where we were standing, and then submissively offered the tray to Fairuzo. I took a quick peek at the serving platter, afraid of what I might see there. I felt a great relief that no sort of animal, either dead or alive, was curled upon it this time.

Instead, there was a small, heart-shaped bowl that looked to be made out of faceted periwinkle fluorite. It contained a luminously glowing blue substance with the consistency of pudding. It seemed to be alive, bubbling and pulsating rhythmically like volcanic lava being pumped through an aorta.

Just then a loud thought popped into my head as if it were being whispered urgently into my ear:

"Electromagnetic radiation is emitted when a charged particle or electron passes through a dielectric medium at a speed greater than the phase velocity of light. The blue glow of an underwater nuclear reactor is due to radiation. When absorbed, radiation causes cellular degradation by damaging the DNA and other key molecular structures within the cells in various tissues."

I glanced over at Procel and he gave a slight nod of his head, as if to acknowledge that those words had indeed originated from him. I interpreted this as his way of warning me that the substance in the bowl was dangerously radioactive. Whatever was lurking in there, it certainly did not look appetizing or even edible.

Fairuzo plucked the bowl off of the tray and held it up high for all to see.

"Here we have our irresistible Dessert of Enticement – a most delectable *con*fection of sugary *per*fection. It has the sweet taste of the ripest blueberries and the scent of a most fragrant floral blend of Blue Belladonna, Lobelia and Blue Cupid's Dart," he proclaimed with obvious pride.

"Not only will you delight in its divine taste but it will make you deliriously happy as well," he added buoyantly.

Unconvinced that it possessed any of these marvelous properties, I peered at the dessert with a great deal of distrust. It continued to throb and quiver, strobing and undulating like a bluefire jellyfish held captive in a bucket.

Fairuzo continued on with his sales pitch: "Oh, yes, you will feel as if you are floating on clouds without a care in the world. Come on, now, just try a little bite and you will see what I mean!"

The harder he tried to convince me to taste it, the more determined I became that I wanted no part of it. Again, as with the wine, there appeared to be some sort of ulterior motive behind his eagerness for me to consume this dessert.

However, I decided I would at least make it appear as if I were cooperating somewhat, and so I bent my head down and warily sniffed the bowl's contents. I did not detect the slightest hint of fruit or floral fragrance. In fact, it gave off the same unpleasant synthetic malodour as the liquid in the goblet had.

"It smells like chemicals," I announced matter-of-factly.

Fairuzo sighed loudly. "Again with the criticisms and excuses not to try anything new," he grumbled. "What does it take to please you, Enmira?"

He picked up a small copper ladle-spoon from the tray and plunged it into the thick phosphorescent mass. He then held out a spoonful of the vibrating blue goop to me as if he were presenting a much-coveted prize to a winning contestant.

"Come on, baby," he said sweetly, giving me a most winsome smile. "At least just take one little bite. You'll never know how much you might like it until you try it!"

He brought the spoon nearer to my mouth and I began shaking my head and slowly backing away.

"No! I do *not* want to try it! It smells awful, just like the wine. And there were snakes in there that you did not bother to warn me about! How do I even know what you have hidden in *this*?" I exclaimed.

"Oh, you are being so silly!" he retorted. "I don't see what the big deal is. I cannot believe you are refusing yet another exquisite delicacy selected just for you! Do you not trust me?"

As I stared back at him, I thought I detected a look of sadness in his eyes. This completely took me by surprise, as I had fully expected him to be furious with me by now for yet another rebuff. Instead, he looked disappointed, crestfallen even – almost as if his feelings were hurt! But was this simply a clever performance to gain my sympathy and convince me to eat the dessert?

Regardless, I had already made up my mind that I was not going to take one single bite of this witches' brew of a concoction. Procel had already discreetly relayed his warning to me and I would be a fool to disregard it.

Whatever sort of toxic ingredients the bowl contained would surely have a most unwelcome and deleterious effect on me, perhaps even putting me in a state where I had no control over my own actions. And the last thing I needed was to not have my complete wits about me when surrounded by so many that wished to do me harm.

And yet I was still undecided: Was Fairuzo one of those wishing to do me harm? I vacillated between wanting to place my trust in him and feeling suspicious of his motives.

The trolls began to express their immense displeasure at my disobedience, shuffling in closer from behind to jab me with their sharp, spiny elbows. I could almost feel their eyes burning into the back of my head as they muttered venomously: "Ungrateful bitch. We don't want you here!" and "You are no better than us. How dare you refuse our gifts of hospitality!"

Just then one of them sidled up to me, grabbing ahold of my forearm, her sharp, ragged nails raking and digging into my skin. I immediately recognized her as the bitter Achlys, otherwise known as the "Viral Lamenter," as Procel had so dubbed her.

"You won't last long as Fairuzo's lover," she hissed maliciously into my ear. "You will be easily replaced, just as I was. Don't be stupid; eat the dessert and become one of us for when he discards you!"

I could smell her rancid breath; her body reeked of death and decay. As I tried to free my arm from her talons, she leaned forward aggressively and knocked her shoulder into mine with a vicious shove, throwing me off balance. She snickered and then slithered away.

The crowd of trolls began encircling me, forming a tighter and tighter ring of hostility around me until it felt as if I were being squeezed and suffocated by a mammoth boa constrictor.

All this time, Fairuzo was standing frozen in place like a marble statue, holding the bowl and spoon out to me with that same forlorn expression. He seemed to be begging me with his eyes not to disappoint him. I felt a flood of emotions then, torn between wanting to please him yet realizing that giving in would result in nothing but the most dire consequences.

Some of the trolls swarming around me began kicking my shins and stepping on my heels with the gnarled, crusty toes of their bare feet, others ripping chunks of hair out of my head as if for souvenirs.

I began to panic and looked around for Procel, but he was nowhere to be found. *What a time he picked to desert me*, I thought in desperation. *And doesn't Fairuzo see or care that the trolls are starting to attack me?*

In fact, they were now grabbing and yanking at my gown, deliberately plucking off as many seashells and rhinestones as they could get their claws on, then triumphantly holding up the handfuls of baubles as if they were trophies. As they busied themselves at this task, they made ferocious grunting noises along with obscene slurping sounds, as if they wanted to devour me along with my dress.

Just as I feared they were about to start taking bites out of my flesh and literally eating me alive, Fairuzo finally snapped out of his daze and sprang into action. He tossed the bowl of dessert back onto the tray. Leaping forward, he backhanded the faces of the trolls nearest me with a wild, forceful sweep of his arm. They flew into the air like a slew of clay pigeons being ejected simultaneously, each landing with a dull thud on the hard limestone floor.

"Back! Back off, you vile, stupid cretins!" he yelled, raising both arms in the air as warning. The crowd of trolls stumbled clumsily backwards, falling over each other in their haste to get out of the pathway of his wrath. Others scattered in all directions to avoid blows from his wide-swinging fists.

He then grabbed ahold of my waist and hoisted me high above his head. Holding me aloft like the wicker basket of a hot air balloon, he began marching us towards the rear of the Ballroom.

With the raw force of a cyclonic tank, he furiously kicked and knocked over any still-standing trolls that were in his way. Like the fragile papyrus reeds embedded in the Lake of Tanis, the ocean of trolls bent and snapped in the wake of his powerful gale, causing them to part and form a dry seaway bed that allowed us smooth passage.

Looking down from my vantage point far above, I felt an exhilarating sense of unbridled power. It was as if I were hydroplaning across the crest of a massive tidal wave rushing out to sea. I must confess it was quite the vindicative thrill to see the formerly-vicious mob of trolls now cowering in fear and being forced to scurry out of our way.

When we reached the back wall of the Ballroom, Fairuzo set me down. "Just one moment more and I'll have us out of here," he promised.

He swung his left leg back and held it rigidly in place behind him as if it were an arrow being drawn taut in a bow. Taking careful aim, he let his foot fly. The toe of his boot smashed through the wall with the force of a steel wrecking ball. Upon impact, an oval door instantly materialized and swung open, revealing a narrow carpeted hallway.

"The Royal Chambers," Fairuzo said simply, by way of explanation. He grabbed my hand and pulled me through the opening. The door slammed shut behind us with a thunderous crash, leaving no indication that a portal had ever existed.

CHAPTER 31

THE DEN OF DATURA

𝕵ust up ahead, two menacing-looking ogres stood guard in front of what appeared to be the very same spiral staircase that Fairuzo had initially led me down on our journey here. I was actually shocked to see that it still existed. I'd had the impression that the entire stairway had simply vanished after we'd reached the bottom.

I distinctly recalled noticing at one point in our descent that all behind us had turned into a vast expanse of black nothingness, including the stairs we had just taken. But perhaps it had just appeared so, and had actually only been obscured by the dense fog surrounding us.

I wondered now if the steps still led all the way back up to the portal in my closet. But when I tried to determine how far up the staircase went, I could not see much more beyond the first five stairs. If it did go any higher, it was well-hidden in the swirling gray mist that floated just above it.

Nonetheless, I began to feel a growing excitement: Might this not actually be the best route of escape back to Earth, possibly even the *only* way? After all, it was the only bridge between Tartarus and Earth that I was aware of.

Although I had no idea if the stairs could be ascended, or where it was they even ended, it was at least worth a try – providing, of course, one could figure out a way around the savage-looking behemoths standing guard. Perhaps there were times when they were off-duty and a short break or lapse between shifts occurred?

As I made a mental note to ask Procel about this, I wondered why he had not mentioned this particular avenue as an escape strategy before. It certainly seemed to me to be the most viable option.

It was not an easy task keeping up with Fairuzo as he walked briskly and purposefully towards the guards. He held on tightly to my hand, effectively pulling me along after him. His fingers entwined with mine were as icy cold to the touch as they had been the first time I'd felt them. Although I still found his glacial body temperature peculiar and a bit troubling, I was actually becoming almost accustomed to it.

As we approached the guards, they greeted him cordially, each bowing deeply and reverently before him: "Good evening, Master Fairuzo."

One of the guards politely inquired, "Has the Initiation come to a close, then, My Lord?"

Brushing aside the question, Fairuzo spoke sternly: "I am going to need each of you to make absolutely certain that this area is completely secure. No one – and I mean *no one* – is allowed back here, even those with keys. I am not to be disturbed under any circumstances. Have I made myself perfectly clear?"

The guards both nodded eagerly in acknowledgement, one of them replying, "Yes, Master. We understand your orders completely. You will not be disturbed; we will make sure of it."

They both bowed again, and we continued on down the hallway past the staircase.

As we walked, I began to wonder: This was obviously where Fairuzo maintained his private quarters, but who else might obtain access, or be allowed back here, that the guards would be on watch for? And who else would have a set of keys?

Procel was the only one who immediately came to mind. But being a Duke, surely his royal status would allow him access to anywhere in the Kingdom. Therefore, it seemed odd that Fairuzo might order he be denied admittance to this particular area – especially if he, too, kept his own living quarters back here.

One thing I knew for certain: it was highly unlikely

that any of the trolls would be entrusted with such a privilege as having keys. And so, who else was there, aside from the slaves and the guards?

The thought suddenly struck me: how was it, then, that Darceva had managed to gain access to the off-limits laboratory area behind the bandstand, along with her accomplice Dantanian? Surely only the scientists should have been allowed to roam freely back there, yet there they both had been, in hiding and anticipating our arrival.

Did I dare ask Fairuzo these things? I decided it would be best not to take the chance of fouling his mood or arousing his temper. He seemed in such cheerful spirits and we were getting along so splendidly.

As we rounded the corner, we came upon a dome-shaped vestibule with the ambiance of an enchanted garden. It appeared to serve as some sort of waiting area, with several wedge-shaped, jute-sack pillows placed symmetrically around the perimeter, allowing one to comfortably lean back. Upon the wall were intricately webbed patterns of creeping kudzu vines with long, hairy pods, intertwined with stalks of black henbane. Various vespertines and witches' weeds were dotted throughout the foliage-web like spiders awaiting their hapless prey.

Mature mandrake plants were strewn about as if tossed randomly out of a basket onto the gleaming blue-and-gold-veined floor. Their fleshy, forked roots were naked and fully exposed, revealing human-like torsos and bent legs that resembled voodoo dolls with exploding bell-shaped heads. The flowers were in full bloom, evidently flourishing without visible aid of soil, water or sunlight.

A thick net made up of spruce root and wild grass hung from the curved ceiling, as if a trawler had placed it there to entice and entrap wayward fish swimming upstream. Colorful garlands of devil's trumpets and moonflowers dangled alluringly through the knotted mesh-holes like ripe, savory bunches of grapes waiting to be plucked and eaten.

On either side of the portal opening hung a dense, parted curtain of wisteria, comprised of long strands of iridescent pearls interwoven into thick ropes of blood-red, black-hearted poppies.

It was then that I noticed a small copper sign that hung in the middle of the archway between the pearls and the poppies. Upon it was scrolled *"Den of Datura,"* and under that, a most curious poem, indicating some sort of enigmatic pact along with an explicit warning:

"Those who linger in the Garden do hereby give consent
For in the Realm of Nothingness lies nothing to lament
Immortal hands of cold will gather all things mortal there
Fair warning now is given to proceed with utmost care!"

The reference to cold immortal hands sent a shiver up my spine. A chilling wave of morbidity washed over me, and I hastily slipped my own hand out of Fairuzo's frigid one.

And even though I did not understand precisely what it meant, I took its warning to heart. I certainly had no intention of giving any such consent for whatever mortal things it was intent upon gathering, nor did a Realm of Nothingness sound at all inviting.

"Just hold on a minute," I said, stopping abruptly. "What does that sign mean?"

I was now quite worried and veering back into distrust.

Fairuzo smiled cryptically and said, "Hiding in plain sight."

"What?" I asked. "But what does that even mean?" I had absolutely no idea what he was referring to.

"It simply means do not linger here for too long or you may come to regret it," he answered. "It also means we're entering the inner sanctum of my Royal Chambers Suite and we need to keep going."

I stood there obstinate, refusing to move. I felt I had every right to be cautious before deciding to venture any further.

"Come, come, Enmira," said Fairuzo insistently, tugging gently on the tattered sleeve of my dress. He reached out his hand and whimsically twirled a piece of my hair between his fingers.

"Let's not dawdle, shall we? We're almost there. You don't want to turn into a pillar of salt just standing here, do you?" He chuckled, apparently amused, but I failed to see the humor.

"If I continue onward, what will I be giving my consent to?" I asked, still trying to decipher the meaning of the sign.

"And why would you need to know that?" asked Fairuzo. "Have you got a better place to spend your time?"

He certainly had me there. As badly as I wanted to get back to Earth, I was basically stuck here and at his mercy. And since I could neither retrace my steps backwards nor remain in this foyer forever, it was obvious that my only choice was to go forward.

I would just have to resign myself to facing and dealing with whatever it was that awaited me after I crossed over that threshold.

CHAPTER 32

THE SEDUCTION

After witnessing the trolls' outrageously hostile behavior towards Enmira in the Ballroom, Fairuzo was even more convinced he had made the right decision to bar them all from participating in her Consummation Ceremony.

The standard procedure was to have all the trolls join in after he had taken his own sordid liberties, passing the hapless neophyte around like a cheap jug of Ripple. Watching them each having their revolting way with his newest initiate always gave Fairuzo a deliciously voyeuristic thrill. He would then drag the spent and worn-out trollop to his private lair for further lascivious activities.

On the way to his Royal Chambers, he would encourage her to linger as long as she liked in the Den of Datura, where he would join her in the leisurely partaking of the myriad of delightfully intoxicating refreshments available there.

But there would be no sampling of the Den's wares this evening for either Enmira or himself. He would be forgoing this part of the Initiation routine as well. He realized that any further attempts at persuading her to consume anything she might perceive as mind-altering would be just precious time wasted.

After all, she had already staunchly refused both the goblet *and* the dessert, and he simply could not afford the luxury of tarrying. He had much more urgent and rewarding pursuits in mind. And what was first and foremost on the agenda was getting Enmira to his bedchambers as quickly as possible so as to have her all to himself.

Unfortunately, without the aid of any inhibition-numbing substances, her still-intact, prudish sensibilities would undoubtedly prove to be a most bothersome obstacle, one that would require massive amounts of wile and beguilement on his part if he wished to achieve his goal.

He would have to depend solely upon his raw seductive charms to woo her into his bed. But he had quite a bit of faith in his own powers of persuasion. After all, he had received many years of explicit, hands-on instruction from the very Master of All Things Lustful: his own father, Lord Phegor.

In fact, it had become the custom over many centuries for Phegor to be present at many of Fairuzo's Consummation Ceremonies. He had simply shown up one day announcing he would be joining in, and thereafter had made it a habit to put in an appearance whenever the fancy struck him.

Fairuzo had always found it curious his father would even be interested in the cocottes he recruited from Earth for his own personal harem, as he already had his pick of the most succulent succubi back home at Mount Hermon. He couldn't help feeling a bit resentful that it was simply another opportunity for Phegor to flaunt his sexual prowess, which usually resulted in making him feel decidedly inadequate in comparison.

It was as if he were in a sort of competition with his own father, who behaved more like a rival sibling than a parent, especially when it came to matching him stroke-for-stroke in any sexcapade.

And even though Phegor had handed over all keys to the Kingdom a long time ago, he still insisted on wearing the cloak of ruling tyrant on the occasions he visited.

Even worse, Fairuzo was forced to endure a full critique of every aspect of his sexual performance by his father afterwards. Phegor took obvious pleasure in reciting a long list of what he'd deemed to be poorly-executed moves and fumbles that weren't up to his level of proficiency.

Fairuzo had come to almost dread those Initiations when Phegor was present; he was always so relieved when his father went back to his own planet and he was free of his overshadowing, domineering presence.

Although Phegor cheerily referred to this ordeal as a father and son sex-bonding ritual, Fairuzo felt it actually drove a deeper wedge in between them, serving only to reinforce the notion that he would never be able to measure up or please his father. And more and more lately, he had basically given up even trying to. Just once he wished he could have something all to himself instead of having his father constantly horning in and taking control whenever he so pleased.

On more than one occasion, Phegor had abruptly shoved him off of a naked vixen right in the middle of coitus, yelling out, "Let me show you how it's done, boy!" Pushed to the sidelines, Fairuzo would burn and smolder in humiliation while the trollop screamed like a mountain lion in heat, apparently having forgotten all about him once his father hopped onboard.

It was not surprising then that Fairuzo was extremely relieved whenever his father did not consider it worth his while to show up for an Initiation, or when he decided not to stay for very long, citing either the unappealing looks of the initiate or some pressing Cabal business he needed to attend to. But, for the most part, he was raring to go, even if the wench was not what he considered top prime grade quality.

The dirtier and sluttier they were, the better Phegor liked them. Those were the kind most eager to please and not opposed to any immoderate roughness or over-the-top crudity. He could impose the most obscene acts of perversion upon those types for hours without a whimper or complaint from them.

Fairuzo had grown accustomed to his neophytes transparently displaying a preference for his father after he'd taken over the reins and ravished them with his sex magick. He had also learned not to let it bother him too much any more.

But it was different with Enmira.

Not only was Fairuzo extremely reluctant to share her with the filthy, vile trolls who had so disrespected her, but the mere thought of anyone else touching her filled him with a jealous rage. This included his own father – *especially* his father.

So his determination to keep Enmira away from all clammy, grabbing hands other than his own was yet another tradition he would be deviating from this evening. In fact, this would be the first Initiation *ever* that he had deliberately not informed his father of.

So far, his father had not put in an appearance. And although this gave Fairuzo a sense of relief, the evening was far from over; he might yet pop in after all. Perhaps he was not even fazed by being left out of the loop, or perhaps he was just busy elsewhere.

But even if he discovered that his father was mightily displeased and insulted at having been excluded, Fairuzo simply did not care; he would do whatever it took to keep him away from Enmira. He felt like he needed to protect her from being soiled and tarnished by all those not worthy of her – and that included everyone but himself.

This overwhelming possessiveness felt new and unfamiliar to Fairuzo; it was totally out of his character. It seemed to have sprung out of nowhere like a crouching beast suddenly pouncing upon its prey. It had a powerful hold over him, and there seemed little he could do to control it.

Frankly, he could not recall even one other Earth-Tart with whom he had been so desperate to lay with in bed, to see unclothed and open to him and willing to submit. There was the usual anticipation with each one, of course, but none of this almost desperate craving he felt now to be in her company every hour of the day and evening, to touch her all over, to hear her declare how she, too, felt the same burning desire towards him.

Ever since he had first laid eyes upon her, he had done nothing but impatiently bide his time until the moment he had her in the most obliging state conceivable, tucked in between the sheets of his bed. He even felt it was within the realm of possibility that he might still retain this delirious longing even after the consummation. But that would remain to be seen; he would not know how he genuinely felt until afterwards.

He had decided this would be the true litmus test: that only after his physical lust had been quenched and satiated would he be able to discern and realize his true feelings, disentangled and separated from the carnality.

Only after experiencing for himself how it felt to be naked beside and inside her would he discover if this covetous yearning was only for something not yet obtained and still a mystery, and not yet a part of his memory.

Only then would he know if this invasive pruritus was merely a prurient itch that, once scratched and resolved, might even just simply evaporate, as if it never held significance or merit.

Aside from not wanting to waste any time, he had not attempted to persuade her to consume any of the Datura treats because he wanted her wide awake for him, fully coherent and cognizant. Having had to deal with other neophytes in various stages of unconsciousness had actually been rather annoying. He'd had to lug and half-carry them to his boudoir, and then give them a series of face-slaps to snap them out of their apathetic drowsiness.

Not that he minded having his way with any of them while they were unconscious. He actually enjoyed using their unresponsive bodies to simulate acts of necrophilia. In fact, for those he deemed not quite attractive enough to be brought back to Tartarus, he would first suck and drain all of the blood out of them until their veins resembled dry creekbeds, and then use their desiccated bodies for a quick and efficient copulation before discarding them.

Fairuzo found it quite humorous to think that the undertaker, upon the discovery and preparation of the corpse, would get the shock of his life when he realized that most of the embalming process had already been taken care of.

But with Enmira, he wanted to see her visibly responding to his sexual stimulation, reciprocating with her own heightened passion. He had pictured this scenario in his mind many times the past few days: having her between his silken bedsheets behaving like the most experienced and skillful courtesan, in complete compliance with all of his wishes and demands.

Of course, Enmira had no idea that such a ceremony was even planned for her. He was also certain she had no inkling of the magnitude of lewd, romantic thoughts he had been constantly entertaining about her.

But she was finally here with him en route to his private quarters where his royal bed awaited their inevitable, combustible union. And, as he had so succinctly reminded her, she really did have nowhere better to be than here with him.

And so, now, Fairuzo held out both hands to her, and she reluctantly stepped through the portal with him into the lobby of the Royal Chambers.

So far, she had not seemed at all impressed by much of what he had shown her in his Kingdom. And so it was with a great deal of pride and pleasure that he observed her reaction to the garish, extravagant décor that lay before her. She seemed appropriately bedazzled and awe-stricken, even overwhelmed, and he knew this would aid greatly in his seduction.

"It's like a palace!" she gasped.

Damned right it's like a palace, Fairuzo thought indignantly to himself. Did she not realize he was royalty?

It had taken many months and dozens of slaves to create this masterpiece of opulence. The ceiling was flecked with glittering scallion quartz chips, the walls encrusted with Paraiba tourmaline gemstones of a most brilliant oceanic blue. The mirrored floors gleamed with amber-blue veins of pyrite and azurite, reflecting both of their images and making the room appear as if it floated upon a tranquil, bottomless lake filled with gold.

Tall orange flames flickered and pirouetted in elegant copper torches ensconced in beautifully detailed brass urns next to scrolled columns, throwing long shadows on the elegant tapestries that hung like draperies from the translucent green ceiling.

Just up ahead was another spiral staircase; but this one led downwards. Each step was magnificently carpeted in an exotic pattern of deepest teal brocade.

Still holding on to both of her hands, Fairuzo pulled her along with him to the landing at the top of the stairs that led down to his private chambers. As her heel sank into the soft, velvety carpeting on the first step, she let out a small shriek. It startled him for a moment, and he was afraid she might be in pain.

"What is wrong?" he asked her, alarmed.

"I've lost both of my shoes!" she exclaimed.

She then blushed, as if she felt foolish for making a fuss over such a trifling matter.

"The trolls must have stolen them," she hurriedly added. "Or perhaps they slipped off when you carried me out of the Ballroom," she ended lamely.

Fairuzo turned to look directly at her, taking in every inch of her appearance: her magnificent turquoise gown was shredded and torn, and minus most of its adornments; she was missing chunks of hair on the sides and back of her head; her eye make-up was smeared and her face streaked with dirt. And yet she looked just as exquisitely alluring as when he'd first lain eyes upon her on Earth.

"Oh, is that all?" He laughed in relief, unable to look away or take his gaze off of her.

"Enmira," he continued, looking directly into her eyes, "there is no need to worry your pretty little head over such trivialities. Don't you realize I will provide for you everything that you crave? There is no need for you to concern yourself with such things! I shall give you as many pairs of shoes as your heart desires!"

He cupped his hands around her chin and pressed his face close to hers.

"Don't you know how much I want you? I'll do anything to make you mine," he purred in a low, sultry voice, his turquoise cat's eyes transmitting intense electromagnetic beams of ardor into her hazel-green ones. Fairuzo could literally feel the electrical current sparking and crackling between them.

This was the closest they'd been to each other since that first night when he'd come into her bed.

He leaned forward and touched his lips to hers. His tongue probed inside her mouth tenderly and tentatively, his frosty breath tunneling and burrowing inside her throat like a wintergreen arctic wind.

Fairuzo felt a searing bolt of lightning burn inside his closed eyelids, jagged and hot; he felt dizzy and hungry and thirsty all at once. When he opened his eyes, Enmira was staring back dreamily at him.

He picked her up, pressing her close against his chest, cradling her in his arms. As he painstakingly made his way down the flight of stairs, he held her as if she were fragile porcelain made of precious clay and bone ash.

He marveled at how light she was to lift and carry. But it was not so much her lack of weight but more her acquiescent demeanor, her eagerness to comply, her willingness to submit. Her face seemed to soften when she looked at him now. He noticed that she no longer seemed so defiant or combative, but actually almost beholden to him.

And as he descended the stairs with her in his arms, he felt an odd sense of hope. It was an unfamiliar sensation, but one he welcomed. He felt nervous yet excited at what was in store for the two of them together. He now had something he had never before even contemplated: hope for the future.

A future with her.

He began to think ahead to what he would do after he carried her over the threshold into his bedchamber. He instinctively knew that she could not be treated roughly or crudely like the others. Throwing her down upon his bed and then pouncing on her aggressively like a barbarian would simply not do at all.

He would be gentle and attentive, ensuring that her needs were met first before his own. He would begin with a masterful massage, kneading her supple body all over with his skilled, capable fingers. She would become quivering putty in his hands for him to sculpt and mold.

The thought then struck him how much more confident he felt whenever his father wasn't around, constantly judging and criticizing and upstaging him. Without him there, he did not have to worry about competing or being pushed to the sidelines, leaving him frustrated and simmering with resentment.

Without his father around, he could take charge of a situation. And he planned to take charge with Enmira – only he must allow her to believe that it was *she* who was in control.

One thing was certain: he must convince Enmira that her happiness and pleasure was really all he was concerned with, and that he meant her no harm. She must understand that he had only her best interests at heart.

Well, that was not entirely true; he would be seeking and deriving his own pleasure too, of course, from their physical fusion. But, really, all he asked was that they enjoy each other mutually.

And surely she must have realized that his having

rescued her from the violent mob of trolls had proven that he was truly on her side and watching out for her. It was only logical she then come to the conclusion that she would require his protection from here on out – and be extremely grateful to him for providing it.

Of course, her submission to him must be entirely voluntarily and of her own volition. He felt the key to a successful consummation would be to ensure she not feel pressured, forced or coerced in any way. But he also needed her to believe that his seduction of her had all been her own idea.

He would tease her. He would use reverse psychology to implant the suggestion that *she* was the aggressor, the one seducing *him*.

And so, while administering this most intimate and provocative massage, he would pretend he had absolutely no interest in her sexually.

Oh, did you think I might want to see you without your clothes on and then engage in certain sexual behaviors? Why, you're just being silly! he would declare coyly; only he would know he was being facetious.

Truth be told, though, he would really enjoy a reversal of roles for once. It would certainly be a first for him, as this had never before happened with any of his other bedmates. They had all been of such libertine disposition, so eager to submit and have him dominate them, that there was never a hint of challenge involved.

Even here on Tartarus, in the world of the Eternally Forsaken, there were certain behaviors and procedures that were followed mechanically and by rote without even a thought of questioning them. But Fairuzo had always delighted in testing the boundaries of the status quo, flipping the dial of accepted norms.

This innate curiosity he possessed was only further aroused and heightened by the arrival of Enmira. Everything about her felt fresh and new, inspiring him to cross unexplored frontiers of tactile and sensuous discovery.

And what would he have her do with him? Perhaps he would suggest she bind his wrists to the bedpost with bloodroot vines, then wildly rip off his clothes and climb on top – oh, but he was getting ahead of himself now.

They had arrived at the entry to his bedchambers. He nudged the door open with his shoulder, then realized it had been unlocked and left ajar. He wondered where the two guards normally present were; they were nowhere in the vicinity. Where had they gone and why had they left their post?

Everyone in the Kingdom was fully aware this was a special night of Consummation for him and, therefore, should have been on full alert – especially after his explicit instructions that he be disturbed by no one.

He began to feel agitated. This was no time at all to have to go scouting around for someone competent and trustworthy enough to guard his chambers.

It was at least a small comfort that the other two guards were still on duty out by the passageway staircase. He could only hope that his personal security guards were simply in the midst of changing shifts and would be arriving back on their post soon.

And in the meantime, he would just have to make do with properly locking his door.

He carried Enmira over to the bed and gently laid her down, trying his best to mask his worry so as not to let on that anything was amiss. He would allow nothing to mar or interfere with the mind-shattering experience he now felt certain they were about to share.

She lay still and seemed quite content to be there with him, open to whatever happened next, agreeable to whatever he might have planned.

He walked over to the door to close and lock it, taking care to ensure it was secure.

"This is a beautiful room," she said admiringly,

looking all about, "and this bed is deliciously soft."

"The mattress is made out of Irish moss, mullein leaves, and fountain grasses: a replica of my father's," Fairuzo replied.

As soon as he mentioned his father, he wished he hadn't; for a moment, it seemed to ruin the mood.

He suddenly realized that, although his bed might very well be a reproduction of one his father owned, he himself was nothing at all like him. Whereas Phegor was only able to view all species of females as whores and harlots to be used and discarded, Fairuzo could not and would not see Enmira as such. And just the fact that he was able to regard her as someone worthy of respect or even veneration was one crucial trait that set he and his father apart.

It was true that Fairuzo had pretty much treated all of his preceding pretties as mere objects to be taken advantage of and conquered until they no longer pleased him, as this is how his father had taught him. But now, with Enmira, it was different. He could clearly see that she was unlike any of the others. Simply being around her had changed something deep within him in a profound way.

He was beginning to realize that he and his father shared nothing in common other than bloodtype. If only he could permanently remove himself from Phegor's cynical presence and degenerate influence, he believed he had a real chance of finally becoming the authentic version of his true self – whatever that might be.

He walked back to the bed. Leaning over her, he began to gently massage Enmira's dainty, doll-like wrists, languorously moving up her arms to her shoulders and then to her soft, vulnerable neck. His eyes were magnetically drawn to the dieresis-like flesh punctures where he had injected his serum into her that first night.

But instead of a craving to sink his fangs deep into the purplish grooves, making the mark even more indelible and prominent, he had a sudden urge to wipe it completely away, to erase it from her body as if it had never existed.

But he could not take it back, nor could he make it vanish. The scar would remain there eternally, marring the perfection of her skin, and it was all his doing. He felt a twinge of remorse for having done this to her.

He bent down and tenderly kissed her neck.

She giggled and squinched up her shoulders as if it tickled, and the teasing smile that played upon her lips aroused him even more.

By now her tattered dress was falling down around her bosom, exposing the fragile bones of her clavicle and sternum, and the pale, pliable flesh of her cleavage. He cautiously, almost surreptitiously, tugged at the fabric, lowering it ever so gradually, waiting for her to resist or stop him. But instead of discouraging him or expressing any sort of reluctance, she reached over and plucked at the front ruffle of his shirt.

"Shall we both discard our clothes?" she whispered suggestively.

Fairuzo needed no further coaxing. He got up off of the bed and hastily peeled off his top. He began to pull down his trousers then stopped.

"Do you want me, Enmira?" he asked her softly, as if he wasn't quite sure.

"Oh, yes," she whispered, "I want you."

He finished undressing then climbed back onto the bed. Kneeling beside her, he pulled down the rest of her dress to expose her nakedness, for she was wearing no undergarments.

It was as if he had unpeeled an exotic fruit to reveal the only sustenance required to attain true bliss: ambrosia, the sacrament of the Deathless Ones. Sweet nectar exuded from her pores and permeated the air; he inhaled her perfume deeply and it intoxicated him.

He eagerly slid over on the bed until he was so close to her he could feel the heat radiating off of her body and seeping into his own frigid flesh. He sinuously climbed on top of her, placing his hand between her thighs.

"Are you ready for me?" he whispered into her ear.

"Please, oh, yes," she sighed.

Immediately upon entering her, he felt the most delicious euphoria. He began making pure, unfiltered love to her: this was not carnal lust or mechanical sex; this was something dreamlike and beautiful and he never wanted it to end.

She began to arch her back and thrash about wildly beneath him, emitting gasps and loud moans. It was as if they were both lost in a labyrinthic trance together, melded into one entity and wandering through sensual mazes for hours. Finally, she let out a feral scream of ecstasy; it was only then that he allowed himself to climax.

As he basked in the afterglow of the Consummation, the sensations from his groin flooding throughout his entire body, he impetuously whispered into her ear, "I think I could love you, Enmira."

He immediately regretted uttering the words as soon as they escaped his lips; the remark had come out sounding so offhanded and casual, so insolently superficial. Why could he not just tell her the truth: that he *already* loved her, that he was, in fact, deeply in love with her?

Especially now, after having finally broken through her long-standing and impenetrable walls of defense, after having been so intimate with her at her most exposed, after realizing that his feelings had grown even stronger. In fact, she had just passed the litmus test: he was now certain that the way he felt about her was indeed genuine and everlasting – or at least he never wanted this bond with her to end.

She did not seem to take any offense at his comment, however; perhaps what he had just demonstrated with his lovemaking had convinced her of his true feelings. As she snuggled trustingly into his arms, his self-reproach at his inability to put into words how he really felt quickly dissipated, and he felt the contentment of a purring cat.

As he wrapped his arms tightly around her, he began to feel something extraordinary seeping over him: a strange lucidity, an awareness, a new perception of reality, intermingled with an unfamiliar sensation of what felt to be an overwhelming and undeniable joy, a noticeable uplifting of his formerly sagging, vacant heart.

But there was something else he could not identify or pinpoint; something else in his being that had been altered irreversibly.

Negative emotions like hate had always come so easily to him, along with a plethora of other base sentiments like arrogance and vanity and scorn towards all beneath him. Indeed, his disdain for others and conviction of self-importance had served him well all this time. It had effectively prevented him from ever feeling the pangs of loneliness or the desire for companionship.

He had always scoffed at the weakness of those who sought and craved love; there was certainly none of that nonsense on *this* planet. He especially sneered at those foolish enough to believe in the mythical concept of soulmates.

All throughout his youth, his father had regaled him with tales of imbecilic Earthlings who wasted all their time dreaming of finding this ever-elusive other-half, with nothing to show for their efforts but disappointment, dashed hopes, deflated egos, and a lost sense of autonomy. It certainly sounded most unappealing.

The entire notion was even easier to dismiss since Fairuzo's own soul had always felt like a burden to him. It had only served to interfere in his constant pursuit of pleasure and self-gratification. Who in their right mind would welcome feelings of guilt or regret, and the constant monitoring and self-policing that a soul forced upon one?

And since he had no use or need for his *own* soul, the last thing he wanted was to be saddled with sharing the cumbersome millstone of someone else's as well.

He had heretofore gotten by just fine without ever having known any love or affection. He had only ever known the sensation of a gaping black hole of nothingness in the vicinity of his chest. And what he had never known, he could never miss.

He had grown accustomed to the blanket of deadness he kept wrapped around himself like a burial shroud. It protected and comforted him like a shield through which no arrows of conscience could pierce.

But now it seemed as if everything inside of him was rapidly undergoing some sort of mystifying transformation. He could feel his own glacial and embittered heart melting and fluttering like the wings of a butterfly emerging from a long-frozen cocoon.

He now realized what this curious new sensation was, and it was this: he felt alive for the first time in his entire existence.

Enmira had awoken him from the dead.

CHAPTER 33

THE CONFESSION AND AN INTRUDER

As Enmira lay there contentedly, her head resting easily upon his shoulder, Fairuzo decided it was time for him to reveal to her the truth about his relationship with Darceva.

It was important that she first hear his side of the story before anyone else had a chance to offer their own skewed and inaccurate version. It was crucial she be given all the pertinent particulars so as to understand that what happened that night was not at all his fault.

"I have a confession to make," he announced.

"Yes?" Enmira asked. "What is it?" She twisted her neck to look up at him with a slightly troubled frown.

"Oh, don't worry; it's nothing really bad," he hastened to add, "and it doesn't have that much to do with us. But it's about Darceva."

"Oh," Enmira said, sounding relieved. "Procel said he was going to tell me about the bizarre relationship you have with her."

"I know he was. And that's why I'm telling it to you now," Fairuzo said firmly. "I'd really rather you hear it straight from my lips than from Procel's. He was not even here on Tartarus at the time, and so he has only second-hand knowledge and hearsay at best. He may be unaware of certain details and unintentionally omit them, and I need you to understand the exact dynamics of our relationship.

"You see," he continued, "Darceva is actually my mother. I mean, my real birth-mother."

"What?!" Enmira exclaimed, her eyes popping wide in surprise. "But she acts like you and her have something sexy going on! She certainly seems attracted to you in some weird, obsessed way, not at all like any mother *I've* ever seen. So why does she behave like that?"

"Well, it all came about on the night of my Rite of Passage," Fairuzo began, "which is an induction ceremony held for all Sons of Royalty when they come of age – a bit like the Bar Mitzvahs you Earthlings have."

Fairuzo paused for a moment, considering whether or not to make mention of the succubus's visit, then quickly decided against it. That little detail was best kept to himself; Enmira would most likely not understand.

"So, after the Ceremony that night," he continued, "I had fallen asleep in my bedchambers here when Darceva somehow snuck past the guards and forced her way into my room. She climbed into my bed and hopped on top of me like a toad on a swamp log. I awoke to find her grotesque face leering down at me."

"Oh, my God!" exclaimed Enmira. "That must have given you a real fright!"

"Well, it certainly turned whatever dream I was having at the time into a real-life lurid nightmare! She weighed more than a bushel sack of limestone, nearly crushing me with her massive girth; she was pressing down so hard on my trachea that I could barely breathe. But I managed to shove her off of me right as the guards rushed in to drag her out of here."

"Now, this is where it gets hinky," said Fairuzo. "I didn't even know who she was at the time. I'd seen her waltzing around the Kingdom like she was somebody important, but I just always thought of her as some unattractive, obnoxious troll I wanted nothing to do with.

"She would come sniffing around me sometimes like she was after something, but was always kept at bay by my personal guards – something they obviously failed to accomplish on that particular night.

"But get this – right after she forced herself upon me, it was actually the guards who revealed to me who she really was! I had not an iota of a clue before that. I mean, I had been told by everyone around me – including my own father – that the nursemaid who had attended to me since birth was my mother.

"I just couldn't believe I had to find out the truth from a security worker, and that my father had lied to me all that time. In fact, I don't think he would have ever gotten around to telling me either, had this incident not occurred.

"As far as what she did," he continued, "I would not even call it an attempted seduction but an outright malicious attack. It was insidious and planned, and she definitely had an ulterior motive – some sort of vendetta or revenge, from what I've since managed to piece together.

"To be completely honest, Enmira, it's something I've never really been able to get over – that feeling of repulsion, the betrayal, the lies I was told for so long – all without a word of apology or even an explanation as to why no one ever bothered telling me the truth before or even considered my feelings..." he tapered off.

"Oh, no!" Enmira exclaimed sympathetically. "That's just horrible! A mother forcing herself sexually on her own son? That's completely perverted. And where I come from, we have a name for it – we call it incest!"

"Well, it's taboo here as well," Fairuzo replied, "but for different reasons – not because it's considered a perversion or anything immoral, but because it screws up the royal bloodline. The mental and physical mutations it creates in the offspring is more than a bit undesirable, to say the least.

"You see, the ancestry of the Mount Hermon Royalty is so dominant that a Lord, Duke or Prince can mate with an uninfected human Earthling and still manage to keep the bloodline potent and pure. Even better is to mate with a sister or daughter of the Cabal. But when a descendant of the infected primeval Dark Hollow Goblins is chosen as womb-vessel, that mother can never come in contact sexually with her son.

"Actually, there's been talk recently of using succubi

bellies to incubate the offspring. They don't have the Beastly Mark and they're a hell of a lot easier to control. Besides, they don't hang around after the Seeding and make nuisances of themselves."

"Oh, I completely understand," said Enmira, "because that's what happens when siblings or close relatives mate together on Earth as well – it results in children being born with horrible, crippling deformities. Inbreeding is heavily frowned upon as being completely inappropriate and out-of-bounds and, in most parts, it's illegal. *Certainly* no one with any self-respect or decency would even consider it! It's just wrong."

Fairuzo nodded absently, lost in his own deep thoughts and painful memories. He realized he had never before told anyone his feelings about that night – or pretty much his feelings about anything, for that matter. But, now, after having finally confided all this in Enmira, it was as if the ponderous boulder that had lain so oppressively across his chest for all these years had been pulverized into a fine, weightless dust.

If only he had known what a relief it would be to talk to somebody about the anguish and betrayal he'd felt that night, he would have spoken out about it a long time ago!

But, then, who would he have told? His leering, taunting father? One of the half-witted trolls? The stiff, austere and scientifically-minded Procel?

He saw clearly now that there had been no one to tell... that is, until Enmira came along.

"So, when she came into your room, did she disguise herself in some way? Or did she just not care if you knew who she was or not?" Enmira was asking.

"No," Fairuzo responded, shaking himself out of his reverie, "there was no disguise. She was fully aware that I had no clue as to whom she really was, and she was hoping that I would welcome her advances. But there was no chance of that; I found her totally repugnant."

"Oh – and I wanted to ask you about this," said Enmira. "I heard one of the trolls in the Ballroom refer to her by another name. Was that --?"

"Oh, yes, that," replied Fairuzo. "She was known as Lamia at the time that she and my father got together for the Spawning; that was her original goblin name. My father has since told me that he had initially found her extremely attractive. But, of course, after he injected his serum into her, she quickly deteriorated into the nasty troll creature she is now.

"Just like what has happened to everyone else here after being given the Mark – except for you, that is," he said thoughtfully, turning to look curiously at Enmira. "You've somehow managed to escape that fate so far."

He stared at her as if waiting for her to offer some sort of an explanation, but of course, she was unable to. Why the same fate had not befallen her was something she herself did not understand.

He would simply have to accept it as a most puzzling phenomenon, and not at all an unpleasant one, either. It was certainly something that worked well in both of their favors. Besides, he really did not think he could bear it if she changed and became like all the others, especially now.

"So, after Darceva had lost all semblance of appeal to my father," Fairuzo continued, "he made it clear he wanted nothing more to do with her. And yet she continued to pursue him like an obsessed lunatic, completely oblivious to his rejection and obvious contempt for her. She became such a pest that he had her carted off somewhere just to get her out of his hair.

"He then ordered she have no contact at all with me, and the nursemaid that had been attending to my needs was assigned full charge. But Darceva was never a mother to me even when she was around."

"I would certainly never imagine her as a motherly type, that's for sure," remarked Enmira.

"But the fact that she was not immediately banished after she attacked me and received only minimal punishment just added insult to injury," complained Fairuzo bitterly.

"I mean, not only did she commit one of the only sexual taboos the Cabal considers to be in direct violation of the Royal Code, but she forced herself upon the son of a Lord. And for this she was not given the ultimate penalty?"

He paused for a moment, remembering all too well the morning after the attack, when he had walked in on his father unclothed in his chambers lewdly laughing it up with the molester herself, and how powerless and outraged it had made him feel.

"And no matter how many times my father rejects her and has the guards drag her away, she just doesn't get it. Even after all this time of being continuously spurned, she's *still* got the hots for him," he said, grimacing.

"And for you, too, obviously," said Enmira with a slight grin.

"Yes, for me too, unfortunately," Fairuzo reluctantly agreed. "Although I'm basically being used as a pawn in this whole cockamamie mess. But something will be done about her soon, I can promise you. I plan to elicit Procel's aid in petitioning the Cabal to have her permanently removed from Tartarus, now that he's been physically assaulted by her as well."

"I hate to say it, but it was most likely because of me that he was attacked at all. I was the one she was really after," offered Enmira.

"Oh, yes, I don't doubt for a moment that you were her intended target and that Procel was simply in her line of fire for being there with you. But what the Cabal will be concerned with is that she's now committed two separate offenses against two Sons of Royalty – a Lord and a Duke. That in and of itself should certainly be enough to persuade them to banish her once and for all."

"Well, that's hopeful news!" Enmira exclaimed. "I'm

just surprised she hasn't popped up again since then."

"Oh, she's been kept guarded and under wraps all this time," said Fairuzo. "Or at least she was the last time I checked. At any rate, she wouldn't dare come after you again while I'm around. Even *she* wouldn't do something that moronic and self-defeating.

"And there's also the matter of the pact she was forced to sign in blood, agreeing to never again force herself upon me or reveal to anyone what happened that night. Because if she ever dares break that, she will certainly –" here, Fairuzo paused in mid-sentence, swiveling his head towards the door.

"Did you hear that?" he asked in alarm.

"Hear what?" Enmira asked, apparently having heard nothing.

"That!" Fairuzo shouted, referring to the now-unmistakable sound of keys jangling in the door lock, followed by the distinct sound of someone jiggling the handle.

"I told those idiot guards that he was not allowed back here!" Fairuzo muttered angrily.

Just then the door was flung wide open and his father burst into the room.

"What have you got the door locked for, boy?" Phegor yelled, his face a dark shade of purple and twisted in rage. "I can't believe I had to hear about this Initiation tonight through the Cabal grapevine. Why did you not bother to inform me?

"And what's with the guards telling me something private was going on back here? What's with all the secrecy?"

His voice rose to a furious pitch. "Don't they know who the fuck I am? I come and go as I fucking please anywhere on this piece of crap planet!"

Enmira had slunk down between the bedcovers as soon as he'd barged into the room. She now pulled the sheet all the way up to her eyes, as if trying to make herself

297

disappear.

"Who's that you've got with you? Is this that special twat you've been going on and on about? And what's so special about what she's got between her legs?

"I'm so disappointed in you, boy," his father spat out virulently. "You know damned well that you and I share everything. You mentioned this wench was special but you said nothing about wanting to keep her all for yourself. Even the imbeciles in the Ballroom told me they weren't given any access to her during the Consummation.

"So what's going on here? And what's this about the guards stopping me, telling me no one is allowed back here?" His voice rose to a crescendo.

Fairuzo started to reply but his father brusquely cut him off, continuing his furious diatribe.

"I told those shit-headed bastards that not only do I have a key to every shit-hole room in this Kingdom, but I used to *own* this place. How dare they try to keep me out! I don't give one flying fuck *what* you told them; I hold the rank here, Fairuzo. And don't you ever forget that!"

Fairuzo realized that whatever he said to his father now would only be met with more yelling and recriminations, and so he chose to remain silent, while inwardly furious and steaming at the intrusion.

What he really wanted to do was leap out of bed and shove his father out the door, locking it behind him. But he was naked underneath the sheets, and he was well aware that Phegor would not miss an opportunity to deride and ridicule him. He was sure to make some snide, disparaging remark about his physique or the size of his genitalia. No one could harangue and humiliate prey more skillfully than his father could, and he simply would not allow himself to be mortified in that way, not in front of Enmira.

"So if you're finished there, boy, why don't you move over so I can take my turn. You know what I always say – sloppy seconds are the juiciest," Phegor sneered, licking his chops. "I'll show her how it's done, who's the top cocksman around here."

He strode over to Enmira's side of the bed and yanked the covers off of her, revealing her naked but for the remains of her dress wrapped around her waist. Smirking, he gave her a leering once-over, sticking his tongue out and waggling it obscenely.

"What, you don't even have all of her clothes off yet? What's the matter with you, are you losing what little touch you had? I'll rip those clothes off for you, honey, if my useless son here can't finish the job."

"No!" Fairuzo yelled. "You will leave her alone!" He reached over and pulled the sheet back up over Enmira.

"I purposely did not invite you here for good reason!" he shouted at his father. "I have decided that my relationship with Enmira is to be private. That was *my* decision and I had every right to make it.

"No one was invited to share her, including you. Not the trolls, not you – *no one*. So I'm going to have to insist that you leave right now, Father. These are *my* bedchambers and we want to be alone."

Phegor stared back at him in disbelief. "You're got to be joking. You're kidding me, right? How *dare* you order me around. Don't tell me she's got you whipped already!

"What about all those tips I gave you, all that advice never to get hung up with any of these juice-holes? These trollops are nothing but trash and trouble!"

Fairuzo shook his head emphatically.

"No! You've got it all wrong. Enmira is different. She is not like any of the others," he insisted.

"You know what?" Phegor snapped. "You can have the whore, for all I care. I certainly don't need to stay somewhere where I'm not wanted or invited. I've got sluts and succubi all over the universe on six different planets. What do I need with your second-hand slop?

"You can keep your private stock until you tire of her.

And you know damned well you'll be sick of her soon; you always are."

He stomped over to the door. Glancing back over his shoulder at Enmira, he tossed out one final, parting shot.

"He's using you, sweetheart. Every word he's saying to you is a lie and you're a gullible fool to believe him. Take it from me; I'm his father and I should know. We've fucked hundreds of broads together and he's a chip off the old block. Don't be stupid; he'll never change. Not for you or for any other cheap whore."

He gave a snort of disgust, then marched furiously out the door, muttering and cursing to himself. He slammed it behind him so hard it sounded like an explosion, wooden shrapnel and splinters flying all around as if a bomb had gone off.

And maybe it had. Fairuzo had no idea of the repercussions this altercation with his father could bring about. Phegor might even go so far as to petition the Cabal to rescind his son's rulership of Turquoise, perhaps even have him exiled from Tartarus. Who knew what type of retaliation his father was capable of? Whatever happened, though, Fairuzo would fight hard to appeal any such decision and assert his Royal bloodline rights.

But right now, he simply did not care; he was just relieved that his father was gone.

He looked over at Enmira, but she had turned away from him. When he reached out to touch her shoulder, he noticed that her body was shaking and she was quietly sobbing.

"What is wrong, Enmira?" Fairuzo asked with genuine concern. He felt even more anger at his father for upsetting her and causing her distress.

"We're okay here now," he said, trying to reassure her. "He's gone and I doubt he will be coming back."

But she did not answer or acknowledge him, continuing to cry softly, her head turned into the pillow.

The realization that she was so unhappy filled him with a rolling sorrow that came in dizzying waves; he felt her sadness as if it were his own.

Even in his rare moments of self-indulgent sorrow for himself, he had never before felt the powerful depths of dolor he was experiencing now. The deep-seated rage and frustration he had just been feeling towards his father had now been replaced with something poignant and sweet, yet profoundly painful.

He was feeling empathy for the first time, and it hurt.

CHAPTER 34

FLOODGATES AND SPLINTERS

𝕴 was still badly shaken from the encounter with Fairuzo's father. Never before had I come into contact with such an overpoweringly evil entity.

Poor Fairuzo, I thought; *that is the only father he has ever known -- and to be saddled as well with such a despicable mother was nothing less than a horrific double whammy of an ancestral heritage.* I couldn't even begin to imagine the mental torment his childhood must have been: the disgust he must have felt to have that grotesque excuse of a mother forcing herself sexually on him, and then to have the whole matter so cavalierly dismissed by all those around him as if it were nothing of significance.

The moment his father entered the room, Fairuzo's confidence had seemed to shrivel and shrink like a deflated balloon. I could literally see the air being sucked out of him as he became first subdued then despondent. It was as if his father's very presence had infected him with insecurity and mental impotence. In fact, it was the first time I'd observed him not being fully assertive and in total control over his surroundings.

But who *wouldn't* feel defeated after being subjected to such an abusively abrasive attitude his entire life? His father was a crude, overbearing whirlwind of sneering negativity, crushing anyone in his path who dared defy him – and that obviously included his son.

I found it flattering that Fairuzo had confided in me, trusting me enough to share the sordid details behind his aberrant relationship with Darceva. It couldn't have been at all pleasant to dredge up and relive such obviously painful memories and deeply-embedded feelings.

Right when his father had burst in and so rudely interrupted our idyllic time together, I had been so blissfully lying in his arms, basking in the afterglow of our rapturous lovemaking session and savoring the intimacy of our new romantic bond.

But now, especially after having to endure that whole nightmarish confrontation, all I could think about was that I wanted out of this hellish place. I just wanted to go home. Even with Fairuzo as my protector and Procel as my friend, I could not forget that I was surrounded by demonic beings who only wanted to harm me.

I shuddered to think what would have happened in the Ballroom had Fairuzo not been there to spirit me off – or what would have happened had I been left alone with his leering father. I had no doubt he would have forced himself upon me had his son not been there to intervene and act as foil. I would not have stood a chance against his menacing aggression and strength.

The floodgates of unhappiness I had been leaning my back against ever since my arrival here were suddenly flung wide open, and I began to cry uncontrollably. Once the waterfall of tears began to cascade down the rocks of my fragile composure, I could not seem to wade out of its deep pools of despair.

Faintly, as if his voice was coming from a great distance, I could hear Fairuzo asking me repetitively if I was all right. He did appear genuinely concerned, but what could he possibly do to help me now?

It was highly doubtful that he would even consider leaving his entire Kingdom behind to flee with me to Earth. He was the Ruler here and this was the only home he had ever known. He garnered such respect and wielded so much power over all the inhabitants, why would he ever want to give all of that up to live the humdrum life of an ordinary Earthling with an uncertain future, one that seemed unbearably mundane in comparison to what he had now?

And what about his cruel and barbaric eating habits? How would he adapt to a diet that was entirely alien to him, such as the one I followed?

As well, his leaving here would be a final, irreversible decision; for once he went AWOL, he would never again be able to return. And what of those bounty hunters he himself had warned me about? Would they immediately go into action hunting him down if he absconded. Or were they only concerned with going after the troll and neophyte escapees?

Fairuzo seemed to believe that all would be well now that his father was gone, but I knew differently: this was a dangerous place, one where I would never be able to feel safe. I would constantly be aware of the ever-looming presence of Darceva and on the alert against the horrid little trolls who wanted nothing more than to rip me apart and eat me alive.

The truth was that I could not even begin to contemplate any sort of future here other than one of utter bleakness and constant wariness.

I kept my face turned away from Fairuzo; I did not want him to see me like this, so wretched and hopeless. Up until now, I had, for the most part, tried to present as cheerful a disposition as possible, as I loathed any public display of self-pity. But now, it had become impossible to pretend that I did not feel incredibly sorry for myself, trapped in such a hopeless situation with no way out – and through no real fault of my own except perhaps my impulsiveness and naivete.

The discontent I'd felt with my former life had played a role in my ending up here as well. But now all I could think about was how much I desperately wanted things back the way they were before.

I realized that Fairuzo was not going to like what I had to say, but I could hold it all in no longer: my words and emotions came gushing forth in a long-pent-up avalanche.

"I want to go home!" I blurted out, lifting my head up

from the pillow to look beseechingly at him. "I want to go back to Earth! I'm so tired of living in a damp cave; I miss the sun and I feel so trapped here – and your father scares the hell out of me! Any minute now, Darceva could pop up again, and those trolls want to lynch me and eat me for breakfast! Please tell me that you'll take me back home and away from here!"

Fairuzo stared at me, a heavy look of sadness in his eyes. He slowly shook his head.

"I am so sorry, baby," he said softly. "But I am forbidden to help anyone escape from Tartarus. Even being the Lord and Ruler here would not protect me from the punishment for breaking that taboo. It is one of the few laws that descendants of Royalty must adhere to, under the severest threat of banishment."

I read an honest sincerity in his face, and realized he was speaking the truth: he really could not help me.

I lowered my head again in utter dejection and my falling tears continued to drench the pillow. When he put his arm around my shoulder to comfort me, I noticed that his skin, although not quite warm, no longer felt so frigid to the touch.

He certainly did not seem at all like the same being I'd woken up to in my bed that first night. He no longer appeared to have some sort of hidden agenda that aroused suspicion and distrust in me. No longer evident was any sort of cunning or deceitful intent. Something inside him definitely seemed to have undergone a transformation.

Suddenly I felt an enormous rush of compassion and love towards him; I trusted him with all of my heart.

"But *surely* there is some way you can help me get back to Earth without getting into trouble yourself?" I implored. "Isn't there some sort of secret tunnel you can at least tell me about?"

Fairuzo looked pensive for a moment, as if mulling over a proposition.

"Well, actually, now that you mention it, there *is* a way I can help you. But I cannot directly reveal to you how the escape could be achieved. I can give you hints, though."

Fairuzo smiled then, his face brightening, as if extremely pleased with his own cleverness for thinking of this loophole.

"So, what – you give me a hint and I try to guess?" I asked, not quite sure I was in the mood for guessing games right about now, but would take whatever I could get.

"Yes," said Fairuzo. "That's how we'll play it. And I'll make it real easy for you, too."

He paused and I waited impatiently for him to continue.

"Here it is," Fairuzo said. "Ready? It's your name."

I thought about that for a moment but it made no sense.

"My name – Ermina?" I asked. "Mean-a-what? What does that even mean? I don't get it."

Fairuzo shook his head, a secretive smile curling up the edge of his lips as if he were enjoying stumping me with this riddle.

"No, not your given name; the name that I call you. Say it out loud."

"Enmira," I said. "Enmira. En-mira – oh!"

The revelation suddenly struck me and I felt foolish for not having thought of it sooner.

"I get it, I get it!" I practically shouted. "En-mira – in mirror! The way out is the same way that *you* first came in – through the mirror!"

Fairuzo smiled broadly, nodding his head emphatically.

"Yes!" he exclaimed. "That's it! But you've still got to figure out how to accomplish it."

"Well, let's see," I said, racking my brain and thinking out loud. "It can't be my own Turquoise Mirror, because that's still stuck back on Earth. But there is that huge replica of it in the Ballroom..."

Fairuzo nodded encouragingly. "Keep going. Keep going. You're getting it."

I thought again. The mirror would need to be broken through somehow; what could I use to smash it? I would need some sort of a large stone or brick, which shouldn't be too difficult to locate. It would have to be light enough for me to toss hard and from a distance. And I would need to wait until every last troll had vacated the Ballroom, for they would certainly physically and violently do everything they could to prevent me from leaving – or, God forbid, crawl after me through the crack in the Mirror's opening!

I shuddered at that frightening scenario; no, I must make absolutely certain that no trolls were around when I made my escape.

Now, there was also the problem of all that glass breaking and flying around. The Mirror was of such monstrous size, and I would need to protect myself from all of those jagged shards of glass raining on me when it shattered.

I couldn't help thinking then about the seven years of bad luck that were said to come with a broken mirror. This, I knew to be just a silly, unfounded superstition, but nonetheless, it still made me uneasy.

"So, you cannot help in the actual act at all? Is that forbidden too?" I asked.

"No, I cannot lift a finger to help you. You must do it all on your own," Fairuzo answered resolutely.

I was silent for a moment, wondering how I was ever going to accomplish such a thing all by myself. But then I got an idea.

"So, what about Procel?" I asked.

"What *about* Procel?" Fairuzo shot back, a fleeting look of displeasure crossing his face. "What does he have to do with your getting back to Earth?"

He seemed annoyed that I had mentioned Procel's

name but I had no idea why. I thought they were friends. And if that were so, he certainly couldn't be jealous of him – or could he? I decided to ask, just to clear the air.

"Wait – you don't actually believe there is anything between Procel and I, do you?" I asked. "Because we are totally the most platonic of friends. I have no romantic feelings towards him whatsoever and I'm absolutely certain he has none towards me either. I've only felt the utmost of respect and, dare I say, asexual vibes from him."

Fairuzo's face softened and he looked visibly relieved.

"Oh, no, I thought nothing of the sort," he lied, then caught himself. "Well, actually that is not true; I *was* feeling a bit jealous and suspicious there for awhile. I mean, you were spending so much time together.

"The truth is that I have always trusted Procel implicitly as a loyal friend – in fact, my *only* friend – but you've got to understand that this type of situation has never arisen before with any woman I've ever been with. Never before have I had occasion to consider him as any sort of rival."

"And you still don't," I assured him. "Procel is still your loyal friend. He has nothing but the utmost respect and regard for you."

"Well, I was pretty sure he had no such romantic notions towards you," he replied, "but I just could not get a read on how *you* felt towards *him*. So I must say this is really quite the relief to find out for sure now."

"But all you had to do was ask me," I told him, "and I would have been perfectly straight with you. And I'm sure you could have asked him as well, if just to ease your suspicions."

"Yes, I do see what you're saying," agreed Fairuzo. "It may take a bit of practice, though, for me to get the hang of this type of open communication; I'm so used to just plotting things out on my own.

"Now, let's get back to the matter at hand. As far as

Procel being able to help you, I will tell you this: he is not bound quite as tightly by the same Royal Code as I am as Ruler here. As I believe he told you, his official job title here is the Gatekeeper of Hidden and Secret Knowledge.

"So, even though he is forbidden to reveal any secrets that might constitute a breach of confidentiality or a threat to the security of the Cabal, he can technically directly participate in helping someone escape as long as no information is shared.

"In fact, he and I will put our heads together and come up with just such a way that will allow us to get around those annoying little statutory obstacles. What I'm saying is, Procel knows exactly what will unlock the mirror and open it as a portal."

"Oh!" I exclaimed. "So, the mirror can be simply unlocked instead of being forcibly shattered? But how will –"

Fairuzo gently put his forefinger on my lips as if to hush me.

"Do not worry, my love. We will put together a most ingenious plan and you will back on Earth in no time," he reassured me. "Now let's go to Procel's chambers and get started on this straightaway!"

He energetically threw off the bedcovers and reached for his trousers and top.

"Quickly, get dressed!" he urged while pulling on his pants. "We must act fast while all the trolls are still sleeping. I'm sure they're pretty knocked out from all the punch and festivities, but we don't have much time before they wake up and start milling about."

I reluctantly began to pull my tattered dress back up over my torso. It felt slimy and unpleasant next to my skin, and was beginning to emit a most unappealing odor.

"Fairuzo, is there some way I could get something else to wear?" I asked hopefully. "I've been wearing this dress for so long that it's really starting to smell pretty badly. I know worrying about something as trivial as clothing seems so petty, but --" I trailed off.

"Well, if you don't mind wearing something of mine for now, I'll get you a million new dresses later," Fairuzo promised, walking over to his bureau. Pulling open a drawer, he selected a long tunic top.

"Here," he said, offering it to me. "You can make do with using this as a dress."

I gratefully took it from him. It was a vibrant color of turquoise, soft as velvet, and had a large peacock embroidered in great detail all down the front.

"You have the most beautiful clothes," I said admiringly as I quickly yanked off my smelly dress and pulled the top on over my head. The hemline went all the way down to my shins, but otherwise it fit quite snugly.

"Lucky for you that I do!" Fairuzo laughed.

"I only wish I could see what I looked like; I must look quite the mess," I said, looking all about for a mirror or a piece of glass.

"Well, there will be ample opportunity for you to see what you look like when we get to the Turquoise Mirror in the Ballroom," said Fairuzo.

"Oh, yes, of course," I said, laughing and feeling a bit foolish. "After all, that's what mirrors were designed for!"

"All right, let's get going then," said Fairuzo, striding purposefully towards the door – or what remained of it after his father had left it in splinters. When he pulled on the handle to open it, it snapped off in his fingers.

"Damn it. He ruins everything he touches," Fairuzo muttered. "I hope I never have to see his sneering face again!"

In a fit of pique he grabbed ahold of either side of the door and pulled hard, effectively ripping the entire panel off of the jamb. He then tossed the remnants off to the side like a pile of pulverized firewood.

"There. Now I have no door at all," he grumbled.

He stepped nimbly over the threshold and into the hallway, with me following closely behind.

CHAPTER 35

THE WAY OUT FROM WITHIN

$\mathfrak{I}$ had been wondering where Procel kept his living quarters and I was soon to find out.

Out in the hallway, Fairuzo turned a hard left and began walking in the opposite direction from which we had come. I tripped along after him, trying to keep up with his hurried pace.

After turning a corner, we came to a few cobblestone steps, which led us down to a vestibule. Inside, on either side of an oval door, sat two chairs.

"What the hell is going on?" Fairuzo muttered, frowning. "There are no guards here either! Where have they all trotted off to?"

"Oh, does Procel have guards too?" I asked.

"He's certainly entitled to them, being Mount Hermon Royalty," replied Fairuzo, "although it would be nice if they actually showed up for the job. I have no idea why none of these idiots are here at their posts. I really would like to know what's going on."

He was just about to knock on the door when it opened. Procel peered out, looking extremely preoccupied and a bit worried, then a relieved smile crossed his face when he saw it was Fairuzo and I standing there.

"Oh! It is you! I was so worried that Phegor or some of the Cabal would be coming back here after all the commotion."

"The commotion?" Fairuzo asked, puzzled.

"When your father burst into your room – I heard it all, every word of it."

"Oh, that's right," Fairuzo said, laughing. "You and your supersonic hearing; but of course you heard it all. The bastard is gone now and I don't think he'll be returning. Even so, we don't have much time."

"Much time? Much time for what?" asked Procel.

"Much time to get Enmira back to Earth," replied Fairuzo.

At this Procel looked completely surprised. "Back to Earth?" he asked.

"Yes," Fairuzo answered. "What, you didn't listen in on that part of our *private* conversation?" He gave Procel a playful jab in the arm to let him know he was just teasing him.

"No, I did not," said Procel, looking extremely solemn. "I would never listen in on any personal conversations. That would be rude of me and I totally respect your privacy."

"I know you do, my friend; I was just kidding around with you," replied Fairuzo amicably. "But now you and I are going to put our two Royal heads together and figure out how we're going to accomplish getting Ermina back home. And we'll have to do it without breaking any laws or taboos – or as few of them as possible," he added. "But come now; we'll talk as we walk."

Procel stepped outside into the hallway. He and Fairuzo walked ahead of me, talking in low voices. I could only make out a few phrases here and there. But even though I could not hear much of what was being said, I felt totally confident they were going to come up with the most perfect plan, and that soon I would be back home on Earth.

I felt a buzz of excitement and anticipation at the prospect. When I'd left my home, I'd had no idea how much I would miss so many things about it! But now I was just grateful that I had a home to return to. And with my two new friends coming along with me, I would no longer be lonely or unhappy there; I was just sure of it.

After a few minutes more of discussion, Fairuzo turned back to me and said, "All right. It is all settled then. Procel knows exactly what to do when we get to the

Ballroom. He has confirmed that all of the trolls went back to their bunks late last night before he himself left, and that no one is in there now."

"So, we will be leaving immediately then? We can do this today?" I asked.

"As soon as you position yourself in front of the Mirror, you are as good as back home," Fairuzo reassured me.

For a moment I felt elated – until I remembered all of those poor miserable creatures languishing in cages back in the laboratory, the salamander slaves swaying back and forth in their chains, the servile praying mantis musicians so fearful of being punished – what about them? Were we just going to leave them all behind?

I began to feel agitated; surely there was some way they could be freed from this place as well.

"But what about those chained-up slaves and all the animals in the laboratory? Are we just going to leave them here?" I asked Fairuzo.

"Well, Enmira," Fairuzo said, "I'm sorry, but we just don't have time to worry about all of that. The trolls will be waking up shortly, not to mention my father could be filing a disciplinary report with the Cabal this very minute. Things could start getting ugly around here real quick, so we've got to make our move while the coast is still clear. Besides, where would you put them all, anyway?"

I was just going to insist that we at least try to help free them, even going so far as suggesting that I'd be willing to risk waiting one more day, when Procel spoke up.

"I believe I know of a way we can bring them all with us that would not interfere with our escape plans. It would be something I can do fairly quickly on my own. If you like, I will get to work on that right away."

"Oh, so, you will be able to free them?" I asked hopefully.

"Yes, I believe that would be extremely likely," Procel

replied, nodding.

Addressing Fairuzo, he said, "It should not take me long at all to collect all of the animals and then join you both in the Ballroom. What do you say? Would this slight alteration of our plan be acceptable to you?"

"Now wait a minute, Procel," Fairuzo said, "I don't see how that would even be plausible. There must be dozens of them back in the lab and in the slave caves. Once you unchain them and let them out of their cages, how would you ever manage to get them all corralled?"

"My dear Fairuzo," Procel said almost haughtily, "have you forgotten that I am not only a Whisperer of Hidden Knowledge but an accomplished Animal Whisperer as well? Why, with my ability to communicate with our furred and feathered friends in their own language, they will listen trustingly to every word I say and be extremely cooperative," Procel replied.

"You can speak their language and talk to them? Like Doctor Doolittle?" I asked, intrigued.

"Oh, dear me, no – not Doctor Doolittle!" exclaimed Procel, looking appalled. "A lovely, heartwarming story, no doubt, but a complete fabrication. You see, the character of the good doctor in the book who speaks to animals was actually based upon a very sinister fellow in real life – a surgeon and vivisector who went by the surname of Hunter.

"Throughout his career, he sliced up thousands of animals to use their skeletons and organs as anatomical specimens – hardly someone who talked to them! Not in any friendly sort of way, that is.

"This vivisector also collaborated with a very well-connected and diabolical Master Mason whom he took on as apprentice, and whom was responsible for developing the first-ever poison injection in a syringe. It contained a filthy virus derived from the ulcerated udder of a cow that had been cultivated in the festering sores on a calf's abdomen. He injected this vile, diseased pus-substance into children under the guise of preventing illness.

"I dare say this son of a Vicar and medical fraud with a purchased doctorate degree was responsible for centuries of suffering and disease, with the deliberately fallacious propaganda he peddled still persisting to this day."

"Oh, my goodness," I exclaimed. "I had no idea! That sounds positively disgusting! In the book, Doctor Doolittle is portrayed as being such a kind man whom all the animals just adored and flocked around."

"Well, that's the whitewashed fictional version," replied Procel. "But things are not often what they seem, especially in the medical world or when it comes to public relations. In reality, he did not surround himself with gentle animal friends at all, but with dissected corpses and colleagues involved in wickedness and deceit."

"Walk faster, you two," Fairuzo urged, glancing back at us with a decidedly irritated expression. "Keep up with me. Less talking and more walking." I could tell he was becoming a bit annoyed with all of our extraneous chatter, but I found Procel's endless tidbits of information quite fascinating.

"Let's just say I can speak the universal language of all animals and that they implicitly trust me when they are in my presence," Procel continued, lowering his voice so as not to further aggravate Fairuzo. "Their senses are so finely tuned that they instinctively know who means them harm and who is there to help them. I shall have no problem whatsoever gaining their confidence and obtaining their cooperation."

"All right, but then what, Procel?" Fairuzo asked. "After you get all of these creatures to follow you, how will you get them through the Mirror?"

"I suppose we can sort that out once we get them all gathered together in the Ballroom," Procel replied. "The important thing is giving them their freedom."

I could tell he was getting rather excited about the whole idea, but Fairuzo still did not look too convinced.

"I don't know, Procel," he said, shaking his head. "That's an awful lot of animals to bring back with you. And how long will this task take you?"

"Oh, not long at all!" Procel asserted brightly. "I will simply cyclone-spin down to the Slave Quarters, undo the amphibians' chains, round up the Mantidae, and then have them follow me to the laboratory, where I will open all the cages. The entire facility should be unmonitored and void of staff now, as all of the scientists have flown back to Mount Hermon to celebrate the completion of their Creoboros project."

Turning to me, he said, "You remember those three-headed dog experiments I was telling you about? And the prototype that brought out the dessert in the Ballroom?"

"Oh, yes," I replied, "how could I forget?" That disturbing image was imprinted firmly in my memory.

"Well," Procel said, "they have finally finished patching a batch of those creatures together. They've got them all up and working, positioned as guards at all of the planet's exits.

"But, fortunately for us, their grand planetary security scheme will be utterly useless in preventing our escape, as we won't be needing to use any of those exits as a way out!" Procel managed a wry chuckle at the thought of outwitting the Cabal.

"So, why don't you two continue on to the Ballroom, and I will be there very shortly with all of the creatures in tow. It should be quite the procession!"

Before either of us even had a chance to reply, Procel began spinning rapidly backwards faster and faster until he was just a blur. After he turned the corner of the passageway, he vanished from our sight.

"That is so amazing how he does that," I marveled. "And at that rate of speed, he might even beat us there!"

"Yes," agreed Fairuzo, "but I really wish I'd had time to teach you how to shapeshift. Traveling as insects would save us so much time and get us there within seconds. 'Tis a shame also that I never got an opportunity to demonstrate how to make use of those fabulous wings on your back. It's unfortunate that they will disintegrate the moment you and Procel enter the connecting tunnel back to Earth. They were only meant for use in the atmosphere here on Tartarus."

"Wait a minute," I said, a knot of dread starting to gather itself into a tight ball in the pit of my stomach. "You're coming with us, right?"

"Oh, no," he answered, slowly shaking his head. "I won't be coming with you. I must stay here."

Then, seeing the look of dismay and disappointment on my face, he added, "But don't you worry. I can visit you on Earth whenever I take my trips there."

He paused for a moment and then continued, "I'm terribly sorry, Enmira, but I just cannot leave my Kingdom. It's the only world I've ever known – even if it *is* inhabited by wretched simpletons. But, like I said, I will be dropping in on you as often as you want me to."

All this time I had simply assumed Fairuzo would be coming along with us; I had deliberately avoided dwelling on the possibility he might be staying behind.

At the thought of only seeing him occasionally and sporadically, a somber cloud of melancholy wafted over me, dampening my buoyant spirits. I could hardly bear the thought of having to say goodbye to him each time he went back to his own planet, and then having to wonder when and if he would be returning.

But perhaps there was some way I could convince him to reconsider.

"What if you just came along with us now and then came back here later?" I asked.

"No, Enmira, I would not be permitted to return after using the Ballroom's Turquoise Mirror as a portal," Fairuzo explained patiently. "I am free to pass through Earthly mirrors, but must use only the guarded staircase for my journeys back and forth. I am still ultimately under the Cabal's rule and supervision, you know, when it comes to leaving the planet."

"But maybe when you come visit, you will decide to stay?" I asked hopefully.

"We'll see," he replied thoughtfully. "We'll see how everything goes."

I felt the edges of my heart unraveling, as if sharp embroidery scissors were snipping at the threads that held it in place, rendering it bare, exposed, and desolate. The ocean of contentment and wholeness I'd felt just moments ago was slowly receding, leaving me feeling parched and incomplete.

How ironic it was, I thought, *that before I'd met Fairuzo, I'd unquestioningly preferred solitude, even to the point I'd embraced my own isolation and seclusion. But now, at the mere thought of being separated from him, I felt a disquieting sense of aloneness, of being disjoined, of unrequited longing.*

Was not my former contentment and sense of autonomy much preferable to such discontent and dependency? And was losing a love really better than never having loved at all? It did not seem so, if this is what it felt like.

However, I really had no choice but to accept his decision. There was certainly no way I could stay here, and so I would simply have to go on without him. I could only hope that he kept his promise to visit me and that he did not forget me once I had gone back home.

My one consolation was that I would at least have my kind and wise friend Procel with me. No doubt he would be a tremendous amount of company and a great comfort to me between Fairuzo's visits.

But perhaps I was being unduly pessimistic and things would not turn out so miserably after all; I would manage somehow. I should just be grateful that I would finally be going home to Earth!

As we hurried along, I began to wonder how Procel was going to unlock the Mirror. But I knew it would be futile to ask Fairuzo, as he would not be permitted to tell me. I would be finding out for myself soon enough anyway.

"All right, we are getting near the staircase," Fairuzo said, "so be sure not to give the guards posted there any indication that you are at all nervous or up to anything that might be deemed suspicious. They're not exactly the sharpest scythes in the cornfield, but they have been trained to spot anyone acting shifty. So, whatever I say when we walk by them, just nod and agree."

We turned the corner and Fairuzo came to a dead halt.

"Stay back," Fairuzo hissed, putting out his arm to shield me. "Let me handle this."

Peeking around him, I saw that the two ogres who had previously been standing guard at the ascending staircase were no longer there. In their place was one of the monstrous triple-headed dog-spiders that Procel had just been speaking of.

Upon catching sight of us, all three heads of the Creoboros mutant began growling ferociously, baring its fangs and waving its tentacles menacingly.

Fairuzo stepped forward and shouted at the creature in a booming, autocratic voice: "It is I, Fairuzo, the Lord and Ruler of this Kingdom, and I command you to stand back and let us pass!"

The beast gave no indication of hearing a word Fairuzo had just spoken. It was as if it had been programmed to respond to any and all stimuli in full-attack mode.

Around the neck of each dog-head was a red spiked collar with a small black box connected to it, very similar to the ones I'd observed around the necks of the salamander slaves. I wondered if these devices emitted electric shocks as well for punishment and behavior modification. A heavy chain was attached to each of the collars, the looped ends of which were anchored to a rail next to the bottom stair.

"The monster looks pretty well-secured by its chains, Fairuzo," I said, "so I don't think it can lunge too great of a distance at us."

"Yes, yes, I can see that," he answered impatiently, "but I'm not sure how long those chains can extend or how resistant they are to being snapped when full weight is placed upon them. I do believe we can manage to get past the creature, though, if we give it a wide enough berth and do so quickly."

Although it bothered me greatly to see any animal in chains, I must admit I felt a blessed sense of relief that this particular one was being restrained – especially since he had apparently been turned into some sort of killing machine automaton, either by genetic manipulation or through abusive obedience training that utilized a combination of beatings, proddings and electric shocks to instill compliance.

As we began walking towards the snarling Creoboros, I prayed that the restraints would hold up under all the stress of it straining so violently against its multitude of chains. Frothy strands of saliva dribbled from its gaping jaws as it exhaled thick clouds of hoarfrost, the needle-like ice crystals splashing and sparking on the ground all around it like chucked frozen spears.

Each of its glowing red eyeballs darted constantly and frantically in every direction, pivoting wildly on the ends of rubbery tendril stalks.

I was just thinking how much the eyes reminded me of infrared camera lenses, when Fairuzo said, "You see those red dots blinking? You hear that faint whirring sound? Their eyes are filming us."

"Whatever for?" I asked. "To keep a record of all who pass by?"

"Basically, yes. The Cabal had its scientists create these mutants as the ultimate security device to deter anyone even entertaining the idea of escape while visually documenting the attempt."

As we drew closer to the growling beast, Fairuzo instructed me: "Now keep your eyes focused straight ahead, Enmira. Whatever you do, do *not* look in the creature's direction! You do not want to give its mainframe a vantage point of being able to perform an iris recognition scan. And you must do your best to keep your mind a complete blank as well, as it is most likely also programmed to detect thought crimes."

My mind was now flooded and racing with so many worries and fears that forcing it into a state completely devoid of thought would not be an easy task. As we began to pass by the creature, I kept my eyes averted, staring straight ahead. I could still hear the sound of its vicious snapping and snarling from just a few yards away. I imagined myself floating in a sky full of distant stars, in an endless void of nothingness; it was the closest I could come to removing all the chaotic thoughts and images from my mind.

After a few moments, Fairuzo nudged me to let me know we were in the clear and out of immediate danger.

"Okay, you can relax now. We're safely past. Apparently nothing was detected that would set off any alarms, so great job there, Enmira! You handled that with real aplomb," he said. "And I'm quite proud of you," he added, giving my shoulder an affectionate squeeze.

I breathed a huge sigh of relief. Thank God those chains had held and I was able to conceal my fear and plans of escape! I couldn't help wondering if the creature really did have the capability of reading my mind, of probing it for any disobedient thoughts as if it were sweeping a minefield for bombs. But, truthfully, with all of the other fantastical things I had witnessed here, that really didn't seem so farfetched.

I could only hope that what we had just encountered was going to be the last obstacle we'd have to face until I was safely back home, and that there would be no more stumbling blocks ahead.

We continued on and soon arrived at the same portion of the hallway where Fairuzo had kicked open the door from inside the Ballroom. Placing the palm of his hand upon the wall, he gave it a firm push and the outline of a door appeared, swinging inward.

"Hang back here for one second," Fairuzo told me. "I'm going to scope it out first."

He crossed over the threshold and went inside. I could not resist poking my head in to take a quick peek for myself.

Just as Procel had reported, the Ballroom was completely void of all activity, the exhausted trolls having gone back to their cave-holes to sleep it off. What they had left behind looked like a garbage dump. There were huge piles of trash strewn all about, and what appeared to be thick puddles of green puke intermingled with black blood. Obviously, those in charge of cleaning up the mess hadn't bothered to show up yet or were sleeping on the job.

The stage where I'd last seen the Insect Pulse playing was now bare. Apparently they had packed up all of their equipment and instruments, save for one tall bank of modules with blinking red and blue lights, and retired to wherever their quarters were.

Fairuzo came back to the door and, taking my hand, pulled me into the Ballroom.

"As you can see, everyone is gone – but, like I said, we don't have much time before they start to wake up. Now all we have to do is wait for Procel. He better get here soon or else –"

Just then, I heard a loud rustling noise and a sound like the shuffling of many feet. Through the doorway behind the bandstand appeared Procel, closely followed by a horde of animals of just about every shape and size.

There were dogs and monkeys and cats, and pigs and lambs and rabbits, and rats and mice and hamsters. Apparently they had all been crammed into the cages of the laboratory, slated to be experimented upon and then sacrificed after serving their purpose.

They all walked together in harmonious unison with an almost military precision, following trustingly behind Procel. At one point he stopped and turned towards them, speaking in a language unlike any I'd ever heard before. It consisted of chirps, clicks, purrs and trills, although I caught a few words that sounded vaguely like the language of humans. It was much closer to Greek than English, however, including some words that seemed as if they were being spoken in reverse.

Bringing up the rear was the Insect Pulse band. Each of the praying mantis musicians walked alongside a blind salamander, holding on tenderly to his forepaw, acting as a seeing eye guide to steer him along.

I was struck then by how much Procel reminded me of the Greek legend of Orpheus, who had charmed all of the animals in the forest by playing his lyre and singing melodious sonnets to them.

As he approached us with his impressive flock of followers, I exclaimed, "Oh, Procel, this is absolutely amazing! I have never seen such a thing in my entire life. And what language were you just speaking to them in?"

"It is the universal language of the Web of Life called Creats, which all non-humans can understand, even the detached spirits that reside in the shells of trees and flower petals," he explained.

"In fact, Earthling children are actually born with the ability to speak this language, which just sounds like meaningless babble to adults. They have a natural proclivity to pronounce words in reverse, even before they are taught to speak in the recognizably normal/forward manner. This is because they are subconsciously reverting back to their former lives as a non-human species."

"You see," he continued, "the soul transmigrates from animal to human and from human to animal in no particular order, and so the child is also born with this innate bond and fascination with all non-human animals. Until, that is, it is methodically crushed and stolen from them by the indoctrination of a perverted society. And --"

At this point, Procel stopped speaking abruptly as he noticed that Fairuzo had begun to glare at him.

"That is all very interesting, I'm sure, Procel," Fairuzo said impatiently, "but we don't have time for a complete zoology and linguistics lesson right now. We need to get on with this before the trolls start wandering around and poking their noses in!"

Procel nodded eagerly. "Yes, yes, of course," he agreed.

"Come, Enmira," Fairuzo said as he took ahold of my arm and pulled me forward in the direction of the bandstand.

When we reached the platform, he pressed a pulsating blue button in the center of one of the modules. An enormous screen began descending from the ceiling, just as it had before. When it was just a few inches away from the ground, the middle began separating into two panels like a grand theatre curtain, revealing the Turquoise Mirror in all of its splendor.

As we stood before the Mirror's reflection, it reminded me of a gorgeous framed painting from the Renaissance – Fairuzo and I standing together as a couple, then Procel with his impressive collection of mammals, insects and amphibians right behind us. I could see them gazing all about in wonder and amazement, as if they could still scarcely believe their luck at being free of their cages and chains.

Fairuzo turned to Procel and said, "Okay, my friend. You know what to do."

Procel hesitated for a moment, then said, "Well, I must admit that I have never before attempted this – but, not to worry," he hastened to add. "I have the entire incantation somewhere within my memory banks; I simply have to conjure up the words in their proper sequence. I do believe it is the precise reversal of the key that authorizes entry, if I am recalling it correctly."

Fairuzo nodded encouragingly. "Come on, Procel, you know this – it is simply the positive of the negative."

Procel stood there for a moment, as if deep in thought, then replied, "Yes, I realize it is the opposite of vanity and hate that unlocks the Glass Gate. But you cannot give me any hints at all as to the actual phrasing?" he asked hopefully.

"Now, Procel," Fairuzo chided, "you know damned well that I cannot utter any of the words. You're going to have to summon them up completely on your own.

"And you had better make sure you've got them precisely in the proper order before speaking them," he warned.

"Yes, yes," said Procel, nervously nodding his head. "I understand you cannot speak aloud any of the words, but please bear with me for a moment. I just need to make sure I recall all verses of the invocation in both tongues."

He stood still for a moment, frozen, as if silently rehearsing what he was going to say. Then he deftly twirled around to where he was facing the mirror's glass dead-on and raised his fist high up in the air.

He then said, in a firm, bold voice, louder and more confident than I had ever heard him speak:

"Ta solipsis pas da misola laptan vi fatalis, valit sim vun borus tudis vas belids! Sim tonis pas batind! Vidis braz tulunta naristan!"

He paused for a moment then continued, his voice rising even further in volume and intensity:

"A soul that is pure cannot be corrupted, even by the most potent of evils! All life is sacred! Good will always triumph!"

He paused again then chanted in a measured rhythm:

"These words I have spoken will act as the key;
O, Mirror, I beseech thee to let us pass free!"

For a moment there was an eerie silence all around. It was as if we were all collectively holding our breaths, including the animals. As I waited to see what would happen next, I fervently hoped that Procel had spoken all of the right words. I had the feeling he would not be getting a second chance to do so if he hadn't.

Just then, I heard a deafening crash, and a long, jagged crack suddenly snaked and ripped through the mirror. Instinctively, I ducked my head to avoid any flying shards, but surprisingly, there was none. There was now a deep chasm in the center of the glass that belched forth great plumes of smoke. The crevice slowly expanded like a zipper exposing the innards of a hot pie crust – only it spat no volcanic debris. Clouds of steam and swirling wisps of vapor continued to pour out as the hole split wider and wider, until it was a huge gaping isosceles triangle with its base nearly touching the floor.

I could now see that there was some sort of drawbridge inside that was slowly being lowered, apparently to allow us passage once we climbed through the Mirror's opening.

I looked hesitantly at Fairuzo, wanting so badly to run through the Mirror to freedom yet torn at leaving him behind. I wanted to plead with him to come with me, but my pride would not allow me. He had already made his decision and I would not beg.

He looked at me for a moment as if he, too, desperately wanted to say something, then threw his arms around me, hugging me tightly to him.

"I will see you on the other side, Enmira," he murmured into my ear while softly stroking my hair. "I promise I will come visit you as soon as things blow over here." At that moment I thought I detected a slight waver in his voice; I myself was holding back my own tears.

I suddenly had a strange and foreboding feeling that I might never see him again. I had no idea what sort of trouble he might be in for his role in helping us escape; and how would it even be possible for him to resume his journeys to Earth? The monstrous Creoboros automaton was now aggressively blocking all access to the ascending staircase!

I did not want to release my hold of him for fear it might be our last embrace. I only knew that I would worry constantly and feverishly until I saw him again.

"Come quickly, Enmira!" Procel urged from his position now ahead of us, interrupting my doleful thoughts. "I am unsure as to how long the Mirror will remain open before it slams shut, so we must leave *now*!"

As I reluctantly let go of Fairuzo, he grabbed my face between his hands and kissed me long and hard.

"There," he said firmly, mustering a bittersweet smile. "So you will not forget me."

Forget you? How could I possibly ever forget you? I thought wistfully to myself.

He gave me one last look of longing then slowly began backing away from me, reaching out with his hands to wave me onward.

"You must go now, my love," he called out, as I stood there affixed to the spot, my eyes glued to his. The distance between us was growing as if there was now a moat betwixt us, swollen to overflowing from a torrential rain that would not cease.

I finally managed to tear my gaze away in time to see that Procel and his eager army of creatures were now almost all the way through the Mirror. I suddenly wanted very much to join them.

I turned to give Fairuzo one last look. He stared back at me so forlornly it was all I could do to keep from bursting into tears; I managed a weak wave of goodbye.

I began to run towards the Mirror. Just as I got within inches of it, it began to vibrate and emit a high-pitched hum. The glass appeared to be rippling like undulating ocean waves, and the triangular fissure was perceptibly beginning to shrink and close up. I realized I only had a few moments to spare before the crack would be completely sealed shut.

Just as I was stepping through, I heard Fairuzo's voice behind me, and I froze in place.

"Wait! Wait!" he was yelling urgently.

I spun around to face him.

"I'm coming with you!" he cried.

With one great leap, he flew over to where I was. He was just reaching for my hand when, out of the corner of my eye, I saw four trolls suddenly emerge through the door behind the stage. I recognized two of them immediately: one was Darceva and the other was the shapeshifter Dantanian.

"Oh, my God, look!" I gasped, turning towards them. "It's Darceva!"

"Well, I'll be damned," muttered Fairuzo in disbelief.

Spotting us, Darceva immediately gave chase, stomping and lumbering clumsily towards us.

"Hey!" she yelled. "You bastard! Where do you think *you're* going without *me*?"

"Come on, there's no way she'll ever make it in time; let's keep going," Fairuzo urged me.

At this point, the triangular gap in the Mirror had narrowed to just a thin, jagged slit. After maneuvering our way through the crack, we stood triumphantly on the other side. I felt completely safe now with the both of us tucked snugly away inside the swiftly-closing Mirror, Darceva still waddling desperately towards us.

When she realized there was no possible way she was going to reach us in time, she stopped short, wheezing and rasping. She bent over to catch her breath, her face mottled and purple, swollen with a seething, choking rage.

"You'll pay for this!" Darceva screamed at Fairuzo as she huffed and puffed. "You can't just leave us all here and go off with your fancy new slut! The bounty hunters will hunt you down and find both of your asses!"

"As for you, you dumb little bitch," she screamed directly at me, "I'm his mother and I have first dibs on him – I fucked him good that night and he loved every minute of it!"

"You were never my mother, and Enmira already knows all about you and what you did," Fairuzo retorted.

"And oh, by the way," he continued, "since you've just now publicly revealed what happened that night, you have officially broken the blood oath you signed! And don't doubt for a second that your troll pals there won't turn you in for a nice, fat snitch reward. So it looks like you just fucked *yourself*!"

He laughed uproariously at the dazed and stunned look on her face as she realized she had just inadvertently set herself up for her own banishment.

It was mere seconds later that the crevice in the Mirror slammed completely shut, echoing and reverberating on the drawbridge, mercifully erasing the hideous presence of Darceva and forever cementing her fate.

I could see Procel ahead of us on the bridge with his animal friends still following closely behind. Some were starting to run and leap about, chattering excitedly amongst themselves as the realization sunk in that they were finally free.

Fairuzo was literally beaming; I had never seen him so elated.

"She'll most certainly be banished now," he said exuberantly with a wide grin. "But even if she isn't, I really don't care any more. I'm free! Free of Tartarus and free of my father and free of the trolls!"

He was practically skipping along the bridge beside me. His joy was infectious and I felt it too.

Not only was I going back home to Earth but I had Fairuzo by my side; Procel had managed to save every last one of the animals, and Darceva was now left to stew in her own karmic juices. She would be reaping the punishment she fully deserved, for she had brought it all upon her own self.

After walking along the bridge for a few moments, we came to the tunnel that Fairuzo had alluded to earlier. I heard a soft, soothing sound like the whispering of the wind, which seemed to be emanating from the gently revolving spiral vortex inside. The vaporous walls were comprised of swirling clouds, spinning multicolored stars, and rings of smoke the color of palest green chrysopase.

A long, winding pathway made entirely of glass ran lengthwise up the tunnel's center, twisting and bending, and glittering like spun gold.

At the very end of the tunnel was an ornate gate that stood slightly ajar, covered in vines and pink strands of margarite. On the other side of it shone a brilliant white light in the shape of a perfectly-formed equilateral triangle. It was so luminous that it looked as if it could illuminate an entire planet – or perhaps even the Heavens.

The light felt warm and comforting and magical, as if it had healing powers and harbored the secrets of the Universe.

I could see that Procel was nearly halfway through the tunnel now, leading the animals onward like a mystical piper on a pilgrimage to the gates of dawn.

"Is that the sun I see shining just outside that gate?" I asked hopefully.

"I believe it is, Enmira," said Fairuzo, smiling. "I believe it is."

As we entered the tunnel, he leaned close to me and put his arm affectionately around my shoulder. His body was radiating such intense heat that, for a moment, I thought his touch might scald my skin. But, instead of it burning me, I felt an all-consuming and rapturous contentment, as if I were lying next to a blazing fire in the deepest spell of winter, hypnotized by the blue-tinged flames that danced and leapt about like joyous sprites.

"Oh, but your body is so warm now!" I exclaimed.

"Yes," Fairuzo replied, a look of awe upon his face. "Isn't that the most peculiar thing?"

And together, hand in hand, we walked toward the light at the end of the tunnel.